SHIP IT

BRITTA LUNDIN

 **FREEFORM** BOOKS

Los Angeles   New York

If you purchased this book without a cover, you should be aware
that this book is stolen property. It was reported as "unsold
and destroyed" to the publisher, and neither the author nor the
publisher has received any payment for this "stripped" book.

Copyright © 2018 by Britta Lundin
All rights reserved. Published by Freeform Books, an imprint of Disney
Book Group. No part of this book may be reproduced or transmitted in any
form or by any means, electronic or mechanical, including photocopying,
recording, or by any information storage and retrieval system, without
written permission from the publisher. For information address
Freeform Books, 125 West End Avenue, New York, New York 10023.

First Hardcover Edition, May 2018
First Paperback Edition, May 2019
10 9 8 7 6 5 4 3 2 1
FAC-025438-19081
Printed in the United States of America

SUSTAINABLE FORESTRY INITIATIVE
Certified Chain of Custody
Promoting Sustainable Forestry
www.sfiprogram.org
SFI-01054
The SFI label applies to the text stock

This book is set in Arial/Monotype; KG Happy/
Fontspring; Kozuka Mincho, Melior/Monotype
Designed by Marci Senders

Library of Congress Control Number for Hardcover: 2017034202
ISBN 978-1-368-02115-9

Visit www.freeform.com/books

For the Claires and the Tesses.
One day, you will run the world.

EVENTUALLY THIS WHOLE BUSINESS WITH HEART
is going to kill him.

But Smokey hopes it's not today.

Ignoring every screaming signal in his body pleading
with him to stop, Smokey forces his legs to carry him faster,
through the woods, away from danger.

Away from Heart.

Finally, his lungs on fire, his legs rubber, gasping for air,
Smokey breaks into a clearing, drops his battle-ax with a
thud, and falls to his knees as a dozen birds take flight in
alarm. Letting his chin fall to his chest, he notices he's drip-
ping blood on the ground from a long gash across his forearm.

Shit.

In the furor of the battle, he'd underestimated how badly
he was hurt. Smokey had seen worse injuries in his long history fighting demons, but still, each new slash reminded him
how fragile his mere human body was.

He presses his palm to the wound and closes his eyes, letting his breath return to him. He decides to take a short break here before continuing on, feeling certain Heart couldn't have tracked him, particularly not after he spent half a mile wading through that river an hour back. He lets his shoulders relax. He's alone, he's safe—for the moment.

Smokey had vowed to spend the rest of his life trying to atone for the damage he caused by allowing the demon portal to open. In the long run, he doesn't stand a chance against the onslaught of horror pouring out of the portal every day, but still he fights, killing demons one by one. Doing his part. It's the least he can do, considering.

So when the Dragonbeast emerged from the portal, Smokey had no choice but to fight it. He'd heard the rumors about the Dragonbeast, that it had killed eight hunters already, that it was fearsome and mighty ... yadda, yadda, whatever. None of that mattered, because at the end of the day, he's a hunter and the Dragonbeast needed hunting. He'd waltzed into the fight with the same swagger he used in every situation, and look, it had worked, hadn't it? The Dragonbeast lies dead and Smokey is alive—although his damn arm hurts like hell.

And the demon portal? It's still perfectly functioning and spitting out demons faster than he can take them down. But he's yet to find a way to deal with that particular shitshow.

Lord, he needs a drink.

"He got you good, didn't he?" Heart's voice cuts through the silence.

Smokey leaps to his feet and draws his ax with his good arm in one swift motion as Heart appears from the shadows, looking like he just stepped out of a Lands' End photo shoot, not the depths of demon hell.

Damn. He may have underestimated Heart's tracking skills. Or is he just that bad at hiding his trail? Because Smokey managed to slay a Dragonbeast—a Dragonbeast!—and escape with his life, only to be tracked down by Heart, the most annoying demon on the planet.

He and Heart had rumbled before, of course, but Heart had always managed to escape Smokey's ax. Heart insists to anyone who will listen that he's different from other demons because he has a (wait for it . . .) heart. Like the organ, like in his chest. *Yeah, we get it, you on-the-nose asshole, you're a demon with a heart. Love the name.*

But Smokey suspects that what really sets Heart apart is the fact that he's the most self-righteous, obnoxious, soapboxing ass he's ever met. And he's always *there*, showing up at inopportune times, making a nuisance of himself, and refusing to get killed. He's even provided the cover Smokey needed to escape danger one or two times. By accident, Smokey is sure. Because they're enemies. They have to be. Internal organs or no, a demon's a demon, and demons all belong in hell.

"Not another step," Smokey warns Heart, his ax trembling from exhaustion.

Storm clouds rumble overhead, threatening rain. Smokey ignores them.

"You're bleeding," Heart notices with . . . is that *concern*? He reaches up and rips the sleeve off his own shirt, exposing the thick bicep underneath. "Give me your arm," Heart growls, stepping toward Smokey.

"I said stay where you are." Smokey keeps his ax in battle position, but Heart just brushes past it and Smokey finds he doesn't have the reserves to keep up the struggle. Heart starts wrapping Smokey's wound with his torn sleeve.

"What are you doing?" Smokey demands. *Is this a trick?*

"Trying to keep you from bleeding out," Heart says simply.

"Why, so I can be alive and healthy when you kick me down to hell?" Smokey growls.

Heart just levels him with an annoyed look and continues to work on Smokey's arm. It already hurts less, under the pressure of Heart's makeshift bandage and his hands, too warm from demon blood. Smokey curses himself for his weakness. Heart is a *demon*, Smokey is a *hunter*. They're mortal enemies, not *soldier and nurse.*

"The opening of the demon portal," Heart murmurs as he works. "You know it's not your fault."

Smokey scoffs. That's not remotely true. It's *entirely* his fault. Smokey failed to stop the seven commandments that led to the demon portal opening and the Commander stepping foot on earth for the first time in millennia. No one else was there to stop it but Smokey, and he 100 percent, no-doubt-about-it *failed.*

"You did everything you could," Heart says.

Smokey feels Heart tie the bandage off tight, his hands strong, secure.

"Why are you saying this?" Smokey asks, afraid of the answer.

"Because you're a good man," Heart says. "Maybe the best."

Smokey knows he shouldn't trust the demon in front of him, that there's a more-than-fair chance that this is all a trick to catch him with his guard down, but the truth is, he's *tired*. Tired of the battle. Tired of being on guard. Tired of fighting solo. The demon portal is open. The Commander has returned. The world is on the brink of total demon rule.

Nothing matters, except that Smokey screwed up yet again. And he's alone.

But Heart, for some reason Smokey can't comprehend, forgives him.

Smokey keeps his eyes firmly on the ground in front of him. "I tried to stop it, but it wasn't enough. I didn't change anything."

Heart grasps his hand, and the heat from Heart's fingers sends a wave of warmth up Smokey's arm. "You changed me," Heart says, low and rough, and it seems impossible. "I know you think we have to be enemies because of how we were born..." The pain in Smokey's arm is barely a whimper now, ignored as he tries to make sense of the words coming out of Heart's mouth, the feeling of Heart's fingers lacing into his. "It doesn't have to be that way. We want the same things."

What does Smokey want?

He knows, of course. He's always known.

"Heart..." Smokey whispers.

Heart smiles. "If you want me, I'm here, I'm not leaving." The two lock eyes as the rest of the forest fades away. "I'll stay with you..." he starts, then waits, the words from their first meeting hanging in the air for Smokey to finish.

"'Til the dirt hits my chest," Smokey says.

And like that, Smokey's head feels light, his eyes are clear, his arm doesn't hurt, and everything makes sense.

Smokey meets Heart's deep brown eyes and sees him waiting for an opening, waiting for permission. Smokey tips forward, and before his brain can stop his body, their mouths fit together, hot and solid and exactly what Smokey has been waiting a very long time for.

Smokey wraps his hands around Heart, one of them traveling up to curl into his hair, the other pressing into his back, bringing him closer, closer. The heat of Heart's breath sends a thrill through Smokey's spine, and he can't believe they're finally kissing, and he can't believe it took this long.

As Heart's mouth grows more insistent, Smokey feels an aching heat grow in his stomach, like a sun threatening to turn supernova, the enormity of this kiss overwhelming his senses, blinding out his brain.

There's a crack of thunder and a flash of lightning, and Heart is pulling off his shirt, his warm brown skin smooth over taut muscles, bearing the marks of many battles, including one scar that runs long and thin down his chest that, Smokey realizes with horror, he remembers inflicting.

Doubt creeps in.

This isn't right. They're enemies, not lovers.

Smokey pulls away and turns his back on Heart, all the feelings hitting him in a crush at once. He's tried to kill Heart so many times. What if this is a trap? What if Smokey's letting his feelings get in the way of good sense? Does he even know where his battle-ax is?

"What is it?" Heart asks, worry in his voice. He follows Smokey's line of sight to the ax, lying on the ground a few feet away. "You want to kill me? Now's your chance. I won't even fight back."

Smokey shakes his head. "I've already hurt you too much."

"Oh, these?" Smokey peeks over his shoulder to see Heart trace the shapes of the scars on his body. "My skin heals. Just don't hurt my heart"—he pauses, smiling at his joke before he even says it—"because I have one of those, too, you know."

Heart's eyes twinkle annoyingly, but Smokey isn't in a joking mood.

He has to know. Smokey turns back and fixes his eyes firmly on the dirt in front of him and asks, low, "Is this real?"

He hears Heart take a long breath in, then step forward, hooking his chin over Smokey's shoulder. Smokey tenses, but as Heart slides his hand across Smokey's stomach, lifting his shirt, he feels the tension leave his body. When Heart subtly rocks forward so Smokey can feel the swell straining stiffly against the fabric of his pants, Smokey gasps out a breath and closes his eyes, letting the desire course through him.

Heart whispers in Smokey's ear, breath hot on his skin, "It's real for me. Is it real for you?"

And so, like a book sliding into place on a shelf, Smokey makes the decision to allow himself to find a home in Heart's arms. He leans back into Heart, letting their bodies notch together. Heart is all skin and steady pressure, and Smokey wants nothing as much as he wants this. Heart slides his open hand down Smokey's chest, over his belly, dipping under his waistband, and curls it around his—

2

HMM. SOOOO...HMM. I HAVE TO PAUSE WRITING
for a moment because this is the first time I've ever tried to do
a scene with this kind of choreography, and I don't actually
know how the next part works.

Frankly, it can be a challenge writing explicit gay fanfic
as a teenage girl virgin who's never done any of these things
before.

I glance around the school library, but the only other person here is Ms. Wignall, our librarian, who's shelving books
and not paying any attention to me, so I go ahead and try to
mime Heart's movements. He's about to give Smokey the handjob of his life, but, like, from behind? Is that a thing? I feel like
it could be. Having never given a life-altering handjob—from
the front *or* behind—I'm a little mystified as to how it works.
Does the wrist go *this* way or *that* way?

Whatever, that's what Google is for.

I know from experience that the school's internet filters

won't let me access sexually explicit information, so I connect to Pine Bluff's terrible public wifi instead. It takes forever to load my homepage, during which time I try to figure out what to search. Handjob? No . . . *reacharound*. That's it. I knew it was a thing.

Googling *gay porn reacharound* leads you to a sparkling variety of sites that all seem useful to my research. I click on the first video and loud moaning comes out of the speakers.

Shit. Mute. *Shit.*

Ms. Wignall gives me a look over her glasses, but miraculously she goes back to shelving books. I scootch the laptop closer and examine the video on mute. Ahhh, the wrist goes *that* way, okay, got it.

I could stop there, but I keep watching the video a minute longer than I need to. Their faces twisted up, their muscles working, their movements syncing until they're not two separate people anymore but one, connected, a unit. It's mesmerizing. One of them blond, one of them dark-haired—I'm already imagining them as Smokey and Heart. Why anyone would watch porn videos rather than read fanfic is beyond me. Isn't imagining sex better, more compelling, when it's between two people you know and care about and *feel* things for, rather than these tanned, oily strangers?

Stopping the video, I open up the fic again. It's not really about the sex. Okay, it is, but the sex is also about Smokey learning to trust another person, even if that person is a demon. And about Heart sacrificing everything he knows for the human he accidentally fell for. The sex—the thrusting, the low moans, the rain pelting down on their naked, strong bodies, washing away their pain until finally, the release—that's all just gravy. Really, it's about *love.*

When I finish the fic, I post it to my fanfic page and hit PUBLISH. Then I post a snippet and a link on my Tumblr. It belongs to the internet now. Smokey and Heart's love, no matter how many times I write about it, always feels new and incredible and joyous. I know it's only a matter of time before the notes start coming in—people liking, commenting, responding to my work. I would be writing these stories whether anyone read them or not, but I'd be lying if I said it wasn't nice to know other people like what I do. Even if I don't ever really talk to them, or have any real friends in fandom, just knowing they're out there, feeling what I'm feeling, shipping what I'm shipping. . . . It feels good to not be alone, even when I'm sitting by myself in an empty library.

Or at least, I *was* by myself, until Andrea Garcia slides into the seat across from me, asking before I even look up, "Are you working on the assignment for Mrs. Fitz?"

I snap to attention, awaking from my post-fic buzz, and stare at Andrea, with her perfect winged eyeliner, delicate fake lashes, and exquisitely groomed thick, dark eyebrows. She's the daughter of the couple who own the feed store downtown, so her family is basically Pine Bluff royalty. She has very nice skin and a very nice car, and she's Kyle Cunningham's girlfriend. There's a million reasons why Andrea and I don't really ever talk, but that list is a good start.

Which is why it's super weird she's talking to me now.

"Oh, uh, no," I mumble as I covertly close the porn tab that was still open on my laptop.

"Well, have you finished it yet? I can't figure out the last question."

"No, I usually just do it right before class."

"Okay, well, some of us aren't that smart," she says bitterly.

"Oh, I didn't mean..."

"Yeah, I know, whatever," she says, frustrated. I have this effect on people.

That's when Kyle Cunningham saunters up and kisses Andrea obscenely. I know, *I know,* how can this kiss possibly be considered obscene compared to what I was just writing, but the difference is Smokey and Heart are beautiful and in love, and Kyle Cunningham is a gross popular farm kid who doesn't deserve to share the same zip code with Andrea.

On TV, high schools never have popular farm kids, so I get the sense this isn't a nationwide phenomenon. Maybe at other schools, popular kids play guitar or have a tattoo or listen to their parents' vinyl or something, I don't know. But in Pine Bluff, Idaho, the cool kids wear Carhartt work pants with chewing tobacco stuffed in the side pocket and camouflage hunting T-shirts that match their John Deere baseball hats with the brims bent all the way in half. Their shoes are always muddy because they had to, like, milk the cows that morning before they came to school or something (I don't know because I'm not friends with them). Honestly, it sounds like a lot of work, and I'm sure it's difficult balancing farming with high school *and* being popular, but I don't feel like empathizing with them because they've never really made an effort with me, either.

Why don't I have friends in Pine Bluff? Maybe they don't like me because I'm a "city kid." (Pine Bluff with all of its four thousand people is actually considered a city to people who live twenty miles into the country.) Or maybe it's because I only moved here five years ago and wasn't born and bred in Pine Bluff. But probably they don't like me because they expect me to be obsessed with country music and elk hunting and prom instead of a dumb TV show about demons in which the two lead male characters are not yet—*but totally should be*—dating.

I realized a long time ago that making friends wasn't really going to be a realistic goal, and a better mission was to keep my head down, get into a good college a long way from here, and never talk to anyone from Pine Bluff again.

Kyle readjusts his John Deere hat so that it's sitting on the very back of his head like it might fall off if not for the sheer charisma of his farmer-boy hair. He looks at me like he's just now realized I was here. I'm used to the popular farm kids treating me like I'm invisible, but it's particularly irritating when Kyle does it, considering the fact that I used to be *very* visible to him.

"What's your shirt?" he asks me, kind of out of the blue.

I move the sides of my hoodie out of the way and look down at my shirt. It's my second favorite *Demon Heart* T-shirt. "It's for this show, *Demon Heart*."

I know he doesn't know the show because it hadn't started airing yet when we were hanging out last year. At the time, I was pretty obsessed with this series of books called Citybreakers and only wanted to read/talk about/write fic about them. Kyle thinks reading for pleasure is for "chumps." Also, the only thing he likes to watch on TV is ultimate fighting. "Because I'm *a man*, Claire," he would say.

In case it's unclear, Kyle is literally the worst.

Andrea takes her hair out of her ponytail, brushes it with her fingers, and then starts putting it back up again exactly the same, but slightly tighter. I never do this with my ponytail, I just tighten it throughout the day until it's time to take it out. Is that what Kyle likes about her? That she has really clean, tight ponytails? But what could Andrea possibly see in him?

"*Demon Heart*?" Kyle squints at my T-shirt again. It's the one with promo photos of Smokey and Heart gazing deeply into each other's eyes, ostensibly locked in eternal conflict, but the shirt, like the show, is open for interpretation. And I choose to see love.

So does Kyle, apparently. "Why do they look like they're about to kiss?"

Andrea snorts and punches him. "Be nice," she says.

"I'm serious, that's the gayest thing I've ever seen," he says.

For a second there, I almost pity him. *This shirt* is the gayest thing he's ever seen? Okay, sure, it's a pretty gay shirt. But a gayer shirt would have them *actually* kissing. Or shirtless. Or it would show Heart taking Smokey from behind and... Well, there's plenty of fic out there going into the details. The fic is pretty damn gay. This shirt? This shirt is just *subtext*.

Kyle snickers.

"Kyyyle," Andrea whines. Their relationship is a mystery to me.

"What?" Kyle feigns innocence.

I straighten my glasses. "You think being gay is funny?"

"I think that shirt is hilarious," he says. I want to reach over and knock the stupid precarious tractor hat off his head.

"Kyle, shut up, she's probably gay herself." Andrea turns to me. "There's nothing wrong with that." How generous of her. How *progressive.*

I look at Kyle to see if he wants to respond. Apparently he does not, so I turn back to Andrea. "I'm not gay," I tell her.

"Yeah," Kyle says, "obviously. She's in love with the gay dudes on her shirt."

It's too much. I suppress a snort, then I catch Kyle's eye and the dumb expression on his face makes me really belly laugh. Andrea leans away from me, confused and a little afraid, but Kyle just gets mad. "What?" he demands. "What's so funny?"

"You know, there are people out there who think we're crazy? That we see stuff that's not there, that the show's never gonna make it canon. But I just wanna state for the record that Kyle Cunningham, *Kyle freaking Cunningham* sees it. We're *not* crazy." Kyle is looking at me like I just kicked his prize heifer and I don't care. "If Kyle Cunningham ships it, we should all be shipping it."

"I don't ship it," Kyle says sharply, his mood turning dark. But I don't care, he brought this on himself.

"Why, does that freak you out? That you ship two dudes?" I ask.

"Give it a rest, Claire."

"Yeah, figures. You know what I never understood? Why they always cast straight men as heroes in everything... because you're honestly the most terrified people on the planet."

Andrea looks back and forth between us with wide eyes. Poor chick has no idea what kind of idiot she's going to prom with. Kyle starts to say something, but I wave him off. "Forget it," I say and grab my stuff. They'll never understand.

I can hear their whispers before I even reach the exit. I close my eyes and shove through the doors.

Screw this place.

On the bus, everyone else has someone to talk to. Row after
row of chattering kids, excited for their afternoons to start, for
summer to start. I slip into the seat next to Joanie Engstrom,
who is eating an apple from the top down, core and all. Joanie
and I aren't friends, exactly, but we're allies—someone to pair
up with in class on group projects, someone to sit next to on
the bus when all the other seats are full. She smiles at me,
then looks back down at her Bible open in her lap—well-worn
and Post-it–noted from a lifetime of use. I'm not sure what
more there is to glean from those pages after she's read them
so many times, but I'm not one to judge since I've seen all the
available episodes of *Demon Heart* upwards of a dozen times.

As Joanie reads, taking another bite of her apple, I look
past her and watch Pine Bluff pass by out the windows, all
six glorious stoplights.

Annoyingly, I can't stop thinking about what Kyle said.
Am I in love with the guys in *Demon Heart*? Maybe. Rico
Quiroz and Forest Reed, who play Heart and Smokey, are
undeniably attractive people. I've spent more than a few afternoons gazing at pictures of them, the slope of their jawlines,
the rough texture of their stubble, the swell of their lips.

Rico, the older one, has amazing dark curly hair, an open
face, perfect soft brown skin, and an easy smile. He comes off
as approachable, kind, warm. I can see why fans are always
tweeting *Dad* at him—I want him to rub my back and tell me
I'm doing a good job, I want him to teach me how to fix my
car, my problems. In my favorite fantasy, I imagine myself
sitting across from him as he reads my college admissions
essay, then looks up over it to tell me he thinks I'm going to
do great things. I trust him, even though I've never met him.

Forest is the younger of the two. Under his wavy blond hair, he has these incredibly expressive watery blue eyes that betray how broken he is inside no matter how tough he's trying to be. He's lean where Rico is broad, young where Rico is experienced, serious where Rico is quick to laugh. Forest has these long, strong arms—I imagine, if I were falling off a cliff and holding on with only my fingers, he could reach down and effortlessly pull me to safety with one hand. After which, I would melt into his chest in gratitude, but he would refuse to kiss me because he wouldn't want to take advantage. He would insist on taking me out on a date first.

But here's where the fantasy falls apart. Do I want to *date* Forest Reed? It's hard to imagine kissing Smokey's lips when I've pictured them kissing Heart so many times.

Am I in love with Smokey and Heart? Or am I in love with their love?

After my run-in with the popular farm kid brigade, I feel tight, like an overfilled balloon. If anyone touched me right now, I would pop right in their face. The bus turns left onto a farm access road. Even though I live in a small town, I still have twenty minutes until I get home, thanks to circuitous rural bus routes. I don't have the energy to start a conversation with Joanie today and inevitably hear about her horses or whatever she's learning in Bible study that week, so I rub my eyes under my glasses and do what I always do when I need to calm down—I cycle through my mental rolodex of fics and pick one.

In episode nine of *Demon Heart*, there's this scene where Smokey is tailing a gnarly demon, and he watches him enter a roadside bar. Then the show time cuts to several hours later, after dark, as Smokey watches the bad guy leave the bar...with Heart. At first you're supposed to think Heart is cavorting with the enemy, but then there's a twist where they reveal that Smokey and Heart are collaborating to bring down the bad guy. It's the first time Smokey and Heart work together, so it's a big moment for their relationship. And there's this four-hour gap of time that's unaccounted for. In my circles, we call that a *fanfiction gap*. I've read a hundred fics that take place in those few hours—imagining the conversation that must have occurred between them to get them to team up, and I've written a few myself. Today, I mentally pull up my favorite. It's one of mine, because the only way to make sure someone writes *exactly* the fic you want to read is to do it yourself.

I skip to the best part because it's my head and I get to do what I want. Blah, blah, blah, Smokey confronts Heart in the bathroom of the roadside bar. Heart wants to work together, Smokey is dubious. They talk, then argue, then fight, then Heart pins Smokey against the wall of the bathroom, and I stop fast-forwarding and enter slo-mo.

Their eyes find each other. The energy changes. All that struggle, all that energy, falls away. This thing they're both fighting, they look it in the face for the first time.

Smokey licks his lips.

Heart glances at his mouth.

They're so close already, breathing each other's air, the next move either a punch or a—

Smokey leans in and they're kissing and my stomach does backflips.

It never ceases to work. That *zhoom* feeling that I assume people get when someone you like actually kisses you. But who needs all the drama and the herpes and the hurt feelings of the real thing when you can get that same feeling reading a great fic?

I feel myself relax. Like a crumpled paper getting smoothed out. SmokeHeart always makes me feel better, like the world is manageable and love is real. There are only a few episodes of *Demon Heart* left in season one, and it feels like they're building to something. The SmokeHeart vibes get stronger with every episode, and I'm not the only one who thinks so—the entire fandom is practically buzzing with anticipation about what's going to happen in the season finale. A lot of people came to *Demon Heart* from other fandoms where they had gotten their hopes up about a gay ship and been disappointed. But *Demon Heart* feels different. Everything they've built so far, all the dominoes they've laid—it all feels like they'll start tumbling into place soon. This time, *this time*, SmokeHeart might be real. The ship might go canon. And then everything will be okay.

"Claire." Joanie nudges me. The bus has pulled over and the driver is looking at me.

Back to reality. It's my stop.

"THAT'S LUNCH, FOLKS," THE 1ST AD HOLLERS.

"Wait, really?" I ask as Rico reaches a hand down to help me up. We've been shooting this fight sequence all morning and my muscles are aching for a break, but I didn't think that last take worked. "I wasn't sure we got it, do you think we got it?"

Rico laughs. "Gotta move on, man. We have four more scenes to shoot before we lose the light."

"I thought there was another beat we could've played after the fall," I say.

The gaffer walks by carrying her burrito lunch.

"Here's a beat I'd like to play." Rico clears his throat and adopts the unnaturally gravelly voice he uses for Heart. "Smokey. I hate to tell you this, but it's burrito Tuesday, and everyone's hungry."

Very funny. "Message received."

He softens. "C'mon," he says, apparently taking pity. "I'll read lines with you over lunch."

It's still wild to me that I'm here, on a set, with a lead role in a TV series. A year ago, I was close to calling it quits on the whole Hollywood thing. It had been years of auditions and acting classes, indie shoots and student films. Of changing clothes in my car because the production didn't have dressing rooms and getting chased off the location by security because we didn't have permits. Of telling my dad I was fine, I was happy, LA was great, even though I hadn't eaten anything in a week that I hadn't stolen from the kitchen of the cafe where I waited tables. The good acting gigs, the ones that gave me hope, were rare. I was a Helpful Honda Guy for four blissful rent-paying months two years ago. That made my dad stop pestering me for a little while about my chosen profession. At least he could point me out to his friends on football Sundays when my spot played. But eventually, the commercial stopped running, the residual checks got smaller and smaller, the new auditions kept turning up bupkis, and I started to wonder if I should just move back to Broken Arrow, a failure at twenty-three, and think about applying to colleges.

When my agent called about *Demon Heart*, it was just another audition in a million for a role I'd never land. I didn't get my hopes up. You can't, in this job, if you want to survive. But then they called me back to read with Rico and for the first time, I started to think I had a chance. I was nervous as hell, but auditions are always like that, so it was nothing new. What *was* new was Rico. I recognized him, vaguely, from his previous work. Not that I had seen *Star Command* or anything, but he'd been on the cover of grocery store magazines enough for me to know who he was. In person, though,

he had that sparkle that successful actors sometimes have—
that alluring mix of charisma, attractiveness, and well-fitting
clothes. He shook my hand, flashed me that smile of his, and
we got down to business. In front of a few casting people,
some people from the show, and a PA running a video camera,
we started the scene. And that was the moment I knew I had
a shot at the role. I'd never had an audition that crackled like
that one did. Rico kept up with me, matching my energy line
for line, as the rest of the room fell away. We *became* Smokey
and Heart that day, for three blissful minutes until the casting
director called cut. And then it was over, and I was sitting
in my car in the parking lot, holding my validated parking
ticket, smiling and hoping.

Four days later, I was standing in a Smart & Final when
my agent called to tell me I got the job. I dropped my basket,
walked straight over to the liquor aisle, and bought a bottle
of champagne. My friends were all out at an improv show I'd
already begged out of well before I got the call, so I drank my
bubbly out of a coffee mug that night, toasting to myself on my
futon in my studio in Koreatown, hoping this was the start of
everything. Even though it wasn't the kind of show I normally
watched or cared about, this was a *dream job*. A series regular on a primetime drama? That is, as my agent would say, "a
career-launcher." I could go anywhere from here.

But then I actually had to do it. The daily grind of shooting
ten, twelve, fourteen hours a day, memorizing lines, working
in the cold, the hot, the rain. Exercising, being careful what I
eat, hitting my marks, finding the emotional beats in a scene
while thirty crew people watch, waiting for me to cry or yell
or break down on cue. The *work*. My Helpful Honda Guy commercial had been a one-day shoot, my indie films shot over

a few weeks. *Demon Heart* shot eight days per episode, for twenty-two straight episodes. The day after we wrapped one episode, we started shooting the next. It was endless work, and I had never had to do it on this scale before. There were days, weeks even, that I was sure the dailies were coming back terrible, convinced the studio would call, the network would call, the showrunner would realize: *We've made a mistake. He can't do this.*

But through it all, Rico, who has done this before, never made me feel dumb even when he probably should have. Every day on set I make mistakes, forcing everyone to wait on me. The grips, I'm sure, are onto me. Karen, the makeup girl, definitely knows. *I'm faking all of this.*

But Rico, Rico the goddamn saint, has never once pointed it out. And for that I love him every day.

Our burritos sit forgotten on the coffee table in my trailer as we play *Red Zone 3* on my Xbox.

"The demon portal could only be opened by a pure heart. There's nothing you could've done, Smokey," Rico says, as Heart.

I shoot at a rebel fighter in the desert, then dodge return fire.

"I can't...think about my lines while I do this," I say.

"That's your problem, you're thinking too much," Rico says, which doesn't make any sense. "Just *react*."

He gives me my cue again: "There's nothing you could've done, Smokey."

TAT-A-TAT. He fires a few rounds at my head in the game, forcing me to duck behind a sand dune to avoid him.

"Jesus, okay! Um...um..." I take a deep breath and sneak a peek at my script, making sure Rico doesn't catch me cheating. "This isn't a game, Heart, it's people's lives," I say, as Smokey.

"It's *our* lives. You wanna spend it fighting me or fighting *with* me?"

This next line's easy. "With you. 'Til the dirt hits my chest."

I see my shot at Rico and I take it. *Bang.* His character drops to the sand, dead. Maybe I can't remember my lines, but at least I'll always be better at *Red Zone* than him.

"Damn you, Reed!" Rico says, tossing his controller away. Then he looks at me and grins that ridiculous, contagious grin of his. "Told you," he says, taking a bite of his burrito. "You got this." And he makes me feel better, like always.

I'm almost able to forget the fact that *Demon Heart* is a show on the bubble without a guaranteed second season, which means everything we've built here could come crashing down with the stroke of some executive's pen, and then I'm out looking for another job.

When I think about what my next gig could be, I just want it to be on a series or a movie that I'd actually watch. That my dad would watch—he'd never turn on some unknown genre show for teenagers and I wouldn't ask him to. When *Demon Heart* ends, I want something *more.* But it was hard enough getting this job. The idea of going back for more auditions, more hoping, more waiting, more sitting alone in my apartment doing weights and eating lean protein and waiting for the phone to ring . . . it's almost too much. Just as I start to feel myself falling down an anxiety spiral, Rico yanks me out.

"You hear they're rebooting the Red Zone movies?" he asks.

I look at him. No. No, I did not hear that.

"Rebooting the whole shebang," he says.

"What about Graves?" I ask. Jasper Graves has been the star of the Red Zone movies since the very beginning. I couldn't imagine the franchise without him.

"Apparently, they want someone new to play Jack Tension. Someone younger." Rico holds up my *Red Zone 3* game box where Jasper Graves grimaces out from behind an assault rifle. My heart springs and I picture myself stepping into Tension's fatigues, picking up his assault rifle.

"What do you think," Rico says, making a tough-guy face, "do I have the look?"

I let out my breath. *Of course* Rico would want to go out for it. Just because I've been playing the game every day for seven years doesn't automatically qualify me for the role. He's a much better actor than me, with a higher profile. Plus, he's got like five million Twitter followers, which my agent tells me is *so crucial*. To which I remind my agent that I'm an actor, not a personality, and the work should speak for itself. But in this case, Rico's probably right that his following, and his general being-good-at-everything-ness will land him that *Red Zone* role if he goes for it. Maybe I can play the villain . . .

"I'm just kidding, dude!" Rico busts up laughing. "Jesus, you should see your face right now. I'm too old for Tension, brother. You should go for it."

Oh. I run my fingers through my hair anxiously. "You think?"

"You got the look, you got the chops, you obviously love the material. I can't imagine someone better. You're destined for more than *Demon Heart*. Someday, I'll be going to cons saying, 'I used to be Forest Reed's co-star.'"

I smile; I can't help it. Sometimes it feels like he's decided to make himself my personal life coach, pumping me up, even when I know it's horseshit.

"I ever tell you how I got my role on *Star Command*?" Rico asks.

"No." Rico's last role was on this heavy science fiction space show where he had to wear prosthetics every single day of shooting and yet he still only has positive things to say about it. The dude's unflappable.

"The show was already in its second season and I was obsessed with it, I *had* to be on it. So I recruited a bunch of friends to come with me to a *Star Command* convention. I bought them all autographs with Gary Levine, you know, the creator of the show? And gave them each one of *my* headshots to have him sign. By the time he signed his eighth or tenth picture of me, he was seriously wondering what the hell was going on."

"You're insane."

"The best part was that I didn't even have to approach him. Eventually he spotted me in the crowd and ran over *to me*. That's when I knew I had him hooked. He demanded to know who I was and I just gave him another headshot, told him to call my agent, and walked away. Gary loved a shtick, though. Told me later he brought me in just to satisfy his curiosity, then I nailed the audition. Nine years later, that character is an icon." He shrugs and takes a bite of his burrito. "Anyway, you gotta get to the director, the new one. Jon Reynolds."

"*Jon Reynolds* is directing the reboot?"

"Yeah, man, didn't you see *Deadline*? It broke this morning."

"How was I supposed to see *Deadline* when I was getting my ass kicked by you all day?"

"Text alerts." He smiles around his burrito.

"So you think I should *harass* Jon Reynolds until he gives me an audition for *Red Zone*?"

"Yup. You gotta convince him one way or another. Tell him this role is the one you were born for. *Sell yourself,*" Rico says.

The very idea of having to sell myself makes my heart clench up in anxiety, but at the same time . . . *Red Zone*. What wouldn't I do to get a role in *Red Zone*?

I'm considering that when there's a knock on my trailer door, and Paula Greenhill climbs the steps to come in.

"Hello, boys."

Paula is our terrifyingly intense publicist. I've only met her once, at a photo shoot for *TV Guide*'s "Hot New Fall Shows," and something about her effortless confidence and tailored pantsuits freaked me out. Still does. Today she's wearing dark red lipstick and has her black bobbed hair slicked back and tucked behind her ears in a look that screams *I'm in charge here.*

"We have great news!" She clasps her hands together excitedly.

Our showrunner Jamie Davies trails behind Paula—he's the guy who invented Smokey and Heart in the first place, which gave us all our jobs. Jamie's the kind of boss who tries to be chums with everyone, but I'm never quite sure where I stand with him. He's got on the same backward Dodgers hat and crisp black Chuck Taylors he always wears, as well as a shaggy haircut that falls across his forehead and makes him look like a college student even though he must be in his forties. Today Jamie looks like a whipped dog, which can't be good.

"Well, it's news, anyway," Jamie says, and Paula shoots him a look. "The numbers are in from last night," he continues. "Point three."

No wonder he looks miserable. "That's not good," I say.

"Yeah, no," Jamie says, "the technical term is *in the shitter*."

Paula takes over. "Now, we're still waiting on digital and DVR numbers, so that will go up, but still, we need to do something. The *Demon Heart* audience, they're young, they're hard to reach. Our team is finding that they don't respond to traditional marketing."

"Damn millennials!" Rico says, giving me a shove. I know he's just trying to lighten the mood, but I hate it when he draws attention to my age. He's only eleven years older than me, but sometimes he acts like I'm still a kid and he's Cary Grant. It's annoying.

"So what's that mean? What can we do?" I ask Paula.

"First of all, *stop worrying*." She takes a seat on the couch across from us. Jamie continues to stand, nervously picking at some old tape stuck to the wall, barely paying attention. "We still have a couple weeks left until the finale. If we can build our ratings, I'd feel a lot better about your chances of a season two."

"Oh, no problem, just grow our audience, seven months into the season? We'll get right on that," Jamie snarks from the corner.

Paula ignores him. "To do that, we need to capture people's attention, get them excited about *Demon Heart*. I want the world to adore you guys—especially you, Forest. They already know Rico, but you're a fresh face. Let's get the internet to fall in love with you."

"The internet's new boyfriend," Rico says with a wink.

"I don't know about that—"

"No, that's exactly right," Paula says. "The first thing I want you to do is start tweeting." Paula knocks on the window of my trailer and a young, hip-looking woman in an army jacket and high-waisted jeans, with curly hair flowing into her eyes, bounds into our space. This is officially too many people in my trailer at one time. "Forest, I want you to meet Caty Goodstein. After this, she's gonna set you up with a Twitter account and teach you how to use it."

My head spins. I've successfully avoided social media my entire career, why should I have to start now that I've actually already made it? Caty gives me a big toothy smile and holds up her giant iPhone, made even giant-er by a bright pink rubber case with bunny ears sticking up from it. "You ready to pop that social media cherry?"

"Not really," I say.

"Well, get ready, because that's only the start," Paula says. "In addition to a big social push, we're also doing a live tour. As soon as you're wrapped shooting the finale, we'll send you out. Three conventions in a row, with traditional media, digital media, online activation, and social integration throughout. It's going to be an all-hands-on-deck straight-up media blitz leading up to the finale. I want viral tweets, I want your faces on the front page of BuzzFeed, I want you trending on Tumblr, I want everyone and their aunt sharing you on Facebook, whatever it takes. I want *eyes on our show*. Sound good?"

Sounds terrifying.

Rico claps his hands together. "Oh my god, I looove conventions!" he moans.

Jamie sighs, apparently feeling just as reticent as I am. "This isn't *Star Command*, dude, these fans are different than you're used to."

"What does *that* mean?" I ask.

"Ignore him," Rico whispers.

"It means *Demon Heart* fans are deranged," Jamie says flatly.

"Stop it," Paula tells him. "They pay your bills."

"You don't know what we deal with," Jamie says. "You're not getting their crazytalk on Twitter all day long."

"Crazy is good, as long as they're crazy for *Demon Heart*," Paula says. "We need to engage them, turn them into advocates. This audience doesn't want me telling them what to watch, they want to hear it from each other." She turns to me and Rico and drills into us with her eyes. "The point of conventions is to get them talking. Your job is to be giffable. These convention fans are more important than any ad buy. It's on you, now."

Paula looks directly at Jamie, who is scowling. "If you want a second season," she says, "this is how you do it."

Jamie looks at us with a resigned sigh. "You guys want to go to some conventions?"

"Hell yes!" Rico says.

"I guess I'm in," I say with a shrug.

"All right!" Caty pumps her fist.

Paula smiles. "You're gonna have a great time," she says to me. "Really. Your first convention isn't something you forget."

Rico slaps me on the back. "Let's go save our show."

claire

I PICK MY WAY UP OUR FRONT WALK WAVING MY
arms in front of me to catch spiderwebs. Our yard is so overgrown that the neighbors have probably considered coming over and trimming everything for us, but I'm sure they
were deterred by the numerous large sculptures of naked
women on display among the greenery. (Okay, they're just one
woman. My mom. Self-portraits. I try not to think about it.)

As soon as I push open the door, I smell pesto. Oh god,
she's cooking something off the internet again.

"Hey, honey bunny, how was school?" Mom hollers from
the kitchen.

"Tremendous." I drop my bag by the door and head for
the stairs.

"Something the matter, kiddo?" Dad asks, rounding the
bend to find me. One thing about your parents being artists
is they are *always home*. Which would be fine if they weren't
incredibly interested in my life at all times.

"Everything's fine, just another day in Pine Bluff," I say on the way upstairs.

"It's eggplant pizzas in an hour!" Mom calls after me. Groan. I knew it was something off the internet.

"There better be bread in that," I say, halfway up.

"No, the eggplant *is* the bread, isn't that great?" she hollers. No. It's not.

"We'll talk more at dinner!" Dad says.

God, parents are so annoying with all their *caring*.

The three *Demon Heart* posters hanging in my room aren't quite enough to completely cover the horrible vintage wallpaper my mom plastered up when we moved in, but they don't make more than three *Demon Heart* posters at the moment, so until the new season two merchandise comes out, I've covered the gaps with some old Citybreakers ads I took from my bookstore, and some *Demon Heart* fanart I printed out at the school library for five cents a page.

I only feel comfortable at last when I have my perfect screen setup—laptop on my stomach, playing last week's episode in the background, and my phone in my hand, scrolling through the comments on my most recent fic. Pretty positive responses so far, with comments like *YOU DESTROYED MY WHOLE LIFE WHYYYY* and *I'M DEAD I'VE FALLEN DIRECTLY OUT OF MY CHAIR AND I AM DEAD NOW.*

Switching over to my Tumblr dash, I start scrolling when I see...

Holy...

What...

Oh my god.

I sit straight up and my laptop falls off my stomach onto the bed. My hands feel heavy and my vision blurs and I can't quite read my phone screen anymore and my head is swimming.

Because the cast of *Demon Heart*—*my Demon Heart*—is coming to Boise—*my Boise.*

THIS. This is what I've been waiting for.

I didn't even know I could hope for this. I didn't even know this was in the realm of things that were possible.

Why the hell are they coming to *Boise*? Why would *anybody* come to *Boise*? Boise is a town you get stuck in, not a town to *travel to.*

Well, unless you live in Pine Bluff.

I have to see them. Me. With Forest Reed and Rico. And Jamie. My brain short-circuits just even trying to comprehend it, so I have to keep saying it. I'm going to see them. I'm going to share an hour with them. Maybe if I'm lucky, the air vents will be pointed just the right way and I can *smell* them.

That's weird, I don't care that that's weird. *DEMON HEART* IS COMING TO IDAHO, I GET TO BE WEIRD IF I WANT.

I take the stairs two at a time and fly into the kitchen.

"Forest Reed, Rico Quiroz, and Jamie Davies are all going to be at Boise Comic-Con! They just announced it!" I am bursting in eleven different directions at once and Mom is taking mini eggplant pizzas out of the oven like this is just a normal Tuesday. *Forget the non-pizzas, Mom, SmokeHeart in Idaho!* Nothing ever happens in Idaho, much less *this*. It hits me all over again, and I have to lean against the kitchen counter because I don't trust my legs to hold me up. My favorite ship, my OTP, my *ONE TRUE FREAKING PAIRING*, is coming to my home state, just a couple hours from me. It's too much, it's too much. My poor heart can't take it. I am but one mere fangirl, how can I be expected to survive this?

Dad looks at Mom for help. "Who?" he mouths to her, uncovertly.

"*Demon Heart.* They're the *Demon Heart* guys!" I cry, gesturing at my T-shirt.

"That's exciting!" Mom says, at a *fraction* of the appropriate excitement level.

"So can I go?" I ask. "I have the money."

"All the way to Boise?" Dad says, his eyebrows furrowing in worry. I can hear it already, his "my little girl" voice he uses when I want to do something he feels is dangerous.

"I've been to Boise by myself before," I say. There's a bus that goes there that I've taken to go to the mall and do school shopping. I mean, for pete's sake, we used to *live* there before we moved to godforsaken Pine Bluff.

"Not overnight you haven't," he says.

"It's fine! I'm old enough!" I take a breath and straighten up and focus on making my voice as serious and calm and adult as possible. "This is *Demon Heart*, Dad."

He looks like he's about to say something else when Mom interrupts him. "I'll take her," she says.

"Hon..."

I stare at her. "Really?" I literally can't picture my mother, Trudi Strupke, at a convention.

"What? A grown woman can't enjoy herself at Comic-Con?" Mom asks, puffing up.

"Yeah, cool! Cool!" I'm not gonna argue with her when she's trying to help. I can feel my heart starting to pound because it looks like this might happen.

"When your father moved us to this town, he promised it would be more relaxing than the city. That we'd get *so much* work done," Mom says. She gestures at the wall in the living room where a bunch of her self-portrait oil paintings hang, and, like, half of them are of her, naked, just like the sculptures in the front yard. It's humiliating. Or it would be, if I ever had anyone over. If I *had* anyone to have over.

"And you know what?" she continues. "Your father was right, I *have* gotten a lot of work done. But Mama misses her Vietnamese food. I'm coming with you."

"Fine!" I say. As long as I get to go, that's the important thing.

"S'okay with me," Dad mutters.

"Wooooooooooo!" I holler and punch the air. *It's happening!*

"I'm going to the city!" Mom squeals as Dad grumbles and waves his hand dismissively. High emotion isn't his strong suit. But he'll be all alone for the weekend—I'm sure he's excited to get some poems written without us around. Mom French-kisses him.

"Gross," I say out of habit, but my heart's not in it. I'm soaring right now.

Back up in my room, I go to one of the posters on the wall—the one where the characters are in profile, just inches from each other. Carefully, I unpin one side and fold the poster along a worn crease down the middle, bringing the sides together so that Smokey and Heart can kiss.

I get to see Forest and Rico. In person.
SmokeHeart.

My heart swells just thinking about it.

"So Heart is the hero, he's the demon with a heart."

"*Demon Heart*," Mom says, piecing it together.

"Exactly. But Smokey's the one everyone really likes," I explain. "We're supposed to root against him because he's Heart's antagonist or whatever, but who could hate that face?"

We're in the car coming into Boise, and I'm trying to give Mom a crash course in *Demon Heart* so she doesn't humiliate me when we get there.

"So why does Smokey hate Heart if he's a good guy?"

"Well, because Smokey's a demon hunter, and Heart is a demon. But Smokey just won't believe that Heart isn't like other demons just because he has a . . . ?" I raise my eyebrows and wait.

"Heart?"

"Ding, ding, ding. Basically Smokey's discriminating against all demons without thinking of them as individuals. And yeah, most of them are evil, but he already knows Heart isn't like the others, he just doesn't trust Heart yet. But they'd actually be really good partners, if Smokey would ever get his life together and learn to trust another person." I sigh. This show is just *so good.* "You know, that classic thing where the guy acts all tough because he doesn't want to let anyone in, and the person he's pushing away the hardest is actually the one who'd be best for him? Yeah, that. That's why everyone ships them."

"Ships them?" Mom asks.

"You know, it's, like, short for *relationship.*"

"Okay . . ." Mom nods, keeping her eyes on the road, but I don't think she really gets it.

"Like how some people might ship Harry and Hermione, because they want them to be together forever and ever. It's like that, only I ship Smokey and Heart."

"Well, I ship myself with your dad," Mom says. "Or maybe Barack Obama."

"Okay, ew, and also that's not really how shipping works."

"I wouldn't want to split up him and Michelle, though," she says.

Very considerate. "I'd join your ship, but I'm really just focused on slash at the moment."

"And slash is..."

"The gay stuff."

"Right." She takes her eyes off the road for a second to look at me. "So these guys, Smokey and Heart, they're gay?"

"On the show? Well, no. Maybe. We don't know. So far they've only dated women, but some people think they're going to get together in the season finale," I tell her. "They *should*, anyway. It's the only obvious thing to do with all the sexual tension they have."

"Oh." She frowns. "So you ship them, but they're not even gay?"

"They might be bisexual!"

"But they haven't said so?"

"Mom, you don't understand, they're *meant* to be together."

Mom gives me a look out of the side of her eyes. "Hon, is there anything you want to tell me?"

"What?" I stare at her, and she raises her eyebrows innocently.

"I'm just *asking*, that's all. That's my job, to ask you about yourself."

It's not the first time she's asked me if I'm gay, but every time it makes me more exasperated. I just wish she'd stop prying.

"Just because you ship slash doesn't make you gay, okay? Lots of people do it," I say, then sigh and look out the window. "If you watched the show, you'd understand."

"Okay," she says, and leaves it alone.

I've seen the queer kids on Tumblr, with their proud statements on their profiles and their pictures throwing rainbow glitter at Pride. I get it, I'm happy they know themselves. But I don't understand how anyone gets to that point. Did they just wake up one day and say, *I see it now, I'm definitely gay!* Or was it a long, slow, difficult process? And if it was long and slow, how did they eventually know they'd reached the end of it? Honestly, I can't really imagine putting on some rainbow suspenders and going to a Pride parade with those kids. I also can't really imagine putting on a cheerleading outfit and going to a football game like the straight girls from high school. Maybe I'm not gay or straight or bi or anything. Maybe I'm just nothing.

We pull up to the hotel and I can already see people coming out and headed for the convention down the street. I see a tiny woman dressed like one of the Ghostbusters and I feel a warmth inside of me. *These*, these are the people who are like me.

Once we get upstairs to our room, I fling my duffel onto the hotel bed and go straight to the window. Throwing open the blinds, I can see we have a full view of the convention center across the street. There are already so many people down there, picking up their badges, taking selfies, *convention-ing*. I'm itching to join them. They all look like they have friends with them, and I'll just be with my mom. But still.

Mom comes out of the bathroom wearing a mom swimsuit. "I'm gonna check out the hot tub," she says.

"You're not coming with me?"

"How are you gonna make friends with your mother hanging around? Besides, I'm not actually here for the convention,

I just had to get out of Pine Bluff for a while," she says, slipping a shower cap on. "Don't do drugs. Unless it seems like
everyone else is doing it. Then make sure you know the name
of everything you take so you can tell the EMTs later." She
slips into a fluffy white towel and winks at me. "And don't
tell your father."

"Okay." I wasn't exactly looking forward to having her tailing me around the convention, asking questions, but somehow now that she's not coming, I feel a little intimidated.
Everyone else will be with someone and I'll be alone.

"Hey, are you gonna ask any questions at the panel?" she
asks.

"Oh god, no."

"Why not, this is your chance, right? Tell that Jamie fella
what you think should happen in the finale, face-to-face."

"*Oh my god*, Mom, go away now." Yeah, I can just see her
waving her arms during the Q&A and forcing them to call on
me. I decide it's definitely better she's not coming.

Mom shrugs. "Suit yourself. Have fun out there!"

She sweeps away in search of the hot tub.

I take in the scene at the Boise Convention Center as I cross
the street. The building isn't much to look at—a big corporate-
looking slab of concrete and glass—but today the premises
are *alive*, crawling with other weirdos who have chosen this
place to spend their Saturday.

I push through the glass front doors, and the noise over-
whelms me. People talking, cameras going off, somewhere
in the distance, lightsabers fire up and I turn to watch a

full-grown Kylo Ren cosplayer battle a toddler dressed as Rey as everyone in the vicinity melts at the adorableness. There's no one for me to share the moment with, so I make a mental memory of it. Maybe I can tell Mom about it later tonight. Or Joanie, when I get back home. I'm not sure Joanie's interested in *Star Wars*, but who doesn't love stories about little kids?

The people are flowing around me and I realize I'm causing a traffic jam, so I move toward a column, press my back into it, and take in the scene. There's an energy in this place, and it doesn't even matter that the carpet is ugly and the fluorescent lights wash out everyone's skin—it's beautiful. The whole lobby is humming with excited fans—I see lots of young people, but also middle-aged couples, moms and dads with tiny kids. I see every body type, every fashion style, and, like, so much more racial diversity than you'd ever find in Pine Bluff.

And then there are the cosplayers. There's a guy sitting against the wall who's dressed as Black Lightning, chatting with a female Winter Soldier. In the line to pick up badges, I see a very tall Brienne of Tarth laughing with a short black Hermione Granger. By the stairs, I smile as I watch a Waverly Earp spot a Nicole Haught across the room and dash over to greet her and take a picture. My *Demon Heart* T-shirt doesn't even raise an eyebrow here.

Against the wall, I see little pods of friends sitting in circles. At one pod, they're splitting a pizza while one woman talks animatedly, gesturing wildly with a slice in her hand as the rest of the group looks on, nodding furiously between bites of pepperoni. I recognize the image of an "overexcited fan" immediately, but for some reason it doesn't feel embarrassing here. The woman isn't downplaying how excited she is about whatever she's talking about. She's just 100 percent geeking out, and her friends love her for it.

That's when it really hits me. There are absolutely no Kyle Cunninghams here. There are no Andrea Garcias. There isn't a single John Deere hat. There's no shame.

These people get it. These people get *me.*

I want to cry. I want to shout. I grin like an idiot to myself and tuck my head down so no one wonders what I'm smiling at. I realize I need to find the line for the *Demon Heart* panel. My heart zips because I remember suddenly that Forest and Rico are somewhere in this building, getting ready for their panel. And I get to see them in just over an hour. How could I forget? The best is still to come.

forest → 5

WE'RE SUPPOSED TO BE MAKING OUR WAY THROUGH the service corridors to VIP registration, but Rico has taken a detour because the guy couldn't follow simple instructions if they were tattooed on his arm. Promising me that he's "done this before," he pushes through a pair of doors and I hear people milling below us. *Lots of people.*

"Check it out," he says, pulling me toward a balcony that overlooks the enormous main hall. I peek over the railing and ... *wow.*

I mean, okay, people-wise it isn't *that* many. Wouldn't even put a dent in OU stadium. But they're packed in, and excited, and loud. Like this is the social event of the year in Boise for these people, which it probably is.

They're also all dressed like it's the Halloween dance at the United Methodist Church, which is to say they're in *real* costumes, not sexed-up versions of everyday professions. Some of the costumes I recognize—there's a lady who's a dead ringer for Doc from *Back to the Future* standing by the entrance with a guy who looks like a hipster millennial version of Jughead Jones from the Archie comics—but most of them, I have no idea who they're supposed to be. I point at a girl with elaborate face makeup and a dark, witchy outfit.

"Good god, how long do you think *that* took? She looks like she stepped out of a horror movie," I mumble to Rico.

Rico drops his mouth open in shock. "Don't tell me you don't know Dark Willow!" He grasps his chest. Because *of course* he knows every character's name here. "Willow Rosenberg? From *Buffy the Vampire Slayer*? Season six? Oh my *god*, Forest, what have you been doing with your life?"

"Dude, *auditioning*," I say. I don't have time to catch up on old shows that were on the air when I was in diapers. I push myself away from the railing. I'm ready to go find registration now.

"Well, I know what I'm getting you for Christmas," Rico says, not leaving his lookout. "All seven seasons, and I'm not leaving your place until you've watched every episode. Yes, even the ones with Riley."

"C'mon, dude, let's go." I'm eager to get out of another conversation where Rico (intentionally or not) reminds me how much older and more experienced he is than me, but Rico's off pointing at another fan.

"Hey, look at that Groot!" he says delightedly.

I follow his gaze and see a guy dressed like a giant tree. "Wow," I say. "He hasn't had a free weekend in a year."

"Tell me you know that one," Rico pleads.

"Of course. From the first *Guardians of the Galaxy*. Made almost a hundred million opening weekend. Launched Chris Pratt as an action hero. Dude's got an amazing career."

"Are you thinking what I'm thinking?" Rico says, still gazing out at the crowd below.

"I'm thinking I hope Chris Pratt's too busy to go out for *Red Zone*."

Rico laughs. "Well, *I* was wondering whether there are any Smokey and Heart cosplayers down there." Rico raises an eyebrow at me. It hadn't even occurred to me.

"Do you think?"

"Maybe. First time I saw a *Star Command* cosplayer, man..." Rico shakes his head nostalgically. "Magical." He props one elbow up on the railing and looks at me. "That's when you realize that people really care."

"You think these people...you think they know us?" I say. I mean, I know rationally that our show has viewers, but our ratings are pretty low, and we've been shooting out in North Carolina for the better part of the last year, so I've never actually met any. Our fans are purely abstract concepts to me at this point.

"Definitely. But probably not many. We have what they like to call a cult fan base. Which means small," he says. "But, you know, *passionate*."

"Isn't it kind of weird that people would be so into our show that they'd come to see us talk?"

Rico smiles at me. "Get used to it, brother."

I look back out over the crowd, searching for guys wearing Smokey's iconic leather jacket. I don't see any.

"There," he says, nodding at two girls passing below us. "I bet they watch the show."

"Them?" They don't look like the type of nerdy sci-fi comic-book-loving geeks I pictured as the audience for *Demon Heart*. They look like they belong in a record store, honestly—one of them in glasses and the other one rocking an oversize denim jacket with the sleeves cut off. But like magic, just after Rico says something, one of the girls glances up and spots us and it's like her body lights up from the inside out. She straight-up *whacks* her friend on the arm, and soon they're both screaming and waving.

I wave back, sort of in amazement. No one has ever reacted like that to me before. Rico cracks up and blows them a kiss.

"Never gets old," he says.

Rico pulls away. I follow but my eye is drawn by two people working to unfurl a banner for . . . Red Zone.

"Holy shit," I say, gripping Rico's arm. "Holy shit, Rico, Red Zone is here!"

"Oh yeah, I meant to tell you! Jon Reynolds did a panel this morning on video game adaptations in the post–Lara Croft world. You have to go find him."

Wait. Jon Reynolds is here? Jon Reynolds . . . is *here*?

"Forest," Rico says, jiggling my shoulder. "We still have, like, forty minutes before our panel. You have time. Go find him. Get that face-to-face, brother."

I meet his eyes. "Yeah, yeah. Okay." I turn to find the stairs down to the floor. I have no idea what I'm supposed to say if I find him, but I'll go. I have to try.

Jamie cautioned me against venturing down to the convention, but Rico said Jamie is a fool and I should experience what he calls "The Floor" at least once per con. But I'm not going downstairs for the *life experience,* or whatever. This is a mission.

Thankfully, I'm already wearing a big sweatshirt, and I

tug my Sooners hat down over my eyes. The idea of being approached by a fan while I'm on my own sort of freaks me out, so I'm hoping to avoid attention by being generically bland-looking.

The floor is crawling with people. It's claustrophobically tight, like when everyone leaves at the end of a Thunder game, except with more costumes and nerds. Thankfully, I don't see the two *Demon Heart* fans we waved to earlier. Hopefully they're off somewhere, tweeting about it.

Oh god, *tweeting*. I flinch thinking about the account Caty set up for me that I haven't used yet and then push it out of my mind.

The Red Zone booth sits right in the front of the whole convention. Prime real estate. They have game systems set up promoting the new version that will come out soon, *Red Zone 4*. I'm itching to play it—I've already played through *Red Zone 3* many times and I'm ready for a new challenge— but I don't have time for that right now because I have to get back for my panel soon. I find the banner with a photo of Jon Reynolds off to the side advertising that they'll be doing sign-ings at the booth later today. He looks like exactly who you'd want to helm an action movie—a perfect balance of wise and badass. He has this distinguished haircut, hipster glasses that probably cost more than my monthly rent, and a strong jaw and thick neck that indicates he works out. I wonder what he benches.

I called my agent from the staircase to ask him how he thought I should approach this. To his credit, he promised to do what he could to get me an audition, and then he said, *and I quote*, "Just get in there and talk to him. Face time is huge." Like that's just a thing. Like Jon Reynolds is just some dude and not a famous multimillionaire director in charge of one of the biggest film franchises in recent memory. Thanks for the tips, Mr. Agent Man. No sweat. I'll take it from here, I guess. I wonder if Rico's agent treats him like this.

As I approach the booth, there's a guy setting up the signing table. Between his perpetual scowl, his tight red jeans, and the very modern, large, solid black rectangle tattoos covering both forearms, he's putting out pretty clear *too cool for this* signals. I don't see Reynolds anywhere. I wonder if he's behind the curtain right there or somewhere else altogether, far away from the crowds and noise of this room. I gather myself up and approach the guy.

"Hi, can you tell me when Jon Reynolds will be around?"

Tattoo Guy barely glances up. "The signing starts at five."

A nerd dude standing in front of the booth pipes up. "There's a line," he says, jerking his thumb behind him, where there are already about eight guys waiting.

Like, *yikes*, it's not even three p.m., y'all, isn't there something else you could be doing?

I turn back to the Tattoo Guy and lower my voice. "I'm not here for an autograph, I just wanted to have a few words with him." I tip the brim of my hat back, giving him a look at my face. "I'm Forest Reed, I'm an actor?" The guy finally looks at me, but his flat expression doesn't change. "*Demon Heart*? Mondays at nine?"

Nothing. I start to feel my cheeks turn red. This was a bad idea, why do I ever listen to Rico? I start talking a little faster. "Okay, no problem, my agent's getting in touch with him anyway, but I just wanted to see him face-to-face, have a quick hello since we both happened to be in Boise...." I give a little chuckle here, but he is giving me nothing in return.

I take a step to go and then turn back because like, *god*, if I've already started to make a fool of myself, might as well bring it home, right? "You know, hey, if he's inclined to swing by, my panel is today at three thirty in Hall C."

"Okay" is all Tattoo Guy says.

"You'll let him know?" I want to run away from here, but I need to hear him say it first.

He eyes me one last time. "Yup," he says, and goes back to work.

And that's it. The nerd at the front of the line gives me a nasty smile and I get out of there, pulling my hat back down and hoping this wasn't all a waste of my time.

THERE'S A LINE FOR THE *DEMON HEART* PANEL, and it looks, well, *lively*. There's maybe fifty people already waiting, chattering and buzzing with excitement. It looks like they all know one another, even though there's no way that's possible, right? Could I be the only person here who came alone? I wonder what my mom is doing right now. Probably convincing the Holiday Inn to make their pool area clothing-optional.

Taking my place at the end of the line, I lean against the wall, pull out my phone, and run my fingers over the fading *Demon Heart* stickers on the case. I get to see Smokey and Heart soon! It's almost too much, so I open Tumblr, but I'm too jittery to actually look at my dash, so I open my email, but there's nothing new, so I open Facebook, but I hate Facebook, so I reopen Tumblr. My own personal endless loop of being an anxious person with a phone in public.

"Here you go." A voice forces me to look up from my phone. It's the girl behind me in line, she's handing me a clipboard with a name/email signup on it. "In case you want to join the *Demon Heart* mailing list."

I'm totally already on the *Demon Heart* mailing list. *Obviously* I'm on the *Demon Heart* mailing list. But the way she smiles at me flusters me for some reason.

"Oh, okay," I say, and start putting my info down anyway.

As I scribble my email address, I can feel her watching me. I glance up, and she looks away. She's black, and her hair is shaved short on the sides, but the longer tight curls in back and on top stick out in every direction, including over her forehead into her eyes. She's not in cosplay. Or if she is, it's for, I dunno, *Pretty Little Liars* or something. She's wearing a gray dress that curves over the top of her body but is flowy at the bottom, with little orange foxes dotting it. I finish writing my info and pass the clipboard down the line. I kind of want to say something else to her, but what is there to say? Besides, she probably already has friends here. She looks pretty and put-together, and she has a very cool haircut. There's no way she's not popular.

I pull my phone back out and open Tumblr, but as I scroll, I can feel her looking at my phone. When I glance back at her she blushes, caught in the act.

"Sorry," she says, and gives me an apologetic smile. She's wearing the brightest pink lipstick I've ever seen. I don't wear lipstick, couldn't even imagine wearing that shade. But on her it looks perfectly natural, like she sells it with confidence alone. She busies herself straightening her skirt over her hips, smoothing the wrinkles out. When she looks at me, I'm still watching her hands move across her legs. Now it's my turn to be embarrassed.

"Sorry," I say. Then I laugh, because this is dumb, and then *she* laughs, thank god.

"This is my first convention," she says, almost like she's apologizing for something. But she has nothing to apologize for. It's weird to see someone wearing such confident lipstick be nervous. Like they don't go together.

"Me too," I say.

"Oh, good!" she says. "I just assumed everyone here had already done this before."

"Not me." And then I run out of things to say. I feel my cheeks warming, so I look away, and then I click open my phone again, needing an excuse to stop talking to her.

"I . . . I love that gif," she says, nodding at my phone.

I glance at the screen, open to Tumblr. The gif is from a scene in the *Demon Heart* pilot. One of the first moments I picked up on the presence of something *extra* in Smokey and Heart's relationship. Smokey's been tracking a demon the entire episode, until he finally corners it at an abandoned warehouse (because *of course* it's an abandoned warehouse). They have a foot chase through all the shadows and the towering, vaguely industrial equipment, and up onto the roof, until the demon jumps off and lands three stories down on the ground, leaving little old human Smokey stuck up top. The demon pulls himself to his feet, unharmed, and looks up . . . and that's when Smokey recognizes the demon is Heart, his old acquaintance. They share a long, subtext-fueled look, until Heart escapes into the shadows and Smokey is forced to grapple with what he's just seen. *That look* is what got the pilot a first-season pickup. And *that look* is what captured the heart of, well, me, and probably everyone else in this line right now. What was in that look? What did it mean? Where was this headed? That's the whole thrust of *Demon Heart*. So yeah, it's an important gif.

"It's one of my favorites," I say, and I watch in amazement as her shoulders relax.

"Me too," she says, then adds, "I'm Tess."

"Claire." Until now, she's been grabbing one elbow across her body, her sleeveless dress showing off her arms, wide and soft and this deep smooth brown and just *out there* like they belong out there. Sleeveless dresses—another thing I couldn't imagine wearing. How does she make it look so easy? But now she lets go of her elbow and reaches over. I slip my phone in my pocket and shake her hand, which is cool and soft. Her smile spreads across her entire face.

"It's nice to be around people who get it," she says. "My friends, they don't do, you know…" She waves her hand around. "*This.*"

It's my turn to comment on whether my friends do *hand wave* *this* or not, but…friends? Yeah, *no*. I guess I have Joanie, and my parents, and none of them get it.

I say, "Heh." Vague enough to sound like I'm agreeing without offering any additional information. I wish I hadn't put my phone away, because now would be a good time to start looking at it again. I want to try to extricate myself from this conversation, but I also don't. Tess is much easier to talk to than anyone at my high school, and I get the feeling I could start talking about anything at all and she'd be happy to join in. But I'm somehow paralyzed by what to say next. Obviously she likes *Demon Heart*, so we could talk about that, but everything I think to say sounds stupid. *So, you like* Demon Heart, *huh?* Ugh, dumb. *Who's your favorite character?* Agggggh, gross. For a fleeting moment there, I had become one of those chatting, social people in line I was intimidated by before and I want that feeling back. Finally, I come up with something and before I lose my nerve, I just blurt it out.

"Do you want to trade Tumblr URLs?"

"Oh," she says, and frowns. My stomach sinks.

"We don't have to." I adjust my glasses. "Never mind."

"No, it's fine! I just..." she says hesitantly. "I've never done that before. I, uh, have a lot of *Demon Heart* stuff on there."

"Oh. Yeah, so do I."

"And some of it's kind of..."

Kind of what?

"You know," she says. "Between Smokey and Heart..."

"Oh, yeah," I say. "Totally."

"So you..."

"Ship them? *Definitely*," I say confidently. About this one thing at least, I'm 100 percent certain. She lets out a breath and starts to smile. Wow, she has really nice teeth. "I don't know how anybody who's paying attention could *not* ship them. I mean, come on."

I unzip my hoodie to show her my other favorite *Demon Heart* T-shirt. Smokey's holding his battle-ax to Heart's neck, and Heart is gripping Smokey by the throat. It's supposed to be suspenseful, I guess—men on opposite sides of an eternal battle. But to me, it just looks like two incredibly attractive guys playing a high-stakes game of Twister with props.

Tess squeals in delight. "I haven't seen that one! Oh my god, they're so close. If they would just..."

"I know," I say, and I pinch my shirt between my fingers causing a wrinkle, bringing their faces even closer together.

"There it is!" she shouts.

Then, by hunching and straightening my shoulders, I'm able to bring their lips together and apart, again and again, and Tess is dying laughing and I can't help but giggle with her. Her laughter is contagious.

"Okay, but you can't add me until later, okay? I don't want to see you looking at the dumpster-fire stuff I reblog." She pulls a sketchbook out of her bag and tears a blank page from the back. Holding the paper against the wall, she writes her URL on it, then hands it to me.

"Pan-labyrinth," I read. The paper feels heavy and nice in my hands. Her handwriting is loopy and large.

"And don't laugh at my fanart," she says.

"I would never!" I tell her genuinely. I take her pen, my fingers brushing against hers. It's a nice pen, with silky black ink. I write *heart-of-lightness* on the other half of the paper and tear it off and I don't even pause before I give it to her, but when she reads it and looks up at me with big eyes, I realize with a cringe that she knows who I am.

I can see her image of me changing as she looks me over brand-new.

It's not that I'm famous, *I'm not.*

No, really, there are people on Tumblr who are legit famous, and I'm not one of them. But I write fic, and a lot of people follow me so they can ask when the next chapter of whatever WIP I've been posting will come out, that kind of thing. But I don't really have *friends* online. Acquaintances, sure. Mutuals, definitely. It's just that most of the time on Tumblr I feel like everyone else is friends with one another and I'm just *around*, reblogging gifsets and posting fics and trying to avoid any drama. We're a community, for sure, but

I'm kind of like the old lady in the creepy house at the end of the lane who never comes to the block parties. It didn't even cross my mind that Tess would recognize my name.

"You're heart-of-lightness?" she asks incredulously.

"Uh, yeah."

"I love your fics!" She says this with, let's be honest, far more weight than I really deserve. The line starts moving, and I feel grateful to be able to escape what has suddenly become a much more intense conversation.

"Thanks," I say as we shuffle forward.

"No, seriously, you're really good. Oh my god, don't reblog any of my fanart, you probably have a million followers."

"I don't. At all. But don't worry, I won't. I'll, ah, see you online," I say, and slip into the hall.

Before I'm out of earshot, I hear her mutter "heart-of-lightness" to herself again. And I feel a little stuttery. I think about the look on her face when she read my name and I smile to myself, and mutter under my own breath, "Tess."

THE CONVENTION CENTER ISN'T BIG, NECESSARILY, but that has never stopped me from getting lost. As I'm wandering the service corridors, peering through doors, searching for the greenroom Paula told me about, I hear a familiar voice.

"Hey, Z-Dawg!" It's Jamie. I follow the voice and round the corner to see "Z-Dawg" is Zach Sanchez-Anderson. I didn't even know Jamie knew him. Maybe they're both in some secret showrunner society. He's the creator of this show called *Time Swipers* that my agent tells me has "franchise potential" and is apparently "blowing up with the demo." All I know is that three years ago he was a nobody and now he has a hit TV show and—according to the *Hollywood Reporter*—a very tasteful historic Spanish-style house in the Hills.

I hang back, not wanting to interfere with their little showrunner catch-up session. Looking over Zach, he has almost the same style as Jamie—sneakers, baseball cap, hoodie—but he stands a little straighter, keeps his haircut a little fresher. Jamie's the only showrunner I know personally, so I sort of assumed he was par for the course, but I see now that slob-chic isn't necessarily the required style.

"What's cookin'?" Jamie asks him. "Your network got you out here, too, huh?"

"You kidding?" Zach says. "I begged them to let me come. Our panel had to move to a larger room. *Twice.*"

"Well, you got a great show, Sanchez. People love it."

"Started out as assistants and look at us now, right?" Zach says. Then he spots me hanging down the hall. He calls out at me, "It's your time next, man. Get used to the love out there today, you deserve it." Jamie turns around to see me approaching.

I didn't realize Zach Sanchez-Anderson would even know who I was. "Thanks," I say, and start to make my way toward them, embarrassed that I was caught eavesdropping.

"I'll catch you later," Zach tells Jamie. As he strides past me, he slaps me on the back. I amble up to Jamie, who stares after him, curling his lip in disgust.

"His show blows," Jamie mumbles once Zach is out of earshot.

God, Jamie really just hates everything. How did he ever manage to create a show as emotional as *Demon Heart* with that kind of attitude about everything?

Jamie takes off in the other direction, dragging his feet in a pouty sort of shuffle. "Where you been, anyway? Our room's this way."

When we reach it, the greenroom is just an unused conference room with a large table of snacks. It's not that I expected

Boise, Idaho, to offer up the lap of luxury, but this is so utili-tarian that I'm reminded of my LA apartment. IKEA furniture and Lärabars—ahh, feels like home.

Rico is already there, scoping out the snack table. I join him just as he stuffs three Red Vines in his mouth. "You talk to Reynolds?"

"Just his assistant. Can you believe he's here? In Boise? In this building, even?" I'm disappointed I didn't get to talk to him, but remembering how close I got makes me buzz with anticipation. What if Tattoo Guy tells Reynolds about the panel and he *actually comes*?

I catch Rico's eye and he looks amused. He probably doesn't get excited by his favorite directors anymore. It's all old hat to Rico Quiroz.

"Anyway..." I start inspecting the bananas on the table.

Rico puts his hand on my shoulder. "Don't ever let Hollywood kill your spirit, hombre. You hear me?"

"Have I ever told you I'm super into your bromance?" Jamie says from across the room, leaning back in a conference chair and putting his brand-new black Chuck Taylors on the table. I pull away from Rico, reinstating a personal bubble, but Rico only chuckles and whacks me on the shoulder.

The social media girl Caty saunters into the room. I avert my eyes—I don't want her asking me how my feed or whatever is going. After she set me up with an account, she told me to "just start tweeting." I haven't opened the app since. Rico mentioned on the flight to Idaho that I already had 42,000 fol-lowers on Twitter. *Without a single tweet.* The thought of try-ing to come up with something clever to say to 42,000 people makes my throat close up and my fingers twitch. I don't know what she expects me to do. I'm an *actor*. If she wants me to be interesting on Twitter, she's going to have to have the *Demon Heart* writers' room get together to write me something.

As she comes over to the snack table and starts casually looking over the options, Rico chats to her about garlic versus red pepper hummus and the benefits of each. Meanwhile, I sneak a look at Caty. She's young, maybe recently out of college. Today she's wearing a small-patterned floral shirt under a very loud large-patterned floral blazer. I can't believe she's pulling it off, but with her confidence and her dark curly hair in a messy-chic bun (or is it just messy? I can't tell) it looks pretty good. I wonder what she studied in college to end up here, setting up Twitter accounts for reticent actors. She snort-laughs at something Rico says, and I feel a pang of jealousy that this all comes so easy for them—the small talk, the traveling, the social media. Rico seems perpetually comfortable with himself, and so does Caty. I wonder how they do it.

Caty looks over Rico's shoulder at me. "Hey, Forest," she says. "Saw you're up to sixty-five thousand followers now. Think you might like to tweet something soon?"

No, not really, I think.

"Yeah, totally," I say.

"Just say hi," she says. "It doesn't have to be groundbreaking. People will be excited just to hear from you."

"Okay, yeah," I say, ignoring the pit in my stomach at the idea of "just saying hi" to a group of people rapidly approaching the size of my hometown.

"Hey, did you guys hear the glee club singing in some Star Trek language out there?" Jamie sneers.

"Pretty sure it was Elvish." Rico corrects him effortlessly, taking his bagel and sitting down in a plush chair. He shrugs at Jamie's eyeroll and adds, "I went to a million of these cons when I was on *Star Command*. You pick up things."

"Yeah, well, nothing against the geek-apella, but this convention tour blows. If the network's gonna cancel us, I wish they'd just do it already instead of turning us into PR indentured servants," Jamie grumbles.

"Nobody's making you do anything," Caty says almost under her breath, not looking up from her giant pink phone. Her thumbs are zipping around, typing at mach speed.

"Sorry, who are you again?" Jamie snaps.

"Caty Goodstein. We've met. Many times." She finishes typing, then looks up at Jamie, slipping her phone into her blazer pocket, the bright pink bunny ears sticking out the top.

"Uh-huh," Jamie says, looking her over, "I remember."

"Do you think they will? Cancel us?" I ask. It's starting to feel more and more likely. I *have* to get that *Red Zone* role. *Demon Heart* can't be my only option.

"No one's getting canceled yet," Paula Greenhill says, waltzing in, wearing a charcoal-gray pencil skirt and matching fitted jacket, all straight lines and authority. She's followed by an entourage of four or five assistants.

Paula puts her enormous purse down on the table with a thud, then flicks Jamie's shoes with her fingers until he takes his feet down. "They don't need to come to any renewal decisions until well after the finale," she says. "We still have plenty of time to get people excited about our little show.... Is that what you're planning to wear?" Paula looks directly at me. I glance down at my black jeans and white T-shirt.

"Um, yes?"

"Donna"—Paula nods at one of her assistants—"a little help?" Donna jumps to action, rummaging through a tote bag.

"What are you, a medium?" Donna asks me.

"Yeah."

Donna pulls a black T-shirt out of her bag and rips the tags off it. It's a Wonder Woman shirt—brand-new, but weathered to look old.

"See if this fits," Donna says, handing it to me.

"Got any Red Zone shirts in there?" I ask, craning my neck to see what else is in that bag. Does she have other clothes, other sizes, other styles? Is her whole job to walk around with nerdy clothes in case people like me didn't dress ourselves with the appropriate care?

"That's not really the brand we're going for," Donna says.

"Put it on, Forest," Paula calls.

I sigh, because *yes*, I take off my shirt for the cameras all the time, but that's for work. I don't like the expectation that just because they've seen me shirtless once means they're invited to look at my body whenever. But there's no dressing room here, so I pull off my T-shirt, very aware of the army of publicists probably checking out my abs. Not to mention Caty and Jamie, and *Rico* for crying out loud. And yes, they're nice abs. I work really hard on them. But still, they're *mine*.

The shirt fits. Donna pokes at my hair a bit before she leaves me alone, satisfied.

"You look great," Paula says. "Perfect for this crowd."

"Yeah, how big is this panel even going to be?" Jamie grumbles. "This entire convention couldn't fill a courtroom."

"We've found it actually doesn't matter how many people are physically in the room so long as we generate great content. *Demon Heart*'s audience are internet people. Caty's going to be live-tweeting and blogging the panel, and we're livestreaming the feed. All you have to do is be interesting."

Awesome, that's not terrifying or anything. I wander over to the plush chairs where Rico is sitting, hoping that by staying in his orbit, he'll keep some of the spotlight off me. As I sink into the chair next to him, he nudges my boot with his shoe.

"You'll be great," Rico whispers to me, which I take to mean my nervousness is written all over my face.

"Everyone take a deep breath. This is a strategy that's worked before. We've done amazing things using social engagement on *Ice Queens*, *Darkness Falls*, and *Time Swipers*."

Jamie snorts at the mention of *Time Swipers*. "So basically it's all on our shoulders now. Just don't say anything to screw it up," Jamie says.

"How could we screw it up?" I ask. My nerves are already running high, but my stomach clenches even more when I remember that Jon Reynolds might be out there, too. A lot could be resting on this.

"Don't worry, it's a friendly crowd," Rico says. "You've talked to fans before, right?"

"Not really," I tell him.

"Handsome *and* lucky. Some people get it all," Jamie mutters.

"Everyone just be yourself," Paula says. "Except you, Jamie, you should try being someone else. Someone excited to be here."

"We don't really get a lot of fans out there in North Carolina," I tell Jamie. It's true, though aside from a few random locals, we didn't have many fans come by set. Rico always said it was because our fans weren't the "Confederate flag types," which we do see a lot of on the trucks that drive past the woodsy areas we shoot in. But what does that mean? Who even watches *Demon Heart*, anyway? And what do they think about Smokey?

What do they think about *me*?

"You'll be great," Rico says. "Convention fans are the most supportive audience you can imagine. They're here because they already love you. I mean, you know what fans are like."

I conjure up an image of the people I saw out on the floor. "They're nerds."

"Sure," Rico says.

"Geeks."

"Yeah."

"Fanboys," I say.

Jamie, Rico, Paula, Caty, and the assistants all look at me. I've said something wrong.

"They're not fanboys?"

I hear the cheers before I even see the door, and it takes me a few beats to register that they're for us. My heart is beating in my ears, and I feel distant and shallow. There's a nudge at my elbow, and I turn to see Rico running his hand through his thick curly hair and winking at me. I hear the moderator call our names from the stage and somebody opens the doors for us and I keep my eyes locked on Rico's feet in front of me, stepping where he steps, climbing the stairs, finding my chair, the lights bright.

I shade my eyes and look out and see...*girls*. Women. Moms, daughters, friends. All screaming.

"Fan*girls*," I whisper to Rico, and I can tell he's dying laughing at me on the inside.

Some of these girls are even dressed like us, wearing heavy yellow Carhartt jackets for Heart and carrying battle-axes for Smokey, faux stubble drawn on painstakingly with eyebrow pencil, looking tough in leather jackets a bit too large for them. But someone should tell them that screaming that much is very out of character for either Smokey or Heart.

There's a girl in the front row, maybe fifteen years old, who has broken down sobbing and I'm not sure why. Have we already disappointed her without even opening our mouths? She notices me looking at her. I give her a small smile, but she only cries harder.

The moderator, some comic-book website guy I'd never heard of before, quiets the crowd, somehow bringing order to the chaos, and starts the panel. I glance around the room, searching the faces for Jon Reynolds, but there's no sign of him. Then the back doors open, and I see Tattoo Guy sneak into the back and stand against the wall. Okay! It's not Reynolds, but at least someone came. This is my chance to show him I'm capable of being a star.

As the moderator introduces us, I pick up the mic, cool and heavy in my hand. Let's do this.

8

SMOKEY IS SITTING, LIKE, FORTY FEET FROM ME right now. I'm smiling, no, *grinning*, and I can't stop. I might break into hysterical giggles at any second. I don't even know why. I mean, I know why, Smokey is *right there*. But my body is outside my control. There's a girl in the front row who is all-out bawling, and I know how she feels. Emotions are, like, leaking out my *pores*. Crying actually seems like a pretty minor reaction. All things considered, I might literally explode.

"Local girl explodes at Boise Comics Convention. Doctors mystified, but witnesses suspect she had too many feels. Details at eleven."

The moderator starts the panel and he has prepared a slew of easy questions about the show (it's great), life on set in North Carolina (very rainy), and what's coming up at the end of the season (can't tell us). Forest is wearing a Wonder

Woman T-shirt, and I realize I didn't even know he was a fan. I love that he loves Wonder Woman, how great is that? The shirt looks old; I wonder how long he's had it. There's still so much I don't know about him—I wish the questions were more about his feelings and background and personality. What does he think about the new Star Trek movies? Is he a dog person or a cat person? Does he ship SmokeHeart? *Will it go canon?*

There's a chick in a really cool bright floral blazer wandering around, taking pictures of the panel and the crowd with her phone and posting them somewhere, her thumbs flying over the screen. I assume she must work for the show; it seems like a cool job and I wonder how she got it.

Before I know it, it's time for the audience Q&A, and I'm trying not to think about my mom's dumb suggestion that I should ask a question. I just want to enjoy this, I don't need to be a participant, too.

There's a palpable shift in tone once the Q&A portion begins, as fans stand up to ask questions I've seen percolating on Tumblr that haven't had an outlet until now. A girl with pink hair asks whether the demons on the show are intended as a metaphor for race relations in America. A woman in an electric wheelchair asks why her favorite female character was killed off after just three episodes. Jamie glides through one answer after another. "It's just where the story took us," he says breezily, as though the story were somehow sentient, like a jungle guide leading him through a forest of ideas, showing him the only possible path.

Which is obviously wrong. I might not know exactly how TV works behind the scenes, but I know story decisions are consciously made. *By him.* He's trying to anthropomorphize the story to make it sound like the episodes spring to life and write themselves, but it's just not true.

I listen to Jamie sidestep another question about why the only Asian character on the show was a hacker computer wiz—something that hadn't even occurred to me but is definitely a tired stereotype. He deftly avoids answering the question by talking about how the show is actually really popular in Japan.

The anger feels like sand on my tongue. I don't understand how this guy could create this show that's such a tender and thoughtful story about friendship and loving others despite our differences. He doesn't seem capable of it.

I check the time on my phone. The panel will be ending soon. I'm waiting for someone to ask what I really want to know. Someone in her twenties with buzzed hair steps up to the mic. She has the look—maybe she'll ask the question. She leans in, her mouth too close to the microphone. "Hi, my name's Heather and when Smokey says in episode seven that he finally feels like he knows where he belongs, is he talking about working with Heart?"

Yes! This is the kind of question I came to hear. *Sing to me of SmokeHeart, O Muse, sing.*

"Forest, you wanna take this one?" Rico says. Forest looks a bit unsteady. He hasn't spoken much so far.

"Um, sure," he says. Then he pauses before continuing slowly. "When I played that scene, I was actually thinking that Smokey was talking about literally finding a home in this world. His apartment in town. His place to hang his hat."

That is *not* my interpretation of that line.

Forest adds, "You know, Smokey's a pretty independent guy. He doesn't really need anyone else."

And I can't really explain it other than what he said is so wrong it's *absurd* and that part of me that loves Smokey down to my bones knows that. Smokey doesn't need anyone else?

"BULLSHIT."

The adrenaline hits my system as I realize that I just said that. Out loud. And *loudly*.

As eyes turn toward me, I feel my blood thump in my ears, and I wonder what the hell I did that for. To my horror, I see Forest squint into the bright lights and find my eyes.

I'm making eye contact with Forest Reed. Not through a computer screen, but in real life. It's a little *too* real. I came here to look at my favorite actor, not have him look at me.

But Forest Reed *is* looking at me. And he's frowning.

"Did you have something to add?" he asks sarcastically.

I look around wildly. A few rows up, Tess is staring at me. Everyone is staring at me. More than a few phones are pointed at me. My palms start to sweat. I wipe them on my jeans. I remember what my mom said. This is my chance to tell them what I really think. I should take it.

"Yeah, actually." I stand up.

A volunteer runs over to me. "Say your name and ask your question," she whispers and puts a microphone in my hand. It's heavy and holding it feels like power. I take a deep breath, look somewhere above Forest's head, and pretend I'm just telling my mom what I think about Smokey and Heart, not *Forest freaking Reed.*

"My name is Claire Strupke, and *of course* Smokey needs other people. Everyone does. You can't go through life alone, it's not healthy," I say. "Smokey's whole problem is he doesn't realize how lonely he really is, until he meets Heart."

I notice Rico nodding along. Forest seems to be actually thinking about what I said. Is he *considering* my interpretation of his character? What is even happening? When I woke up this morning, the last thing I thought I'd be doing today is talking to Forest Reed. *What?*

The chick in the wild floral blazer comes up the aisle and takes my photo. She does it too fast for me to be nervous about how I look. I straighten my hair and push up my glasses, but it's too late. Whatever it's for, I'm sure I look like a freak. Then she winks at me and blows a giant pink bubble with her gum as she types on her phone.

Jamie smiles politely. "Thanks for that, thank you," he says. And as I look at him, I realize I'm not done. I can't be.

I steel myself. "I...Actually, Jamie, I have a question for you."

"Oh." Jamie exchanges a look with the volunteer standing next to me, who reaches for my mic, but I draw away from her, closing my fingers over its cold metal even tighter. I have a question and I have this microphone and I'm not going to sit back down until I've asked it.

"You've built this really strong relationship between Smokey and Heart," I say, and the volunteer steps away, unsure what to do now that I've seized control. "They presumably hate each other, but they're also kind of obsessed with each other."

Jamie narrows his eyes, but I can't stop. I have to know if my idea of Smokey and Heart is what the show intends; I have to know if what I feel about them is real.

"Some people would even suggest..." I say, my lips close

to the microphone. "Some people would even suggest that Smokey and Heart..." I can feel Tess's eyes on me from three rows up. She wants to know, too. We *all* want to know.

"Are they *in love with* each other?"

Dead silence.

I continue, "I think they are. So I guess my question is, are they going to *realize* they're in love with each other by the end of this season... *and kiss*?"

There's a collective holding of breath as all the eyes and phones in the room turn to Jamie, and I swear to god my heart simply stops beating for a second while I wait. Jamie looks at me with a completely neutral expression that I can't read, as he probably deliberates what to say next, but already the pause has gone on too long. Was this a big mistake?

Jamie is raising the microphone when another voice interrupts him.

"You think Smokey is gay... for Heart?" Forest asks slowly, like I'm an idiot. He's smirking at me. *Smirking.*

His accusation just hangs in the air.

"Forest—" Rico starts, and Forest shoots him a look.

"Obviously they have a strong connection..." Jamie says diplomatically, finally finding his voice.

"Yeah, but not *that* kind of connection." Forest talks over him.

"We'll see their conflict play out in the coming episodes," Jamie says.

"No disrespect to people who are, but Smokey definitely *isn't*," says Forest.

"You'll have to keep watching if you want to see more," says Jamie.

And then Forest just cracks. He drops the mic into his lap

and lets his head fall backward. "Jamie!" he says to the ceiling, then turns to stare at him. Jamie meets his eyes and it's a battle of wills. Rico looks back and forth like a kid watching his parents fight.

Forest hisses, "What are you doing? What are you talking about? This is crazy. *She's crazy.*"

And he's covering the mic with his hand, so I genuinely don't think he means for us to hear it, but we still do, and the hall is silent. The volunteer takes my microphone back from me and my ears are burning hot and I start gathering my things because suddenly this room is too small, they are too close, and all of this needs to be on a laptop screen and not happening in real life.

I vaguely hear Rico's admonishment: "Forest. Dude."

Then Jamie fills the dead air. "The finale is coming May twenty-second. You'll just have to tune in to see what happens." But I'm already edging out of my row and speed walking down the aisle to the back of the room as the moderator wraps up the panel and there's sparse applause and I push out the doors and I'm gone.

I shove through the crowds of still-happy nerds in the lobby laughing and chatting and pretend-jousting with each other, but they no longer feel like my people. They feel like strangers, because they are.

Just because I like something doesn't mean it likes me back.

I don't stop running until I make it to my hotel room. The tears start welling as soon as I close the door. Mom isn't there, so I drop my bag on her bed and crawl into mine and let myself sob in private.

Forest's voice still rings in my ears. Did he have to be such a dick? He could have just said, "No, that's not in the plans." But instead he scoffed and sputtered and acted like I had suggested the most ridiculous idea in the history of television. But, like, what show has Forest Reed been working on? Because it's not ridiculous in the slightest. It's *right there* on the screen for anyone to see. I just happened to be the one to point it out.

I suddenly have the need to do what I always do these days when I get stressed—watch *Demon Heart*. I pull my laptop off the side table and click open episode four, one of my favorites. As the cold open begins, Forest's face fills the screen and I glance away as anger floods my belly. *Dammit.*

No. I'm not going to let Forest Reed ruin *Demon Heart* for me. I look back at him and force myself to think of him as Smokey, not Forest. Smokey I have no problems with. Smokey I still love. It's Forest Reed who I wish would just disappear.

"NOW WE HAVE TO CLEAN UP THIS MESS, AND you're going to do whatever we tell you to do to fix it." Paula towers over Jamie and me in her black heels as I slouch even farther down into my chair. She's been lecturing the two of us plus Rico—although let's be honest, Rico didn't do shit—for fifteen minutes with what should've been a five-minute speech that keeps getting interrupted by phone calls, emails, and taps on the shoulder from her staff. She seems to be wrapping up now.

"Do you understand me?" she asks, her eyes slicing back and forth between us.

"I understand," I say, although what I'm supposed to understand, I don't know. What did she *expect* me to say? Some girl called Smokey gay, and I'm supposed to, what, agree with her? Give her a damn award? Like, *good for you, you're delusional, here's a trophy.* She stood up and spewed a bunch of nonsensical fantasies, and when I shut it down, *I'm* the asshole?

Paula turns to Jamie next.

"Paula, what did you want me to say? I don't think I did anything wrong up there." Jamie sounds exasperated. He lets his hands fall in his lap, his legs spread wide in the plush chair next to mine. I adjust my knee so it won't touch his, tucking myself into the far crack of the chair. Rico is pacing somewhere behind us, weirdly silent. I wish he'd defend me.

"I want you to say whatever it damn well takes to get them to tune in to the finale."

"You want me to lie to them?" Jamie shoots back. "You want me to tell them these two bros kiss each other in the final episode?" He jerks his thumb at me and Rico. "Because unless we're going back for reshoots, it ain't happening."

I wince at the thought. Why are we even talking about this like it's a legitimate thing? Why can't we just ignore it and move on?

"I don't want you laughing in their faces." She looks at me. "I don't want you smirking at them and telling them they're crazy. These people *pay our bills*, do you understand that?"

I can't look her in the eye. I dig my knuckles into my thigh and wait for this to be over. I just want to get out of here and change out of this damn Wonder Woman shirt.

"Oh, hardly." Jamie stands up in order to get out from under Paula's oppressive towering. "That girl's just the radical fringe, I don't think *all* our million and change viewers have *quite* as little grasp on reality as she does." Jamie grabs his coat off the back of his chair and slides into it. "Look, you got a job to do? Do it. Let me know what the plan is. In the meantime, I'm done being lectured by someone who has no idea what it takes to write a TV show."

Jamie slams out the door, leaving Paula to glare at me.

"From now on?" she says to me coolly in a tone that makes my tongue shrivel back in my throat. "Your ass is mine."

I don't trust my voice, so I give her a nod that says *I understand.*

She takes a deep breath. Her gaze lands on Rico, who's finding the carpet very interesting in the far corner of the room. "Rico, you got anything to add?" she calls to him.

He looks up at her like he just noticed she was there and says brightly, "Sure am looking forward to Portland!"

Oh right. We have two more conventions ahead of us. Can't wait. Rico gives me a little shrug. Then I see his eyes raise up over my shoulder, and I turn to find Caty standing in front of me.

"Hi," she says with a big smile. "Ready for your first tweet?"

10

claire

BY THE TIME MOM RETURNS, I'M DEEP INTO EPISODE seven, digging into a room-service cheeseburger and reciting along with my favorite lines.

"I'll keep coming for you 'til the dirt hits my chest," I murmur with Smokey, and I feel that familiar lightness as they stare into each other's eyes, this long, loaded look.

Just. *KISS*. For crying out loud!

Mom comes back from wherever, barging into the room in a fluffy towel. "My god, the sauna in this place. I love the city," she says, interrupting the moment. She slides onto the bed next to me, her hair still wet. "How'd it go?"

"Fine."

She frowns and looks me over. Then she picks up my jeans, which are lying on the bed, and holds them in front of me. "You took your pants off?"

"Yeah," I mumble.

"Okay, tell me what's up." She knows, of course, that pants are critical shields against the outside world and are only to be removed for showers and sleeping and times of great emotional distress.

I sigh, but I know the look in her eye, and she won't leave me alone until I tell her what happened. "I asked a question. I asked about SmokeHeart."

"Oh!" She clutches a hand to her chest. "And?"

"I don't want to talk about it."

She gets that sad mom face and rubs my knee. I can tell she doesn't really know what I'm talking about, but she's searching for something to say anyway. I wish she'd just leave it alone. "I'm sorry, honey bunny, I know that was a big moment for you," she says. "But hey, the important thing is you got up there and tried, right?"

I wish I hadn't. If I had just kept my mouth shut, I would be perfectly happy living in fantasy land right now, still believing that my ship might go canon. I would still have *hope*. Instead, I'm publicly shamed and humiliated. So. Yeah. Great. I tried. Whoop-de-do. Look where it got me.

When I don't say anything, she picks a new topic, whacking my leg. "Tell you what, how about tomorrow we go to that Thai place on the way home? A little pad see ew solves everything, right?"

"Sounds good," I say, even though at the moment I can't really bring myself to care.

"Okay, you hang in there, kiddo. I'm gonna change clothes." She leaves me alone, and I let out a long breath. It's so much more exhausting being around people when you're sad, especially when they're not as sad as you.

As soon as she's gone, I open up Tumblr to scroll through my dash. I search for *pan-labyrinth* and find Tess's blog so I can follow her. She has a cool layout, very cute and well designed. Her bio says:

tess || she/her || pan || p much just demon heart atm.

She's...pansexual. I know the word, I've seen it around Tumblr enough times. It means she's attracted to all genders. It means she likes girls.

I'm a girl.

I think about the way Tess wouldn't stop looking at me, the way she kept trying to make a conversation happen between us. I think about how my fingers trailed along her soft, round hand as I borrowed her pen.

Is it possible that Tess might like *me*?

But I'm not gay, so why do I care? This is literally the dumbest thing to be freaking out about.

I remember how her legs looked really cute in her dress today. I'm allowed to think that and not be gay. There's no rules that say I can't think other girls' legs are cute. She has *objectively* cute legs. It's just fact, not opinion. I wonder if she thinks my legs are cute. Maybe if I didn't wear old, dirty jeans all the time, she'd be able to see them. Ugh, I hate my clothes. Why don't I own anything that fits me right like Tess does? I'd never be able to pull off a cute patterned dress. Not like she can. She did tell me she liked my T-shirt, though.

I spend a moment remembering her laugh when I pinched Smokey's and Heart's faces together. I look down at my shirt, which I'm still wearing, and the memory floods back to me. The feeling of being funny. The feeling of being understood.

I scroll down to see what she reblogs, but I don't get very

far before I find it. My breath catches. Everyone's already been talking about it for hours, but I've been too mopey to check Tumblr and I almost missed it.

Forest *tweeted*. To his almost 100,000 followers.

His first message? *Thanks to everyone who watches* Demon Heart *and comes to conventions to support us. Your passion is why we keep making the show.*

Maybe I'm being narcissistic, but is that tweet about me? Did Forest Reed just make his first tweet ever about *me*? It sounds like it was vetted by about fifty PR people before he published it, but still. Forest Reed might have just sub-tweeted me.

Then I see Rico's last tweet. *Demon Heart* is doing a prize giveaway on the floor of the convention in—I check the time—*fifteen minutes.*

What kind of prizes? Maybe I could win a new T-shirt!

But no. I can't go. Not after today. I don't have it in me.

But what if they have new poster designs? I could finally finish covering the walls of my bedroom....

NO. I'm *not* going.

It's in fifteen minutes, though. I could go and be back in half an hour tops.

But what if Forest Reed is there? There's literally no one I want to see less.

But Tess might also be there....

What do I care about Tess?

She's a potential friend! Of course I care. A *friend*. It's not like I'm exactly rolling in friends. It might be my last chance to see her before I go home to Pine Bluff and we never meet again. How sad would that be?

Okay, that settles it. I haul ass out of bed. "Mom, I gotta go!"

She sticks her head out of the bathroom in only her bra. "What?"

"*Demon Heart* is doing a prize giveaway! I gotta go!"

"Ooh, prizes? I want to see this," she says, wriggling into a shirt and jeans.

"I thought you wanted nothing to do with the convention," I say, yanking on my pants and shoes.

"Well, now my daughter is sad and I want to be with her, is that so wrong?"

"Okay, well...Hurry up, then."

Fine, Mom can be sweet sometimes. Still annoying, though, don't get me wrong.

forest ➡

PAULA ALMOST DIDN'T LET ME GO, BUT CATY TOLD her I tweeted exactly what I was asked without hesitation, so I'm starting to get back in their good graces, unlike Jamie, who hasn't been seen since he stormed out of the greenroom. Paula did force me to bring Caty with me, though, because apparently I can't be trusted without a chaperone anymore.

"God, don't you just love the floor?" Caty says as we speed-walk through the wide, busy aisles on our way back to the Red Zone booth.

I don't answer, I just pull my hat down farther over my eyes as I skip sideways to avoid running into a man bending over to pick up his toddler. Caty is practically jogging after me to keep up, but I don't care. I have to get back to the Red Zone booth and explain the situation to Tattoo Guy before he has a chance to report back to Reynolds about the panel. I have to explain *Demon Heart* isn't like that. Smokey isn't a gay character—*I'm* not gay. Of course, there's obviously nothing

wrong with being gay, I've known a ton of gay guys in the acting world, but I don't want to be thrown in with that group
just because some wack-a-doo fangirl reads my character that
way. That way lies trouble. That way lies a lifetime of gay
roles. That way lies the death of my *Red Zone* dreams.

But when we reach the booth, there's no one there. No
Reynolds, no Tattoo Guy, no nerds in line, just a banner hanging over an empty booth. I slam my hands down on the table
and bow my head. *Dammit.*

"Guess they're not here. We gotta get going, anyway," Caty
says, checking her phone.

I try not to think about the worst possible scenarios Tattoo
Guy could report back to Reynolds. Option 1: *Oh sure, he's
got a following, but they're all girls. . . . Not really Red Zone's
brand.* Worse, option 2: *Guy seems great, but there's something about him, I don't know if he can do action hero. People
seem to think he's a little, you know, GAY.*

Gay, gay, gay. Why is this happening to me? What did I do
to deserve this?

And then, of course, there's option 3: Nothing. He could
just not mention it at all. And my career could sputter and
die, and this could all be over five seconds after it started.

I can't wait to get out of Boise. To get away from this convention tour, to never have to see another teenage girl again.

Caty's phone dings. "Seriously, Forest, we gotta go."

I remember when I used to wait tables and we'd get busy,
I wouldn't think about how many tables I had, or how many
hours left in my shift, or how much I'd made in tips so far. I
just did the work, and when someone told me to go home, I'd
go home. I'm good at that. I'm a workhorse. But back then, at
least, I could choose how to be. I could charm customers with

my jokes and get tips. I could choose my shift, my outfit, my haircut. I could choose how to act and what to say.

I'm not in charge of my schedule anymore. I'm not in charge of my shirts or my hair. I don't get to decide who I talk to or don't. I am the property of *Demon Heart*. I'm no longer a workhorse, I'm a show pony.

I stand up straight and look at Caty, who is tapping her fingers on her phone case impatiently. "Okay," I say. "Let's go."

Caty guides me through the aisles, around clumps of people, past vendors and artists, checking back to make sure I'm with her. At times I put my hand on her shoulder to keep her with me so we don't get separated.

Once, I hear someone shriek and say, "Forest, Forest!" I just keep my eyes on Caty's shoulders as she tells them she's very sorry, but we're in a hurry and we can't stop just now. I feel the flashes of their phones anyway as they take photos.

I can hear the cheering before we see the reason. A large gathering of fans is being led in some kind of contest to see who can cheer the loudest. We round a corner and at the back of the floor, there's a stage set up. Rico stands confidently up there, goading on an electric crowd of fans.

"Is that the best you can do, left side?" he screams at one side of the crowd, and they lose their shit at him.

"That's right, that's better," he hollers, and pulls out—*you gotta be shitting me*—a T-shirt slingshot and flings three *Demon Heart* T-shirts into that side of the crowd. Fifty pairs of hands strain to catch one.

He's so comfortable on that tiny stage, so easy and happy, giving out merch and hugs and making the day of everyone here. I imagine myself up there with them, and the crowd going quiet. Paula seems to think they might all hate me now, but Jamie said that's only a fringe group of the fans. What's the truth? I don't know. If they hate me, will a couple of free T-shirts make it all better? I really don't want to find out, but Caty grabs my hand and leads me toward the front.

"Oh, and look who decided to join us!" Rico says, pointing me out from the stage as everyone starts craning their necks. The fans closest to us pull out their phones to snap photos or take video. I pull off my Sooners hat and smooth down my hair.

Caty brings me around to the stairs up to the stage as Rico waves at me to join him. Another stage, another chance to embarrass myself. But we're just handing out free shit, right? How hard can it be?

I glance back at Caty for any words of support, but she only brings her thumb and forefinger to the sides of her mouth to indicate that I should smile. I smile with my lips closed. She indicates to smile bigger, so I do, opening my mouth and baring my teeth, and feeling like a cheeseball. She takes my picture.

"Perfect. That's your power pose from here on. Now get up there and do your job." She gives me a little shove and I climb the stairs to the stage.

Don't fuck up, don't fuck up.

Rico reaches into his bag of merch for another T-shirt, then feels around exaggeratedly. "I think that's it," he says, and tips the bag upside down to prove it. The crowd moans. Rico grins at them, then turns to me. "What do you think, Forest, can we scrounge up something else to give away?"

Rico hands me another microphone, eyes twinkling. Now I'm standing on a stage holding a microphone in front of an expectant crowd, not entirely sure what I'm doing and what to say next. So I do what I've been doing for the last six months: I trust Rico.

"I think we can probably find something," I say, and the crowd cheers.

"How much do you guys love *Demon Heart*?" Rico turns and asks the crowd. They scream their heads off. "And how much do you love coming to meet us at conventions?" They cheer even louder.

"Well, *Demon Heart* loves you, too," Rico hollers over the madness. "So as a special thank-you to all you fans out there supporting the show, we'd like to offer one all-expenses-paid trip to join the cast for the rest of the convention tour!"

Wait, *what?*

The crowd freaks the fuck out.

Paula steps up to the stage and hands Rico a bowl, which I recognize as the Bowl of Holding—a prop from the show, decorated with "ancient"-looking symbols that are really just nonsense squiggles dreamed up by our art department. Paula gives me a pointed smile, and I know this is all because of what happened in the panel today. This is their apology to the fans, their new game plan. But why does Rico know all about it and I've been kept in the dark? I watch Paula carefully as she heads back to the sidelines, always behind the scenes, never in the spotlight.

"We have the names of all the attendees of the *Demon Heart* panel today," Rico says. "Or, at least, the ones who signed up for our email list." The crowd grows quiet as they all hold their breath.

"Forest, would you do the honors?" Rico holds the bowl up high so I can't see in. I reach in and feel around, then look at him. He holds my gaze. *Just do it*, his look says.

I pull out a name, then peer out into the audience and pause as the room completely stills in anticipation.

I don't want to read it. I already know who it is.

Rico leans over into my mic and reads the name for me. "Claire Strupke."

There's a scream as the crowd turns to look, and there she is, that outspoken girl from the panel, in a hoodie, with the ponytail and smudged glasses, standing frozen, staring blankly up at Rico and me. I look at Paula, who has her arms crossed in front of her, glaring back at me as if to say, *I own you, Reed.* And she does. Because this convention nightmare is far from over. We're headed to Portland next, then Seattle, and I'm going to have to do this all over again, and again, but this time I'll be side by side with a wild-eyed superfan teen. One who thinks I am—or at least should be—gay.

I toss the paper with Claire's name on it back into the Bowl of Holding.

It was the only paper in there.

12

UM.

Wait.

What?

Wait.

WHAT?

Everyone is looking at me.

Probably because my mom just screamed pretty loudly.

A moment ago, my name was inside Rico Quiroz's mouth. *WHAT?*

Mom pushes me toward the front. Rico gives me a hand up to the stage, then sweeps me into a giant hug.

"Congratulations, Claire!" he says, his voice in my ear. He pulls away and grins at me, and I'm just straight-up dazzled, lost in his broad smile, in his happy eye crinkles. He brings me back to reality with a wink. "I can't wait to get to know you."

Forest shakes my hand. I don't really want to talk to him,

but he gives me a bright smile that may or may not be fake, and says, "It's nice to officially meet you, Claire." It's not wildly enthusiastic, but whatever, it's fine.

Then Rico takes my hand and raises it up, and we turn toward the crowd and they're cheering for us and Blazer Girl, who I swear is like this omnipresent angel of photography, takes my picture. I spot my mom, who is grinning. Rico is grinning. I am grinning.

I'm literally holding Heart's hand and he's looking into my eyes with excitement and I've just won something and I never win anything. What even is my life right now?

"You'll come along with us for the remainder of the convention tour," the woman says. She's tall and her black bob is tucked behind her ears like an evil Taylor Swift, but she doesn't look evil, she just looks in charge. Her name is Paula Greenhill. I like the way she stands very straight. I pull my shoulders up and back and try to mimic her posture. Maybe if I feel as powerful as she looks, I won't be shaking so much about what the hell I just won. I glance down at my hands and, nope, still trembling, so I stuff them in my pockets.

Ms. Greenhill hands my mom a manila folder full of papers. We're standing in a back room, just off the stage where I won the contest. It's blank, with no furniture or anything on the walls. Empty.

"This is our itinerary, including where we'll stay, when we'll travel, and all the events and media interactions over the next few days. Take a look and make sure you can agree to all of this. If it looks good to you, we have some releases for you to sign regarding using Claire's photos and likeness in our media campaigns."

Mom flips through the papers, her brow furrowed. Oh no, I can tell already she's taking this way too seriously. "And what are we talking in terms of *financial* compensation?"

"Mom!" I hiss at her.

"Honey, I'm only asking. Haven't I taught you it's always important to ask for things?"

Ms. Greenhill smiles patiently. "We don't have anything in the way of that. This is a contest your daughter won. The compensation comes in the form of meals, lodging, and, frankly, a once-in-a-lifetime experience."

My mom puts a pair of reading glasses on. I know she can't see anything farther than about two feet away with them on, but they do make her look Smart and Sophisticated.

"But isn't it true, Ms. Greenhill, that my daughter was 'selected' for this contest"—she puts fake quotes with her fingers around *selected*—"after asking a particularly pointed question at a Q&A?"

My eyes bug out of my head. I can't believe my mother is playing hardball with the woman offering me the Trip of a Lifetime. But also . . . it *is* weird that I won this trip, out of everyone at the panel today. Why me? Was this more than just a coincidence?

Ms. Greenhill shakes her head. "I assure you, Mrs. Strupke, your daughter is merely very lucky."

My mother stares Ms. Greenhill down, and for a moment I'm terrified Mom is going to make this into a big deal and they'll take it away from me and I won't get to go. And I really, *really* want to go. No matter how I feel about Forest and what they said to me earlier. If I don't go I'll always wonder. I *have* to go.

As subtly as possible, I stick my elbow into Mom's side, and she breaks her deadlock eye battle. "Hon, this is something you want, right?"

"One hundred per-freaking-cent," I say.

She nods, turning back to Ms. Greenhill. "Okay. Let's talk specifics. What's the situation with the hotel rooms?"

And Ms. Greenhill starts to get into it. Mom has a lot of questions about how many school days I'll miss, and what's the deal with the saunas in each city, and how close the Vietnamese food is, and how much downtime she'll have, because she's beginning a series of oil paintings of vulvas disguised as hotel-painting-style landscapes, and she's hoping to be able to do some research while she's there, so long as she's not needed 24/7. And I know she's only half kidding about the saunas and the Vietnamese food, but she's also half serious and Ms. Greenhill is treating every question like it's a nuclear disarmament negotiation, promising to get answers back immediately.

Forest disappeared directly after we left the stage. I'm starting to get the impression that he, well, hates me. And I have to take a beat to remind myself that Smokey is not Forest and Forest is not Smokey and everything is going to be okay and, oh my god, I just won this and how is this actually happening to me?

I look over Ms. Greenhill's shoulder and see the Bowl of Holding sitting on a table behind her. Since she and Mom are deep in it right now, I'm able to easily duck away and check it out. It's large, about the size of a mixing bowl. In the show, it's an ancient artifact, first uncovered by old-timey

archaeologists, then stolen by conniving demons looking to use it to open the demon portal to help usher in the
apocalypse, then chased down and ultimately recovered by
Smokey. Now the bowl is empty, and I wonder where all the
people's names went from inside it. Slowly, I reach out and
pick it up. It's lighter than I thought it would be, and I find
that instead of stone, it's made of plaster and painted to look
like stone. It's fake. But of course it is. The Bowl of Holding
never existed, it was just dreamed up by Jamie and his writing staff for the show.

But I'm still touching it. I have the Bowl of Holding in my
hands and it's real and it was in the show and now it's here.
It doesn't seem possible that this thing that I have seen on my
screen a hundred times before could be here in my hands, but
it is. And my name was in it.

"Hey, Claire," a voice says, and I turn to see Jamie Davies
coming up to me. I scramble to put the bowl down on the table.

Dear god. This is really happening. The creator of *Demon
Heart* knows my name. I hope he doesn't say anything about
me touching the props. It seemed like it would be okay! I con-
centrate on not locking my knees so I don't faint.

"Hi, Mr. Davies," I say.

"Jamie, please. Jesus, no one calls me Mr. anything," he
says, looking horrified. "I just wanted to say, ah, well, *thanks*,
I guess."

"Thanks?" I'm not sure what he's getting at.

"Yeah," he says. "It's nice to have so much support from
LGB...T...Q...A fans," he says slowly, like he's trying to
remember all the letters in the acronym.

"Oh..." I start. *Crap, does he think I'm gay?* I don't know
how to correct him. That's not me, I just happen to think

Smokey and Heart are in love. That doesn't determine my sexuality.

"I love the subtext you guys pick up on in the show," he says.

"The subtext," I repeat, frowning, trying to understand.

"Between Smokey and Heart," he says, rubbing his face with his hand. "I think it's great."

"So it's intentional?" I ask. This feels like a 180 from what Forest said at the panel earlier.

"All we do is make a show," he says. He flips his hoodie hood up so it covers his shaggy dirty-blond hair. "It's up to you guys to figure out where we're headed." He yanks the strings on his hoodie so it constricts around his face. He looks like Elliott from *E.T.*, but old.

My heart thumps in my chest with what feels unexpectedly like hope. "So, wait. Are you going to make them gay, or not?" I have to know. I can't keep following this show if they're just going to toy with my emotions, but it also feels like Jamie might actually get it. Is it possible? Can this bro have really made a show about a gay demon hunter and the demon he loves?

Jamie smiles at me like he knows a secret that I don't.

"No spoilers," he says.

Then he winks.

Then he walks away.

And I'm left standing there wondering WTF just happened.

Was that . . . confirmation? Is he telling me there's a chance that they could get together? But then, why did Forest act all weird? Maybe it's the long-term plan and Forest doesn't know yet? Mulder and Scully didn't get together until, like, season seven. . . . Maybe he's stringing us along with the slow build.

I have no idea. My shipper heart is too weak for this. I need a long nap.

My mom, having signed all the necessary papers, joins me.

"We're good!" she exclaims, full of positivity for the world and all that it offers. "Ready, honey bunny? We leave in the morning!"

Am I ready?

"That Forest is so *cute*," Mom says as we head back to our room. "Forget Obama, I ship myself with *him*."

I barely hear her. Tomorrow my dad is dropping off my Social Studies textbook and homework assignments, and clothes for Mom and me for the trip, and then we're getting on a bus to go on tour with the *Demon Heart* guys. *Me.* On tour. With *them.* There's a pit in my stomach as I consider that I might have to talk to Forest again.

I follow Mom into our hotel room as I try to ignore the growing knot of anxiety. "Are you sure you're okay with this?"

"Why wouldn't I be?" Mom asks.

"We're going on the road to faraway big cities," I say. "I mean, I could end up doing drugs."

"The important thing is you have fun."

"Maybe I'll have sex. Or get a tattoo. Anything could happen! I could get pregnant!"

"Those all sound like important life benchmarks."

"I could get a B," I say, more realistically.

"Your father is going to speak to your teachers and they'll email you any assignments you don't already have. Don't you even worry about that." At this point, so close to the end of the school year, I would have to actively *try* in order to get a B in any of my classes, but I don't say that. I'll do all my work. I'd hate to miss something interesting.

Mom pats me on the back. "And if you want a tattoo, you know all you have to do is ask. I'd be happy to go with you." She really is the worst mother sometimes.

"I need a shower," I say.

I take a long shower and let the tension release from my shoulders. When I get out, I towel off and put my hair up in a second towel, and I put the toilet seat down and I sit in the heat and the steam and the privacy of the bathroom and look at my phone.

It's been three hours since I won the grand prize, and that photo of me the Blazer Chick took is already up on the official *Demon Heart* social accounts for Facebook, Twitter, Snapchat, Instagram, and yes, Tumblr. I might have hoped that no one would put it together that the very lucky girl who won was also minorly famous fanfic author heart-of-lightness, except that my account is tagged in all the posts.

My stomach drops. I just went from internet nobody to Big Name Fan in nothing flat. I didn't really think about the fact that this might happen, but there's no turning back now. I steel myself and scroll through my mentions. They're a mess of people wondering who I am, what's going to happen, and what it means for SmokeHeart fans that one of their own was selected for this. They're sharing the video of me from the panel asking my question and then leaving the hall in tears after Forest's smug answer. They're wondering the same thing I'm wondering: is this purely a coincidence, or is there a connection between me asking the question and me winning? A lot of the messages are supportive, but some of them think I should never have bothered Jamie and the cast with my ship. Some of them think fandom should stay in fandom, and canon should be canon, and never the two shall meet. Some of them think I'm an "entitled teenage bitch." Some of them think I'm a hero.

I have two thousand new followers.

Hands shaking, I log out.

So. Now everyone knows who I am and they all want different things from me. But what do *I* want?

First of all, I don't know if I want to get on a bus to Portland in the morning with the entire *Demon Heart* team, including Forest Reed. I've already put myself out on a limb once, and he shot me down. Do I want to do it again?

Maybe some of those Tumblr people are right. Maybe I should let fandom stay in fandom. I never asked to win this prize. Although, deep down, I know that it can't possibly be an accident. Whoever's in charge over there, that Ms. Greenhill woman probably, figured out who I was and decided I would make a better ally than enemy. And now I'm just taking their little handout like a patsy? They probably think they can woo me with a bunch of VIP experiences and Rico's dreamy eyes and I'll do whatever they want me to and say whatever they want me to.

So what do *I* want?

I want SmokeHeart to be canon. I want a SmokeHeart kiss on the show. And I want the whole world to see it. There's a whole community of fans who want the same thing, including Tess. But none of them have the access I have. I can't just throw away this chance. I've been given the tools to actually make a difference. How can I put them down and ignore them just because Forest Reed might laugh at me again?

Whatever. I don't need his acceptance. I just need him to do his job: act what's in the script.

And who writes the scripts? Jamie Davies and his team of writers.

So that's it, then: I'm going to be the one to convince Jamie Davies to make SmokeHeart go canon.

At the crack of dawn the next morning, I'm rolling my suit-case across the hotel lobby, following my mom. Through the glass doors, I can see the charter bus waiting outside. Forest hands his bags to the driver to put underneath the bus and climbs aboard. I'm really doing this. I'm really getting on a bus with Forest and Rico, and I'm going to pretend that's super normal.

When we get to the bus, Mom says, "Now, I gotta sit up front or I'm gonna get carsick and nobody wants that. You sit wherever you want, okay?"

"Yup," I say as she hands her bags to the bus driver.

"Okay, honey bunny. I'm excited!" she says, and climbs the stairs.

As I hand my bag to the driver, I hear the *thwick-thwack* of running flip-flops hitting the pavement. I turn and see Tess rushing toward me. A smile spreads across my face so fast I can't stop it. She's wearing a charcoal-gray jumpsuit that looks really classy while also seeming really comfortable. I try not to dwell on what she looks like, since this might be the last time we speak.

"Holy shit, heart-of-lightness!" Tess says, a little out of breath, finally catching up to me. "I caught you!"

"I was hoping to run into you again!" I say.

"I literally *cannot* believe you won this contest. I literally . . . I can't even!" She gestures broadly, taking up the space around her with her excitement.

"I know, me neither," I say.

"Are you nervous?" she asks, and at first I think she means am I nervous to be talking to her, which is ridiculous. What, just because I found out she's pansexual? That doesn't make me nervous.

"You know . . ." she says. "Like, what all are they going to have you doing?"

I realize she means am I nervous about the trip. Of course I'm nervous. I'm about to get on a tour bus with Forest and Rico. What if I say something wrong? What if I fart? What if Forest decides to humiliate me publicly again? Anything could happen.

"I'm always nervous," I say, and she laughs.

"My whole dash is talking about you, by the way. You're, like, famous now."

"Yeah, I, uh, noticed that," I say.

"Is that weird?"

"So weird," I say. "But it's going to be worth it if I'm going to get anything done."

"What do you mean?"

"I decided last night. I mean, I'm closer to Jamie Davies on this trip than any fan has ever gotten. I have the chance to convince him to"—I lower my voice—"you know, make SmokeHeart canon."

She furrows her brow at me. "What?" she says. "Why?"

"What do you mean, why? I thought you shipped it."

"I do, but I'm not going to tell Jamie Davies what to do with his show."

"*His* show?" I can't believe what she's saying.

"We have our fanfic. We don't need it to be canon," she says.

I stare at her. "Of *course* we do."

"Why?"

"Not for me, or for you, but for...for all the kids out there who are watching the show and didn't even know that someone like Smokey could be gay."

"But it's not a kids' show, Claire."

"Then for teenagers, *whatever*! Not everyone reads fanfic, Tess. Do you know how many people this show could reach?"

"Okay, okay, fine." She throws up her hands like I'm coming at her, but she's the one who started this. "Do what you gotta do."

I gape at her. I thought we were on the same side.

"Well, uh, I guess let's hang out in Portland?" she says, and it takes me a second to compose myself and realize what she's saying.

"Wait, you're going to Portland?"

"Hell yeah, and Seattle, too!" she says. "I got a sleeping bag in my car, fifty bones in my pocket, and a Wizard Rock playlist for the road. *Demon Heart* road trip!"

"You're...sleeping in your car?"

"Yeah, totally. I wouldn't miss these cons for the world. But don't tell my friends." She laughs. "They all think I'm visiting my grandma in Phoenix."

"Wait, you didn't tell your friends?" I thought that was the whole point of friends, that you told them things.

"You kidding? I wanna still have a social life when I get back from this. I mean, if they knew I was a groupie for *Demon Heart...*" She trails off. Too unspeakable to even think about, apparently. "Why? Do your friends know where *you* are?"

I pause before answering. "Everyone knows."

At least, everyone on Tumblr.

"Whoa."

Yeah. "I'll see ya."

"Damn right." She gives me a wave and starts off toward her car. I can't believe she's on this trip, all on her own, just because she loves the show that much. How cool is that? Tess is honestly unlike anyone else I know.

Then, over her shoulder, she shouts, "I hope you find someone to sit with!"

Well, *great*. I didn't even think about *that*. I take a breath as I look up the steps to the driver, and then gather myself. No big deal. Just sitting on a bus with Forest and Rico. I can do this. I climb aboard.

My mom is sitting in the very front seat, reading her paperback novel, but I'm *not* going to sit up here with her. Behind her, a few of the seats are full with Ms. Greenhill's entourage. Farther back, I see Jamie, working on his laptop. Near him is Caty, who I met yesterday. She's got on a red plaid shirt with a blue plaid bow tie and it's the most extreme look, but I'm into it. I consider sitting with her, but she's got her bag out next to her and her laptop open, and she seems hard at work. Sitting together toward the back are Rico and Forest.

My heart zips just seeing them again. Right here. On a bus. With me.

Rico's in the middle of telling Forest some story that I

can't hear, his hands gesturing animatedly, his eyes all lit up. Forest is laughing along, not taking his eyes off Rico. I can't turn away from them. Their proximity, their ease with each other... My heart lurches. Do they know how they look?

"Excuse me," someone says, coming up the stairs behind me—one of Ms. Greenhill's assistants, I think—and I tear my gaze away from the shipper's paradise happening in the back of the bus.

"Sorry," I mumble, and find an open seat across the aisle from Jamie. This travel day seems as good a time as any to begin work on my mission, and also to avoid thinking about Rico and Forest snuggled up to each other in the back of the bus and how terrifying it is that one of them might try to talk to me. But Jamie's typing away on his laptop with head-phones in. I don't want to interrupt him, because what if it's important? What if he's working on *Demon Heart*? I push the button to lean my chair back in order to get a better view of his screen. He's composing an email. But I see a messy array of documents cluttering his desktop. What if one of those is the script for the finale? Or a rough cut? My mind boggles at all the secrets that Jamie's sitting on, but I hold it together. I need to be calm when I talk to him.

A few minutes later, the bus driver turns on the engine and closes the doors as Jamie takes off his headphones and closes his laptop. I seize the moment.

"Hey, Jamie."

He looks a little startled to find me sitting across the aisle from him. "Hi," he says curtly.

"Hey, this is so cool, the way you guys get to ride on a bus all together like this," I say, looking for some kind of casual opening.

He squints at me. "Is it?"

"Yeah, I mean, I think so." He kind of turns away from me and I sense that I'm about to lose him, so I just dive into what I want to say. "Hey, I was wondering what you guys had in store for the Portland panel."

"In store?" He takes his glasses off and rubs at his eyes with his palms.

I press on. "Yeah, I just think, you know. You don't want a repeat of what happened in Boise . . . with me."

"Sure, sure, sure," he says, putting his glasses back on and finally focusing on me.

"Especially since it seemed like, after we talked, you were maybe a little bit open to—"

"Totally."

"—SmokeHeart being—"

"Claire, we're keeping all our options open," he says.

Why won't he just let me speak? "Okay, so if someone else asks the question again . . ."

His phone buzzes. "I'm sorry, I gotta take this," he says, picking up. "P-Dawg!"

I sigh. Did that go well? I can't tell. I can feel the stress growing in my belly. I need a break from reality for a minute.

I know what I would normally do in this situation, but can I do it here? Surrounded by these people? I take a quick peek over my shoulder and see Forest and Rico are still deep in conversation. Everyone else is either working or sleeping because it's still so early. I think it's safe. I pull my laptop out, open a blank document, and start typing.

13

THE FIRST THING SMOKEY FEELS IS PAIN, FOLLOWED by relief. *He's alive.* He tries to look around, but even moving his head releases stripes of searing agony down his side. He takes a beat to get his wits back and assess his situation. He can tell from the beeping machines over him that he's in a hospital, but he has no memory of how he got here. The last thing he remembers is the Dreadful Gorgon bearing down on him, and his absolute certainty that he was about to die.

But he didn't die.

Heart had been there, too, showing up in time to stop the demon portal from ushering in hell on earth, etc., etc. Heart had actually *helped*, but then he'd skedaddled as soon as the Dreadful Gorgon took flight, and Smokey didn't blame him.

Smokey hears the door to his room open and a nurse appears over him. "How we feeling?" he asks, and Smokey fights through the cloud of painkillers in his brain to put together an answer that feels true.

"Shitty."

The nurse smiles. "Yeah, I'd imagine. You were in pretty rough shape when they brought you in. Another few minutes and we might've lost you."

"Did..." Smokey struggles to get the words out, and the nurse waits patiently for him to finish. "Did they find anyone else out there?" When the Dreadful Gorgon wakes from her slumber, she's hungry and grumpy and willing to scorch the land in order to find some fresh meat. Also, she has thermal vision, so yeah, pretty hard to get away once you find yourself in her territory.

"Just you," the nurse says gently.

Smokey thinks about Heart running away and wonders if he was able to escape. Maybe Smokey distracted the Gorgon long enough, maybe Heart found a hiding spot, but most likely...

Smokey closes his eyes against the thought. *No. Heart can't be dead.*

"Well, you and the guy who brought you in."

Smokey's eyes snap open. The nurse nods his chin to the corner just behind him, out of his peripheral vision. Smokey turns his head, slowly, slowly, swallowing the pain, and hoping.

Curled into a chair next to his hospital bed, one arm in a sling, the other wrapped protectively around his stomach, looking at Smokey with a furrowed brow and two blackened eyes, is Heart.

He's alive.

And he's looking on with such tenderness, like Smokey is this wounded bird that he's just *willing* to fly. Like he isn't just as banged up as Smokey is.

"Hey," Smokey says.

"I'll be right outside if you need anything," the nurse says, wisely making his exit.

Heart saved him. Heart *saved* him.

Heart saved *him.*

"I thought..." Heart's voice catches. He's crying, Smokey thinks wildly. Heart composes himself. "I thought you were a goner."

"I'm here. I'm not going anywhere," Smokey whispers.

"That's for sure," Heart says, and chokes out a laugh. Smokey's in no shape to be moving for a while. But then Heart's brow knits, and he gets serious again. "I'm not going anywhere either," he says.

And even though it hurts, even though his whole body hollers at him not to move, Smokey lifts his arm and reaches his hand out. Heart spills over then, two tears running down his cheek as he uncurls his body and leans forward, gently taking Smokey's hand in his good one and—

"WHATCHA WRITING?" FOREST PLOPS DOWN ONTO the seat next to me.

Why is he talking to me?

"A story." I minimize the document so he can't read it. But my desktop wallpaper is fanart of Smokey and Heart in each other's arms, so I slam my laptop closed. When I finally get the courage to look up at him, Forest's eyes are dancing. Ugh, did he see that? Is he going to make fun of me again?

"A story, huh? Anything I'd like?" He looks down at me with his bright blue eyes through long lashes. I blink hard to shake Smokey out of my mind. Ten seconds ago I was imagining him hurt in a hospital bed, leaning forward, about to kiss the love of his life, and now here he is, sitting next to me, his knee touching mine, warm and solid and real. But he's not Smokey, he's Forest. This is reality. He's not wearing a leather jacket and carrying a battle-ax. Instead, he's got on a weathered college sweatshirt from the University of Oklahoma that looks about forty years old, and he smells musty and sweet, and a little like coffee.

"I doubt it's your style," I say.

"Mind if I sit with you awhile?" he asks casually, like we're old friends or something. "Rico keeps trying to make me watch YouTube compilations of returning soldiers surprising their dogs, and it's driving me bonkers."

"Oh, um. I guess?" I'm not sure what he wants from me, but maybe he's going to apologize. I look past him and see Ms. Greenhill making her way to the front of the bus from the back. She gives me a warm smile as she passes, but now I'm suspicious. Did she tell Forest to come talk to me? I can't be sure what's real and what's not with her.

"So, where you from?" Forest asks, and I wonder if there's a chance he's just being friendly.

"Pine Bluff, Idaho?" I doubt he's heard of it. "It's small."

"Oh sure, I know all about small towns. I grew up in my share of tiny Coast Guard towns," he says.

"I thought you were from Oklahoma," I say. Then, realizing that sounds stalker-y, I add, "Sorry if that's weird that I know that." Even though that's only the tip of the iceberg of things I know about Forest Reed. I don't mention that I also know his birthday (May 7), his favorite food (bibimbap), his childhood dog's name (Lady Bark Johnson), his first car (1995 silver Ford F-150), and a lot of other things. Forest hasn't done a ton of interviews, but I've read everything I could find.

"My dad was in the Coast Guard, and we moved around a lot," he says. "But when he retired when I was a teenager, he said he wanted to move as far away from the coast as possible.

Thus, Broken Arrow, Oklahoma." He flourishes *Broken Arrow* like it's a fabulous getaway destination. I haven't been there, but I'm guessing it's not that fabulous. It's weird that I didn't know this, too. He must be private about it because he's never mentioned it in an interview.

"But enough about my old man. Tell me about Pine Bluff. How small is small?"

"Minuscule."

"How many Dairy Queens y'all got?"

"None."

"None?! Claire, that is *unacceptable*. Good god, you gotta get out of Pine Bluff immediately." He turns to the rest of the bus, and hollers, "Can someone get this girl a Peanut Buster Parfait stat?" A few people turn around and look, but most ignore him. It makes me laugh, in spite of myself.

He turns back to me and whispers, like it's our secret, "I cannot *live* without DQ. It's my one weakness."

"Pretty tame, as far as weaknesses go," I say.

"Yeah, maybe so."

He smirks in such a way that he looks just like Smokey, and for a second, that's all I see, like I've been transported right into the show.

There's a *click*, and I look up to see Caty has just taken a photo of us. I look back at Forest, and he arches his eyebrow in a way Smokey never would, and suddenly he's the actor again and this is the real world. I blink hard and look back at Caty.

"For social," she says. "You guys should do a selfie, too." I stare at her. I had almost forgotten that this is all just for show. "Only if you want to, though. It's not in your contract or anything." She shrugs and goes back to her seat.

Forest seems unfazed. Of course he is; he knows all of this

is an act. Something that looks good on camera, online, but isn't actually real.

"So what's old Pine Bluff have to offer, anyway? You got a boyfriend back home?" Forest nudges me playfully.

I am *not* going to tell Forest about Kyle Cunningham, but I still have to hold back a shudder as an image of Kyle comes unbidden to mind. He and I were never officially dating, but we did, well, some of the things people who are dating do. It makes me question myself every time I think about it. If I couldn't see how gross and dumb Kyle Cunningham was then, how can I trust my own instincts about anyone ever again?

For instance, I used to think Forest Reed was sensitive, intelligent, and handsome. Now I wonder if he's a Kyle Cunningham in celebrity's clothing.

"No boyfriend," I say.

"Cool, cool. This trip'll be more fun that way anyway. Maybe we'll find you someone in Portland, huh?"

Oh, so now we're going to just hang out in Portland like old buddies as he plays wingman to help me pick up boys. What makes him think I even want that? There he goes again, just assuming people are straight, just like he assumes Smokey is straight. *Am I* straight? I don't know, I don't know, *I don't know*, but I sure as hell am not going to say that to Forest Reed, who thinks being gay is something to laugh at, or be embarrassed of.

I watch the highway and trees whipping past out the window.

He leans over to try to catch my eye. "Hey, what's up, what's wrong?"

I look at him squarely. "You're being nice to me now, but it doesn't really change anything, does it? You think I'm crazy." He starts to protest. "You *said so*, Forest. And now you have to be friendly to me because some PR lady is telling you to, but you're still exactly the same. You think I'm watching your show for the wrong reasons."

Forest stares for a moment. "I'm sorry if I made you feel bad."

"That's not really an apology."

"Well, I can't change everything I know about a character just because you want me to."

I pull away from him, pressing my shoulder up against the cool condensation of the window. "So it would change *everything*?"

Forest sighs. "I'm not sure what you want from me."

He doesn't get it. He's never going to get it. He's just a pretty-boy actor who wants to find the path of least resistance so that everyone loves him.

"Here's a start. The next time someone asks you about SmokeHeart, you can try not being a condescending dick. You can try to understand where they're coming from."

He shakes his head. "So I guess this means you don't want a selfie?" he asks drily, then stands up and finds another seat.

"GUESS WHAT PORTLAND COMIC-CON HAS?" RICO turns to me excitedly as soon as we pull into the Portland Convention Center VIP parking area. "Gina's Poster Emporium."

Far ahead of us, at the front of the bus, Claire is the first to hop off, grabbing her backpack and heading out without looking at me, her weird mom right on her heels, asking her what's wrong. It's fine with me if she doesn't want to talk to me, I didn't have anything more to say to her anyway.

"Sounds amazing," I say to Rico in a flat tone, but if he senses my sarcasm, he doesn't react.

"There is literally no reason someone who has *the greatest* selection of rare and vintage Japanese movie posters in the world should also be just so darn nice. But that's Gina for you!" He grabs his messenger bag from the rack and slaps me on the shoulder. "She's also a looker. C'mon, I'll introduce you."

I had been planning to spend the rest of today working

out and then playing *Red Zone 3* in my room, but I know that hanging out with Rico will probably make me feel better than solitude, so I shake my head in defeat. "Okay, okay, let's go see Gina."

"Great! I've been looking for an original Japanese edition of *Alien* and she promised to hold on to one if she finds it."

"I *love Alien*, it's my favorite movie!"

"Right? Perfect film," he agrees. "Perfect."

As we deboard the bus, Paula is waiting for me, with Caty standing right behind her. "Forest, you're free for the day, but we need you back by five."

"Why?"

"We're livestreaming interviews from the *Demon Heart* booth," Paula says. "You and Claire."

"Oh, *come on*. Can't Rico do it?"

"No. Did you patch things up?"

Last night, Paula sat me, Jamie, and Rico down to tell us that there's a strategy shift in how we're approaching these conventions. Claire, in Paula's opinion, is a silver bullet. *A digital influencer*, Paula had called her, because apparently she has a lot of followers online. So now I have to be nice to her and do everything it takes to make her like me again. Like it's so easy to get on the good side of a moody teenager who's already made up her mind about you.

"She hates me," I tell Paula. "No amount of small talk is going to change that."

"Forest, figure it out. You're charming, you're gorgeous, and you're her number one favorite actor in the world."

"Yeah, I'm pretty sure I've fallen in that ranking."

"Then claw your way back up," she says fiercely.

"Seriously, Paula, I'm not trying to be difficult here, but I think it would be better for everyone if Rico did the media stuff with her; she and I are like oil and water."

"Caty?" Paula steps aside and looks pointedly at the social media maven.

"The buzz online is about *you*, Forest," Caty says, brandishing her ridiculous pink phone. "People want to see you and Claire come together after the Boise snafu."

"Snafu?" I know it wasn't great, but I think that's putting it a little strongly.

"The point is," Caty says, "you have ground to make up. We think if we can show the two of you as friends, it will go a long way toward repairing what was broken in Boise."

"Or what?" I say.

"Excuse me?" Paula draws herself up. In her heels, she's exactly the same height as me, and she makes sure I know it.

"I said, *or what*? I don't think what you're asking me to do is reasonable, or possible. So what are you going to do if I say no?"

"Forest," Rico says, low.

"No, Rico, it's okay," Paula says. "This is important." Her voice is hard when she speaks again. "Forest, you may be under the same illusion a lot of young actors are under: that their job ends when the cameras stop rolling. But that's not true. Your show only matters if people watch it. Publicity is *just as important* to the process as production, or writing, or editing, okay? So let's dispense with this belief that the work I do is somehow frivolous or unnecessary."

"I just—" I start to say, but she cuts me off.

"And if you can't be motivated by wanting to help the show that *you're one of the stars of* succeed, then I am happy to motivate you another way." She narrows her eyes, and I can't not feel intimidated anymore. I don't know what this woman is capable of, but at the moment her powers feel limitless. "Caty tells me you're looking to cozy up to Jon Reynolds and the Red Zone folks." I pale, realizing where this is headed. "Do I need to remind you what studio has Red Zone? That's right, the same one that has *Demon Heart*, the same one that pays me. I can pick up the phone right now and call the president of the studio and tell her that you're too difficult to work with, and how do you think that will play once casting gets under way for your little video-game movie?"

My hands feel clammy. She can't do that, can she? But she's solid and unmoving, and I don't doubt that she could do anything she wanted to. Rico gives me a little shrug, like *Just do what she asks*. And I know it's over.

"Okay," I say. "I don't think it's going to work, but fine."

"Great. I'll see you at five."

"Let's go," Rico says under his breath. We start across the parking lot toward the convention center.

"Oh, and, Forest?" Paula says sweetly. I turn, wondering what the hell else she could possibly want, but it's Caty who speaks.

"We need you to tweet again," Caty says. "Something real. Something personal. Rico, will you give him a hand?"

"You got it," Rico says, and pulls me away before I can respond.

The bustle of the convention floor seems to not affect Rico at all as he glides along, cutting a path through clumps of people. The Oregon convention center appears to be about twice the size of Boise's, with a larger attendance, too. More costumes, more vendors, more people getting in the way of where I'm trying to go.

"The thing about a crowd like this," Rico says over his shoulder as we navigate, "is that there are so many people, but they're all here for their own specific thing, and the *Demon Heart* fans are just a drop in the bucket. So, weirdly, you get recognized *less* than at a smaller convention." Still, Rico has swept up his distinctive thick black hair into a beanie and he's wearing sunglasses indoors, which gives him kind of a rock-and-roll-Unabomber look, but it works for him. I slip my sunglasses and Sooners hat on and try not to let him get too far ahead of me.

When we reach Gina's Poster Emporium, the woman behind the counter throws her arms around Rico.

"Rico!" She almost sings his name. "My love, my main squeeze!"

"I told you she was a looker," Rico says to me.

"Oh, stop it," she says. Gina is probably around seventy-five years old, Asian, and tiny but lean, like she works out every day. She's wearing a faded U2 tee from some tour in the '80s and loose-fitting jeans. There's a youthfulness about her that is compelling. I have to admit that, yeah, actually, Rico's not wrong. Gina's hot.

Rico introduces me, and Gina gives me a kiss on the cheek that I'm pretty sure leaves behind an imprint of red lipstick. She doesn't have an *Alien* poster for Rico, so we start flipping through her collection, looking for anything else that sparks our interest.

"You know, it's weird," I say to Rico as I browse the '90s section. "There are so many vendors here I don't really, well, *get*. But this one..."

"Pretty cool, right?"

"Actually, yeah."

"I'm just happy people like Gina exist in the world," he says. "She loves Japanese movie posters more than anything, and she's been able to carve out a life going to cons and buying and selling them. It's so weirdly specific, and yet everyone here has their own weirdly specific thing. It's the one place in the world where being weirdly specific is totally the norm."

"Whoa." I pull out a poster from the stacks. Rico takes one look and busts up laughing.

"See what I mean, man? Everyone's a fan of something."

It's a mint-condition, gorgeous *Red Zone* poster from the 1999 original film. Jasper Graves's face fills the frame, giant and dotted with sweat and grease. The title is scrawled in black lettering across his nose: レッド ゾーン.

"I'm gonna hang it in my living room," I say. That room needs something on the walls. Anything at all.

We poke around a bit longer until Rico finds a vintage *Who's Afraid of Virginia Woolf?* one-sheet, which I have to ask what it is, because I don't think I've ever seen an Elizabeth Taylor movie in my life, but apparently she's one of his favorite actresses. We try to give Gina money for them, but she won't take it, insisting that we more than paid for our purchases by signing the Japanese *Demon Heart* posters she had on hand. Apparently Jamie is right when he's always saying *Demon Heart* is big in Japan.

It's while Gina is wrapping up our posters that Rico

suddenly lights up and smacks me on the arm. "You know what you have to do, right?"

"What?" I furrow my brow, suddenly suspicious.

"You have to tweet about this," he says, eyes dancing.

"Aw, dude, c'mon."

"You have to tweet *something*, Reed," Rico says, reaching over and wriggling my phone out of my sweatshirt pocket. "Seven-four-two-six, right?" He watched me punch in my phone passcode on set once, and he's been using it against me ever since. He opens Twitter and hands it to me. "Might as well tweet now, about this."

I know he's right, so I take the phone from his outstretched hand and stare at the blinking cursor on the white tweet box. *Don't think about how many people will read this.* I don't know what my follower count is up to and I don't want to know.

"Be sure to mention I'm booth two forty-four!" Gina calls from behind Rico, and I laugh.

"Okay, okay, I'm doing this one for you, Gina," I say, and I type out a message about how much I love Gina's Poster Emporium and I found something amazing for my walls back home. Then I mention Booth 244, and before I can overthink it, I hit TWEET. It has 114 likes and 12 retweets by the time I even click over to my notifications tab. Intense.

When I look triumphantly up at Rico to tell him that wasn't so bad, his eyes are locked somewhere over my shoulder.

"What is it?" I say.

Rico murmurs, "We've been spotted. Two girls, two booths down."

"What? Already? I just tweeted, like . . . fifteen seconds

ago." I don't dare look around lest I accidentally make eye contact.

"They must have been nearby. Never underestimate fans," Rico says. "Looks like they're too scared to come over."

"Can we get away, do you think?"

Gina hands us our posters as Rico gives me a funny look. "Why would we want to do that?" He smiles, kisses Gina on the cheek, and takes off toward the girls.

"Wait, Rico, jeez." I basically have no choice but to scurry after him. Rico walks right up to the two fans, who at this point are kind of hyperventilating.

"Hi, I'm Rico." He sticks his hand straight out. They gape for half a second before quickly shaking it one by one, a little too enthusiastically.

"Betty," says one.

"Riley," says the other.

"Forest," I say.

Riley blushes. "We know."

I'm not sure what to say next. What do I possibly have in common with these girls? And that's when I notice. "Oh my god, are you *me*?" Riley is wearing Smokey's trademark leather jacket, holding a replica battle-ax, her hair pulled back in a bun.

"Yes!" She strikes a pose. "I love you! I mean, I love Smokey. I don't know you." In that outfit, in that stance, she almost looks like me. I'm weirdly impressed.

"I love you, too," I find myself saying, because I'm that overwhelmed, and she looks like she's just about to faint.

Betty is dressed like Rico's character from *Star Command*, and she and Rico are taking a selfie next to us.

I turn back to Riley. "Wow, you even have the broken

strap." I reach out and touch the shoulder strap of Riley's leather jacket that's busted in just the same way as my real costume is. The attention to detail is incredible. I notice her tense under my touch, and I pull my hand back. "Sorry."

"No, it's fine," she says, and laughs breathily, but she's wound tight like a coil. It's weird to interact with someone who has so many feelings about me. She knows me, but I don't know her at all. What does she expect from me?

"That strap"—I indicate her jacket—"I actually broke it myself my first day on set by accident. I was afraid I'd get in trouble, but it turned out they liked it so much they did it to all the jackets." I realize she might not know how the costume department works. "They have a lot of jackets that are all the same, just in case we need backups." I rub my hand around the back of my neck. "Anyway, I didn't think anyone watching would notice."

She smiles at me. She noticed. Then she looks down at my chest, like she can't make eye contact for too long.

"Forest, I want to tell you that *Demon Heart* is . . ." She fiddles with the bracelets around her wrist as she searches for the words. I give her a second to find what she wants to say. "It's *important* to me."

I think of *Demon Heart* as some little Monday-night show on a minor network that no one really watches. Obviously I try to do my best at work, but I never thought what we were doing was a big deal or anything.

I didn't think it was *important* to anyone.

"This last year," she continues, "I was in AP classes? And Advanced Calc. And my best friend went to Switzerland to study abroad . . ." She glances over her shoulder at Betty, who is chatting excitedly to Rico. "It was a hard year."

"I'm sorry to hear that," I say.

"No, you don't get it." She looks at me very seriously, gripping the battle-ax in front of her with white knuckles. "I didn't think I was gonna make it through. Like I was *really close* to just..." She shakes her head and looks away, biting down on her lip. "But then I found *Demon Heart*."

She starts to well up, and I have *no idea* what to do.

"*Demon Heart*..." she says, wiping tears off her cheek with her sleeve, "it saved my life."

"I'm..." I say, unsure how to respond to that. I don't know how that could possibly be true, but she's looking at me so genuinely that I know it is. "I'm glad we could help you."

She nods, trying to keep the tears back.

"Do you...uh...want a hug?" She nods, her lip quivering. I step forward and wrap my arms around her. She tucks her head into my sweatshirt, and I can feel the tears spilling out of her.

"Thank you," she murmurs into my chest.

I look up and Rico is smiling at me. Betty covers her mouth with her hands, and has this expression on her face like I've just given a home to a shelter dog. I have no idea what's happening.

"Can we get a picture with all four of us?" Betty asks.

"Of course," I say. Riley pulls away from me and swipes at her eyes and tries to look like she hasn't just been sobbing into my hoodie. We all get together, and Rico takes the photo because he has the longest arms.

After, Riley asks me, "So, um, where's heart-of-lightness?"

"Where's what?"

"Not *what*. Who," Rico says. "They mean Claire."

"Oh, she's...I'm not sure," I reply. "She's around. What did you call her?"

"Heart-of-lightness," Riley says. "Oh my god, she's one of my favorite fic writers. I can't believe she won this trip with you guys. She's incredible."

"I'll, uh, I'll have to tell her you said so," I say. So Paula was right about Claire. People know her.

Rico and I head off with a wave, leaving Betty and Riley to grip each other and giggle and look at the photos we took. As Rico and I slip our sunglasses on and maneuver our way back through the crowd toward the exits, he smiles at me.

"I don't always have the time or the energy to do that," he says. "But when I do..."

"Yeah," I say. I feel this fullness inside me that I didn't feel before. It's weird, having that kind of effect on people, but to be able to make them happy like that? With just my presence? It's kind of an undeniably great power. It makes me feel like I have something to offer.

16

THERE IS SO MUCH MORE AT PORTLAND COMIC-Con than at Boise. Like, *so, so* much more. I already went through the over-the-top booths for Marvel, Warner Brothers, Netflix—all the big companies spending lots of money to build out these ridiculous displays with screens and sound effects and areas to take selfies, just to try to wow fans like me. I know it's a blatant cry for my attention, but I'll be honest, I kind of like it. It's nice to feel catered to, even if it's in this flashy, impersonal spectacle.

My mom walked around with me for fifteen minutes before it was too much for her, and she went off to find some froyo and read a book. She gave me $40, half of which I promptly spent on a T-shirt that reads, SHOW ME YOUR FICS. I don't have anywhere to be until five p.m., so I'm determined to soak in as much of this convention as I can, but it's *a lot*, and I'm getting tired of fighting the crowds.

I check out another room off the main floor that seems

quieter, and I find an area with a bunch of tables set up where people are playing tabletop games. The bustle of the con is a little more muted here, and I'm considering finding a chair and checking out what they have to offer, when I hear a voice call out, "Hey, show me your fics!"

I turn to look, and it's Tess, smiling at me from the ground where she's sitting against the wall, charging her phone at an outlet.

"Hi," I say, approaching her. "Whatcha doing?"

"Just passing time while my phone charges."

I feel a little thrill that I happened to run into her. We hadn't made plans to get together, and after the sort of turbulent way we left things in the parking lot in Boise, I wasn't sure if I'd see her again, but she's smiling, which is a good sign. Her sketchbook is open on her lap, the pages covered with tiny drawings of hands.

"Can I see?" I ask.

She shrugs, her smile fading a bit. "Don't get your hopes up," she says, handing the sketchbook to me. The hands are gorgeous. Tiny, detailed line drawings done with a very sharp pencil. Hands touching, holding. They make my neck prickle, just looking at them.

"These are awesome," I say.

"You think so?"

"Definitely. You're really good! I thought from how nervous you were about it that you'd be, like, a beginner or something, but, *dang*, girl."

Tess smiles. It's the first time I've seen her look shy since I met her and it's adorable. I turn back to the notebook and flip the page.

"Oh—" Tess reaches out to stop me, but it's too late. I see

that the hands are part of a much larger study. Smokey and Heart, emotionally ragged, holding hands, staring deep into each other's eyes. In love. It's completely G-rated, and yet there's something so deeply intimate about them that I feel like I shouldn't be looking at them in public. Still, I can't look away.

"Wow," I say. "These are *good*."

"Yeah, uh, I don't show a lot of people."

"You should," I say.

"No, you know, I want to be a real artist, not just, like, this stuff."

I look up at her. "This isn't real art?"

"You know what I mean."

I look at the drawings one more time.

Of course I know what she means. To make art in fandom is to follow your passion at the risk of never being taken seriously. I've written dozens of fics—put them together and you'd have several novels—but who knows what a college admissions officer will think of that as a pastime. Where does 12,000 Tumblr followers rate in relation to a spot in the National Honor Society in their minds? Every week I get anonymous messages in my inbox telling me I should write a real book. Well, haven't I already? What makes what I do different from "real writing"? Is it that I don't use original characters? I guess that makes every Hardy Boys edition, every Star Wars book, every spinoff, sequel, fairy-tale retelling, historical romance, comic-book reboot, and the musical *Hamilton* "not real writing." Or is it that a real book is something printed, that you hold in your hand, not something you write on the internet? Or is "real writing" something you sell in a store, not give away for free?

No, I know it's none of these things. It's merely this: "real writing" is done by serious people, whereas fanfiction is written by weirdos, teenagers, degenerates, and women.

I want to say all of this to Tess, my "fanart is real art" speech, but it's almost five p.m., and I have to get going. Plus, I have a tendency to come on a little strong with people, and I'm not ready to run her off quite yet.

"Hey, you wanna go get something to eat?" Tess asks, packing up her things.

"I can't, I have to go to this dumb livestream thing."

"Tomorrow, then. Dinner? After the panel?"

Something in me twitches. She wants to make plans like we're real people, like we're friends.

"I mean," she says, "it doesn't have to be a date thing...."

"What?" My stomach drops.

"Just 'cause, like, I'm queer. Pansexual, actually. Which I didn't know if you knew, and I don't know if you are...."

"Oh, no..." I feel my palms begin to sweat.

Dang it, Claire, pull yourself together.

"No?" She looks disappointed.

"I mean, yeah, let's do it," I say.

"Only if you want to...."

"Yeah, no..."

"It doesn't have to be..."

"No, it's fine."

"Cool."

"Cool."

A beat passes. Where was I?

"I better go," I say, and spin to leave, then realize I'm still holding her sketchbook and I turn back around and hand it to her, then I practically run away.

"See you tomorrow!" she calls after me, and I'm certain I hear her laughing, because who wouldn't laugh at me? I'm acting like a three-year-old.

What just happened? Did I just agree to a date? Does she think I'm gay? Everyone else seems to, so why not her, too? And maybe I am. Or maybe I'm not. How does anyone know?

But if I'm not, why can't I stop thinking about the way she smiled when she saw me?

"When I say five p.m., it's not a gentle suggestion." Ms. Greenhill is reaming out Forest as I approach. It's 5:05. I wince, knowing I'm next, but she just gives me a smile and a "Hi, Claire, good to see you." Which, to be honest, is almost worse. Forest looks miserable.

We're at the *Demon Heart* booth, and there's a throng of fans wrapping around the outside of it, trying to get a glimpse of Forest. They all have their phones up, taking photos. I stare at them a moment, amazed that I'm on this side of the ropes, inside the booth instead of crowded on the other side. How did this happen to me?

The booth is shared with *Witchcraft*, *Ice Queens*, *Time Swipers*, *Darkness Falls*, and all the other shows at the same studio. There are screens above our heads showing a loop of nonstop promos, and two false walls surrounding a carpeted area with tall chairs set up in front of a camera. The walls are covered in enormous images of the cast members of all the shows. It's disorienting to see Smokey standing next to a medieval knight, who's next to a spunky young doctor, who's next to Heart. I'm so used to seeing Smokey and Heart alone, but here in this environment, it's hard not to view them as cogs in a much bigger network machine.

Ms. Greenhill is bustling around, making sure everyone's on task. I wonder if she watches *Demon Heart*. She must, to do her job properly. I wonder if she likes it.

Since no one's watching me for the moment, I wander over to the area of the booth selling officially licensed swag for the shows, and I see a wall full of T-shirts, tote bags, prints, and toys. My breath catches in my throat when I see a numbered *Demon Heart* print from a graphic designer featuring the quote: *'Til the dirt hits my chest.* It's large and hand screen-printed and gorgeous. It would look amazing in my room.

"What can I get you, miss?" the vendor asks, coming over to help me.

"Yeah, how much are those prints?" I point to the one I like.

"Two hundred," he says. Then, seeing the blood leave my face, he adds, "Limited edition."

I don't have nearly enough money for something like that. I gaze at the print a bit longer, then start to move away.

"It's fine, Eduardo," Paula says, coming up behind me. "Go ahead and give it to her."

I turn around to look at her. "Really?"

"I can't think of anyone who deserves it more than you," she says.

Eduardo rolls the print into a tube for me, and I can't believe it. I take the tube from him. How can I put this print up in my room with my cheapo $14.99 posters, knowing how much this costs? How could Paula just give it to me without a second thought? How is this my life?

"Okay, now," Paula says, "let's go over a few things about

this interview. I just want you to be super positive, which shouldn't be too hard, right? Just keep smiling, you're happy to be here, you're excited, this is a dream come true. Sound good?"

She looks at me to make sure I understand, and I realize the print she just gave me is more than just a kind gesture. She's trying to keep me happy. I remember that nothing here is free, not really. They're buying my loyalty—or trying to, at least.

Of course, I could use this opportunity in front of the cameras to make a scene, talk about SmokeHeart, speak my mind. And maybe I should, maybe this is my only chance. But making a scene here isn't going to help convince Jamie to make it canon, it's only gonna piss him off, and possibly get me sent home. This interview is small potatoes, and I'm gunning for the whole hog. So I look at Paula innocently and nod, the poster tube clutched under my arm.

"This *is* a dream come true," I say, which is completely true.

She smiles and hugs me. "You're gonna do great." She gestures to a woman in headphones who comes over with audio equipment and starts attaching a tiny mic to my shirt.

Across the booth, Forest is getting mic'ed up as well. He's completely ignoring the crush of fans taking photos and video and calling his name. I realize, horrifyingly, that some of the fans have their phones pointed at me, too. I tilt my head down, letting my hair fall in front of my face, and take a few breaths. Okay, okay. No big deal, right? Just answer some questions on camera with a hundred jealous fans watching me from the sidelines and thousands more livestreaming it at home, as I sit next to a guy who thinks I'm a joke. No sweat.

An assistant guides me to the tall chair I'm supposed to sit in. Forest is seated in a second chair already. He's wearing a NASA shirt.... Was he wearing that earlier? I can't remember. We make flickering eye contact.

"'Show me your fics.'" He reads my shirt slowly like he doesn't quite process it. Then he looks at me and says, "Heart-of-lightness, right?" He seems hesitant, like he doesn't know how to behave around me, his hands clasped in his lap.

"What?" I ask tightly, my stomach falling like it's made out of lead. How does he know about my Tumblr name?

"That's you, right? Heart-of-lightness? I like the name." We're both talking low so the fans nearby can't listen in.

"Where did you hear that?" I demand.

"I met some fans. They like your writing," he says with a shrug. "Is that what you were working on earlier? On the bus? I'd love to read your stuff sometime."

"I don't think so," I say flatly. "If you're going to get defensive about a basic SmokeHeart question, you're definitely not ready for fanfiction."

"You know what, at least I'm *trying* here," he says with a hint of frustration. "What do I have to do to prove that I'm not the homophobic asshole you think I am?"

"I never said you were—"

"I have gay friends," he says. "I love them. I went to a gay wedding once. I'm glad *Moonlight* won the Oscar." I roll my eyes. "I once told my dad I thought Jasper Graves from Red Zone was handsome, and he didn't speak to me for a week."

Whoa. That stops me. "That's terrible," I say, my eyebrows furrowing. I've never even thought about what kind of environment Forest might have grown up in.

"Yeah, well, guess what? Flash forward ten years and now

Graves is fired and I'm trying to replace him." He holds out his hands and smirks. "Wait'll my dad hears about that."

His arrogance really knows no bounds, does it? I was almost feeling sorry for him, too. "Good for you, Forest," I say, and look away.

"Claire, what's it take?" His smirk disappears. He's practically begging me now. "Can't we just start over?"

It's like he wants absolution, but I'm not his priest. I'm just some "crazy" girl, right? I glance over at Paula, who is watching us from behind the cameras. I know she put him up to this, that he wouldn't be even trying unless she was forcing him to. Forest doesn't actually care about me, he just wants me not to hate him anymore because it looks bad. Well, that's not my problem.

I lean over my chair to get closer to him, and I make eye contact so he knows I'm being serious. "When will you understand that you're not the center of the universe, Forest Reed?" I don't say it cruelly, just matter-of-factly. This is true: "You think all these people are here for you? They don't know you. They love the character you play. You? You're just a haircut with a battle-ax."

His jaw is tight as he holds my look, then gives me a brief nod and sits back in his seat.

I'm a little amazed that I may have actually rattled him. I didn't think anything could shake his confidence. I almost feel bad, but I remind myself that he's a grown adult man and he can handle a little criticism from a teenager. Right?

"Everyone ready?" Paula asks, coming over.

"Let's do it," Forest says stiffly.

"Sit up straight, Claire. Don't forget to smile. We're rolling in three . . . two . . ."

As the camera rolls, Forest puts on his big charmer-boy smile, his eyes crinkling at the corners. He combs his hair back off his forehead with his hand in a perfectly practiced move. He looks fine again, normal. He looks like the Forest I know from my computer screen. And I remember...he's an actor. He's always acting. I don't really know him at all.

I'VE NEVER HAD MORE FAITH IN THIS PUBLICITY team than when they asked Claire literally one question and gave the rest to me. The girl's a loose cannon. If it were up to me, she wouldn't even be allowed in front of a camera, but apparently they think she's "good for the brand," so what do I know.

Haircut with a battle-ax.

After the interview, a large-necked security man leads us through the crowd as fans snap photos, calling out my name...and Claire's. He leads the two of us to the service corridors, where Claire is shuffled in one direction and I'm put into the back of a black town car to be taken to my hotel. I'm shuttled everywhere these days. My schedule planned for me, my days no longer my own. I'm surprised they let me pick what I want to eat.

Haircut with a battle-ax.

I could have this driver take me through the Dairy Queen

drive-thru right now. I could get a double cheeseburger and a Blizzard, and no one could stop me. I could rip off this NASA T-shirt, I could shave my head, I could tell Paula and Jamie and Claire to go fuck themselves.

But I won't.

I'll go home and get whatever high-protein, low-fat option I can find from room service and I'll work out in the hotel gym and I'll say all the things I'm supposed to. My career depends on it.

People don't realize just how much work it takes to be a haircut with a battle-ax.

"Hey, it's me again." It's a new day and I'm back at the Red Zone booth. Red Zone appears to be on the same convention circuit tour that we are, and I'm grateful for it. Tattoo Guy looks unsurprised to see me, but I've never actually seen him show any emotion beyond *waiting for all this to be over.*

"That last panel back in Boise," I say, "I just wanted to apologize. Things got a little out of hand."

"All right."

"Do you think there's a chance he'll show up today? I have another panel in half an hour. It's going to go smoother." And it will. I have a plan. I stayed up half the night playing *Red Zone 3* and figuring it out. Who's the haircut now?

"He's very busy."

"Can you just...can you tell Mr. Reynolds that I play Red Zone every single day, and I love it—as much or more than these fans he's meeting—and I'm...I'm just very interested in this role."

He nods distantly. "I'll let him know."

I manage to make it to the greenroom with a few minutes to spare. Paula shoots me a look for being late but doesn't say anything, just waves her assistant Donna over to me. Donna wordlessly hands me a Batman T-shirt, and I put it on. Then she tuts over my hair before walking away, and I have just enough time to steel myself before Hurricane Claire touches down on my coastline.

"Hey, Forest," she says, and before I can greet her back, she dives into it. "Look, we have to talk about this afternoon's Q and A, because the questions aren't going to be written by your publicity team today. You have to have a good answer to the SmokeHeart question. Someone out there *will* ask about it."

Looking down at her now, it strikes me just how much authority Claire tries to pack into her small frame. She must only be about 5'3" or so, her blond hair tied up in a messy bun on the top of her head that gives her the illusion of a few more inches. Some women might wear heels or boots to accomplish this, but she seems pretty attached to her scuffed-up high-top Vans. I take a minute to wonder how this stubborn, obnoxious high schooler became such a real and unignorable part of my life. At least it won't last much longer.

"I took care of it," I tell her. Across the room, I see they've set out little bottles of Perrier. I start to head toward the craft table to grab one. Claire follows me.

"What do you mean you took care of it?" she demands.

"I mean don't worry about it, it'll be fine."

"I don't believe you," she says. "Tell me specifically."

I take a mini Perrier. Ahhh, it's in a glass bottle and still cold. I crack it open and take a sip.

"Forest, are you listening?" she says. "You have to reach

down somewhere deep and find a way to not be a dick out there."

I finish the whole thing in one drink and burp. *Refreshing*. Claire flinches.

I look her in the eye. "I said I took care of it."

From the door, Paula waves at us. She's waiting with Rico and Jamie to head toward the panel. I take the opportunity to squeeze Claire into a hug.

"What are you doing?" she asks, looking confused.

I glance over her head to make sure Paula is watching, and she is. She gives me an appreciative nod.

"I'm just glad you're here, Claire. Keeping us on track." I pull away.

Claire frowns at me. "Okay, I guess."

"See you after."

I suppress any instinct I have to feel bad or protect her. Just because she's small doesn't mean she's helpless. She's done enough damage. It's time I take back control.

18

WATCHING A PANEL FROM THE SIDE OF THE STAGE instead of the audience is weird and suboptimal. There aren't chairs to sit in, people are whispering and not really paying attention. No one here is a fan, they're all just working. Ms. Greenhill has gone to stand in the back of the hall so she can "read the crowd," which means the only people left here are me and that chick Caty, who is typing madly on her phone as usual, and a few of Ms. Greenhill's minions—who, in the absence of their strong parent figure, are horsing around and laughing.

But as the panel starts, Caty leans over to me and whispers, "It's a good view from here because you can see everybody, the panelists *and* the attendees." And I find that she's right. There's something powerful about being able to watch over the sea of faces looking up at the stage. There's a girl in the middle of the front row shaking with excitement, her friend holding on to her hand to keep her calm. I recognize her joy because I feel it, too. I see thumbs racing over phones as they

live-tweet for the folks back home who can't be here. I see
Tess, happily perched in the third row. She notices me and
winks, and I have to bite my cheek to keep from breaking out
in a grin. I wish she were here watching the panel with me.
And then there's Rico and Forest, right there on the stage. I'm
so much closer to them than any of the audience members.
Close enough to see the gray hairs among Rico's thick black
curls. Close enough to see the worry lines in Forest's forehead as he waits for his first question. And I'm struck again
by how amazing it is that I'm here, that they know my name,
that this is happening.

"You know," Caty whispers to me, taking a break from typing, "I've been following your blog basically since we premiered. You were always one of the tastemakers in the fandom."

I tear my eyes away from the stage to look at her. She knew
who I was from the *beginning*?

"You might not have the most followers out of everyone,
but you're smart, Claire. You don't wade into every petty little
fandom debate, but the ones you do comment on, well, you
have a good voice. People trust you."

Something's nagging at me, and I recognize my chance to
get confirmation. "Caty, did you guys... did you fix the contest so that I would win? Because of everything that happened
at that panel in Boise, and because I have a lot of followers?"
I'm not sure what I want the answer to be. Do I want to believe
that I was selected because of the quality of my writing and
my ideas? Or do I want to believe that the world is fair and
any fan could have had the same chance I'm getting?

Caty smirks. "Just a crazy lucky happenstance," she says.
But the way she says it, I know.

I was *chosen*.

"Hey, if you wanted to liveblog this panel, nobody here would stop you," she adds, nodding at the phone sticking out of my front pocket. "Use the hashtag #demonheartpdx."

I take my phone out and do as I'm told, liveblogging mindlessly through the moderator-led section of the panel, waiting for the Q&A to start. I'm itching to know what Forest has planned for any potential SmokeHeart questions.

When they finally turn it over to the audience, there's a scramble as people move to the microphone in the aisle. As the first fan steps up to the mic, a convention staff member intercepts her, speaking to her low, off-microphone. As they exchange words, the fan starts to tear up, then heads back to her seat, but I can't tell why.

Another fan steps up to the mic, but again the staff member exchanges words with her before she can ask her question.

I look at Caty. "What's going on?"

She shakes her head slowly, frowning. "I'm not sure."

The second fan starts to get angry with the staff member, and I can tell her tone is rising, even though I can't make out what she's saying. Another staff member guides her away from the microphone.

The third fan in line steps forward and speaks to the staff member. This is honestly getting ridiculous. Are we ever going to get a question? This time, the fan is permitted to step up to the mic.

"My question is for Forest." I lean forward. Could this be it? Could this be *the* question? "How are you liking Twitter?" she asks.

I groan. Like a full third of the audience groans. I think people in other panels in other rooms in other buildings groan. This is not what we came here for.

And I realize then what's happening. Somehow, he got the convention staff to step in and weed out any questions he didn't like. Forest is flat-out refusing to engage on the topic of shipping.

Fans are talking about something he doesn't like?

Ignore, block, mute, reject.

I look down at my phone, open to a new text post. Blinking cursor. He might be able to moderate what people say in a Q&A, but he can't moderate this.

"Claire..." Caty looks down at my phone with concern. It's like she can read my mind.

"No," I say. "You guys chose me for this because you liked what I post online, right? Well, now you're stuck with me." Yesterday I was afraid to make waves in my interview because I didn't want them to kick me off the trip. Now I know that this wasn't random, I don't feel quite so careful. They picked me for my voice, and I'm gonna let them hear it.

I start typing.

Forest Reed doesn't care about fans. I tag it #*demonheart pdx* and publish it. Then I open a new post and keep typing.

Let them silence this.

I didn't know how long I'd have to sit here until he showed up, but I was ready to wait all night. At every ding of the elevator, I raise my head to see if it's him. I've twice had to assure the cleaning crew that I'm fine, I'm not locked out, I'm just waiting for my "dad."

After two and a half hours, my phone is nearly dead from me incessantly checking Tumblr to watch my text posts spread at ridiculous speed like demon blood through the veins of the infected. Fans in other fandoms are piling on in support, recognizing the battle call of a fandom in need, and reaching out to help however they can. Until now, my Tumblr had been mostly fic, fic recs, reblogs of gifsets and fanart, and the occasional meta. But now, my angry text posts fill the first several pages of my blog. I'm sure I've lost followers over this, but I've also gained several more thousand. The mentions are pouring in faster than I can read them, which is fine, because I don't need to read them to know that some people agree with me, some people hate me, and some people can't decide.

But it's time to take this conversation offline. It's time to talk to the guy who can do something about all this. I'm sitting in front of Jamie's hotel room door, and I know he has to show up sometime. The elevator dings again, and this time it's him. He doesn't notice me at first, but as I scramble to my feet, he flinches, then turns on his heel and heads back toward the elevators.

"Jamie!"

He hits the elevator button over and over again. "Oh, hey, yeah, sorry, I just realized I left something downstairs."

"I was hoping we could talk," I say, walking down the hall toward him.

The elevator doors open. "Yeah, me too!" he says. "I gotta—sorry, I'll be right back!" And the doors close behind him and he's gone.

I sigh against the wall and slide back down. I guess I'll wait some more. He has to come back eventually. I pull out my laptop and open a blank document while I wait.

HAMMER CURLS, PULL-UPS, TRICEP DIPS, UPRIGHT rows, reverse flies, skull crushers. Arm Day. It's the good kind of pain. The kind that I can handle, that reminds me that I am stronger than I was yesterday, and I'll be even stronger tomorrow. Weight lifting is a contained pain that I can control, and I can decide whether to end it. It's small and comprehensible and *mine*.

This hotel gym isn't the most extensive, but it's got weights and it's empty aside from me, which makes it perfect. I'm putting new plates on the bar when Rico comes in. He's not dressed for a workout, so I'm guessing he wants to *talk*.

"Hey," he says as I start my bicep curls. "We have to talk." I knew it.

Four... five... six...

"Forest." He's waiting for me to stop. But he doesn't understand Arm Day.

"There's nothing to talk about, Ric. I'm doing what I have to do."

Rico comes over and sits on the bench across from me, but the nice thing about bicep curls is you do them bent over, your elbow on your knee, lifting the weight from the ground to your chin. It's real easy to do them with your eyes locked on the ground.

"You put moderators out there," Rico says to the top of my head. "That audience was pissed at us today. Did you see Paula's face?"

Ten...eleven...twelve.

I switch arms. "I did that for both of us. We're going to be looking for new jobs soon, we both know it. And this is the worst time for either of us to be seen as anything less than masculine."

Rico watches me do reps.

Five...six...

"Did you know," he asks slowly, "that they were thinking of going with another guy for Smokey?"

"What?" I look at him, but don't stop curling.

"When we were auditioning. Some guy—Mark somebody. He was good, I could tell they liked him."

I finish my reps and put the weight down. A line of sweat slides down my cheek, and I swipe it away. "What, did he have a schedule problem or something?"

"No, man, *you* happened," Rico says, knocking his knee against mine playfully. "When you and I read together... *fireworks.* No one could look away." He levels me with his gaze. "Do you remember that?"

"Yeah." Of course I do. I'd never had an audition like my

read with Rico, so full of energy, the connection between us immediately crackling to life, consuming the room. It scared me a bit, that day. And it scares me a bit even now, even here.

"So why do you keep denying our characters have chemistry?" Rico asks.

"Of course they have chemistry, but not the way those girls think," I shoot back.

"They can only see on the screen what we put there," he says, and I'm suddenly aware of how close we're sitting. I can feel the warmth of his body coming off him, his leg a hairbreadth from mine. I wonder how many reps he does to get his quads to pop like that. I wonder how much he lifts. I raise my eyes to find him looking at me.

"You never played it that way?" he asks. "Even a little?"

Did I? No. I couldn't have. Could I?

"What do you mean, *that way*?" I fake ignorance. I'm stalling for time. I'm not sure what's happening anymore. This conversation is slipping out of my control, I'm grasping for a handhold, finding none.

"*You know,*" Rico says, like we have some secret together. "We always do the first take straight up. Then, take two, maybe it's a little looser. And take three..." He pauses, reading my face. "Stripped down."

I don't move. My blood is pumping, but it's probably from the weights. It *must* be from the weights. Right?

Rico shrugs. "Is it our fault they like to use take three?"

"No," I whisper, my mouth dry and rough. I wet my lips, and Rico's eyes flick to my mouth.

"No," he agrees. "It's not our fault."

His gaze continues down my body, and my mind empties.

I uncross my arms.

Don't think, don't question. I open up.

Rico slides his hand across my cheek and behind my head and pulls me toward him and his lips are on—

20

claire

I STOP TYPING AND TIP MY HEAD BACK AGAINST the wall.

I mean, it's not that I haven't written real-person fic before, I have. But it feels different writing it about Rico and Forest now that I've met them. It's not a fantasy anymore, it's more of a wish. Let me re-create Forest as I'd like to see him. Let me make him vulnerable, let me make him uncertain, let me make him love Rico. Let me make him *understand*.

There might be some people who find this gross or mean, but right now it's just super cathartic. I turn back to the document and keep typing. It just got to the good part.

THE THUNDER ARE LOSING AGAIN. I HAD TO CHARM the bartender of this faux-froufrou hotel bar to get him to change the channel away from—I swear to god—the Portland Timbers soccer game, just to watch my team fall apart in the fourth quarter. My only consolation is the fact that I can now afford to drink top shelf on my TV salary. But even killer bourbon won't salvage this inane trip.

Tucked away in this far, darkened corner of the bar, I'm praying Paula doesn't find me. I managed to escape without running into her after the panel, but I'm certain she's gunning for me now. I could have run the idea of question moderators past her before I went ahead and set them up, but I was pretty sure she'd tell me to fuck off. So I didn't ask permission, and I figure I don't have to ask forgiveness until the next time I see her, which I'm delaying as long as possible.

After these godforsaken conventions are over, I'm going to

go home to LA, pray the guy subleasing my place didn't leave it a disaster, and play *Red Zone 4,* which will be out by then, and eat Korean food for like three weeks straight. I've been away from home so long I don't know if I still even remember which exit is mine.

I'm still thinking about the 101 freeway when someone slides a glowing phone in front of me, a blank text message open on its screen. I look up to see Jamie straddle the stool next to mine. I breathe a sigh of relief it's him and not Paula.

"Just tell me what you want me to say and I'll text him right now," he says.

"Who?"

"Jon Reynolds," he says, like it's no big deal. My heart skips a beat.

"You know Jon Reynolds?" I ask incredulously. How did I not know this? How did this not come up? Hollywood is small, sure, but Jon Reynolds is...*Jon Reynolds.*

"USC Snowboarding Club," Jamie says with a shrug. "We were tight for a while after school, but then he made one little indie movie while the rest of us were still assistants and, like, three months later, he was getting hired to direct these huge action blockbusters. Don't see him much anymore. You know, I don't get out to Calabasas much." He says it with more than a touch of bitterness. This town is full of friendships that fizzled because one person became a megamillionaire success story and the other, say, created a minor genre TV show with shit ratings that might get canceled after one season.

This is huge. A personal introduction to Reynolds from an old friend? This will go a long way. I can see the road to *Red Zone* unfurling in front of me.

"I would love it if you would do that," I say.

"Great, happy to. I appreciate everything you've done so far on this trip. You've been awesome." He takes his phone back and looks me dead-on. "There's just one thing I need."

He pushes away from the bar and waves to someone by the door. *Paula.*

"No, Jamie, c'mon..." I start, but he cuts me off.

"You gotta do this, Forest. For the show. For me. I just want to be able to get to my bed without being harassed, you know?" I frown at him, not sure what he means. He barrels on, "If nothing else, then to get this witch off our fucking backs." I look over at Paula striding toward us and breathe a long sigh of resignation.

"It better be a damn good text," I say.

"You got it," he says, slapping my back. He moves off and stands to the side as Paula sits down on Jamie's stool with a fierceness I haven't seen in her before.

"Get me a vodka tonic and put it on his tab," she says to the bartender, jerking her thumb at me. She shrugs out of her blazer, and I can see her arms for the first time—she has fucking *muscles*.

"That was pretty stupid what you did today," she says. "Here's what you're gonna do next."

"Peace offering," I say, holding out the box of Voodoo doughnuts I had delivered to the hotel for this purpose. Claire is right where Jamie said she'd be—camped out in front of his hotel room door. This girl is nothing if not determined. She actually reminds me a bit of myself, only way more unhinged.

If she can get a slightly better grasp on reality, she might be able to use that grit to do some great things in life.

Big *if.*

Claire looks at the doughnut box, then up at me. I crack the lid and waft the incredible scent over to her. She just continues to stare flatly. Yeah, she really doesn't want to talk to me. Even for doughnuts.

Paula told me in no uncertain terms that I was supposed to meet her on her level, not try to convince her to come to mine. Jamie said just to get her to move away from his door so he could get to his room in peace.

I was hoping this would be easier than it's turning out to be. I take a deep breath and try apologizing.

"I wanted to say I'm sorry. I know you're pissed about the moderators. Honestly, I was hoping to avoid drama, not make more of it."

"Ever notice how *drama* is the word people use when women start standing up for what they want?" she asks.

My god, can I get anything right in this girl's eyes?

"I feel like I only understand about half of what you say," I tell her honestly, and watch her roll her eyes and return to her laptop, ignoring me and the doughnuts. "These are *Voodoo* doughnuts," I say, wiggling the box around. "They are *very good* doughnuts. I didn't know what kind you liked, so I got a dozen." I peer inside the box. "Maple bacon bar your speed? Peach fritter?" She looks up at me over her glasses. "Froot Loop cruller?" She scowls. She would be cute if she wasn't so surly all the time. She peers around me down the empty hall.

"Where's Caty?" she demands.

"I'm alone."

"This isn't a PR thing? You're not gonna try to take my picture?" She looks skeptical.

"I promise. I'm here solo." I choose not to mention that Paula practically strung me up by my balls to get me to come, and Jamie offered me one free text to Jon Reynolds.

She studies me for a minute. "What do you want?"

This is it, my opening. I chew on my lip for effect, then say, a little haltingly, "Look, I...I know I haven't been the best. With this stuff. But I want to learn." I rub the back of my neck with my free hand. "I want to understand where you're coming from. Show me what y'all are up to on Tumblr. Show me what I'm not getting."

She narrows her eyes. How long am I gonna have to hold this damn box?

"No," she says.

"No?" I thought for sure she would leap at this offer.

"Tumblr is"—she waves her hands—"it's full of fanart and fanfic and gifsets....It's not there for you."

"But it's *about* me." I start to falter....Did I misjudge this? "Isn't it?"

"No, it's about a fictional demon hunter who happens to look just like you," she says.

I sigh. There's never a right answer with her. "Claire, I keep pissing people off doing what I'm doing and I don't even know why." This started out as an act, but this part is true. She makes me feel like an idiot *all the time.* "I've never felt as helpless as when I'm talking to you. And here you are sitting on a throne of answers and you won't show them to me. You're the only person I know I can ask. You're like this small girl Yoda and I'm big, dumb Luke Skywalker, and I'm asking you to train me. Help me be better," I say, and I actually mean it.

She bites her lip and thinks about it. "You like *Star Wars*, huh?"

"Yeah, who doesn't?"

She sighs. "Okay," she says, taking the doughnuts from me. "Teach you I will. But when you get uncomfortable, just remember, it was your choice."

I let out a breath. "Awesome."

"Have a seat," she says, patting the floor beside her.

"Oh, nuh-uh. I have worked very hard to get where I am in life, and part of what that means is I don't sit in hotel hallways. I like chairs. And rooms."

She squints at me. "You want me to leave Jamie's room alone so he can get in, don't you?"

"Yes."

She sighs. "Fine. But tell him this isn't over."

"I'm sure he knows," I say with a smirk. "Trust me, no one around here is underestimating you anymore."

Five minutes later, we've found an empty hotel conference room to hang out in, and we've already polished off a doughnut apiece. I had a maple bar, and it was so delicious I want to cry. I can't remember the last time I had refined sugar, but I can't eat another one or I'll have to double my cardio tomorrow morning.

Claire flips open her laptop, and I see again the fanart of Heart and me, in a very intimate embrace, gracing her desktop wallpaper. All her documents are neatly arranged around the edges of the screen so as not to cover the image. What the hell am I getting myself into? I raise an eyebrow at her.

"Ignore that," she says, quickly opening an internet browser. "That's too advanced for you right now."

She navigates to Tumblr. "Okay," she says. "Here's my dash."

The first post at the top of the page is a moving gif of, well, *me*. It looks like cell-phone footage, shot over the tops of people's heads. I'm onstage and I'm wearing a Wonder Woman shirt. It's Boise, I realize. The gif shows me covering my mic with my hand, leaning over to Rico and whispering. The caption below makes explicit what my lips are mouthing: "This is crazy. *She's crazy.*"

It repeats over and over.

"Not that," I say, feeling a pang of regret about that moment, and wishing it didn't have to be giffed, destined to repeat over and over forever. "I don't want to see that."

"Okay, moving on." She scrolls down and stops at the next post. It's a series of gifs of Rico and me—Heart and Smokey—from the show. This one doesn't have dialogue, just us staring at each other. Whoever made the gifs slowed it down so the eye contact lingers *fooorever*. When it reaches the end it loops back to the beginning automatically. So it's just us. Staring. Until eternity.

Claire watches me watch the gif. "Do you know what shipping is?" she asks, taking a bite of a Bavarian cream-filled.

"That much I picked up," I say. "SmokeHeart."

"Right," she continues. "You can ship anyone. When characters actually get together on the real show, the ship is considered 'canon.'"

"Like Mulder and Scully," I say.

"Exactly. Do you ship anyone?"

I think about it. *Do I?* I mean, I guess I root for couples to get together in a romcom or something. . . . Not that I watch that many romcoms, unless I'm dating some girl and trying to get her to think I'm sensitive. I can't remember ever thinking about a fictional couple after the film or TV show ended. "No...I don't think so," I say.

"That's okay. Not everyone does." She polishes off her doughnut, licking the glaze off her fingers. My stomach rumbles. *God*, I'm hungry. I haven't had dinner yet, and the doughnut is mixing with the bourbon in my system and giving me serious munchies. "Here's the thing to understand, though: a lot of ships will never go canon, and that's okay. Chewbacca and Princess Leia are never going to hook up in *Star Wars*, but that doesn't stop some fans from writing fanfic or drawing fanart of it."

"Ew. Chewie and Leia?" Please.

But Claire just shrugs. "Something for everyone. Some people have a kink about height differences."

I try to picture Leia standing on her tiptoes, reaching up to kiss Chewie's furry lips. Then I imagine Han watching them from the doorway, pushing away in anger when he sees his best friend moving in on the girl he likes. I bristle. "It would never happen. Leia and Han belong together. And even if she were into Chewie, he would never do that to Han." I shake my head in disgust. "It's obvious."

She turns to look at me excitedly. "That's it! That's shipping!"

Oh, okay, yeah, that makes sense.

"The point is, some ships are just for fun, like Chewie and Leia. And some ships..." She scrolls down. More gifs of Smokey and Heart. Heart is telling Smokey, *I'll never let that happen to you.* "Some ships are more important," she says. She scrolls again. I see another gif. Smokey tells Heart, *You're the only one.*

Below that, another gif: Heart stares at Smokey from a distance as a single tear runs down his face.

Another. Another. Another.

"Some ships," Claire says, "are *supposed to be* canon."

"Okay. Smokey and Heart care deeply for each other, I grant you that. But it doesn't make it romantic. They're just friends. Comrades on the battlefield."

"Do you even *watch* TV?" Claire says. "This is the language of romance on-screen. If Smokey and Heart were a man and a woman, everyone would just *understand* that they're in love with each other. It would be a given. Mulder and Scully were never this explicit—they didn't need to be. People could tell from the pilot that they would eventually fall in love.

"You can take any man and woman, put them in a TV show together and have them look at each other like this"— she gestures at the computer screen—"and it wouldn't even be a question. But because Smokey and Heart are two men, it makes a perfectly normal reading of the show delusional, fantasy...."

"Crazy," I murmur.

"Yeah," she says. Then, almost as an afterthought, she adds rotely, "but you shouldn't use *crazy*, like, to describe people you don't agree with; it diminishes the struggle of people who actually have mental health issues."

"Um, okay." Jesus, is there anything I'm allowed to say with this girl?

All this is fine, but there's this one piece that's still missing. "I get what you're saying but the thing about Smokey and Heart is . . . *they're not gay.*"

"Who says?" She levels me with big eyes.

"Everyone. Jamie, the writers, *me.*"

"What if I disagree?"

I don't know what to say to that.

"He's not real, Forest. He can be anything we want him to be."

The gif is on the screen again. Smokey and Heart, gazing deeply into each other's eyes. I recognize the episode.

"That's a famous moment, by the way. Everyone in fandom knows it," Claire says. "Do you remember shooting that scene?"

"Yeah, of course. We were in the middle of the woods. It was freezing. Rico told wardrobe to get me another shirt to wear under my coat."

What I don't tell her was that I didn't know I could ask for more clothes, but Rico saw me shivering and spoke up. He didn't have to, and he slowed down production for it as wardrobe ran back to their trailer to get something warmer for me, but he still did it. You only get so many cards you can use in situations like that before you get labeled "difficult," or worse, even when you're number one on the callsheet. You try to use your cards on things that really matter. Rico used one on me.

It was a big moment in our relationship. I realized that night that he would always have my back—in this case literally. "We shot this scene right after that. I was much warmer."

The gif plays again and again.

"Do you remember what you were feeling in that moment?" Claire asks.

"I don't know. A lot of things."

"Name one."

"Gratitude?"

"Okay."

"I don't know what else."

"Love?"

"Claire—" This girl doesn't give up.

"I'm just asking."

"I don't know, okay? It was a split second captured six months ago. I didn't know it would be analyzed in this detail."

She shuts up then, and we both go back to watching the gif repeat. I take another doughnut. Old-fashioned. It tastes amazing.

"I never really thought about it before, but this thing'll just play forever?" I ask.

"Forever," she says.

"Forever."

Rico and me. That night in the woods. I have no idea what I was feeling. I have no idea what I'm feeling now.

I watch my eyes glance down at his lips. What *was* that? Why did I do that? Was I thinking about kissing him? It's impossible. Isn't it?

What was I feeling? Friendship, trust, intimacy.

Friendship, I reiterate. Friendship.

Forever.

22

I'M EXPLAINING SHIPPING TO FOREST REED.

Never in a million years would I ever think that I'd be doing this. How many times have I stared at his face on the poster on my bedroom wall, finding comfort in its familiar lines, lulling myself to sleep under his watchful gaze? And here I am sitting inches from him, gazing at that same jaw, that same nose, those same eyebrows. His eyelashes are so long they graze against his skin when he blinks. I could reach out and *touch* those eyelashes, that's how real he is and how *right there* he is. But I won't, because that would be *incredibly* creepy, and also because I don't want to do anything to distract him from what he's doing right now.

Because Forest Reed is thinking about shipping. He's deliberating about SmokeHeart, and it's all because of me.

Some fans might not like what I'm doing right now. Fans like Tess, who think fandom should stay in fandom. *But he asked!* He demanded I show him Tumblr. I could have said no, but he would have just looked it up himself, and he's honestly better off with me as a chaperone. If I weren't there guiding him, he probably would have searched for my fanfic straightaway, and that's like jumping into grad-level classes without taking the prerequisites first.

Maybe I'm totally off base, but it feels like he's starting to understand. When he looks at those gifs, is he able to see what we see? Does he notice the obvious chemistry, the yearning emanating from their every torrid glance? Or does he just see his bro Rico and a cold night in the woods? I can't be sure, but I think maybe, somewhere beyond his high walls, there's a glimmer of a shipper, fighting to make it out.

It makes me want to hug him, to tell everyone in this hotel that there's hope for Forest Reed, there's hope for SmokeHeart. It makes me think the future could be better. Maybe he can talk to Jamie, convince him that this hyper-masculine heteronormative vision of demon hunting is beyond old-fashioned. Maybe he can be the ally we need to get SmokeHeart to finally become the canon it was always meant to be. It feels like a real possibility. For the first time in a while, it feels like *hope*.

If SmokeHeart ever had a chance, it's right here, right in this moment. I have to say something.

"So . . . what do you think?" I ask, softly, gently.

He blinks hard and breaks his gaze from the computer to look at me. "What do I think about what?"

"About this." I nod toward the computer screen. "About SmokeHeart."

He frowns; he doesn't know what I'm trying to say.

I try again. It's now or never. "What do you think about its chances? Can you take it to Jamie, talk to him about it?"

He looks away, rubs his knuckles over his eyes. *Shit*. I thought I was getting through to him, I thought...

"Claire..." he starts.

"Don't."

"It's just... It's not going to happen like that. For a thousand reasons," he says. He's trying to be kind, I can tell, but there's nothing kind about this.

"So you won't even *try?*"

"There would be no point," he protests.

"Just *think about it*," I say, a little more fiercely than I intend to. I can feel my cheeks flush hot and the pressure building behind my eyes, but I won't cry in front of Forest Reed. Not about this.

I hold his eyes and refuse to look away first.

"Okay," he says finally, quietly. "I'll think about it."

"Thank you." I start packing up my things. I have to get away from him, now. My phone buzzes with a text and when I glance at it, my stomach does a single, perfectly executed backflip. It's from Tess.

We still on for dinner?

"Shit," I whisper to myself. I had kind of forgotten we made plans.

"What is it?" Forest asks.

"Nothing, it's just..." I sigh. "I'm supposed to get dinner with this girl."

"Oh!" Forest exclaims, like this is some big realization. Then he says, "Ohhhhhhhhhh," like the shoe is continuing to drop.

Good god, literally everyone I meet thinks I'm gay. Why do they keep wanting to decide my sexuality for me? Can I just have this *one thing*?

"It's not like that," I tell him. "It's not a date. I date boys." Well, *a* boy. Once. And it was bad.

"Ohhhhhh," Forest says some more, like everything is finally clicking into place for him. And now he's just being an asshole.

"Stop it," I say. "Seriously. I'm gonna tell her I can't make it." I pick up my phone to text her back.

"No, you gotta go! Why wouldn't you go?" He reaches out and covers my phone with his hand to stop me from texting. God, he's so obnoxious.

"I'm not talking about this with you," I say, jerking my phone away.

"Claire, seriously, dude. I'm not just saying this so you'll stop stalking Jamie," he tells me, "I actually think that's pretty funny. I'm saying this *as a friend*—you gotta put yourself out there."

"As a friend?" I repeat incredulously.

"What?" he says, taken aback. "We can't be friends?"

This is a supremely weird conversation.

"Tell me about this girl," he says. "What's her name?"

"Tess."

"What's she like?"

"She's kind of... She's..." How do I explain Tess and Everything She Is? "It doesn't matter, I'm gonna tell her I can't come. If I tell her I'm with you, she can't complain."

"No!" He hits the table softly with his fist. "You will *not* use my name to get out of a social engagement. If you try to do that, I'll... I'll tweet that I'm playing Red Zone alone in my room and then she'll think you're lying!"

I gasp. "You wouldn't!"

"I would! I absolutely would!"

I start laughing. "You don't even know how to *use* Twitter; you'd have to call Rico and have him help you."

"Stop changing the subject. You text that girl back right now and tell her you'll meet her in five minutes."

I look at my phone, but I can't bring myself to do it. My stomach twists in knots at the very idea. Why? *Why?*

"I get it," Forest says, getting serious. "It's scary, meeting people you like."

"I'm not *scared*, I'm just..." I trail off.

"What?"

Great question. What? *What*? What, Claire? What's the problem? Tess is cool and she wants to get dinner, what could possibly be wrong with that?

Maybe because she might like me, and that's scary as hell. Maybe because I can't seem to stop noticing things like her cute legs and her smile and her lipstick, and I don't know why. Maybe it's because I don't even really have friends, so why should I have a date? Not that this is a date. Because it's not. And if it were, I would definitely ruin it somehow, by talking too much, or not enough. Or getting too personal, or not personal enough. Whatever. It's just safer not to go.

"I'm not good with other people, I'm not good at...talking," I say, gesturing back and forth between us. I mean, prime example. Forest has disliked me since practically the first moment we met. Most people do. That's fine. I've accepted it. Tess just hasn't figured it out yet, but this dinner tonight is sure to turn that around.

"You're fine at talking. What do you mean?" Forest asks, and I honestly can't tell if he's being genuine or if he's just acting, like always.

"You don't get it. She's just supersmart and very cool, and

she wears dresses with little foxes on them. I could never do that. She's just... She's *more* than I am, you know?" I sigh. "No, you probably don't know what that feels like because you're rich and too pretty for this world and you're famous and you're not a teenager anymore. But Pine Bluff is *so much less* and Tess is *so much more*. Maybe if I didn't put people off so much, but I do. She'll want to look at her phone, but she'll be too polite to. That's just what happens to me; I'm not good at being interesting."

I stop rambling, and I can't look at him. This is the most I've ever told him, the most I've maybe ever told anyone. Shit, why did I do that? Now he probably thinks I'm some small-town loser with no friends and social anxiety who can't talk to people about anything more personal than a TV show. Which is *completely accurate.*

"Never mind," I mumble as I close my laptop and slide it in my bag, then grab the power cable. I don't bother winding it, I just shove handfuls of it in my bag, probably hopelessly knotting it forever.

"Claire," he says, but I don't look at him, I just zip up my bag and grab the box of doughnuts. I'll keep those for later tonight when I have nothing else going on except room service and a three-hundred-thousand-word fic.

"Claire," he says again, soft but firm. I shoulder my bag and, slowly, turn to face him. He's still sitting in the chair where I left him, his arm looped over the back of it as he's turned around to watch me leave. His expression is serious, genuine. "Trust me when I say, you're good at being interesting. Interesting is not your problem."

And maybe it's just because he's an actor, but when he says it, I almost believe him.

"Text her back," he says.

And I close my eyes and let all the air out of my lungs in one long exhale. When I open them, I look at my phone, type as quickly as possible, **I'll meet you in five!** and hit SEND before I can talk myself out of it.

"Okay," I say.

His eyes start smiling first, then his cheeks, then his mouth breaks open and his whole face brightens. God, what an image. I wish I had *that* as a gif.

"Have fun!" he says. "Tell me everything tomorrow."

It was Tess's suggestion to go to a place she read about online called the Roxy. It lights up the whole block with the red neon in its windows. The inside walls are covered with faded ancient signed 8x10s of famous actors from twenty years ago (everyone's a fan of something!). On the far wall there's a jukebox underneath a life-size hanging sculpture of Jesus on the cross, bloody and anguished. My eyes about bug out of my head when we walk inside. We don't have anything like this in Pine Bluff. Or Boise. Or all of Idaho.

As we walk in, our server hollers at us from the kitchen that we can take a seat anywhere. It's pretty empty in here, just us, a group of four punks in ripped denim jackets and dyed hair by the windows, and two elderly gentlemen by the jukebox who are...holding hands. Oh my god, are they on a date? That's so adorable!

I notice they're selling T-shirts in a glass case, including ones that say PORTLAND FUCKING OREGON and GAY FUCKING PRIDE. And maybe I should have figured it out before then, but *that's* the moment I realize that this is a gay café. Blood rushes to my cheeks as I wonder if everyone in here assumes we're on a date. *Are* we on a date? How am I supposed to figure it out?

Tess leads us to a table by the wall, and we sit down. Our server comes over, and I realize I can't tell what gender they are. I must be making a wide-eyed *Where am I?* kind of face because our server smiles warmly at us and says, "Welcome to the Roxy, this your first time?" Their voice has just a touch of Southern lilt to it, which is a nice change from the bland Northwest accents around here.

"Yes," Tess and I say in unison, then look at each other and laugh.

"Well, my goodness, aren't you two just the cutest?" the server says. "I think you might have just usurped that couple in the back as the most adorable date of the evening."

My ears get even hotter as I stare so hard into my menu that my vision starts to develop spots around the edges. Tess doesn't say anything to correct the server, and they leave us alone with a pair of epic menus.

"So," Tess says, somehow acting normal. "Are you planning to go to any other panels while you're here?"

"Oh, um, I don't know." Does that make me boring?

I take a sip of water, then crunch on an ice cube. I'm not sure what else to say.

Tess tries again. "That was a pretty great panel today, huh?"

"If by *great* you mean *train wreck*," I say, because there was literally nothing great about that panel.

"Oh, well, yeah, I guess so. I was surprised by the question moderators, too." She glances at me. "I saw your text posts about it. But, I don't know, it didn't seem that bad to me?" She chews on the inside of her lip. "I mean, I guess I just feel like, he shouldn't have to answer any questions he doesn't feel comfortable with, you know?"

Wow. Yeah, this was a mistake. I start wondering if I should try to make my exit now before we order anything. Tess drove us here in her car, but I could figure out how to take the streetcar back if I needed to.

Tess must register my hesitation because she says, "Sorry. We don't have to talk about *Demon Heart*." But without *Demon Heart*, what do we talk about? It's the only thing we have in common, and the only thing I really ever think about. I've got nothing else in the conversation bank.

But Tess doesn't believe in my mission. Why *not*? No matter how popular I get on Tumblr, I'll never be able to compete with network TV for views. Not that I want my writing to be über-famous, but I *do* want to see a queer reading of these characters reach people. Does Jamie even know what kind of power he wields every time he opens his computer and starts typing? Does Tess see the difference between what he does and what I do?

Tess. Tonight her dress is blue and meant to look vintage. It comes in at her waist with a red ribbon that ties at the back. I wonder if I pulled on the ribbon if the dress would flow out or if it's sewed down and just for show.

I like that Tess wears a lot of dresses, even though she's queer. The only lesbians at Pine Bluff High (there are two that I know of, and everyone always assumes they're dating, even though they're like three years apart) both play sports and wear folded hats and dirty Carhartts like the rest of the farm kids. Tess isn't like them at all; she isn't like anyone in Pine

Bluff. I want to ask her about her clothes, but now too much time has passed without either of us talking, and it would be weird to ask her about her fashion sense anyway when I clearly don't have any.

Tess catches me staring at the ribbon and I look away, praying my ears don't turn red again. She probably thought I was checking out her boobs. I wasn't checking out her boobs. The ribbon is right *under* her boobs, but how do you explain that to a person? *I know it seemed like I was looking at your boobs, but honestly, I wasn't. I just think your dress is really nice even though I don't know anything about dresses, and that ribbon is lovely, and I was fantasizing about tugging on it, but not looking at your boobs, I promise.*

My palms are sweating, so I surreptitiously wipe them on my jeans. My mouth is dry. All the water in my body seems to be going to the wrong location at the moment.

Tess reaches for her phone. Shit. Why can't I be normal? She's already on her phone and our freaking server hasn't even come back yet. I should have just left when I had the chance, but now it's too weird.

Then my phone buzzes.

Oh.

I look at it.

Hey, do you see the guy by the window in the really bad Wolverine cosplay?

Relief. She isn't bored with me yet. I sneak a peek at the disheveled-looking guy, who must have just come in because I didn't see him earlier. He grimaces as he drinks a steaming cup of sludge brown coffee, his chest hair sticking out of his white V-neck in big tufts. I text back.

Omg

She sends another text. **I'm not one to shame a cosplayer, maybe that's his best effort, but C'MON, REALLY?????**

I write, **Tess . . .**

She writes, **Where are his claws? GROWING UR NAILS LONG DOESNT COUNT, DUDE!!!**

I giggle out loud. I look up from my phone and see that Tess is grinning, but she's on a roll now, she doesn't stop typing.

His hair isn't even spiked, like this is BSAIC SIHT HERE, CLAIRE.

"Tess!" I say out loud.

"What?" She looks up from furiously typing, a gleam in her eyes.

"That's not a costume," I hiss.

We both look at him again, and yeah, that's just some guy in a T-shirt eating a pancake. Our eyes meet, and we crack up laughing.

Not-Wolverine looks over at us and scowls, which only makes us laugh harder.

"Okay, Fun Table, who's ready to order?" our server says, coming over.

"I am!" I say.

We don't bring up the panel at all for the rest of dinner. It turns out we have lots of other things to discuss. We trade stories about our high schools: I tell her what it's like to go to the grocery store while the football team is playing a game—so empty it's like a zombie apocalypse hit. She can't conceive of a school where the 4-H program is more popular than the drama program and the county fair is the highlight of the year, not the battle of the bands. She tells me her Seattle public school has a gender and sexuality alliance that's basically like a club for the queer kids. I take a moment to picture Pine Bluff doing something like that and...yeah, no. Maybe in fifty years. Or a hundred and fifty. She says there are straight kids in the club, too, and also "questioning" kids. She doesn't press it, but I wonder if she's trying to tell me something or if I'm just reading too much into it.

Then, because neither one of us can go more than thirty minutes without talking about *Demon Heart*, we start gushing about it. There's just so much we agree on, like how the show balances emotional stories with action so well, and how Heart has the most tragic backstory of any character on television, and how the elaborate mythology just keeps getting more interesting the more we learn about it. And we're both dying to know what happens in the finale that's just around the corner. Will Smokey and Heart finally make their peace? Will they be able to defeat the Commander and send him back to hell? Will Smokey be able to forgive himself for his mistakes? Will they cry? (We both hope they cry.) It's cathartic to finally get to talk about all this with another person, instead of just online, and Tess knows just as much or even more about the show than I do. Our dinner flies by, and our server is bringing the check before I even realized how long we've been sitting there.

After dinner, we still have plenty of time left on our parking meter, so Tess and I walk down to the path that runs next to the Willamette River. It's cool but not cold, with a breeze coming off the water, and clouds overhead threatening to sprinkle on us at any moment, but there are a lot of other people out for an evening stroll as well. No one's afraid of a little rain in this town. Tess pulls a knit shawl out of her large fabric purse to wrap around her arms; meanwhile I'm over here in my faded Gore-Tex jacket I've had since sixth grade. I swear to god, who wears knit shawls besides grannies and Tess? I don't know, but I love it.

The lights of the city reflect off the dark waves of the river. Portland's bridges repeat into the distance as other pedestrians and bicyclists pass by us, bundled up in their rain jackets and hats. A gay couple in their twenties passes us in the other direction, holding hands. One of them gives us a little smile. Did we just trip his gaydar? For the five-hundredth time I wonder if Tess thinks this is a date.

I wonder what it would be like to kiss her.

Then I wonder where that thought came from.

I've imagined kissing people before. I used to picture myself marrying my old middle school librarian, Mr. Washington. He was tall and thin, black and bald, and I would picture our life together—working side by side in the library, then going home to our cottage where bookcases line every wall. I would pick out his next book and he'd pick mine, and we'd share a kiss before settling into our individual armchairs with mugs of cocoa to read for the evening.

I used to spend my lunches in middle school reading in the library rather than eat in the cafeteria. Mr. Washington seemed to always know when to give me a kind word, and when to leave me alone. On my last day of middle school, he hugged me and told me I was going to be okay, I just needed to make it to college, and then he forgave my overdue fines. I waited until I was back in my bedroom later that day to cry.

The next year, there was a boy, Curtis, in my trigonometry

class who would ask me for help on problems, and I would whisper explanations to him. Curtis was a senior, and I was a freshman, and he would improvise compliments about Mrs. Newton's elaborately quilted vests under his breath that would make me laugh. "Now, Helen, how *did* you pull off that saddle stitch on the center panel?" he would say, mimicking an old woman's voice. His jokes were quiet, just for me. He had unruly dark hair and he was trying to grow a mustache and beard, but it was coming in patchy. I thought about what it would be like if he gave me a ride home in his muddy old pickup one day so I didn't have to take the bus, if he told me he thought I was hot, not just smart. If he kissed me right there in his truck, where anyone could drive by and see that yes, a boy liked me, and yes, a boy kissed me, and yes, I could be loved. And I would blush and run into my house and he would watch me go, yearning.

But Curtis never offered me a ride home. He just stopped coming to class one day. I overheard someone say that he had joined the marines and dropped out of school, but I don't know if it's true.

Then, of course, there's Kyle Cunningham. That one, I don't have to imagine.

It happened on the long afternoon Kyle and I spent sharing a beanbag in the basement of his family's farmhouse this past fall, his hand on my leg as we watched Netflix and ate popcorn and peanut M&M'S. It felt good, being that close to him. He smelled musty, like earth and maybe horses. He had taken off his hat to lie down with me, and his dirty hair stuck up in every direction in a messy look I had found endearing. When the episode ended and Netflix asked us if we were still watching, I said, "Another?" and he turned to me and whispered, "How about this instead?" Then he kissed me, the slight prickle of his would-be stubble scratching my chin, his lips warm and wet and needy. He tasted like chewing tobacco—sweet and bitter.

I remember thinking over and over, I'm kissing someone. I'm *kissing* someone. I'm being kissed right now. This is kissing.

It felt like how kissing looks, like two people pressing their lips together. I thought of Curtis, and whether he would have kissed this well. He probably would have stopped to make a joke, and we would never have gotten back around to kissing again. But Kyle Cunningham was persistent, single-minded. Still kissing, Kyle slid his hand up my leg, up, up, until he was cupping my crotch. Then he just kept his hand there, still, like he was holding a grapefruit. I frowned into the kiss and burrowed my butt deeper into the beanbag chair, away from his hand, but he followed me, kept it there. Then he squeezed.

I broke off the kiss and wiggled away from him.

"What?" he asked.

I just looked at him, not having any words. The TV had gone dark, a logo bouncing around on the screen. His parents were making dinner for us upstairs.

"What, Claire? Don't tell me you don't want to." He tipped his head down and looked at me, his eyebrows furrowed into that pout that I'd seen him do before. His eyes were blue and intense, and I think he probably knew that they had an effect on people. "I see the way you look at me," he said with a slight smile.

It was true, I had looked at him a lot. I had liked his arms, his muscles, his wavy hair. I had liked his dumb folded-over hats. I had liked his jeans, and how they wrapped around his butt. I had liked his saunter-y walk and the casual way he had rolled up to my locker and asked if I wanted to hang out, like it was no big deal, like he wasn't upending the entire high school social structure with a simple offer. Like we were *allowed* to talk to each other.

For an afternoon, it was almost something, until he undermined it.

"I want a ride home," I said.

He swore and balked, but eventually gave me a silent, angry ride back to my house.

As I got out of the car, my hands shaking around my JanSport, I heard him mutter under his breath, "Only trying to do you a favor."

That night, I ignored my parents, took my dinner straight to my room, and turned on the TV for noise.

That's the night *Demon Heart* premiered.

I watched it and became obsessed. With Smokey, with Heart, with their love.

The way Smokey kisses Heart in fanfiction, it's like everything I wanted Kyle Cunningham to be.

SmokeHeart kisses are enormous, emotional affairs. Years of longing built up behind a dam that bursts, and unleashes a wave of emotion spilling out onto each other all at once. SmokeHeart is about two people connecting, on equal terms. It's about caring about another person more than yourself.

Does Kyle Cunningham care about anyone other than Kyle Cunningham?

The wind picks up off the Willamette and tosses my hair back. I sneak a peek at Tess, who pushes her hair out of her eyes. The streetlights hit her soft, curved, dark cheeks, giving her a gentle glow.

What would kissing Tess be like?

Tess is no Kyle Cunningham. She's no Mr. Washington, no Curtis from trig class, no Forest Reed, either. Tess is brightness and life.

I realize with wonder that this feels like a *real date*, not a watch-Netflix-and-grope afternoon in a basement. Maybe my future will be full of dates and nighttime walks along rivers and waffles-for-dinner-just-because-we-feel-like-it. Mr. Washington seemed to think it would be. For the first time, I wonder if he was right.

"Can I ask you a question?" Tess asks, tipping her head back to look at the moon as we walk.

"Sure," I say.

"What's the first fic you ever read?" She shoots me a conspiratorial smile.

"Oh man, no way."

"C'mon!" she protests, laughing.

"Are you kidding? Too embarrassing. We barely know each other!"

"Yeah, but I feel like you already know me better than my friends back home do," she says, and she's kidding, but I can tell she's kind of not, also. She looks at me shyly, and it makes me want to tell her, but then I remember what the answer is, and I just can't do it.

"You first," I say.

"Cheating, but okay. So. It was the summer I was eleven. My brother had given me a Jonas Brothers album for my birthday..."

"Oh no." I clutch my face in embarrassment. I can already tell where this is going. Tess is laughing, too, totally aware of how shameful this is, but she barrels forward anyway.

"It was a tough summer for me. My boobs had just—
BOING. And my best friend at the time, Harper, was dating
this lifeguard, so she wanted to spend the whole summer at
the pool and I couldn't find a swimsuit that didn't completely
mortify me." She shakes her head, taking a minute to relive it.
"So I was alone a lot that summer," she continues, her voice
a little rougher than it was before. "I spent a lot of time in
my room, sitting on my bed, listening to that damn CD on
my pink-and-purple boom box. There was something about
the Jonas Brothers that just . . . *helped.* I could create a whole
world around their songs that was just in my head, that no
one else knew about. All for me."

"Yeah," I say, nodding. She could be describing any number of my own summers in Pine Bluff, not going out, just
diving inward, into my own brain, into my computer, into
my fandom.

"So I started reading JoBro fanfic. First the ones where
they fall in love with Miley Cyrus, or a fan or something.
The self-insert stuff was fun because no one ever writes about
Nick Jonas falling for a black girl, but if it was written in first
person, I could imagine she was me."

I nod. I get it, but I don't get it. That's something I haven't
had to deal with.

"But anyway, then I read this *slash* fic . . ." Her eyes sparkle
with delight.

"Tess!" I interject.

"I know!"

"They are *brothers.*"

"I know, I know, but slash is just so much more interesting.
And when you're in Jonas Brothers fandom, the best slash is,
you know, brother!fic."

I bust up laughing, I can't help it. Of course I relate. I couldn't tell you a single Jonas Brothers song, but I'm sure if I'd received that CD at that time in my life, the exact same thing would've happened to me. Tess is laughing, too, and her smile is a lantern in the darkness, lighting up everything around us.

She says, "I mean, brothers or not, isn't it just way more fun to listen to the songs if you're imagining they're singing all those love ballads to each other?"

"Obviously."

"I think I still have a list of fic recs I could send you..." she says with a sideways smile.

"Thank you, that's very kind, but I'm good."

"Okay, I went, now it's your turn. What was *your* first fandom?"

I screw up my face. Crusading on the importance of queer representation? That I can do without batting an eye. Carrying on about *Demon Heart* and why it's appealing to young women? Easy, done. But talking about my first fandom? That's *personal*. Now we're sharing little pieces of ourselves, and I'm really, *really* not used to doing that.

But Tess is looking at me so expectantly, and she told me hers and how can I say no to those wide brown eyes?

"So...my parents don't believe in TV," I start, and she squeals, hopping back and forth on her toes. "Okay, I'm telling you! Relax!" I laugh.

"What do you mean, they don't *believe* in it?"

"We never had TV growing up. No cable at least, just an ancient old TV with bunny ears they kept in the closet and pulled out for, like, presidential debates."

"You kept your TV in a *closet*?" She looks incredulous.

"I know, *ironic*. Look at me now. Anyway, when we moved to Pine Bluff, I didn't know anybody, and all the kids at school had already been friends for a decade. So I didn't go out much, and I ended up hauling the TV out and watching movies at home. We had a few DVDs, but there was one tape—on VHS, I'm not even kidding you—that I watched *constantly*." I glance at her. "*Teenage Mutant Ninja Turtles*."

She cracks up. "Are we about to talk about inter-turtle romance?"

"No! Okay, I mean, there *was* some of that, obviously, but I was more interested in April. You know, O'Neil?"

"Yeah, of course. The reporter."

"Yeah. We know so little about her in canon other than she's a crusading young journalist, and all the turtles want to bang her. But who is she? What's her story? Why does she spend all her time getting captured and sitting around waiting to be rescued?"

We step off the path to let a large, rowdy bachelorette party pass, all the ladies drunk and chattering, wearing sashes. Rather than yell over their noise, I keep the conversation going by leaning in close to Tess. I can smell her shampoo, something botanical and sweet.

"So I googled her—April. And I found a whole world of people, mostly other girls, asking the same questions that I was, and they were answering them..."

"In fanfiction," Tess finishes. She turns her head just a bit, and despite the parade of women tottering by in heels, all I see is her. I can almost feel her breath on mine. The scratchy wool of her shawl rubs against the back of my hand. My eyes drift to the part of her chin that softens into her neck, and my skin erupts into goose bumps, even though I'm wearing a jacket. I watch as the corners of her mouth turn up—just the hint of a smile touching her lips. I swallow. Then the women pass, their cackles fade, and the moment subsides.

We step back onto the path and keep walking. I try not to think about whatever it was that just passed between us. She felt it, too, right?

I intentionally direct my brain back to the conversation at hand. "April never gets to be the hero in the movies, but in fanfic, *finally*, she's the lead. We get to discover all sorts of things about her backstory. What happened to her parents? Car accident. How does she feel about sewers? Unsavory but necessary, and kind of cozy. What's her favorite food? Oysters"—I raise my eyebrows—"on the half shell."

"Cowabunga," she says, laughing.

"So that's how I found fanfic, which led me to Tumblr, which introduced me to so, so many other fandoms. And so I was an old fandom hag ready for a new obsession when *Demon Heart* premiered."

"*Teenage Mutant Ninja Turtles*," she repeats, shaking her head.

"Yeah, well, they say you don't get to pick your first fandom, it picks you."

"So why do you think April picked you?"

I shrug. "I'm not sure. She was smart, she was fearless, she didn't get enough story...."

"She was the only woman," Tess points out.

Oh. Yeah, *huh*. That, too, probably.

Tess gives me a little look and says, low, "Do you often find yourself thinking about women, Claire?"

The way she says it gives me shivers. I look at her, and she's giving me these eyes that are asking me a question I don't know how to answer.

Do I?

Am I?

I honestly don't know.

I sidestep the subtext and answer the question literally. "We're hardwired to look for the character who's like us, right? That's just reality. I guess I saw myself in the intrepid woman reporter. Not so much in Rafael."

"Maybe if she'd been Rafaela..." Tess jokes, and the mood seamlessly shifts back to fun banter.

"Ooh, do you think we could get Jamie to reboot TMNT with all lady-turtles?"

"Oh my god, can you even imagine?" We're both giggling now. The idea is so absurd. Jamie making a movie about women? Ridiculous.

"Rico can play Shredder!" I offer.

"And Forest is April, no, wait...*Abe* O'Neil!"

"Oh my god, in a little yellow bodysuit, he'd be so cute!" We're dying laughing now.

Tess stops walking as we cross to a sidewalk, where her old red Toyota Tercel is parked under a streetlight. I hadn't even realized we'd made it back to her car.

"Well, this is us," she says. "I'll give you a ride back to your hotel. This was a nice night."

"Yeah," I say. I can't believe I almost didn't come tonight. This was more fun than I've had in a long time.

On the short drive back to the hotel, I feel a sort of dread, for the end of the night, for the end of this trip...for being alone again. Back to Pine Bluff, back inside my own mind, my only escape the internet and the occasional conversation about horses with Joanie on the school bus. Tess drums her deep purple–painted fingernails on the steering wheel, nodding her head along to the radio, her hair bouncing over her forehead, down her neck. I finally made a friend, and soon we have to say good-bye. What then?

Tess pulls into our hotel parking lot, puts the parking brake on, and turns the car off. She rubs at the ribbon around her dress, worrying the wrinkles out. And I finally have my answer because I can tell from the way it moves that it's not sewed down, that it's keeping her dress snug around her middle, that if I reached over and pulled on one end...I blink hard, pushing the mental image away.

"So, ah, I guess I'll see you tomorrow in Seattle. That's my last stop."

"Yeah, mine, too," I say. We're flying out of Sea-Tac Airport in two days.

"We should hang out there, though, you know? I heard they're doing a big screening for the finale. Outdoors in a park, like a thousand *Demon Heart* fans all watching together. Should be rad."

"Yeah, definitely! Let's do it." I feel a little sick thinking about *Demon Heart* ending for the season, but it has to happen sometime, and I'd rather watch the finale next to Tess than all alone in my hotel room.

"Cool, cool," she says.

And it's time to make my exit. She looks at me with the same look she had back on our walk—casually upturned mouth, intent unblinking eyes, and I wonder, is she thinking about kissing me? Am I thinking about kissing her? I guess I am now....

Her gaze is so intense, I have to look away. Out of my peripheral vision, I can tell she drops her eyes, too.

"I, uh, I better find a place to park for the night," she says.

"Wait," I start, putting together what she's saying with what she told me back in Boise. "Are you really sleeping in your car?"

"Yeah. It's no big deal," she says. "My sleeping bag is warm, and I lock the doors."

"No," I say. That's not acceptable.

"Claire, relax, it's fine."

"No. Nope. You get a bed. You can sleep in my room."

She looks at me a moment, as though trying to decide what I mean by the offer. *I* don't know what I mean by the offer.

"How many..." she starts, and stumbles, then tries again. "How many beds does your room have?"

"Two," I say quickly. "You can have your own, I'll sleep with my mom. She won't care, I promise. You're not staying in this car. Can you even stretch out? I mean, jeez!"

"You're sure?" she asks.

"A hundred percent. Come on." I open my door and step out, then bend over to look back in at her.

"Okay," she says, and reaches into the back for her stuff.

What am I doing?

forest → 23

BACK IN THE PRIVACY OF MY OWN ROOM, I TYPE *heart of lightness* into Google, hesitate a moment, then hit ENTER.

It's time I figured out for myself what the hell Claire's been writing about me online. Well, she *says* it's not about me, but that's just semantics, right? Because Forest is Smokey, and Smokey is Forest. And all of this, whether she likes it or not, is inextricably tied up in *me.*

I click a link, which takes me to her page on a fanfiction site, and the first thing I see is she has *so many* stories.

"Whoa."

I scroll through the titles but they just keep coming. I don't know what I'm waiting for, I just click one at random. It says 48,000 views. *Jeeeeeesus.* She's not messing around.

Okay, Claire, let's see what you've been up to.

24

THE FIRST TIME SMOKEY KISSED ANYONE, HE WAS twelve years old, impressing his friends by surprising Tammy Rose with a peck on the lips as she came out of the movie theater. Immediately after he pulled away, she'd spat on the ground, screwed up her face, and hollered curses after him as he and his friends ran away. Smokey had laughed with his friends all the way back to his house until he closed his front door behind him, and, alone, sighed against it with a feeling he couldn't name.

The next time he kissed anyone, he was seventeen, pressing that neighborhood boy Tyler against the shingles of his house, their scuffed-up sneakers nudging together. Smokey's dad moved them three states away the next day. He never saw Tyler again, but he sometimes thought about him, hoping his life was easier than Smokey's turned out to be.

The first time Smokey went down on a man was three years later, dropping to his knees in a soybean field in front of the son of a farmer whose name he never quite caught. The farmer boy-nearly-a-man leaned his broad, tanned shoulders back against the enormous tire of the family John Deere and urged Smokey on, the lights of the farmhouse just hidden from view behind the tractor in the dimming evening Iowa light. When Smokey finished, the farmer boy buttoned up his Wranglers and practically ran back into his house, leaving Smokey with a hard-on and a hurting heart. Smokey was always living his life outside, never quite welcome indoors.

The first time Smokey had sex, it was with the pretty and curvy young bartender of a dusty hole-in-the-wall just outside Austin who'd been shamelessly flirting with him all night. What the hell, he thought, and let her drive him back to her apartment, a studio by the airport with a fuzzy orange couch that was missing most of its fuzz and a live oak brushing against the outside of her window. He poured whiskey for them both, but it turned out he didn't need it. As soon as she guided his hands on her, letting him run his fingers over her belly, her back, reaching down her skirt to find she had lost her panties somewhere between the door and the kitchen, he was ready to go. If he was nervous about performance, he didn't need to be, because she was assertive and wasn't afraid to tell him exactly what to do and how slow to do it. He left town three days later with her number in his phone and explicit instructions to text her the next time he was in Hill Country. And he would have, but then the portal opened, and hell literally broke loose, and Smokey met Heart and found that he had a purpose larger than himself.

Smokey and Heart were always meant to be enemies. A man dedicated to sending demons back to hell wasn't supposed to just up and befriend a demon. But Heart wasn't like the others—he was smarter and seemed to understand Smokey, and unlike every other demon that crossed Smokey's path, Smokey couldn't kill him. They were an even match, and not just physically. Like Smokey, Heart's words seemed to suggest a past that was less than sterling, and a deep well of pain that he could cover up for polite company but that haunted him in moments of solitude, or toward the bottom of a bottle. Smokey knew that pain well and didn't wish it on anyone else, not even a grossly attractive Hellhorn Demon who didn't know how to stay in his lane.

Yes, Smokey had met so many people in his short life, had kept track of most of the ones who didn't piss him off or end up dead, and he was certain that despite many attempts, he had never fallen in love with anyone.

This September, after he and Heart had accidentally worked together to send a Redbeast Demon back to his home in hell, they had decided to attempt a tenuous truce at last. And, to make it more official, they sealed it with a clink of glasses of Bulleit and a game of pool in the back room of a roadside place they both happened to know outside Denton.

The bar was dark and smelled of day-old chicken, fried steak, and spilled beer. Lit mostly by the neon signs hanging on every wall, it did two things right: good billiards and cheap prices. The other patrons—looked to be mostly regulars—eyed Smokey and Heart but gave them no guff, just tossed their peanut shells on the ground and ordered their doubles in peace.

The first game of pool nearly ended early after Smokey accused Heart of moving the cue ball when he wasn't looking. Heart laughed him off, which only made Smokey angrier. Strong words were exchanged, and the whole ordeal

would have blown up in their faces if Heart hadn't gener-
ously offered to buy the next round. Then, while he was at
the bar, leaning over the counter, Smokey caught a glimpse
of Heart's shirt riding up in the back to show off a tiny sliver
of pale brown skin above his waistband and felt a familiar
hitch in his chest.

Stop it, he whispered angrily to himself. *Not now, not here.*

Smokey could slay demons all night long. He could stare
down the dirtiest, ugliest dreck that hell chose to spit out at
him, and he could do it with a fire in his eye until his legs
gave out from exhaustion. He could do all that and keep the
fear in his belly at bay, but he couldn't have a straightforward
conversation and game of pool with Heart without feeling like
he had to lob a bomb in the middle of everything and make
his escape. His bravery had a county line, and Heart was far,
far on the other side of it.

Half a bottle later, Smokey found himself subject to an
impromptu pool lesson from Heart. A patronizing one—
Heart explaining that Smokey's bridge was too stiff, that he
needed to put a little give in it, *here, like this*... and then
Smokey found Heart's fingers molding his own, Heart's body
brushed up against his side, the unnatural heat from the
demon blood that coursed through his system making the
hairs on Smokey's arm stand up.

"I...I got it," Smokey coughed out weakly, softly, not
nearly rough enough to get this man away from him.

No, not man, demon. *Demon.* He couldn't let himself forget that.

Heart didn't move away. Instead, he leaned into Smokey's
ear, his whiskey-thick breath warm on Smokey's neck, and
whispered, "Are you sure that's what you want?"

Smokey shivered, the goose bumps crawling unbidden up his arms. His heart jackhammered in his chest as he tried to ignore the growing knot in his stomach.

Smokey couldn't take it, the warmth in his voice, as if Heart gave a shit what Smokey was feeling. As if Smokey *mattered*. He focused on steadying his breath so that his next words came out clearly, without wavering: "I said, *I got it*," he growled, rough and low.

Heart let go, almost immediately. "Okay," he said, "sure." As Heart pulled away, the cool air flowed back in between them, and Smokey felt only disgust in himself for his cowardice. How long had he thought of a moment like this, and he had just let it slip right through his fingers. The swirl of emotions in his gut blackened into anger—at himself, at Heart for making him feel this way and for being a demon, at this bar for existing, at the world for going to shit, at himself, always at himself.

Heart stepped farther away as Smokey spiraled. "I'm sorry," Heart murmured low. "It didn't mean anything."

Smokey had snapped the pool cue before he even realized he was going to do it, sharp splinters of wood flying across the green felt. He took a swing at Heart, who leapt back, surprised, but ready for battle, always—the life of a demon, perpetually hunted.

"Whoa, man, what're you doing?" Heart cried as he scrambled to put the pool table between them, but Smokey sprang onto the tabletop and took another swing, this time connecting with Heart's shoulder. The cue shattered across his granite-hard demon muscles, leaving Smokey with just a shard of wood and his own fists. Heart let out a string of curses in demontongue as Smokey tossed what was left of the pool cue away and dropped from the table to a spot in front of Heart, who had the perfect opening to land a few blows as Smokey caught his balance, but he didn't take it.

Smokey didn't know why he was doing it except that he was already doing it and couldn't stop now. He picked up a chair and sent it splintering against Heart's abs. Heart staggered back but still didn't fight. Instead, he hollered at the barman and patrons to leave out the front doors and not come back in, not for anything. Then he used his demon strength to flip the pool table a full turn and a half, sending the balls flying across the room, rolling under tables and chairs. The superhuman action was more than enough to convince the other patrons that leaving was wise.

Heart turned back to Smokey. "Just you and me now, let it out," Heart said, low and warm, like he was Smokey's mother or some shit, and the fact that Heart still wouldn't hate Smokey, even after this, made him even angrier.

Smokey kicked a few pool balls aside, then lunged at Heart, who tried to dodge, but they had fought too many damn times before, and Smokey knew just how Heart would react. Smokey tackled him hard, landing with a crack of bone and muscle on the slick, dirty floor. Smokey managed a few blows across the face before Heart was able to judo Smokey off him, spitting blood and getting back to his feet.

"That's it," Heart said. "Keep it coming."

Smokey could stop and think about what he was doing. He could open that part of his heart that felt feelings other than *run* and *snarl* and *fight*. He could talk, or he could cry. But instead, he curled his fingers in against his palm so they didn't break, tucked his shoulder, and slammed Heart against the wall of the bar so hard that the Miller sign dropped off its nail and shattered on the ground, sending shards of the glass tubes skittering across the dirty cement floor.

Smokey fit his arm against Heart's neck and pinned him against the wall. "Why aren't you fighting back?" he barked.

"I don't want to hurt you," Heart said simply.

"Well, I want to hurt you," Smokey growled into him.

"I don't think you do," Heart whispered, their faces so close together now, Smokey could see the grain of yellow in Heart's brown eyes.

But Heart was wrong. Smokey *did* want to hurt him. Wanted him to disappear back into the hellhole he crawled out of. Wanted to wipe him from his memory so that he didn't have to face what Heart made him think about every time he looked at him with those fiery eyes that reminded Smokey of a hearth on a cold day. Of safety in a storm.

"You don't have to be scared," Heart said, so low Smokey almost couldn't hear him over the thumping pulse in his ears. "You deserve to feel this way."

That wasn't true, not even a little, but looking into those eyes, Smokey felt the cold beat of anger still into quiet. Heart believed it, even if Smokey didn't.

"It's okay, it's okay. I forgive you," Heart said, still pinned against the wall. And why should he forgive Smokey before the fight was even over? Or maybe it *was* over. The muscles in Smokey's shoulders released, his forearm fell away from Heart's neck, but he didn't step back. It was true, he didn't want to hurt Heart; he had wanted Heart to hurt him back, had wanted to feel the sharp crack of his nose breaking, the taste of blood in his mouth, the comforting wail of his muscles afterward.

"I'm not going to hurt you," Heart whispered. Smokey

wanted to believe him. He knew Heart wasn't going to fight him, but he wasn't so sure this wouldn't hurt. He wanted Heart to grab him, to flip him against the wall and press their lips together. He wanted Heart's hands in his hair, on his chest, down his pants. But he couldn't say it.

No, there's no way this wouldn't hurt.

Smokey was still standing so close he could smell the demon's blood, but he didn't step away. He let his gaze drop down Heart's body, over his chest, his shoulders where he was bleeding a bit from the hit from the pool cue. Smokey wanted to take it back, undo the pain, fix the damage.

When he met Heart's eyes again, Heart was smirking.

"What?" Smokey demanded.

"Dude, you just kicked my ass pretty good, so if you're waiting for me to make the first move—"

So Smokey kissed him.

He felt a little dizzy, but not from the alcohol, and Heart's lips were warm and heavy. Heart hooked his hands around Smokey's hips and pulled Smokey against him so their bodies fit together like a knife and its sheath. Heart's mouth opened, and Smokey slipped his tongue in and found he tasted like Bulleit and demon blood and firewood, and he wanted more.

Smokey's defenses fell away faster than he would've liked, and before he knew it, he was moaning softly into Heart's mouth as Heart half smiled and pulled Smokey even closer to him so that Smokey could feel the unmistakable bulge pressing into his hip, his own erection growing uncomfortably thick in his Levi's. But the only important thing right now was the feel of Heart's hands hot on his back, dipping under the waist of Smokey's jeans, the taste of Heart in his mouth, the feeling of being held and needed and loved.

He didn't fight back.

When they finally pulled apart, Smokey thought Heart might make an excuse to leave, but instead Heart only said, "You got a room in town, stranger?"

Smokey bit his lip as his heart leapt. A huge, knee-jerk part of him wanted to run away from that implication, wanted to spit or crack another pool cue. But he bit back the fear. Instead, he said, "Yeah. Yeah, I do." And he fished a motel room key out of his pocket.

Heart smiled and kissed him again, warmly this time, soft. "You gonna try to beat me up again if we go there?"

Smokey felt the heat hit his cheeks as the shame at what he'd done overcame him. He looked away, and Heart said, "Hey, hey, it's okay," and brought his hand up to Smokey's cheek to guide his face back to his. Heart kissed him quickly, then pressed his hips forward to remind Smokey of the thrumming issue that requested his attention below.

Smokey got the hint. He wrapped his fingers in Heart's, and they picked their way through the mess they left behind. When they pushed out the front door, hand in hand, the barman looked on in shock, but before he could comment, Heart dug a couple of twenties out of his pocket and pressed them into his hand. "Sorry 'bout the mess," he said, and he and Smokey burst into laughter as they crossed the parking lot.

The first time Smokey fell in love, he was twenty-four. High from a fight, a little drunk from whiskey, and not entirely sure any of this was going to end okay. In the parking lot of that roadside place outside Denton, Smokey squeezed Heart's hand, looked him in the eye, and decided, with a thumping shot of terror, that it was better to try than not try.

I CLOSE THE LAPTOP.

Okay.

All right.

So *that's* fanfiction.

claire

WE MAKE IT BACK TO OUR ROOM, AND I'M SO BUSY
worrying about what Tess is thinking that I don't even remember that my freaking *mother* might be in our room when we
get there. I open the door and say, "Mom?" but there's no
answer. She must still be out. Where does she even go all day?

The hotel Ms. Greenhill got for us is absurdly nice, and
seeing it now, through Tess's eyes, I'm a little embarrassed of
it. A "suite" is, I guess, what it's called.

"Nice room," Tess says, impressed, putting her backpack
down by one of the beds.

"Yeah, we don't pay for it or anything," I feel obligated to
say so she doesn't think I'm rich. "Our food is free, too. We
can order room service if you want...."

"Do you know how lucky you are?" she asks, running her
hand along the shiny countertops.

"I do," I say.

"Not just the room. This whole trip. Meeting Forest and

Rico. Getting to *know* them, being ridiculously lucky enough to be the one chosen for this out of *everyone....*"

I feel a pang of guilt because I'm here and a lot of other people wish they would've won instead of me. All I can do is try to represent the fans the best I can and use my brief position adjacent to Jamie to try to get him to see the show from our point of view.

"Because you're *super* lucky," Tess repeats. She must be warm because she takes her shawl off, and now she's all bare wide arms.

"Let me give you the tour of the place," I mumble and move away from her—all the way across the room—and open the curtains. "This is our amazing view...of that strip mall over there."

She laughs and comes over to look out the windows, her shoulder nudging up against mine. Why is she undressing? Why is she touching me? Is she just warm? Or is it a secret signal? I'm not good with secret signals. I'm better with clear and direct communication. Surely she's picked that up by now. I close the curtains and move back across the room to the kitchenette.

"This is the kitchenette. It's mostly useless, but I use the coffeepot to make tea. Do you like tea? I have peppermint, chamomile, green, Earl Grey—it might be too late for Earl Grey, I guess, but I have it." I'm rambling. I know I'm rambling, but I can't stop myself. "Do you want some? I'll make some. Is mint okay?"

I pick up the coffeepot and hold it up to show her. She's still over by the windows, watching me with a funny look on her face. OH GOD, WHY AM I LIKE THIS? I DIDN'T ASK TO BE LIKE THIS.

"Claire..." she says slowly, "I don't know what you're thinking right now, but we don't have to *do...anything.*"

I'm going to puke. What does she mean? Does that mean what I think it means? I'm going to faint. I'm gonna pukefaint.

"Are you okay?" she asks. Why, do I not look okay? She looks okay. She looks more than okay. She looks *perfect.*

"Claire?" she says again. I feel hot. I'm sweating. She's not sweating. She's glowing. She's a glowworm. I'm just a regular worm. A regular gray worm that's sweating so much it turns all the dirt around it into mud. A gross, sweaty, muddy worm.

"Okay," she says. "It's cool. This is obviously too much. I'll just get my stuff...." She goes and grabs her backpack and starts for the door. "No problem, I'll let myself out. I'll see you tomorrow."

She says it like it's no big deal.

Like she's doing me a favor.

She's not doing me a favor.

I want her to stop.

Tess. Stop.

STOP.

"Stop!"

I say that.

She stops.

She looks back at me and waits.

Absurdly, I think about all the fics I've read. I know exactly what to do next. The secret signal I need to give.

I drop my gaze to her lips.

Her lips smile.

I'm still holding the coffeepot. What would happen next in a fic? *Claire puts the coffeepot down.* I put the coffeepot down. *Claire approaches Tess.* I put one foot in front of the other.

She drops her backpack and holds her hands out to me, and when I reach her, she slides her hands around my waist and brings me in tight. *Claire kisses Tess.* And I lean forward and that's how easy it is, because now we're kissing.

And my stomach *zhooms.*

My heartbeat spikes, and I'm tingly from the base of my neck down to my fingertips, and her lips are soft and welcoming, and I just want to burrow in and stay right here in her arms like it's my hobbit home. I never want to leave.

I start to smile, and she must feel it because she pulls away.

"What?" she asks, smiling, too.

I just shake my head. I don't know, I don't know. Kissing Kyle Cunningham was a joke compared to this. Reading fic about kissing is a dim shadow of the real thing.

"It's never felt like this before," I whisper. Our faces are still so close together I can hear her breathing. I can see her pulse in that soft part of her neck, and I want to kiss it, too. I want to kiss her nose. I want to kiss her eyes. I want to kiss her again and again. I realize what I'm thinking. I don't know what this makes me, I can't think about it right now. My mind is a swirl. And I'm lost looking at her, because she's still smiling at me, and her smile makes me want to cry it's so pretty.

"Claire, you are amazing, do you know that?" No, I didn't. "And you're very, very cute."

Glowworm thinks I'm cute. GLOWWORM THINKS I'M CUTE.

The warmth in my belly is overwhelming. Before I know it, the pressure is building behind my eyes, and tears are welling up and I WILL NOT CRY IN FRONT OF TESS but it's too late, she's seen them, and her eyes get big with concern and she lets go of me DON'T LET GO OF ME, TESS and she's giving me space I DON'T WANT SPACE.

"Oh no, what is it? I'm sorry. Too much? It's too much." And I'm shaking my head and I can't speak because I'm afraid it will come out as a sob and now the dumb tears are running down my cheeks and WHY IS THIS HAPPENING? I'M RUINING IT. She's waving her hands around like she doesn't know what to do, then she sees a box of Kleenex and grabs it for me and starts handing me tissue after tissue—way too many tissues—saying, "It'sokayit'sokayit'sokay!"

I wipe the tears away with the tissues and then—oh god—I have to blow my nose so I turn my back to do that, but now I'm this gross mucus-y mess and my glasses are fogging up and it's definitely over. One kiss, that's it, now it's over, and she won't want to kiss again because now I'll forever remind her of snot because I'm the girl who cried after she kissed her.

When I turn back around, she's sitting on the bed with her hands clasped in her lap and not showing her disgust outwardly at all because she is a kind person. I'm waiting for her to make an excuse to leave, when she says, "Sorry."

SHE'S SORRY?

"I know, I always do this," she says. "I fall for straight girls, and then they get confused, but it's cool, it's cool. You're not queer. We don't have to do anything. I can go, or I can stay and we can just watch TV or something. Whatever you want. I promise not to stalk you or tell anyone or anything."

I don't really hear most of that because I'm stuck on . . .

She . . . *fell* for me?

"Tess," I say, and my heart is still going sixty-five down the freeway, but I swallow my fear. "That's not what this is."

She looks up at me. "No?"

"I'm not crying because I'm straight...." Then, because saying that caught me off guard, I add quickly, "I don't know what I am. I'm crying because...It's dumb, but I'm crying because I'm happy."

She stares at me.

I stare at her.

"This isn't gay panic?" she asks hopefully.

I shake my head. She bursts out laughing, and runs her hand over the shaved side of her head and behind her neck. "Oh Jesus, Claire, I thought..."

"Tess..." I know what I want to say, but I'm terrified to say it. But this whole night is uncharted territory, so screw it, right? "Can I kiss you again?"

"Yes," she says enthusiastically. "YES."

So I step forward, and I gently put one knee on the bed on either side of her and kneel so our faces are the same level.

Again, I drop my gaze to her mouth, savoring the moment this time.

Her tongue slips out just a bit to lick her lips.

Slowly, I tip my head forward, and her mouth rises, and just before we meet, I pause again and marvel at the warmth of her, at her openness.

She likes me. And she wants me to kiss her.

So I kiss her.

And I don't cry.

And this time she opens her mouth, and my tongue slides in, and she tastes like maple syrup and waffles and girl.

She brings her hands up my back, and it gives me goose bumps. I press into her, and she tips back onto the bed and our foreheads bonk as we land, but we don't stop, we just keep kissing like that, and there's this feeling building inside, and I definitely know what it means because I've gotten it during a good fic many times.

Tess's hands find the gap between my shirt and my pants, and she dips her fingers into the space, warm against my back, and the feeling in my stomach travels south and I need her to touch me more, so I do the only thing I can think to do, which is roll my hips down, and I feel her breath hitch, and I'm thinking, Don'tstopdon'tstop, and she doesn't. She grabs me by the waist and pulls me somehow closer to her, pressing up into my jeans, breathing into my mouth.

I remember she's wearing a dress. . . . How easy would it be to just slip my hand underneath? She has her hand balled up in my hoodie, and our bodies are pulsing slightly together. I reach down—her thighs are so soft where I graze my fingers against them. I dip my hand beneath the hem of her skirt. . . .

What do I do now? I don't know!

I need to read more femslash, I think wildly.

And then my breathing gets tight as I realize what I'm doing. Thirty minutes ago I was walking along the river and now suddenly I'm lying on top of a girl with my hand up her skirt?

I take my hand back and pull away from her just a bit.

"Claire?" she says.

This is all happening too fast. What am I even *doing*?

"Is everything okay?" she says, her arms still wrapped around me, holding me tight against her.

"Yeah, yeah, I just, um . . ." My voice trails off as I look at her. She looks so beautiful, her hair splayed out behind her on the bed, her lips pink, her cheeks flushed. I did that. *I did that.*

I want to kiss her again, so badly. What does that mean? What does that make me? Is this it? Is this the confirmation I was looking for? I'm definitely gay, no turning back, forever and ever, amen? I feel the sudden urge to leave.

She pulls one hand out of the back of my shirt and brings it to the side of my face, rubbing my cheek with her thumb.

"You are so frigging hot right now," she says.

What do I say to *that*?

So are you, so are you, so are you runs like a refrain in my head. I'm just getting my lips to form the words when...

BEEP.

The door opens.

Oh *shit.*

I leap off Tess and straighten my shirt, wipe my lips on my sleeve. She pulls her dress down and sits up, and we both look toward the door just in time to see...

Mom walk in.

"Claire, I just went to the most *divine* cupcake shop, I brought you a—"

She stops short when she sees Tess.

"Who's *this*?" she asks with a look of wide-eyed wonder. God, Mom, *be cool.* Don't act like I've never had a friend over before.

Friend. I'm burning on the inside. I'm sure my cheeks are neon red right now.

"Tess," she says, putting her hand out. That hand was just up my shirt not ten seconds ago. "It's nice to meet you, Mrs...."

"Good lord, child, please call me Trudi." Mom shakes

Tess's hand, then looks at me in complete delight. "You made a friend!" she exclaims—I swear to god, *exclaims*. I'm dying. I'm dead. Tess and I glance at each other, and her face is tight from holding back a smile and her eyes are bulging and I can tell she's laughing hysterically on the inside.

I look back at my mom. "Um, would it be okay if Tess slept here tonight?" I ask. "She doesn't have a place to stay so I thought she could take one of our beds."

Mom looks back at Tess, then at me, and I have no idea what she's thinking, but I'm mortified.

She just says, "Good thing I got extra cupcakes, then, huh?"

Two hours and two and a half cupcakes later, I'm in bed next to my mom, who is snoring. I look across the gap to the other bed, where Tess is sleeping on her back, her hair up in a silk scarf.

I look at her profile, admiring the way her forehead curves into her nose, the way her lips part a bit as she sleeps.

I want to kiss her again. And I don't know what that means.

Because here's the thing, right? I have a couple options. I could wake up tomorrow and tell my mom I'm gay and I like Tess, and then she'd cry and be so happy for me and probably give me a sex talk, which I do *not* want to hear (but also I probably need to hear from *someone* because if today proved anything it's that I seriously have no clue how sex works when it's not between Smokey and Heart—more research is clearly needed), and then I could announce it on Facebook and come out to my school and everyone would either accept me or not accept me and then I would have to become friends with those other two lesbian girls, even though I don't know nearly enough about basketball to hang out with them, and I would need to buy some rainbow suspenders for the Pride parade in Boise, which I don't even want to go to because parades are just *too many people* and Tess and I could, *what*, be girlfriends? Would I meet her family? Her friends? Would I cut my hair into something edgy and short? Would this be my coming-out story forever when people asked me about it? Would Joanie Engstrom still want to be bus buddies with me? Would I have to decide if I also still like boys? Would I have to start calling myself lesbian? Bisexual? Pansexual, like Tess? The words blur and block out the rest of my brain.

My chest feels tight, so I turn onto my back and look at the ceiling and breathe in through my nose and out through my mouth, long, slow breaths.

I don't know how Tess does it. She seems to know exactly what she is, and who she likes, and why. When did she acquire this certainty? And how can I get some of it to rub off on me?

My cheeks flush in the darkness at the phrase *rub off*, and I shake the visual from earlier that night away.

Because what if... what if I'm *not* actually queer? What if I come out to everyone I know, but then I realize later that this was just a weird night and after this I never kiss another girl? Then what? Then do I have to re—come out as straight? Take it all back? And who would believe me? Everyone I know already thinks I'm gay just because I ship slash and I like to talk about it. I mean, I could never come back from that.

How are you supposed to know? I mean, really know, like *for sure* know? Know enough to tell your mom, who will surely freak out and want to bake a cake or something? Know enough to call yourself gay—in public or even in private, even in your own head?

I don't know. What if I never know? What if I feel like this forever?

Here's one thing I do know: I know that Smokey and Heart are in love.

When I realize that, I can feel all the muscles in my body relax. My shoulders press into the mattress, my eyelids finally soften. This I know with certainty. Sorting through all my own emotions is a mess, but Smokey and Heart's love is no mystery.

And tomorrow I'm headed to Seattle. My last stop, my last chance to make sure the world knows about them. Tonight with Tess was fun, but I can't let something like this confuse what's really important. I have my whole life to figure out my sexuality, but I only have another two days to try to make SmokeHeart canon.

I don't look at Tess again, for fear I'll lose my nerve.

forest ➜ *27*

I DRAG MY SUITCASE DOWN THE HOTEL HALLWAY and curse my six a.m. wake-up call as I hit the down button for the elevator. It's a miracle I'm functioning this morning considering how late I stayed up last night reading—

No. Do *not* think about what you were reading.

Rico ambles up to me and slaps me on the back. "Mornin', hot rod."

I try not to blush, but I can already feel the blood rushing to my face. I avoid his eyes and hope he doesn't notice.

"Hey," I mumble. The elevator doors open, and I get on as he follows me, way too chipper for the hour.

"What's up with you this morning?" he asks.

"Nothing, late night."

"Oh man, I fell asleep at like nine watching QVC. Good thing, too, because I was one more caller away from ordering a squid-ink anti-aging facial serum and moisturizer set."

I really wish he wouldn't say *facial* right now. Or *serum*.

"What do you think?" he asks, touching the skin next to his eyes gently. "Do my wrinkles make me look distinguished or elderly?"

I ignore him because the elevator doors just opened to the lobby and I see Claire... and she's not alone. She's with this girl who must be Tess. A smile grows from deep inside me. Rico follows my gaze.

"Who's the chick with the badass haircut?"

"I'm guessing that's Claire's date from last night."

"Her *date*?" Rico's eyebrows shoot up. *"And she's still here?"* Rico looks over at them and chuckles. "Well, well, well."

Claire and Tess are taking a quiet moment to themselves, talking by the front doors, oblivious to us watching. Claire tucks her hair behind her ears and says something that makes Tess laugh. Claire looks nervous, and that's even *more* adorable.

"They're cute together, aren't they?" I say, and Rico just laughs. "What?" He shakes his head. "What, man?"

He looks at me, endlessly amused, his eye crinkles on full display, and I think, Don't get the squid ink serum, dude, you're fine without it, and he says, "You *ship* them." Oh my god, I would be happy to never hear the word *ship* again in my life, but Claire looks so cute talking to Tess that I can't help it.

He's right, I kind of ship it.

Rico knocks my shoulder. "Go say hi, you dummy."

I tug my suitcase toward them, trying to think of what I'm going to say, but Claire's mom, Trudi, swoops in before I can get there and interrupts their moment.

"Claire, stop dillydallying and get on the bus! We don't want to make these nice people wait on us," Trudi hollers as

she wheels her suitcase past us on her way toward the doors.
It breaks Claire and Tess from their bubble, and they notice
me hovering.

"Looking good, Forest!" Trudi says with a wink.

"Good morning, Trudi."

"It is now, sweet potato." She wheels her suitcase out the
doors toward the idling charter bus waiting outside.

I turn to Claire. "Who's this?" I ask with a big smile.

Claire looks nervous, like she doesn't want to be here right
now, but I figure she's just embarrassed to introduce her new
girlfriend to me.

Claire says, "Forest, this is Tess."

Tess is staring at me, agape. Oh yeah. I'm famous. I forgot
for a second.

"Hi," I say, and put my hand out. She shakes it, trembling.
This is not the cool, confident girl Claire described to me last
night. I guess I have that effect. Claire looks bleary-eyed and
unimpressed, but hey, I also remember a time not so long
ago when Claire was nervous around me, too—standing up
at that convention in Boise, voice wavering, scared shitless.
Now look at her, a little hellion, getting in my way, bossing
me around. How quickly they grow up.

I don't think Tess has breathed in a full minute, so I say,
"I'm Forest Reed. If I look familiar, it's okay, that's normal.
It's because I'm a television actor." And I'm relieved to find
she laughs at that.

"I know who you are," she assures me.

"Oh, good. *Demon Heart* fan?"

"She's a huge fan," Claire says. Tess shoots her a look. "Tess
is an amazing artist; she does this fanart that'd blow you
away."

Is it pictures of me kissing Rico? I don't want to see it, but at the same time I am overcome with curiosity.

"Claire—" Tess says sharply.

"What? I'm not showing him, I'm just saying. You're a good artist."

There's something going on between these two—a tension that I can't quite put my finger on. I wonder what happened last night. Did they hook up? Did they not?

"I draw other things, too," Tess says to Claire, "not just fanart."

"That's awesome," I say, and watch Claire for clues, but she's giving me nothing. "So what's up, Tess? Am I gonna see you in Seattle?"

"Yeah," Tess says. "Well, I mean, *I'll* see *you*. You'll have to look pretty hard at the audience if you're gonna see me." She laughs nervously. "I'm just praying that my old shit-bucket makes it home." She points across the parking lot, where an ancient red Toyota Tercel is parked. Yikes. It reminds me of my first shitty teenage pickup truck. I loved that terrible pile of rust, but I wouldn't want to take it cross-country.

"That's a gorgeous set of wheels."

She smiles shyly. "Yeah, I should probably get rid of it, but I can't really afford to. Besides, my ex-girlfriend gave it to me and she lost the title, so at this point it's practically stolen."

"Oh!" I say, acting surprised. For I am a professional actor. "Are you gay?" Claire rolls her eyes, because of course I've assumed Tess is gay, like I assume Claire is . . . *something*. But this is the perfect opportunity to find out more about these two, and I'm dying to know what the deal is here.

"No, I'm not gay," Tess says. "I'm queer."

I look at Claire, who keeps her eyes firmly on the glossy marble wall behind me.

"What's that mean?" I ask, because one of us has to.

"Well, to be specific, I'm a homoromantic pansexual," Tess says matter-of-factly.

"So you're attracted to cookware?" I ask.

"Pansexual is when you're attracted to all genders."

"So you're bisexual?" I ask, suddenly far more confused than I thought I would be for this conversation.

"Well, bi means two, but it's similar," Tess says, whatever nervousness she may have been feeling toward me somehow dissipating.

"Wait, how many genders *are* there?" I ask, and then I laugh—I can't help it. This is the weirdest conversation to have at seven a.m. in a hotel lobby, with other guests passing by us on all sides.

"Gender is a spectrum, Forest," Tess says, and I suddenly feel bad for laughing; this is really serious to her. I glance at Claire again, and she is definitely *not* engaging in this conversation. I look around the lobby to make sure there aren't any other fans listening in to our conversation, but the coast is clear.

"So when you say homo..." I prompt.

"Homoromantic. It means that even though I feel sexual attraction toward all genders, I only feel romantic feelings for women."

"Oh, okay."

"Like, I'll have sex with whoever, but I'm really only ever gonna marry a lady. I know, it's complicated. You can understand why I usually just say *queer*." She laughs.

"Yeah. Totally."

"People think sexuality is like a light switch: you're either gay or you're straight. It's not. It's not even a dimmer switch. Sexuality's more like...a Tesla Coil. Bzzzzz." She gestures electricity everywhere. "It's up to you to figure yourself out. I just happened to figure it out early. Claire's still working on it. But I think maybe we made a little progress on that front on our date last night," Tess says, playfully elbowing Claire.

"Stop it," Claire whispers to Tess.

"What?" Tess says.

"Stop trying to impress him," Claire hisses, and I suddenly feel very awkward standing here.

"I wasn't."

"It's fine," I say. "I'm fine. Hey, I think I should get going."

"Yeah, me too," Claire says, reaching for her suitcase.

"You're not going to ride with me?" Tess asks.

Claire hesitates. "I think I'm going to take the bus." She shoulders her backpack.

Tess frowns but plays it cool. "Oh. Okay, that's fine."

"Sorry. I'll catch up with you later."

"Okay. Well, um, text me when you get there."

"Yeah," Claire says. Tess goes for a hug at the same time that Claire turns away and Tess's arms fall to her sides. It's awkward and horrible to watch, and I feel like I should do something, but I barely know these people, and what the hell would I do anyway?

"Let's go, Forest," Claire says.

"Nice to meet you, Tess," I say as I follow Claire out the front doors, and Tess just looks mortified.

Outside, we cross the parking lot toward the idling bus, suitcase rumbling on the pavement.

"You okay?" I ask Claire.

"Yeah."

"Did you know all that? About her, like, sexuality?"

"I don't want to talk about it," she says flatly.

I stop walking. "Why are you doing this?" I ask, because I'm not sure what's going on with her, but I think she's about to sabotage something that seemed pretty good.

She stops, too, and turns to look at me with that fiery expression that I've come to expect from her when she doesn't like what I'm saying.

"*What*, Forest, what is it?"

"I just think you should, you know, chill a bit. I kind of got used to you being mean to me, but I didn't think you'd be like that to her."

"You don't know me," she says, and boards the bus.

She's right, I really don't know her at all.

28

OBVIOUSLY, TESS IS ALLOWED TO BE ANYTHING she wants to be.

Queer homoromantic pansexual? That's fine.

She knows herself really well.

And that's supercool.

It's great that she knows who she wants to have sex with.

Who she wants to freaking *marry*.

I'm really happy for her.

I mean, obviously I knew she was gay, she said so, but I didn't know she, like, had it all figured out so clearly. I didn't realize she'd be so *sure* about everything. Goodie for her.

But then she had to go and tell Forest that we were messing around last night? Or, I guess she *implied* it. But I saw the look on his face; he knew *exactly* what she meant.

Look, we never said last night was a date, and we never said we were gonna tell other people about it. I never would have done any of that if I thought she was just going to go around telling everyone we kissed and making them think stuff about me that I'm not ready for them to think. I thought she understood I didn't want to define anything, and then she just goes and blurts out all that stuff to Forest? *Forest*, of all people, who I was *just* starting to feel like was taking me seriously. Now he probably just thinks I'm some closeted lovestruck teenage girl who just wants to make fictional characters gay because she won't come out herself.

No, I'm not doing this. I'm not here to confront major life questions about my sexuality, I'm here for one reason, to make SmokeHeart canon. And I can't let Tess get in the way of that.

That feeling in my stomach I get when I'm with her? I fold it up small, put it in a box, and throw the box into the sea. Tess isn't what I'm here for.

Where's Jamie?

I sit up in my seat. We're on the charter bus, speeding up I-5, headed for Seattle. Out the windows to our right, there are hills covered in evergreens stretching as far as I can see. To my left is the Columbia River, sparkling in the morning sun.

I glance around the bus. Most of the staff members are dozing in their seats. Toward the back, Rico and Forest are separated. I briefly wonder if everything's okay between them. I don't see Jamie at all.

I *do* see my mother making her way down the aisle.

"So," she says, sliding into the seat next to mine.

"Mom, what are you doing? You'll get sick if you're not at the front."

"I wanted to say hi. You know, talk to my daughter whom I never see."

"You're the one who's never around," I mumble.

She shrugs. "Conventions! Who knew they were so happenin'?"

"Please don't say *happenin'*."

"So, *Tess*..." she starts.

"Mom," I say sharply. I so don't want to talk about this. With her or with anyone.

"She's a...?" She trails off with an expectant look.

"Friend. Stop being weird."

"Okay, I just thought..."

"Well, stop thinking."

"Okay, but you know you can..."

"If I want to talk, I know where you'll be, okay? Please leave it alone." The last thing I need right now is my mom asking me to categorize everything I'm feeling into digestible sound bites. Stop. Go away. Leave me alone. I am a small, unhappy rodent, and I will bite the hand that feeds me. Don't open my cage.

The bus lurches around a corner, and she starts to look a little queasy.

"Okay, good talk," she says.

"Good talk," I say sarcastically, and she heads back to her seat.

Since Jamie is apparently MIA, I maneuver down the aisle and lean on the seatback next to Caty, who's nose-deep in her phone.

"Hey, Caty, do you know where Jamie is?"

She looks up. "Oh yeah, he had Paula rent him a car so he could drive himself to Seattle. Said our bus smells like an old gym bag." She shrugs. "I don't smell anything, though. Must've been his crusty self."

Of freaking course. I sigh. Jamie's been avoiding me

practically since we started this trip, why should I be surprised he's ducking out now?

"Thanks," I mutter, and turn to go.

"Hey, Claire, wait!" Caty says. She pats the seat next to her. "Can we talk a sec?"

"Uh, why?"

"I was just wondering how you were feeling about the panel coming up in Seattle," she says.

I furrow my brow and sit. "What about it?"

"Well, I just know how upset you were after the whole ordeal in Portland, with the moderators Forest set up, and all that." She gives me a sympathetic look. "I saw your posts. A lot of people did."

It's weird that my blog is suddenly public knowledge, but hey, this is what I wanted, right?

"I'm not going to apologize for what I said on my blog."

"Oh god, no. I wouldn't want you to! I think it was great! In fact, I'm wondering... do you have anything planned, in, like, *retaliation*?"

I just stare at her. "What do you mean?"

Caty exhales, then glances around the bus, and lowers her voice. "Look, Claire, I get what you want to do, and I think it's really great, but due respect? I think you're going about it all wrong."

I'm... *what?*

"Look, here's the thing. You came over looking for Jamie just now, right? Because you, what, want to try to convince him to make SmokeHeart canon?" I shift in my seat nervously. Well, *yes*. This chick is reading me like a book. "You gotta stop thinking of this as something you can just sit down and convince him of. Trust me, Jamie Davies is never going to willingly turn any characters gay just because someone asked politely; that's not the way he works. When it comes to Jamie, you gotta make a *scene*. You gotta be so loud and public that he feels like he can't say no, because he definitely wants to say no."

She has a good point, but I have no idea why she's telling me.

"And if I do this, if I make a scene," I say, sorting out my thoughts, "you're not going to send me home early?"

"Girl, you're almost done with us anyway!" she exclaims, then lowers her voice again. "But no, no way. Not if I have anything to say about it." She sighs deeply, like she's been down this road many times. "Not everyone agrees with me about this, but listen, when we flew to Boise, I was convinced that *Demon Heart* was dead in the water. That this whole trip was a dying gasp. But then *you* happened, and suddenly we had a prayer. The chatter online about you is off the charts! I'm sure you've noticed it."

It's true, my mentions have been through the roof since I was chosen for this trip. My follower count is higher than I ever imagined it would get.

Caty wiggles her pink phone at me and smiles slyly. "We had more social mentions for that one panel in Boise than any other moment for any of our shows last year. And then after Forest pulled that shit in Portland and you went on a blogstorm about it, we had more social mentions than we had in Boise."

"And you're happy about that even though most of what people were saying was, you know, bad?" I ask.

"TV's not the same business it was before. There's a thousand channels out there for people to choose from, and a million shows to watch. Literally anything that makes a show stand out from the crowd is a good thing." Caty puts a hand on my shoulder. "People were hearing about *Demon Heart* for the first time because of you, and that's *massive*." Caty nudges my elbow with hers. "You have one shot left to make a splash before the finale. I suggest you start thinking about how you're gonna do it."

My brain is swirling with thoughts. I can't believe she *wants* me to make a scene. What can I do? How can I get Jamie's attention in Seattle? Should I stand up in the middle of the panel and just start yelling? Could I get the other panel attendees involved? Maybe we could start a chant, or a song. Maybe we could all hold up signs at the same time. But no, all of that would just drown him out, make him shut down.

I've seen Jamie when he's confronted, he does the diplomatic thing—starts telling you what you want to hear, starts getting slippery, starts lying. He did it to me in Boise after I won this trip, practically told me SmokeHeart was a great idea, got my hopes up. He was bullshitting me then, but what if I get him to say it again, onstage, in front of witnesses? What if I got him to *commit*?

I stand up, itching to get online and search for ideas. "Hey, Claire, one more thing?" Caty whispers, and I look back. "Like I said, not everyone agrees with this strategy, so, you know, keep it hush-hush."

We exchange conspiratorial nods, then she swipes open her phone and goes back to tap-tap-tapping.

By the time we pass through the industrial outskirts of Tacoma, my plan is taking shape. I open Tumblr on my phone and start to type. Before this, I let myself get distracted by Forest, by Tess. That's all gone now. I have a mission. And it's on.

forest ➔

29

SEATTLE IS AN EVEN BIGGER CONVENTION THAN Portland. I have my hat pulled down low over my eyes and a baggy coat on, so I'm hoping to be able to make it to the booth without being noticed, but the floor just keeps going and going. I wish Rico had come with me, but he said he needed a teriyaki bowl, and no one gets between Rico and his lunch. But maybe it's good that he didn't come along, considering I haven't been able to look him in the eye since reading Claire's story last night without being reminded of, well, of SmokeHeart, kissing dramatically in a messy billiards bar.

I try to push the image out of my mind as I slip through the crowds of people. It's not hard to find what I'm looking for—the convention walls are practically wallpapered with banner advertisements for *Red Zone 4*, out this week, all of them plastered with the Red Zone booth number. Bandit Games must have doled out a fortune for this setup, but it's their hometown, and they're launching a new game, so this is their big moment.

When I make it to the Red Zone booth I find it's more of a Red Zone *zone*, with a dozen game consoles attached to giant screens where people can play the new game, and cardboard cutouts of Jack Tension to take selfies with. Gamers swarm the entire area, lining up to get their first crack at the game. I see a few girls in the mix, including one with rainbow-colored hair who's kicking ass on a console in the corner, but most of the gamers fit the image I had pictured of attendees for these cons: a lot of guys, a lot of beards, a lot of backpacks and cargo shorts.

"Can I help set you up on a game?" a woman asks me. She's wearing a very revealing, sexy version of the Jack Tension costume. She must be working the booth. I wonder what Claire would have to say about Bandit Games using sex to sell their video games. I can already kind of picture her going on a tear about it, which brings a smile to my face.

"Um, no, I'm cool," I tell the woman, careful to look her in the eyes and nowhere else. "I'm gonna just buy a game."

"Over there," she says, pointing, and goes off to help someone else. I pick my way through the overenthusiastic knot of gamers and make my way to the purchase desk. "I'll take one for Xbox," I tell the pale, skinny guy working the counter.

"Just ran out here, but hold on, I'll grab more from the other side," he says, and runs behind the curtain. I lean against the counter and take in the panorama of gaming around me.

I watch a dude make a spectacular kill shot in the new game, and his friend full-body hugs him—just wraps him up and lifts him off the ground in this giant, physical display of hetero brodudery. What would happen if they held on a little too hard, if that final backslap lingered a fraction too long, if their eyes accidentally met, and they didn't look away?

Would they awkwardly laugh it off? Make a *yo, get your hands off me, homo* joke? What if they did it again, later, in private, after a few drinks, with fewer people around to see it, to label it? What if they unlocked a room in their hearts that they had always kept bolted tight? What if they *kissed*?

Jesus, Forest, *what*?

I shake my head. What the hell is wrong with me this morning? When I look back, they've returned to their game. Because *obviously*.

She's in my head. She's got me seeing shit that's not there. Just like *she* does. I should never have read that fanfic; now it's goddamn everywhere. Does she do this? Go around imagining every straight person she sees is gay? Is that any way to live?

I look around for the booth babe, and I spot her across the way, chatting with some gamer guy. Boobs, butt, boobs, sex, I think over and over until the Red Zone guy comes back and slaps down my game. I pay him, and as I turn around to leave, I find myself face-to-face with like six wide-eyed girls clutching one another and giggling nervously.

It never ends.

"Hi, Forest," one of them squeaks out. She has a long chain of ribbons hanging off her convention badge, down to her waist. Three of her friends are either filming or photographing on their phones.

I don't want to deal with this today. "I'm sorry, but I have to get going," I say as I attempt to edge by them. The crush of the convention crowd pushes in around us, and people are looking, wondering who I am. Nothing gives me away as a minor celebrity more than a gaggle of teens taking photos.

"Can we take a selfie?"

"It's my friend's birthday, will you call her? She'd flip out if she knew I met you!"

"Where's Rico?"

A flash blinds me. I flinch. When my vision returns, I see another small group of girls down the aisle shrieking and heading toward me. I need to get out of here.

"Forest, have you heard what Claire is planning?" one of them asks.

But I don't care what Claire is planning. I turn away from them, slide into a current in the crowd, and let it take me away.

Rico's picking through the snacks on the craft table like he's defusing a bomb. We're the only ones in the greenroom, and I'm leaning back in my chair, watching him get just the right ratio of Chex Mix to pita chips to hummus to carrot sticks on his little paper plate.

As I watch him select an apple from the fruit basket, I wonder if he's ever googled himself. If he's ever googled *us*. What would he think? Something tells me he wouldn't be bothered by it, but how could he just pretend it doesn't exist? Knowing there's basically . . . well, it's *porn*, is what it is. About us. On the internet. That lots and lots of people read. That *I've* read.

I didn't know this was part of the job.

He catches me watching him. "Yo, this is real Chex Mix over here, not the knockoff stuff." He holds up his plate. "You want some?"

"I'm good," I say.

He looks at me a moment. "You okay?" I shrug. No, not really. "What's up?" he asks.

The greenroom is empty, I know it is, but I glance around anyway, to double-check. I stand up and join him at the snack table. He looks at me, concerned. Of course he's concerned, I'm acting like a freak. *Relax, Reed.*

"I was just thinking about that scene we shot in the woods at night..." I say.

"You're gonna have to be more specific," he says.

"I think it was episode one-oh-three or one-oh-four. I was freezing my ass off and you told Kelsey to get me another shirt."

"Oh sure, yeah, I remember that. One-oh-four, I think," he says.

"Do you remember what we were shooting that night? I mean, after all the fight stuff, we were doing a few pages of dialogue."

"Yeah. That was a good scene."

"I was just wondering..." He takes a bite of his apple as he waits for me to finish picking my words. "Like, how did you—how did you play that?"

He squints at me. His mouth is full. I wait for him to chew. Was this a terrible idea? Oh my god, this was a terrible idea.

"You know what, forget it," I say, waving him off.

"No, no," Rico says and swallows. "What are you asking me?"

"Nothing, never mind. Is this Ranch flavor?" I grab a handful of Chex Mix.

"Are you asking if I played it gay?" He's so casual, somehow.

"Dude, no," I say, my breath catching in my throat. I wish someone would walk in and interrupt this nightmare conversation. I wish an earthquake would hit, forcing us to take cover and never talk about this again.

But mostly, I wish he'd answer the question.

I stare into the Chex Mix in my hand. And wait.

"You can't play a sexual orientation," Rico says finally.

What the hell does that mean?

He shrugs. "I go out there, and I ... react. That's all."

What the hell does *that* mean?

"Why?" he asks, and I dare to meet his eye. "How were *you* playing it?"

He holds my look for a long moment, then I throw my handful of Chex Mix straight into the trash and walk away.

"I gotta pee," I mutter.

"You think too much, Forest," he calls after me as I duck out of the room.

The bathroom is blissfully quiet.

I take the last urinal on the left and drop my head to my chest. What a trip. I can't wait to get back to LA and have this madness be over. I need some distance—from Claire, from *Demon Heart*, god knows I need distance from Rico.

I hear the door open and two people enter, one of them mid-rant: "I remember when this con was actually about comics instead of teenyboppers in TARDIS dresses. Nowadays, if a regular, everyday comic-book fan wants to see Stan Lee talk, he has to wade through, my god, an *endless* stream of sexy werewolves, sexy angels, sexy vampires, and screaming teenage girls."

I tense up. He didn't specifically mention "sexy demon hunters," but I know I'm a part of this.

He carries on, "I mean, this is a *comics convention*. When did this industry start caring what fourteen-year-old girls like?"

And I can't help it, I feel a rankle rising in my chest. I know there are a lot of different kinds of people here, but a lot of those fourteen-year-old girls are fans of my show, and, well, I don't care if this guy finds them annoying, they have as much right to be here as anyone. I zip up, and I'm getting ready to turn around and say as much when I feel a slap on my back.

"If anyone knows what I'm talking about it's this guy, right, Forest?" the man says, and I turn around to find I'm face-to-face with Jon Reynolds.

Holy *shit*.

"Jon Reynolds!" I say, too loudly.

Reynolds is grinning this perfect toothy smile. He's got a face for Hollywood but the demeanor for politics. His jeans are expensive and his graphic tee projects youth, even as the distinguished gray in the temples of his perfect haircut declares aged wisdom. Tattoo Guy stands two steps behind Reynolds, watching us.

"If anyone's had to deal with the onslaught of teen girl hormones, it's a heartthrob like you," Reynolds says, grasping my shoulder and giving me a friendly shake. Jon Reynolds knows who I am?

"I guess so." I mean, he's not wrong, but I don't know if I would put it in exactly those words.

"Don't give them an inch, Forest, or they'll be the ones dictating your next role. Do you wanna be a *Tiger Beat* boy your whole life, or do you want to *act*?"

"I want to act," I say. Definitely.

"That's what I thought," he says, and I worry that he might be done. This is my chance, I can't let this go, so I start talking, not entirely sure what I'm saying yet.

"Sir, I just want to say . . . I *love* Red Zone. I play the video game every single day. If there's a role in the new film, if I could even just read for it . . ."

"We'll see about that," Reynolds says, waving me off. He must get desperate actors approaching him all the time. I probably look like an idiot. "Let's see how this panel goes first."

My stomach drops. "You're coming to the panel?"

"Guess so. Got a text from Davies. Said I owed him one for getting richer than him. Which I probably do." Reynolds chuckles a bit and shrugs.

Jamie came through! I'm swept up in the feeling of holy-shit-ness—Jon Reynolds is coming to my panel today. My career is moving again, my path laid out in front of me. All I have to do is make a good impression today, and I'm on my way to a role in a blockbuster film.

"I can't wait," I say, like a dolt.

"Now get outta here and let me piss in peace, huh?"

"Of course!" And I'm out of there like a shot.

It's all finally happening.

30

AFTER MOM AND I SHARED ROOM-SERVICE LUNCH, she wanted to check out the convention, but I wanted to stay in my room until the panel, checking replies to my post on Tumblr. After some harassment about getting out and meeting people, she finally left me alone. I should have had the rest of the afternoon to plot, but instead, I'm staring at two texts from Tess, debating what to do.

Can we talk? I'm in the food court.

I have fries.

I'd rather not. I need to focus on my work, and Tess is one giant, curly-haired, dress-wearing, queer homoromantic pansexual distraction.

Is she going to consider this another date? If I go eat fries with her, will she tell Forest we're engaged now? Will she drag me back into her chamber of confusion and questions I don't have the time or power to answer right now?

Is she going to ask me to decide what I am?

I keep thinking about last night. When we were kissing.

I still want to kiss her again.

I don't know why.

So I go.

She's wearing her hair in a scarf. I love it, because it means you can see her whole neck all the way around. I never really thought about necks before, but now, seeing hers, I realize how nice they are. This perfect curve from ear to shoulder. Whoever designed necks should get an award.

The food court is located in the back corner of the convention floor, and it's full of lively con-goers sitting down for hot dogs and Diet Cokes and nachos and other terrible, overpriced food of the kind that you'd find at a high school football concession stand. Tess has saved a table for us, a basket of fries in front of her, sipping on a straw that's sticking out of a can of Sprite. I've never seen anyone drink a can of pop with a straw before.

She sees me coming toward her, and I swear, it's like her whole body lights up. "You came!" she says, and slides the fries toward me as I sit down, as though the fries were the big selling point for me, instead of her. Instead of that expression she just made. She has blue paint specks on her face like she just came from Mom's art studio.

"Hi," I say.

"Hi!"

"Why do you have blue paint on you?"

"Oh!" She wipes at her face with her sleeve, suddenly a little embarrassed. "They're doing this thing where you get to screen-print your own T-shirts, and I had a bit of a disaster with the paint." She shrugs. "It's a cool booth, though. It's over near Artists' Alley. You should check it out."

I nod like I will, but I don't say anything, and then she doesn't say anything. We both eat a few fries. I'm starting to wonder why I came. I need to confront her about what she said.

"Tess..." I say at the same time that she says, "Claire..." and we both stop and then laugh, and then she says, "You go." But I don't want to go first because it's awkward to start off a conversation with an accusation, so I say, "No, you go."

"I keep going over and over that conversation we had with Forest," she says. "And you have to be honest with me, was I being an idiot?" She fiddles nervously with the cat necklace she's wearing. "Because I do that, I get going talking about something I care about and it's hard to stop. But I feel like I kind of... went too far for him." She pauses to meet my eye. "And for you, maybe, too."

I pull the fries closer to me and eat another one. They're getting cold and mealy. I can feel her watching me.

"Forget Forest for a minute, can we just talk about us?" I say.

"Okay."

"You told him..." I start, but I can't figure out how to finish without looking petty, or like a scaredy cat.

"What?"

"Tess, you told Forest that we were dating," I say, finally. And I hate that this bothers me, but it does.

"Did I?" she says, straightening up and frowning. "I said we *went on a date*."

"Yeah."

"But we did!" Tess exclaims, and I wish she'd keep her voice down.

"We had dinner, that's all. You specifically said it wasn't a date when you asked me."

"That was before we made out on your bed for, like, the rest of the night…" Tess says slowly, as though that clears everything up, which it definitely does not. It only makes everything more confusing.

I can't argue with what she's saying, I just know that I'm uncomfortable. And it would be easy to back down and agree with her and say it's not a big deal. But it *is* a big deal.

"I just…wish you hadn't talked about it with him before we agreed what to say."

She lets out a breath. "Okay," she says. "I'm sorry."

I look at her a moment, and she seems to really mean it. So I guess that means I'm supposed to just forgive her and we're back to normal, but I don't feel back to normal. I feel like my world is slowly turning upside down and I'm barely holding on.

"I…really liked hanging out with you last night," she says. "I want to do it again."

She reaches across the table and holds my hand. And I try to be okay with that, I really do, but it feels so weird and so public, and so strong a declaration to the world. It feels like *this is who I am* and I have no idea who I am.

I pull away gently.

"Okay, no PDA, got it," she says, but I feel like I can't stop hurting her feelings.

"It's just that I'm not…like you," I say.

"What, *out*?"

"No…" What are words? I never have them when I'm around her. "You're just so…sure."

She examines me. "What do you mean?"

"About your sexuality, like, *how do you know*?"

"I don't know, it just feels right." She shrugs like this is no big deal, instead of literally *the biggest deal ever*. "Did it feel right to you? Last night?"

I remember kissing her. I remember the feeling I got in my stomach. Wanting more. But what if I was just going along with the moment? What if I just got carried away? It seems ridiculous to base this whole huge part of your identity on something so squishy as a *feeling*.

"I don't know how you can be so confident," I say.

"*I'm* confident?" she asks incredulously.

"Yeah."

"Claire, you're the most confident person I've ever met."

I stare at her. Literally, *what*.

"Look at you!" she continues. "No one I know is as comfortable in their fandom as you. It's like you don't even care if the whole world knows *Demon Heart* is your favorite show and you ship SmokeHeart and you write fanfic and you think about their dicks all the time...."

"I *don't* care. Why would I care?"

"Because it's *embarrassing*! Fanfic is embarrassing! *Demon Heart* is embarrassing! All of it. Everything about this is embarrassing."

My heart is thudding in my chest as I pull away from the table. "You're embarrassed by *Demon Heart*?"

"Well, yeah, Claire. I mean, obviously."

I just stare back because of course I know what she means, but I need to hear her say it. "So you're embarrassed of the show, you're embarrassed by all this." I wave around us.

"Does that mean you're embarrassed by *me*, too?" I already know the answer is yes.

"Claire," she says softly.

"No, be honest, Tess. Are you embarrassed by me?" I get a little louder. There's adrenaline pumping through me, now.

"No! Of course not. I like you."

"But you think the things I like, the things we *both* like, are...what? Too childish? Too uncool? Or is it that liking *anything* is embarrassing? The only cool thing is to keep yourself safely detached and protected by actively disliking literally everything? Is that it?"

Tess gestures emptily, but she doesn't have anything to say. "I don't know what to tell you, Claire. It's not fair, it's just...how I feel."

"But it doesn't have to be that way," I say. "Why should liking *Demon Heart* or fanfic be more embarrassing than liking the Buffalo Bills or Bruce Springsteen or like, *America's Test Kitchen*?" Or Jasper Graves, I think, remembering Forest.

"See? That's what I mean," Tess says. "That's the kind of confidence that you have that I wish I could figure out how to get. If my friends knew I liked this stuff, I would never stop getting shit for it. I have no idea how you keep friends when you talk about this. They must be amazing."

And there it is. That's the difference. Because Tess knows what I wish wasn't true—that sometimes you have to make trade-offs. And maybe there are high schools where proudly loving gay fanfic of a cheesy science fiction show won't get you branded a social outcast, but Pine Bluff High isn't one of them. And apparently neither is Tess's high school. So Tess chooses to lie low in order to maintain some kind of social status, and I've chosen to stand proud, but as a result, my friend group consists of Joanie Engstrom, my parents, and the internet. But at least my life isn't a lie.

"Tess..." I say hesitantly. But you know what? Screw it. This is honesty hour, right? "I don't really have any friends."

She searches my face, and I can't really take it. *Why doesn't Claire have any friends?* she's wondering. *Because she's a weirdo disaster who can't relate to people,* she'll determine. And she'll walk away.

"Any friends at all?" Tess asks.

I shake my head. "There's a girl I sit next to on the bus. And I'm on okay terms with my middle school librarian, but..."

Tess laughs a little, because yeah, it's funny. But she catches herself, because it's also not.

"I used to have friends. I used to not worry all the time. I used to go outside and play with kids. I used to talk to people at the bus stop. But then I moved to a new town in sixth grade, and I didn't do so well making new friends because I was awkward, and liked books too much, and I wasn't pretty or rich, and my parents were liberal, and then before I knew it, the transition period was over and it felt like my window of opportunity had passed and I just...I never made any. And then it was settled. That was it. My new reality." I shrug. "Now, my whole life is basically inside my own mind."

"Well"—Tess gives me the softest, smallest smile—"you have a friend now." She looks a little nervous. "If you'll have me."

I let out a long, slow breath. I mean god*damn*, who can resist something like that?

WHO IS THIS CHICK?

AND WHY DOES SHE LIKE ME?

I lower my voice. "If you think I'm weird, or awkward...I mean, I am those things, but also?" I say it before I can convince myself not to: "You make me nervous because I really want you to like me."

She whispers back, "Me too."

My heart is crashing in my chest from the way she's looking at me. I decide to do a thing that terrifies me, but first I need to make sure of something.

"Don't tell anyone what I'm about to do, okay? Not Forest, not my mom. Anyone."

She nods okay.

I reach across the table and lace my fingers through hers as a smile spreads across her face. Her hands are warm, and she gives me a little squeeze and she can't stop smiling and I can't stop smiling and we both must look like toothy, handholding idiots, but I don't care. Or I'm trying not to, at least.

Tess hadn't heard about the secret project yet, so I told her to check her dash before she went into the panel so she'd know the deal. We made plans to meet up after at the revolving sushi place across the street. I've never been to one, and she said they're ridiculous but fun, and it's the only good place to get dinner in this part of town, unless I wanted to go to the Cheesecake Factory. (I've also never been to a Cheesecake Factory, but she scoffed like that was out of the question, so I suppose they're uncool, although a factory that churns out cheesecake sounds kind of like a fantasy land to me.)

I walk her to the door of the room where the panel is taking place and watch her go in. I think she wants to maybe
kiss me good-bye, but she doesn't try, and I'm grateful for that.
Holding hands is a lot already.

Today, there's no one else in the wings with me. I haven't
seen Caty around, so she must be in the audience somewhere,
taking photos or doing whatever it is she does. The Tumblr
post about our plan is up to 3,000 notes, and word has spread
across Twitter and the Facebook fandom groups, too. I wonder
what Caty thinks of it. Is it enough of a *scene*? Will it work?

Onstage, the moderator kicks off the panel by reminding
everyone that they'll be screening the finale of *Demon Heart*
live tomorrow night at nine p.m. in Teatree Park, followed by
a marathon of the best episodes from season one that will last
well into the night. It sounds amazing. With everything that's
happened I almost forgot that the finale is *tomorrow night*!

It's kind of unreal. Before this trip, I would never have
spaced about the finale; I would have been counting down
the days, then the hours until it aired. But now I have all
these other things to worry about, like whether it will get
good ratings, what the media reaction will be, whether the
show will be picked up for a second season, and whether
my plan will be enough to force Jamie to do SmokeHeart
next year. I almost miss the days when I could just relax and
watch the show. When I could just *be a fan*.

My phone buzzes with a text from Tess: **Wanna watch
the finale together?** I smile to myself and text:
Definitely. Bring a blanket. Her text back comes almost

immediately: **Why, are we going to snuggle under it?** The thought makes my heart skip a beat. I just type her the winking emoji. She writes back with the hearts emoji, and I bite my lip smiling.

As the panel goes on, Rico is charming, Jamie stammers through his answers with as few actual details as possible, and Forest is . . . well, Forest is being *weird*. For instance, when the moderator asks him how he feels about shooting the show so far from his home in LA—a question I've heard him answer two times already—his response today is very different. Usually he says, "North Carolina has leeches, but Los Angeles just has *agents*," a joke that I'm sure is funny to a very specific group of people in California but never quite plays with the convention crowd. This time, he says, "You know, North Carolina is a beautiful and welcoming place, and I love being able to travel for a role. It helps me get into the head of my character." I mean, *whaaaat*. Why is he being professional and diplomatic all of a sudden? Who's he trying to impress?

We'll see how professional he'll be once the Q&A starts.

Finally, the moderator asks his last question: "Forest, you recently joined Twitter. So what's next for you, Snapchat?" A groaner—we all know he hates social media, and he barely even uses the account he's on. There's no way this guy is learning Snapchat. But instead of shrugging it off, Forest says, "If the right reason came along."

What does *that* mean?

The moderator turns to the audience. "At this time, we'd like to take some questions from the audience. Please line up behind the microphones in the aisles."

And here's where I hold my breath.

Normally, there's a mad scramble to the microphones as

fans try to be one of the first in line. Today, there's a lot of murmuring and chair rustling and craning of necks, but no movement except one woman toward the back of the crowd and another toward the middle who stand up. The other fans around them whisper urgently until they sit back down. Both fans look older—possibly *Star Command* fans who aren't on social media.

I can't believe it, but I think it's actually working.

Onstage, Forest is frowning into the audience, confused. He looks at Rico, who shrugs.

Again, the moderator announces, "We'll take questions now, just go ahead and go to the mics." And this time, when he stops talking, there is silence in the hall.

Eerie, perfect silence.

I can feel the smile growing across my face, broad and uncontrollable. This is legitimately incredible. The things we can do when we work together. I've never felt more connected to this community.

There are like twenty phones in the air capturing this moment.

Forest looks completely bewildered and a little frustrated, and I wonder again why he's so uptight today. He looks around for an explanation, and he catches my eye in the wings. I see the moment he realizes that this was an orchestrated event, and he looks at me with pure venom. If he had looked at me like that back in Boise, I would have crumbled, but not today.

Jamie figures out what's going on and shakes his head, like he's just so over this whole bullshit. His microphone is in his lap. All I want is for him to pick it up and start filling the silence with promises. I know he's uncomfortable, I know he's itching to make the silence end.

Meanwhile, one of Paula's assistants, registering a distur-
bance in the force, wanders over. She leans toward me and
whispers, "What's going on?"

"Fans feel silenced. So we're literally being silent."

Her eyes widen. "Did you do this?"

"We all did." I might have started it, but everyone came
together to make it a reality.

"Wow," she says, looking back at the audience. "I've been
to a lot of conventions. I've never seen anything like this
before."

Jamie is shifting uncomfortably. The silence has gone on
too long, the lights are too bright, and he's in the hot seat. He
gives a little scoff. "This is absurd," he says and looks at the
moderator like he's asking permission from his parents to
leave the dinner table. But still his mic remains in his lap.

C'mon, Jamie. C'mon. Start *talking.*

The moderator seems to suddenly remember he's ostensibly supposed to be steering this ship, and says, "I suppose if
there are no questions, I'll ask another. Were there any fun
on-set pranks you remember—"

Before he even finishes the question, someone from
the audience boos. The moderator looks up, confused and
insulted. I guess this kind of stuff doesn't happen in *Justice
League* panels or whatever he's used to.

Someone else in the audience hollers, "You know what
we want to know!"

The moderator lowers his microphone into his lap and
looks at his panelists. "What are they talking about?" he asks
them, off mic.

Rico butts in, "You know, there was one funny moment—"

"Rico," Forest interrupts him. Rico stops talking. It was a

valiant effort to save this, but the audience is roiling, now. There's an energy under the surface, everyone's adrenaline pumping. I feel like anything could happen.

C'mon, Jamie. Now. *Now.*

Jamie reaches for his mic. Finally.

But he's interrupted—

"Yeah, I know what you want to hear," Forest spits into his mic. He's pissed and I don't know why. I thought he was starting to come around after our talk.

"You want to 'ship' our characters? You want to pretend Smokey and Heart are grinding against a pool table in a road-house after every episode?"

My stomach lurches. Wait, how does he know about the pool table? Was that a coincidence or . . .

Forest continues, "Go nuts. Seriously. I'm not gonna stop you." He looks at the audience pointedly, waiting for them to quiet down. Waiting for their full attention. When he speaks again, it's slowly and clearly. "But don't ask me to pretend it's real. Because it's not. And it never will be."

He looks at me. As though I didn't know who that message was for.

Asshole.

Jamie keeps his mouth closed. His microphone doesn't leave his lap.

Forest just ruined everything.

As I turn and walk away, the audience roars at Forest, biting mad. Chairs scrape, the silence broken. A rush to the mics. But I don't look back. I can't watch this anymore.

forest → 31

I'M HELPLESS AS I WATCH JON REYNOLDS DUCK
out a back door, shaking his head in dismay. There goes *Red
Zone*. There goes my career. There goes Forest Reed, up-and-
coming star. My Wikipedia entry ends here.

If Claire were really a fan of mine, would she sabotage
my career like this? No. Because despite what I thought, she
doesn't care about me. All she cares about is her goddamned
ship. It has nothing to do with me, or Rico, or anything else.
She just wants these two fictional characters to be gay for
each other, and she doesn't care who gets hurt along the way.

Well, fuck Claire Strupke and fuck these "fans."

I PUSH DOWN THE CORRIDOR, OUT THE DOORS, into the bright Seattle sunshine and across the street, fighting through crowds of hungry con-goers, until I find myself inside the sushi restaurant.

I need to find Tess.

She's not here yet, so I sit at a booth and jiggle my leg with anticipation until she arrives. This place is strange, with a conveyor belt running through the entire restaurant, sending plates of fish around like a lazy river. When Tess finally walks in, I wave her over. I still have so much adrenaline from everything that's just happened that I accidentally kick the table as I stand up, causing our waters to splash.

Tess wraps me in a big hug before sitting down. "Oh my god, that was wild. Did you feel the energy in the room? I had goose bumps!"

"Yeah, but it wasn't enough."

"It was like we were all *one*, you know? Like we were a

team...or in a movie. I mean, that was *huge*!" I haven't seen her like this before, all flushed and wild-eyed. I wish I could share her excitement.

"I have to keep going. Forest's obviously a no-go, but I can still get to Jamie. I can make this happen. He just saw how many people want this. He's got to be ready now." I pound my fist on the table and the waters splash again.

Tess frowns, starting to register my anger, finally. "You can't still be trying to—"

"After that BS out there? How can I *not*?"

"Claire, it's *over*. You heard Forest. It's never gonna happen." The sushi plates stream past and neither one of us even glances at them.

"Forest doesn't matter. Jamie does. I can make him see."

"Claire, *stop*. Just stop," she says. "You have your fanfic, that's enough. I mean, god, poor Forest. He's clearly uncomfortable with it."

"Poor Forest?" I can't believe what I'm hearing. "You're taking *pity* on that homophobic asshole? I don't understand how you're so willing to just give up on this," I say.

"Maybe because I'm used to it," she cuts back. "Maybe it's because I grew up only seeing white people on my television, and it's not like a showrunner can decide one day that a character's *not white anymore*, so I got used to the world being unfair, okay? I stopped caring what the showrunner thinks because a character can be anything in fic. They can be black or queer or fat or whatever the fuck I want, and I don't need anyone's permission. So just ship what you want to ship and stop caring so much about what Jamie and Forest think!"

"But they're wrong," I kind of yell. "And someone has to tell them that. Why don't you see that? The world would be a better place if there were more queer characters, more black characters, more of everything that's not the same old same old."

"But you're not pushing for more black characters, are you? You only care about one thing."

"That's not true."

"Of course it is! You know how many black characters have been on *Demon Heart*? Like two, and they were both demons. Now they're dead. You've never mentioned it. You only care about the thing that affects *you*."

"I *do* care about that. But look, we can still make SmokeHeart queer, but we can't turn them black. That's not how it works." She shakes her head, but I carry on. I know I can convince her. "Let's focus on the things we can change. Just imagine if there weren't so much *hand-wringing* every time people are confronted with the idea that a character they thought was straight actually wasn't. I mean, I thought of all people *you* would understand that!"

I stare at her, and she stares back, and the sushi rolls by.

When she speaks, it's low and steady and cutting. "How can you be so sure that Smokey and Heart are gay when you won't even acknowledge that you are?"

"What?" I can't believe she would drag that into this, when the two things have nothing to do with each other. My blood is pounding in my ears, and my hands are gripping the top of the table. I'm searching for a way to put my thoughts into words when—

Someone screams.

"Eeeeeeeeeee!" It's a high-pitched scream. "Where have you *been*? Oh my *god*, it's been *forever!*" I look over, and there is a murder of teenage girls in tank tops and shoes with heels and dangly earrings and different-colored eye shadow, and they're all headed directly for us. The screamer, the leader, has her arms out and is descending on Tess.

"Oh, heyyyyy!" Tess says, clearly caught off guard. She shoots me a nervous look as she stands up and starts hugging all of them one by one. "Hey, guys, what are you doing here?"

"We're just getting sushi! I thought you were visiting your grandma in Phoenix! Who's *this*?" the leader asks, looking me up and down with a huge gleaming smile. Evaluating me.

"Claire, I want you to meet my friends! Harper," she says, pointing at the leader, then working her way down the line, "Jillian, Augusta, Soraya. Everybody, this is Claire. She's visiting from out of town." Why do I feel like Tess's voice just went up an octave? She motions at me to stand up, so I do, but my hands are just hopelessly by my side, because these look like the kind of girls who air kiss and I'm not going to air kiss any of them.

Tess's friends don't look at all like I thought they would. For one, they're all white. And it's not that I thought Tess could only have black friends or anything, but she's from a big city. I kind of pictured a network-TV-supporting-characters rainbow-of-diversity thing. But they're all of a type—weirdly pretty and too put-together to possibly have anything in common with me. These are not Tumblr people, they are Instagram people. Andrea Garcia people. *Popular.*

Why did I not see it before? This is why Tess doesn't understand me. This is why she can't be honest with her friends. She's one of *them.*

They huddle around us like we're all in a secret clique. One of them smells like perfume. Maybe all of them. Who even wears perfume?

"We're just here to get our spicy tuna on," Harper says, "but, like, did you notice there's some kind of, what, *Comic-Con* happening right now?" She gestures around the restaurant, which is packed with con-goers and cosplayers and all kinds of nerds. "Like, *hello*, I'm trying to walk here, and everyone's getting up in our way with their fake swords and crap!"

The other friends look around at the room like they can't even believe their favorite sushi spot has been invaded. I frown at Tess. Her friends have no idea that we're here for the convention, too. Tess subtly shakes her head at me: *Don't say anything.* I roll my eyes.

"You girls want to sit with us? We were just about to start eating," Tess says.

"Sure!" either Jillian or Augusta says, I'm not sure which one, and they slide into our booth. I really, *really* don't want to do this, but Tess shoots me a look full of daggers, so I squeeze in next to Soraya.

"Oh my god, I totally thought that was that Benedict Cumber guy, but it's a *girl*," Harper says, pointing to a pretty good Sherlock cosplayer in the corner.

"Ew, really?" Soraya laughs. They all crane their heads to look. I glare at Tess—I literally can't believe she's not saying anything to these people, but she ignores me.

"It's called cosplay," I say matter-of-factly. "Hers is pretty good, if you ask me."

They all gape at me. I can almost hear them saying to themselves, *Who are you again?* Tess clearly wants out of this conversation.

"It must have taken her a long time to put together a costume that good, don't you think?" I ask, intently forging on.

"Uh, I guess so," says Jillian/Augusta.

Harper turns her gaze to me. "So, Claire, how do you and Tess know each other?"

"Claire's from Idaho, she's just in town to visit me!" Tess says, wayyy too perky.

"Oh yeah? That's a long way to come," Harper says. Augusta and Jillian start grabbing sushi plates off the conveyor belt and setting them down in front of people. I don't feel like eating a single thing right now. Harper keeps her eyes on me. She can tell I'm not like them.

"And you came to town because..." Harper prods.

Tess is practically begging me with her eyes not to tell them the truth, but it's so dumb because her friends are clearly terrible. What's the point of having friends if you're just going to lie to them to pretend you're as cool as they are? "I'm here to go to the convention, actually," I say, watching Tess. "I love the show *Demon Heart.*"

All the girls glance from me to Harper to see how she'll react.

"What's *Demon Heart*?" Harper asks, all pretty and perky and cute. Tess is full-on glaring at me.

"It's my favorite show," I gush. I'm laying it on pretty thick. Tess can lie to her friends if she wants, but I refuse to. "It's about this guy who hunts demons, and he's secretly in love with this other guy, who *is* a demon, but he has a heart, so he's a good guy. And every week they kill mystical beasts and send them back to hell, and oh my god, you have to watch it, it's amazing." Tess is going to kill me, but I don't care. She should've done this a long time ago. "Well, actually, I said they're in love, but they're not actually gay on the show. That's why I have to write fanfiction where they declare their feelings for each other and finally kiss and have sex and stuff."

Harper's eyes are wide, loving every minute of this. "Wow, Tess, did you know about all this?" she asks. I can tell she's cracking up on the inside. I've seen that look from kids in my high school. They pretend to be interested in what you're saying so that later on they can laugh and laugh. Right now Harper is feeling *so* superior. My lip curls at the way she's judging me, and at how she would judge Tess if she knew the truth about her. No one should have to feel ashamed of loving a TV show, or reading fanfiction, and I hate that they make her feel this way. She deserves better friends than this.

I know I'm sitting on a social hand grenade and all I have to do is pull the pin and let it fly.

"Of course Tess knows about it," I say. "She's obsessed, too. It's how we met!"

The grenade explodes. All the girls lower their chopsticks and stare at Tess. Harper's eyes light up like this is the most delightful piece of information she's heard in a long time.

I did the right thing, I know I did. But my stomach cannot stop turning over at the way Tess is staring, openmouthed, at me. Hurt and betrayed. I've never made anyone look at me like that before. But she should feel so free right now. She doesn't have to lie anymore!

"It's not like that," Tess says to her friends.

"What's it like, then?" Harper asks innocently.

"Claire, can I speak to you outside, please?" Tess says, standing up. All the girls watch her go. I flash them a fake smile and follow Tess outside, ready for whatever's coming.

"What is your freaking *issue*?" Tess is practically yelling at me on the sidewalk outside the restaurant. People stream past us, some of them turn to stare.

I walk down the block, away from the windows of the sushi place. I don't want her friends staring at us if we're going to do this. "You should have told them a long time ago, Tess. You know that."

"It was *my* decision to make. Mine."

"Oh yeah? Like how it was my decision to tell Forest Reed what happened between us? You went ahead and took that decision away from me."

"I already apologized for that, Claire, what do you want from me?"

"I don't want you to be embarrassed of me. Of this!" I point at the convention center, towering above us just across the street. "I want you to be proud of the things you like."

"It's not that simple. They don't understand this stuff."

"What's to not understand? You're obsessed with a TV show. You draw sexy fanart of it. You read fanfic. It's not that big a deal."

"You don't know anything about my life, okay? Look at my friends, I'm already different from them. I'm black, I'm queer, I don't have a damn thigh gap. You think it's easy going through high school like that? I can't just throw 'draws sexy fanart' into the mix and expect everything to stay the same."

"If they're really your friends, they won't care," I say.

"What would you know about friends?" she shoots back.

I take a step back.

Wow.

"I didn't mean it like that," she says in a kinder tone, "but it's true, there's nothing stopping you from being the crazy, beautiful weirdo you are inside. Which is why you should just *come out*, Claire!"

"Tess, stop it." She's being too loud, people are going to hear her. I take another step back, but she doesn't stop.

"Just do it! You're clearly queer, so just own it."

"Tess!"

"Say the words. Gay, gay, gay, bi, pan, lesbian, homo-sex-u-al."

"I said *stop it*!"

"Claire?" a voice says nearby, and my chest seizes up. Because it's Mom.

I spin around, and see she's walking toward us, frowning, clearly able to tell something is wrong. Did she just hear that? How could she have not?

"Mom, we gotta go." I intercept her and grab her arm.

"Hi, Tess," Mom says before I start pulling her away.

"Hi, Trudi," Tess says, then, with a dark look at me, she pulls the pin on her own grenade and lobs it at me. "Your daughter's gay."

We are quiet on the way back to the hotel. I don't know what my mom is thinking. Is she giving me space to express myself? Or is she quietly swirling?

As we enter through the revolving door of our hotel and cross the lobby, I'm still shaking with anger at Tess. I can't believe she would say that to my mom. Maybe I was wrong about her. Maybe she's just as mean-girl bitchy as those trolls she calls her friends. Maybe I never really knew her at all. She said she wanted to be my friend? Well, forget that. Forget her. If this is what having friends is like, I'm better off without.

And then there's that thing she said about me not caring about anyone but myself. Is that why I'm so hung up on queer representation? Of course I care about seeing more black characters, too. Don't I? But why haven't I been pushing for that as much? Or at all? How many things can I advocate for at one time? My ears burn as I realize I could have done more and I haven't. Even if we do make SmokeHeart go canon, there's still no one on the show who looks like Tess.

Mom and I step onto the elevator and the doors close. The silence is heavy. Mom quietly clears her throat.

"What?" I say sharply because I can't take the quiet anymore, and I want her to get it off her chest.

"Nothing," Mom says. "What?"

"Nothing!" I'm mad now. She's playing games. The elevator dings and we step onto our floor. She swipes her card in our door and we walk in. I can't handle the silence anymore.

"Tess and I had a fight," I say, flopping back onto my bed and pulling my pillow over my face.

"I'm sorry to hear that," Mom says. I feel the bed move as she sits down on the edge of it.

"I don't want to talk about it," I say, my words muffled.

"Okay."

I move the pillow a bit so I can breathe, but my eyes are still covered. "And I don't want to talk about what she said."

"Okay."

Mom gives it a long moment before she says. "Are you hungry?"

"I'm starving," I say miserably.

"Room service?"

"Room service."

I get the chicken piccata and Mom gets the crab cakes, and we watch HGTV home renovation shows all night and she doesn't try to make me talk to her, even when I crawl over and lie next to her in her bed instead of my own.

"A DOLLAR THIRTY-FOUR IS YOUR CHANGE." THE girl behind the counter hands me the money, then turns around to make my Peanut Buster Parfait. She doesn't appear to recognize me, even though she seems like the right demo. Maybe she's more of a *Time Swipers* type.

I haven't had DQ in, god, I don't even know how long. Probably since around the time I moved to LA. Dairy Queens are few and far between there for some reason, and besides, as my agent likes to tell me, "Your body is your résumé," and these abs don't make themselves. But honestly, I deserve this parfait. Jon Reynolds is never going to hire me after that disastertown of a panel yesterday. Not to mention the *Demon Heart* finale airs tonight, and unless our numbers are magically higher than they were all year, there's no way we get a second season. And then that's it. My career is over as soon as it began.

I imagine having to pack up my LA apartment, not that there's much to pack up. I picture moving back to Oklahoma, all the kids I went to high school with crowing about how hotshot TV Boy came on home. I imagine my dad telling me over dinner, "We all knew it was a long shot. What'd you think, you were Steve McQueen, son? You ain't nothing but prairie trash like the rest of 'em," then heading out to the porch for a smoke.

As the girl comes back with my ice cream, I hear the door jingle. I look over to see three teenagers come in. I glance away immediately, but it's too late. They've seen me. And they recognize me.

They start whispering and giggling right away. I take my ice cream and start for the door, doing my best to ignore them, but as I pass, I hear one of them whisper, "He really *does* like Dairy Queen."

And another responds, "Do you think he likes Jasper Graves, too?"

Something shifts in my stomach. I stop walking. I turn and look at them. The trio of trembling girls stare back at me, wide-eyed and frozen.

"What did you say?"

They giggle nervously and huddle close to each other for safety, too starstruck to even speak.

I try again, harder. "Why did you just mention Jasper Graves?"

They look at each other, unsure.

My ice cream is sending rivulets of condensation down my hand and I suddenly feel ridiculous, standing in a Dairy Queen, holding a parfait, yelling at teenagers. What has my life become?

"It . . . it's nothing. It's just from a fic," one of them finally gets out.

Of course it is. "Heart-of-lightness?" I confirm, and she nods.

I'm gonna kill Claire.

"I'M GLAD YOU GOT IN TOUCH," CATY SAYS AS WE sit down for lunch in the hotel restaurant. After my fight with Tess yesterday, I'm not sure I have any allies left besides her, and I want to brainstorm with her about how she thought yesterday's panel went, and whether there's anything else to do today. I didn't have her phone number to text her, so I contacted her the only way I knew how—I posted on Tumblr asking her to meet me. And she showed up.

"Order anything you want," she says. "I've got a company card."

"Sweet." When our waitress arrives, I don't hesitate. "Can I please have a BLT and an iced tea and a side of mac and cheese?"

"You are very good at ordering," Caty says, then tells the waitress, "Same for me, but sub pinot grigio for the iced tea, please."

All around us, convention attendees mix with business-suit

types in a weird swirl of conflicting fashion choices and hair-styles. But no one quite looks like Caty today, in a pink furry vest over a dark button-up shirt that's covered in large pink flamingos, open so that her black lacy bra just peeks out the gap, and a wide-brimmed black hat. She makes me wonder if I should try to expand my wardrobe from just fandom tees, hoodies, and jeans.

"So talk to me. How are you feeling?" Caty says.

"Like crap." I fiddle with the sugar packets. "The panel yesterday...I was hoping for a different reaction, I guess."

"Well, I don't know what you had in mind, but from a social media perspective it was a bonanza," Caty says.

"Really?" The waitress delivers our drinks, and I start emptying sugar packets into my iced tea.

"Totally. Huge shock wave across Twitter and Facebook, and practically a sonic boom on Tumblr. You saw the media, right? BuzzFeed picked it up, and a bunch of other sites did, too. It's all over the place. The video is so awkward, it's hard to watch, but you kind of can't look away."

"So what's it mean?" I ask. "What are they saying?"

"They're saying they've never seen a fandom unite this way. Usually there's infighting, self-policing, ship wars..."

"*Demon Heart* doesn't really have any other ships," I say. "All the women get killed off. It's SmokeHeart or no ship at all."

Caty shrugs. "And then of course there are the people who think fans are too entitled and they should just accept what they're given and if you don't like it, watch something else."

I roll my eyes, I've heard that argument before. "No one would say that if we weren't young and women. It's like, when my dad calls in to sports radio to criticize some football coach for making a bad call, no one tells him he's being too entitled and if he doesn't like it, he should just go watch another team. His feelings are, like, *automatically* considered valid. So why aren't mine?"

Caty laughs. "You're good at this. Everyone on our team is feeling very optimistic for the ratings tonight, and that's basically because of you."

I scoff and take a sip of tea.

"I'm serious! You're like this *black hat* publicist. If you ever want to go legit, let me know. I would be more than happy to get you an internship somewhere. I just want to make sure I stay on your good side." She chuckles.

I always thought that after high school I'd go to college in the Northwest somewhere, maybe try to write books or something. The thought of moving to LA? Working in the entertainment industry? Trying to change things from within?

"I'll think about it," I say.

"So." She claps her hands together. "What did you want to talk about?"

The food comes and I talk between bites. I tell her how I was hoping the panel yesterday would pan out, how I only have one day left before I go home, how this is my last chance to convince Jamie. I have to figure out how to make SmokeHeart a reality—it's my last shot.

"It sounds like you have to sit down with Jamie—make your case," Caty says.

"You said before that that wouldn't work!"

"I said cornering him on the bus wouldn't work, but if you really lay it out for him? Explain everything?" She shrugs. "You never know. You're pretty convincing."

"Yeah, well, even if I wanted to, I don't know how to get

him to meet with me. He avoids me at every turn. I don't
know what to do, short of kidnapping him and holding him
hostage."

Caty's eyes light up.

I laugh. "What, you think I should kidnap him?"

"No, of course not, but—" she says slowly, like she's thinking this through as she speaks. "You could kidnap something
of his until he agrees to speak to you."

"What do you mean, like his shoes? His toothbrush?" I
snort. "He's, like, rich. Whatever I take, he'll just buy another
one rather than talk to me."

"It doesn't have to be a physical item," Caty says, her eyes
gleaming. And I start to get a little scared, and a little excited,
because for the first time I might have met someone more
devious than me, and she's willing to help.

Caty outlines her idea, and I have to admit, it's pretty
extreme, but it would definitely get his attention.

"Why are you helping me?" I ask, taking a bite of my mac
and cheese.

Caty smiles crookedly. "Bunch of reasons, I guess. Because
you're right, that Smokey and Heart is, like, the natural direction for the show to go in, and those two studs would look
hot as hell together. Also Jamie's an asshole, and I want to see
you take him down a few pegs." She shrugs. "But also? I like
you and I want you to be happy."

I poke at the last bites of food on my plate. "Are we friends,
Caty?"

Caty pulls her napkin out from under her wineglass, writes
something on it, and slides it over to me.

"What's this?"

"That's my personal Tumblr. Not only are we friends, now

we're also mutuals. Don't show that to anyone or I'll take back my internship offer," she says.

I run my thumb over the napkin's rough surface, then fold it carefully and put it in my pocket, marveling at how many people have called me their friend on this trip.

Caty starts signing the check. "Speaking of friends, I've been meaning to ask, where's that other fangirl you've been hanging around with?"

Oh. Tess. Well. "You know about her?" I didn't realize anyone was keeping track of me like that.

"Sure! News travels fast at a con. You know, everyone is rooting for you guys."

The news brings unexpected tears to my eyes as the pain of our fight yesterday floods back.

"Oh man, I'm sorry. Did something happen?" Caty puts her hands out, but doesn't touch me, not sure what to do.

And maybe it's because I'm tired, *so tired*, or because I can't talk about it with my mom, or just because she's been so nice to me, but something makes me trust Caty.

"Can I ask you a question?" I say.

"Yeah, of course."

"I'm just wondering if you're at all, in any way…" I run my hand over my mouth and let out a big breath. Caty waits for me to finish. "I'm wondering if you're gay."

Her face flashes a look of heartbreak as she realizes what I'm asking, which eventually turns into a smile.

"What gave it away?" she asks, looking down at her wild outfit, running her fingers over her furry pink vest. "Is it the clothes? The give-no-fucks attitude? The so-sexy-she-can't-possibly-be-straight hotness?"

"I just hoped…"

She nods. "Yeah, I am. Bisexual."

I let out a breath, a weird relief falling over me. "When did you know? Like, *for sure* for sure know?"

"I mean, god," she says, "I'm twenty-four now, and I still sometimes second-guess it. I think knowing is overrated." She sweeps her curls out of her eyes and looks off. "It's okay not to know. Just because I like both boys and girls doesn't mean I'm attracted to literally everyone in the world. I still get to decide who I like and who I don't. It doesn't define me."

I get all that, it makes sense. But it also doesn't really help me with my current situation. I slouch down and let my head tip back against the chair and talk to the ceiling. "It's just... Tess. She's pressuring me to, you know, like, *come out*."

Caty takes a moment to sip her wine before she replies.

"There's no time limit," she says finally. "Take as long as you want. Sometimes it helps people to have a name for what they feel. But if it helps you to leave it open, and not decide on a label... that's fine, too. And if Tess is forcing you to do anything you don't want to do... there are other girls. Or boys. Or whoever."

I nod, but I feel a pang of sadness at the very idea of leaving Tess behind. Even though we fought, I still like having her around. I wish she were helping me today, with Jamie. I wish she were here right now, to hear this.

Caty stands up. "Whatever happens with Jamie, keep in touch, okay? Now, give me a hug," she says, stretching her arms wide, not caring at all that there are other people in the restaurant staring at her, at us. I shimmy out of my seat and slide into her arms, pressing my face into the soft fuzz of her vest. "You're gonna be okay, Claire Strupke," she whispers into my hair.

I'm not convinced that's true.

But I'll take it.

My mom texts me as I'm trying room handles on the third floor, looking for one that opens. The convention is only on the first two floors, so I was hoping to find a quiet private space up here, preferably with AV capabilities, where I can confront Jamie.

I try another door—locked—before I swipe open my phone to read her text: **Hi honey Bun I wnt 2 show u what I've been doing Rm203love Mom.**

I sigh. No matter how many times I try to show her how to use punctuation, she refuses. Her texts are a mess. I check the time, and I still have a couple hours before the finale tonight, so I decide I can take a detour to the second floor. I *have* been wondering what the hell Mom's been up to this whole time.

Down on floor two, there are more people around, but room 203 is sort of isolated. As I approach, I hear voices, followed by laughter. Peeking around the door, I see like ten nerds around a table full of crafting supplies. PVC pipe, foam, X-Acto knives, tape, scissors. Plus, every surface is covered with little bits of foam, including the floor. It's a mess.

"Claire!" My mom barrels toward me, crumbs of foam sticking to her with static electricity. The nerds look up from their craft projects to watch with big smiles as Mom wraps me up in a giant hug.

"Mom," I squeeze out as she lets me go, "what are you *doing*?"

"We're making weapons!" she shrieks in delight. "Go on,

show her." The others hold up their projects: a few broad-swords, a mace, a couple shields, and a pair of nunchucks. Mom gleams with pride. "We're larkers," she announces.

I stare. "You mean...LARPers?"

"Yeah, you know, when you go out into the woods and have pretend fights."

"I know what LARPing is." I just would have never guessed that *she* did.

"I want to start a group in Pine Bluff. Do you think your father will join?"

"Mom...*this* is what you've been doing this whole time?"

"Yeah! I've found a way to help out here! I met Winston in Portland." A guy in a Utilikilt at the end of the table waves at me. "He was leading this workshop in weapon construction, and I had a few ideas for him about structural integrity...."

"Your mother is very knowledgeable about this stuff," Winston says with a British accent. This is all so weird.

"And I just started sharing my ideas! You know, finally putting that MFA in sculpture and creative design to work!"

"Great," I say. I'm covered in foam from hugging her, and I start to pick the pieces off. "I'm really happy for you. This is not weird at all."

"What are you up to?" she asks.

"Well, I need a room for something, and it has to be private. Something like this one," I say, flicking a foam piece onto the floor with the others, "but not a mess."

"What do you need a room for?" Winston asks.

Do I tell them? Do I tell *Mom*? I think about how Tess says I'm the most confident person she knows. I'm really not, like really *really* not. But about this? About SmokeHeart? I'll stop at nothing.

"I need to find a room to use to lure the showrunner of my favorite TV show in order to convince him to make his characters gay," I say. "And I need AV, too."

There's a beat of silence before my mom says, "If it's important to you, I'm in."

A weight lifts. Winston waggles a key card in the air. "Will this help, love? Should open just about any conference room in this wing."

I grin. "Um...yeah."

Winston, Mom, and I pop upstairs to the third floor to try his key card in various conference room doors and assess the rooms. As we search for a room, I tell them everything. I tell them about the plan and the video and Jamie, leaving out the parts about Tess. Winston doesn't know what shipping is, but once I tell him, he gets on board pretty quickly, and once I'm done explaining, he's actually excited for me.

My mom gives me a hug and says she's so proud of me and hopes that my plan works, but even if it doesn't, the most important thing is I tried.

"Good luck," she says, just as Winston shouts from down the hall that he's found the perfect room, and it has a projector and everything.

And on top of that, Ballroom 6E is pretty darn big. Holy moly, I'm about to make a splash.

forest → **35**

IT ONLY TAKES A SINGLE GOOGLE SEARCH FOR "heart of lightness Dairy Queen" to find the fic the girls back in the DQ were giggling about. First hit, a fanfiction called "Sugar and Cream" written two days ago. That means it was written after Claire met me.

I steel myself for whatever it is.

And I click on it.

36

FOREST'S FEET ACHED AFTER ANOTHER LONG
night of shooting outside in the woods—always night shoots
in the woods on this damn show.

WAIT—

Fuck. She's writing about me, now?

Not Smokey. *Me.*

She can *do* that?

I hate everything about this. I hate what I think she might say, I hate that she's thinking about me like that at all, but most of all, I hate that somehow she's dragged Jasper Graves into it. This is way, *way* over the line.

But I have to read it to know just how over the line it is. So I set my jaw and start reading.

38

FOREST WALKED THE SHORT DISTANCE BACK TO his trailer, dreaming of the moment he'd get to kick off Smokey's ridiculous boots and tight-ass jeans and slide into a pair of sweats and sleep all day until tomorrow's late afternoon call.

As his trailer came into view, he yawned, but he wasn't too exhausted to gaze at the pink blot of sky on the horizon. Sure, North Carolina was remote and full of rednecks, but it also had some of the most marvelous sunrises Forest had ever seen.

"Mr. Reed!" It always bothered Forest that the PAs here called him that, but North Carolina was in the South and no matter how many times he told them to call him Forest, their upbringing just wouldn't allow it.

Forest looked over to see his favorite PA running (they were always running) toward him. Lynn was endlessly friendly, whether it was midday or four a.m., and never batted an eye, even when the 1st AD—a grumpy old dude in an ancient Yankees hat with no patience—snapped at her for something that was barely her fault.

"Your Dairy Queen," Lynn said in her folksy North Carolina accent. She reached him, out of breath, and held up a paper bag.

"Oh, I didn't order—"

"I did." Forest turned to see Rico walking up to them. Rico took the bag from Lynn, who nodded at him and scampered away toward her next task. "Happy birthday, bud," Rico said, slapping Forest's back lightly.

He remembered. In fact, Rico was the only one who had.

"What are you now, sixteen, seventeen?" Rico added with a chortle. Forest winced. The eleven-year age gap between them seemed endlessly funny to Rico, but to Forest it just reminded him how inexperienced he was, comparatively.

"I'm twenty-four," Forest said, with a little grit in his voice that made Rico shape up.

"I know," Rico said. "Look, I figured you wouldn't want to make a big deal out of it, so I told the producers no cake, no singing, no full-crew shenanigans. Just you and me and two Peanut Buster Parfaits."

And something about the way he said "you and me" made Forest's heart twang.

Me and him.

A team.

"Now, you gonna invite me in before these melt?" Rico asked with a friendly jab at Forest's upper arm. He could feel the phantom touch linger after Rico pulled away. The shadow of contact.

Forest shrugged casually. "All right, come in."

Rico and Forest had been close since the first day of the pilot, before they even knew if they had a series. They had been partners: Rico, joking around, chatting with everyone, playing tricks on the camera crew, and Forest, laughing at his pranks, delighted to be on the inside, letting someone show off for him. It felt good to have someone he could trust. A scene partner, a teammate, a friend.

But outside of work, they didn't spend time together. Rico liked to go out with the crew and cast on his nights off—big group dinners or bar-hopping excursions or karaoke parties. Forest had gone a couple times, but always ended up begging off early; the loud bars and laughing groups were too much for him. He had always hoped Rico knew it wasn't personal.

Once, late on a Saturday night, alone in his apartment, he had started a text to Rico, telling him what his friendship meant to Forest. Halfway through typing, he had seen ellipses pop up on Rico's end. . . . Rico was typing to *him.* Forest had stopped typing and waited. And waited. He fell asleep on the couch, his phone on his chest, still waiting. The next morning he checked his phone: no text. He deleted what he had written, never asked Rico about it. Forest assumed it had been a mistake.

But he wondered. Did Rico feel the same pang when a day went by without a scene between them? Did he think of Forest when he went home at night? Were his incessant jokes a smokescreen for his feelings? Or was it possible that Rico was just as friendly and flirty with everyone as he was with Forest? Forest had no measure of what was in Rico's head, and it killed him, the not knowing. It was impossible to tell if Rico liked him in particular or if he just liked people.

So tonight, with Rico waiting to be invited into his trailer after hours, the sunset glinting pink off his skin like cosmic rouge, felt special. Rico wanted him alone—there was no misreading that, was there? It was a private party, just for them. It felt like progress.

Which is why, when Forest opened the door to his trailer and stepped inside, saw what Rico had done, it hit him extra hard. This wasn't a play to get Forest alone, this was simply a cruel, personal practical joke.

Every inch of the inside of Forest's trailer was wallpapered in full-color pictures of Jasper Graves.

forest ➡ **39**

I SHOVE THE LAPTOP AWAY IN DISGUST. THE FAN-fiction was one thing, but this is completely over the line. I told her one time—*one time*—that I thought Jasper Graves was handsome, and now I get *this* crap? Am I supposed to never tell her anything personal again in case it ends up online in one of her stories as some sort of "evidence" of my gayness? I feel the anger curl into a knot in my stomach. I can't keep reading this, but I need to know how it ends. I need to know what else she put in there.

40

THE PLAN IS IN MOTION. NOW ALL I HAVE TO DO IS
wait. I pick a chair in the enormous empty ballroom and pull
it into the aisle so I have a direct line of sight to the doors
in the rear. Then I sit backward in it, resting my chin on the
back, and opening my phone. I take long breaths to calm
myself as I check my Tumblr dash to see what the current
chatter is about the show, the fans, *me.* Of course there's still
a healthy debate roiling about whether I'm the hero fandom
needs or the loudmouth millennial activist that represents
the worst of entitled internet culture.

I skim my messages—I've been too busy to reply to any,
and I feel bad about letting them stack up, but I've been so
busy. Not to mention, a cursory glance reveals that some are
positive, some are thoughtfully critical, and many are hate-
filled tirades and personal attacks. Definitely don't have time
for *that.* My follower count is up to 44,000, which is only a
fraction of the numbers a typical episode of *Demon Heart*

would get, I remind myself to keep it in perspective. But still, it's at the point that I'm afraid to post anything. I had racked my brain, wondering if I had posted anything too personal on there that I should take down, but I rarely write anything about myself at all. Besides, if this goes well, I'll be a hero, and if it goes poorly, well, I'll delete my account and disappear back into the anonymity of rural Idaho.

But it *cannot* go poorly.

Just then, the rear doors open and Jamie walks in.

He stands in the doorway and stares at me, his arms stiff at his sides, his mouth curled into a snarl.

"You're a goddamn psychopath," he growls.

I knew he'd be angry, but I don't think I was quite prepared for him to be *this* angry. I stand up and put my chair back in its place.

"Hi, Jamie, I'm glad you came," I say.

"Change it back. *Now*," he says, not moving from the doorway.

"You didn't like it?" I ask innocently. "I honestly don't think it looks that much different than any of your official publicity photos."

"They're *making out*, Claire. They're practically playing *tongue hockey*."

Okay, so Caty might have given me the password to Jamie's Twitter account that she still had from when he needed her help changing the settings to privatize his DMs. She told him he needed a stronger password than *PeterParker1976*, but apparently he didn't listen. And apparently he didn't turn on two-step verification like she recommended, either, because it was super easy for me to get into his account, change his password, and then do whatever I liked. So the

first thing I did was change his Twitter icon to a very convincing fan photo manipulation of Rico and Forest kissing.
Then I drafted a bunch of tweets and saved them. Then I took
screenshots of the whole thing and texted Jamie (his number
also came from Caty), and said **Meet me in Ballroom 6E
or I start tweeting**. It only took fifteen minutes for him
to show up.

"You don't know what you're doing here, Claire. I could
sue you."

"Yeah, that'd look really good, wouldn't it? 'Showrunner
sues teenage fan over Twitter hack.'"

He clenches his jaw. "Give me your phone right now," he
says and starts marching down the aisle toward me.

I whip out my phone, and, walking backward, I send the
first saved tweet.

"First tweet published. Want me to keep going?" I say, and
he stops marching and pulls out his phone to look at it.

The tweet reads, *I love all the Demon Heart fans, and I can't
believe I'm so lucky to get to spend these conventions with
you. Thank you for your outpouring of passion and support.*

The likes and retweets are flooding in. He lets out a noise
that approximates a growl.

"What are you going to do?" I say. "Tell people you're
hacked, that you didn't mean that, that you would never tweet
something like that?"

He throws his hands up. "No, of course not."

"Because you wouldn't. Tweet something like that. I know
you wouldn't because I've met you and you don't really seem
to like us all that much."

He glares at me.

"Okay, so what do you want, Claire. What are your

'demands'?" He puts air quotes around *demands*, says it like he's talking to a child.

"I just want to talk this out, that's all." He's being an asshole, but I knew he would be. How did I *expect* him to act, considering how I lured him here? I just hope that by the time I'm done, he can see where I'm coming from. I can feel the adrenaline pumping through my body, and it helps keep the anxiety away. *Remember that Tess said you were the most confident person she's ever met. Remember that.*

"You think this is the right way to open a dialogue with me? Blackmailing me?"

"You didn't leave me much choice, did you? I've been trying to 'open a dialogue' this entire trip; where have you been?"

"You literally have no idea how any of this works, kid." I bristle at being called *kid*, but press on.

"So tell me."

He starts down a row of chairs, away from me, but I don't think he's trying to leave. He can't leave without getting what he came for. Good. Let's have this out. "You think I'm solely to blame for everything you don't like about *Demon Heart*? Do you know how many people work on this damn show?" he calls over his shoulder.

"You're the showrunner, the buck stops at you," I say.

He snorts and chooses a chair out of the thousands to plop down into. "Not even close. The buck barely touches me as it whizzes by. Being showrunner means you're just the guy tasked with keeping everybody happy. From the very first meeting it was made clear to me that I was there to do the network's bidding. And the studio's. And the stars'."

He leans back on his chair's rear two legs to stare at the

ceiling. "God, the 'stars.'" More air quotes. Then, in a sneering, mocking voice, *"Rico Quiroz from* Star Command *wants to do your show! What a get! Congrats, bud!"* He rolls his eyes. "I should've known right then."

"Wait..." I try to keep up. "What are you saying?"

"That some old-ass C-list actor from a space show on SyFy wasn't exactly my first choice to lead my show? Yeah. But apparently you can't do a series these days with two white leads or you get yelled at on the internet *by people like you.* So you make sacrifices, and you do what it takes to get your show made." He looks directly at me. "And you finally find two leads that all the execs can live with who are racially diverse, handsome enough for primetime, in our price range, look the part, and, hopefully, can actually act. Then the people on the internet yell anyway because they aren't also gay."

I'm floored that Rico wasn't his first choice for Heart. He's so perfect in the role, it's difficult to imagine anyone else... and straight-up impossible to believe that Jamie wouldn't like him in the part. Rico *is* Heart.

"Look, this isn't the only compromise I've had to make on this show. Every single script needs approval from the suits at the studio and the network, and they always have notes. '*Make it less enigmatic, spell it out. Think* NCIS, *not* Mad Men.' Then I get yelled at by production in North Carolina that what we've written is ungettable, and we need to cut five pages, oh and also we're running over by a hundred grand. Then I get actors calling me telling me that they'd never say this thing or that thing and I'm trying to tell them *I know it's unwieldy, but the network wants it spelled out. Think* NCIS, *not* Mad Men. But what do the actors care about the network? They just want critics to love them. And then after all that, by some miracle, we make a pilot and put it on the screen and get a full season, and everything's supposed to finally be clicking into place except now the fans, the very people who are supposedly obsessed with the show, are hollering at me that it's actually not quite up to their standards. Well, please, *pile on*." Jamie runs his hand through his hair and then carefully plumps it back up to its proper volume.

"I know you think everything that ends up on-screen is intentional," Jamie says, looking over at me, "a perfectly crafted story that sprang whole from the writers' minds into reality, but it's just not like that. Half of it is compromise, the other half is just happy accidents."

"Which half is SmokeHeart in?" I ask.

He starts to respond, then catches himself. I wonder what snarky thing he was about to say. He tries again. "SmokeHeart," he says slowly but firmly looking me right in the eyes, "isn't real."

I sigh and click a button on my remote control. At the front of the room, a screen descends with a buzz.

"Oh goodie," Jamie says drily, "visual aids."

I hit another button and a video comes up. It's a clip from episode six. Heart is confronting a minion of the Commander, and trying to get information out of him before he kills him.

"Oh god, this guy was such a nightmare to work with," Jamie says as the clip comes up. "Wanted to be paid extra because of the prosthetics. Like, excuse me, you're a *day-player*. I can find a hundred guys to replace you."

I ignore his commentary and let the clip play out. On the screen, the minion—a skinny guy with a prosthetic forehead made to look demon-ish—is squealing that he already told Heart's partner everything he knows. Heart doesn't understand;

he doesn't have a partner. I look at Jamie for this part because the important line is coming. The minion scowls at Heart and says, "You know, that pretty little boyfriend you run around with." Heart frowns and says, "Smokey?" The minion nods. And Heart shoots him through the chest. Scene over.

The screen goes dark. Jamie shrugs. "That's it? Because some meathead nobody called them boyfriends, now it's canon? It was a *joke*, dude."

I hit another button, play another clip. In this one, Smokey and Heart wrestle over ownership of the Bowl of Holding in a biker bar. As they smash into barstools and dartboards, one bar patron wolf whistles at them, while another says, "Get a room!"

The clip ends. Jamie sighs deeply. "That's also a joke."

Another clip. An unnecessarily sexy lady-demon tells Smokey that if he really wants to get information out of her, she's open to bribes, especially "biblical ones." Then, when Smokey hesitates, she says, "I knew it! You got a hard-on for that demon of yours, don't you? Richard owes me fifty bucks...." Smokey gags her and tortures her for the information instead.

Jamie throws his hands up. "I don't know what you want me to say."

"I want you to say these are shitty jokes. I want you to say you knew that the fans were shipping your two lead characters, and you thought, 'Hey, we'll throw them a bone.' But you had no intention of actually following through. I want you to admit—"

"That we were queerbaiting?" Jamie asks.

I stop short. I didn't expect him to know the term. Because if he knows what it is, why the hell is he *doing* it?

"Yeah, I know what queerbaiting is. I get accused of it about every other day on Twitter," Jamie says bitterly. "And okay. Yeah. *Fine.* We were queerbaiting. We knew what you fangirls like, and we were never gonna follow through, but we thought it was fun to joke about it. Aren't you glad we did? Because otherwise you would never have loved our show. The only reason you liked it in the first place is because we were queerbaiting you."

Oh my god, *why am I not filming this?* I want to put that admission on YouTube and have it go freaking viral. He just admitted they were playing into it on purpose. I *knew* we weren't crazy! My brain is racing a million different directions at once. I pull my thoughts together into a coherent sentence.

"How could you *intentionally* layer in gay subtext and then go out there and call us crazy for seeing it and asking about it?" My voice is shaking I'm so frustrated right now.

"I think you're confusing me with Forest," he says, leaning forward in his chair. "I never called you crazy. Or if I did, it was for a totally legitimate reason, like how you *hacked my fucking Twitter account.*" He stands up, getting agitated again. "Are we done now? Can this be over? Is that all you wanted to hear?"

"It's not that easy," I say, and with my heart thumping in my chest from anger and adrenaline, I open Twitter, and post the second tweet.

He grabs for his own phone to see what I've posted. He stares at it, then looks up at me.

"Where the hell did you get that?"

41

FOREST'S FACE FLUSHED HOT AS HE STEPPED INTO
his trailer and turned around to see every wall, every surface, every chair, table, window, covered in the same photo
of Jasper Graves's square-jawed, heroic face.

Behind him, still standing outside in the dying light, he
could hear Rico cracking up. Forest wanted to light a match.
Send the whole trailer up in flames. He reached out and tore
down a picture. Then another. Then a whole swath of them.

"Hey, hey!" Rico complained, climbing the stairs into the
trailer two at a time.

"What the hell is this?" Forest waved a crumpled handful
of pictures around wildly.

"You said you liked him," Rico said.

"So you thought you'd . . . *Goddammit, Rico*—" Forest
ripped pictures off the couch, Scotch tape sticking to everything, little pieces of Jasper Graves fluttering around. Forest's

stomach was tight, hard, screaming at him to get these down *before anyone sees*.

"Relax, Forest, man," Rico said, "I'll get Lynn to take them down."

"Did she see these?"

"Yeah, she helped me put them—"

"Did anyone else?" Forest interrupted.

"Just Lynn," Rico said slowly, calmly. "Hey, have a seat, relax."

Rico started helping Forest pull pictures off the wall, a small blank area growing as he worked. Forest let him take over, falling onto the couch and dropping his head into his hands. Rico paused to move to the door and make sure it was closed (it tended to stick) and throw the dead bolt, just in case. Then he crossed back to the wall and continued to take pictures down.

"I'm sorry," he said, "I didn't know it would upset you. You said one time that you had wanted a Jasper Graves poster as a kid. I just thought I'd make Li'l Forest's dreams come true."

"Yeah, well." Forest breathed into his hands. "What I never mentioned is I got that poster."

"You did?"

Forest nodded miserably. He hated this story, but he needed Rico to understand. "I bought it myself from the cool record store downtown. Brought it home and hung it up in my bedroom. It stayed up for all of three hours. And then my dad came home..." He trailed off.

Rico put down the pictures he was holding and turned to look at Forest, his brow furrowed in concern. Forest raised his head but didn't make eye contact yet; he just twisted to one side, lifted his shirt, and showed a portion of his back—smooth pale skin punctuated by long, angry, raised scars.

"Forest..." Rico whispered.

Forest swallowed hard as he lowered his shirt. "Yeah."

Rico moved to sit next to Forest on the stiff trailer couch. He put his hand on Forest's arm, a soft, sad touch. "I'm sorry."

Forest felt dumb then. He hadn't shown Rico for pity; he had wanted him to understand. Now his birthday party had become a mope-fest. But Rico didn't move his hand from Forest's arm. And feeling it there, warm and solid, Forest thought of that text he had wanted to send Rico. Now was his chance to tell him, away from everyone, everything he wanted Rico to know.

Well, maybe not *everything*—not the thoughts that crept in after Forest had had a few, or late at night on the precipice of sleep, when he would imagine a warm body next to him, keeping him safe, telling him it would work out.

No, not just a warm body. *Rico.* Rico, with his strong hands, his easy laugh, his effortless confidence in Forest. Rico with the deep brown eyes that held on to you tight and didn't let you pull away, even when everything in you begged to walk away. Those eyes were on him now, waiting for him to talk, pulling honesty out of him. Forest couldn't meet his gaze, so he focused on that hand on his arm and spoke to Rico's fingers.

"I know I don't...go out that often. With you guys," Forest started.

"Yeah," Rico said. "That's okay."

"I wanted you to know, that it's not personal, I'm just more of a one-on-one kind of a guy," Forest said. Out of his peripheral vision, he could see Rico nodding, but he kept his eyes on the sharp curve of Rico's hand, still touching him. His hands were brown and limber and deft with a pair of chopsticks, he knew, but he wondered what else they were capable of. No—not *that*, he thought, pushing the image aside, but then admitted, Yes, also that. Of course *that*. Wasn't *that* what all this fear was about? "When I came to *Demon Heart*, I was still pretty green, so I wanted to thank you . . . for helping me out . . ." *Shit*, this wasn't what he wanted to say. This wasn't a damn exit interview.

"Of course, yeah. I'm really glad we got to work together." Rico patted Forest's arm, then let go.

Goddammit, Forest thought angrily, why can't I just say what I mean?

"Yeah, and . . ." Forest started. He scrunched his eyes closed and spit out the next words. "And you've been wonderful I couldn't have done this without you and I wanted you to know how much Iloveyouisall." He slowly reopened his eyes and peeked at Rico, who watched him with amusement. "So . . . thanks," Forest finished limply.

Rico's eyes flashed with delight as he let Forest dangle in the wind, waiting for his response. "A one-on-one kind of a guy, huh?" Rico said, and Forest flushed red. Rico laughed, "Forest, relax, man. I never thought you hated me because you didn't come out with us. I just figured you were one of those people who needed recharge time."

"Yeah."

"Truth is, I always had half a mind to call you after those things, but I was afraid of pressuring you into something you didn't want to do, or making some big dumb gesture and screwing it all up." Rico waved around the trailer. "For example."

"No—" Forest started, but Rico cut him off.

"Yeah, no, I know when I've screwed up; let me own it."

"I wish you *had* called me sometime," Forest said, growing bolder. "I would've liked to."

"To what?"

Rico looked at him carefully and Forest silently begged him to read between the lines; understand what Forest was saying. It's okay, it's okay, I want you to, Forest thought, and willed the words toward his mouth. It would be so easy right now to break eye contact, to stand up, make an excuse, and leave. To never allow himself to get into this position again. Every single instinct in his gut told him to run, to scream, to *look away*.

But Forest didn't look away.

Forest looked at Rico's lips.

Rico cocked his head, reading the signals, following instructions, and leaned closer.

His last chance to back away disappeared as Rico's lips met Forest's, warm and concrete, and real, and any misgivings evaporated as Forest's mind emptied of everything but the taste and smell of Rico. Forest opened his mouth and let him in.

MY HEART RACES IN MY CHEST. I WANT TO SLAM the laptop closed and toss it across the room, but I need to know what else she put in here about me before it ends. I scan the remaining pages. Just a few paragraphs later, I'm stroking the place behind Rico's ear. After that, Rico is unzipping my pants, then he's giving me a blowjob, then I'm "slotting our dicks together" and fucking my fist, I mean, Jesus Christ what the fuck, Claire? By the end, we're happy and satiated and we eat our melted parfaits, naked and snuggling, and I want to scream at her to leave me out of her little fantasies. I want to call my lawyer and have it taken down. I want it erased from the memory of every one of the thousands of people who have already read it. But I can't make that happen and I feel so helpless that I want to hit something or cry or both.

Fanfic is one thing. But this is different. This is targeted.

She knows me. And she wrote porn about me. Using information I told her that I didn't tell anyone else. She implied that my dad *hits me*, which I don't even want to talk about how offensive a leap of judgment that is. And she dragged Jasper Graves into it, which is...

I grind my knuckles into my knees. I will end this. And I will end the reign of heart-of-lightness.

JAMIE IS STARING AT ME LIKE I JUST PERSONALLY
went to his house and paged through his old yearbooks.
Relax, Davies.

How did I find this? "I'm a fan, I can find anything as long
as it's on the internet."

Jamie gapes at his phone. "This photo must be, what,
twenty-five years old? How is it even online?"

"Your high school recently digitized their school newspaper archives." I shrug. "Wasn't too difficult to find."

The photo in question is from the early '90s when Jamie
was a teenager—probably around the age I am now. The photo
is old and yellowed and poor quality from being printed on
a newspaper, kept in a box for twenty-five years, and then
scanned and posted online, but it's clearly him. He's standing
in a high school hallway wearing a Spider-Man costume, a
backpack slung over his shoulder, smiling sheepishly at the

camera. The costume looks homemade—blue tights tucked into red high-top Converse, under a red-and-blue T-shirt with an elaborate spiderweb design made with what has to be puff paint. I tweeted the photo with the caption, *Once a fan, always a fan. ;)*

"So, you really liked Spider-Man, huh?"

"This is ridiculous, I'm not..." Jamie stands up, turns around in place, trying to decide what to do. "I don't have to put up with this bullshit."

"It's weird, right? I feel like most kids like Batman the best," I say, baiting him.

"Batman?! Are you kidding me, that douchebag?" he yells, whirling to face me. "Batman's just a rich asshole with a fast car. Spider-Man had to *work* for what he's got. He was just a scrawny, uncool little weirdo and look at where he is now."

There it is.

"So he's like you?"

He huffs through his nose. "I wasn't bitten by a radioactive spider."

"But otherwise..."

"What, you want me to say it? Okay, yeah," he admits, "he's like me."

"I want you to picture something for a second. Just a thought experiment. I know you feel like an underdog. The unlikely hero, growing up in Ohio, overcoming circumstance through talent and determination. But imagine if you were a teenager again, and instead of being a scrawny, uncool, nerdy kid, you were a scrawny, uncool, nerdy *gay* kid. Or..." I think of what Tess said to be about being black *and* queer, about how she has to battle a variety of prejudices. "What if you were all that plus black? Or disabled? Or trans? Or anything? Who would your superheroes be then? What costumes would you wear on Halloween?"

Jamie is shaking his head, already rejecting the premise. "I'd love to see a gay superhero as much as the next person. I hope they make one. I hope they make a bunch of them. But Smokey and Heart are already straight."

"They don't have to be. I don't think they are."

"If you care about gay characters so much, go make your own TV show."

"I'd like to, but I'm too busy rewriting yours for you."

"That's it, yes! Stick to your fanfic. Love fanfic. Write fanfic. Great compromise."

"Do you know how many people watch your show?"

"Not enough," he sneers.

"You have a reach that is so, *so* much bigger than mine. With fanfic, I'm already preaching to the choir. They know what they're going to get. But *you*. You have this opportunity to change everything. You can add more characters of color, more of every kind of diversity, with every new character you introduce. You have that power!" I lean forward and drill into his eyes. "And as for Smokey and Heart? What if you took these tough-guy characters that America thinks they already know, and you flip them upside down? 'Hey guess what, these dudes were queer the *whole time*!' It would be revolutionary! You have the chance to *make a difference*."

"Wow," Jamie says brusquely and stands up abruptly, starting down the row toward me. It's such a sudden, unprompted move that I'm suspicious.

"Thank you, Claire! There's so much I didn't know about myself that I learn from people like you," he snarks. As he approaches, I go the other way down a different row, keeping chairs between us. "I didn't know that I was given everything in life, just because I was a straight white man. And here I thought I worked my ass off for it." He picks up the pace. I start to walk faster, keeping my distance. Is he *chasing* me? "I didn't know that I was *upholding the patriarchy.* I thought I was telling monster stories for an hour a week."

Unable to catch up to me, he starts literally *climbing over rows of chairs.*

"What are you *doing?*" I ask, but he doesn't stop. I start running down the row away from him, my heart beating.

"It's people like you who think you own *Demon Heart,* but you don't," he yells.

"Jamie, stop it!" He's scaring me now. He's out of control.

He stands on a chair, one foot up on the back and roars, "You don't get to decide what happens! *I DO!*"

He stops all of a sudden.

I watch him from two rows away as he steps off the back of a chair. Closes his eyes.

Then turns around and starts walking toward the door.

"Jamie?" I almost whisper.

He keeps walking, doesn't even look at me.

"Jamie!" I say louder. "Where are you going?"

Still walking.

"I'll send these tweets if you walk out that door!" The adrenaline is back, racing through my system.

He reaches the door, puts his hand on the handle, and looks back at me.

"I'm going to leave here and call my lawyer, who is going to call Twitter and shut down my account. And then he's going to ruin you."

He can't do that. Call Twitter maybe, but he can't "ruin me," whatever that means. *Can he?*

"Oh, and, Claire?" I look at him from across the empty ballroom, my phone hanging helplessly from my fingers. "SmokeHeart is literally never going to happen."

Then he leaves, the door closing behind him, and with it, my last chance.

I sit in the ballroom for a long time after that.

Maybe I pushed him too hard, maybe I shouldn't have stolen his Twitter, maybe I shouldn't have confronted him directly. It *was* a pretty extreme idea, I admit. And probably unethical. Boy, the nerd media would have a heyday writing thinkpieces about the entitlement of fans if they ever found out. I go over it in my brain again and again, and I see a million things I could have done differently, but I don't know if any of them would have worked. Maybe there wasn't a right answer. Maybe there's nothing I could have done. Maybe this was all futile.

I open Jamie's Twitter and consider sending some tweets. But I don't. I just change the password back to his original one and close out of the app.

I check the time. I have twenty minutes until the finale airs. I should get to the park if I'm going to watch it, but I was going to watch it with Tess, we were going to snuggle under a blanket. I wonder if she's still going. I wonder if she even ever wants to see me again.

I open up a blank text to her, and I think a long time before deciding what to say. Finally, I text, **I'm sorry. I was an ass.** and send it.

I stare at my phone, willing the little ellipses to appear. Three minutes later, they do. My heart leaps, and I inch to the edge of my seat, my foot tapping uncontrollably on the carpet as I wait for her message to appear.

Finally, it comes: **I was an ass, too. I should never have outed you like that. I've been beating myself up over it ever since.**

I type back: **My mom was chill about it.**

Then, because that doesn't seem like I'm standing up for myself enough, I add: **But I'm not, like, ready to make any big declarations about that stuff. Not yet.**

I chew on my lower lip as I wait for her to respond. Finally, she writes, **My friends were definitely NOT chill.**

I wince and type, **I'm sorry again.**

Then I add, **I told Jamie to add some more characters of color fwiw. I'm not telling you in order to get credit or anything, it's just . . . you were right. I wasn't focused on anything but myself.**

She writes back, **You talked to Jamie???**

I type, **I have a lot to tell you.**

She writes, **I wish I could talk, but I'm going over to Harper's house tonight for an emergency slumber party. Everyone's coming. We have some stuff to talk out.**

My heart sinks. **So you're not coming to the finale watch party?** I can't believe she would miss it. For a *slumber party*?

Her text comes back. **Tell me what happens.**

She's not coming.

It's fine, though, it's fine. I've watched every other *Demon Heart* episode alone, I can watch this one alone, too. And I won't even be alone, I'll be in a crowd of *Demon Heart* fans! So it's fine. I try to tell myself I won't even miss her, but I know it's a lie.

The park is packed with people, sitting on lawn chairs and blankets, sharing snacks and bottles of wine and sparkling waters. It's a cool night, with a breeze coming off Puget Sound, but the skies are clear. The vibe is high energy, everyone's excited, buzzing for what's going to happen. Maybe this is too much. I start to wonder if maybe I should just go home and watch it on my hotel TV. What if people talk during it? What if the sound quality is bad? I like to be able to really immerse myself in the episode, and what if I won't be able to do that here? Also, most of the good watching spots are taken. I start to feel the hollow knot of anxiety building in my chest, and I'm thinking about turning around and running back to the hotel when I hear a voice call out to me.

"Claire, hey!"

I turn around, and a tall guy in a rubber mask is coming up behind me. I frown—I recognize the mask. It's a replica of an evil alien bounty hunter from *Star Command*. The guy lifts the mask just enough and I see Rico, grinning at me. He holds a finger to his lips—"Shh"—and drops the mask again. I'm weirdly comforted to see him. A friendly face in this crowd.

"I'm undercover," he says. "I wanted to come see what the turnout is like. Pretty good crowd. God, I love events like this, don't you? Can't you just feel the energy?" He shakes his arms like he's buzzing with electricity.

I have to laugh. "Yeah, I guess I can."

He puts a hand on my back, strong and stable, and all I want to do is close my eyes and lean into it. He opens his arms to offer a hug, and I take it, sinking into his body and letting him envelop me, smelling his body through the soft cotton of his flannel shirt, feeling his warmth take off the chill from the wind, his rubber mask bending over the top of my head.

"You're okay," he says.

This whole trip has been so many ups and downs, and it's been easy to forget that I'm just a *Demon Heart* fan and right now I'm standing in the arms of Heart, feeling his blood pump against my cheek, holding him around his waist, listening to him tell me that I'm going to be okay.

This is the actual, literal fantasy.

"Hey, I gotta get going before someone susses out who I am from the mole on my neck or something," he says into the top of my head, but he doesn't let go yet.

"Okay," I say, and I take a long slow breath in and then let it out and I release him.

"Have fun, Claire. And no matter what happens tonight, remember that you're doing just fine," he says, pulling away but letting his arm linger on my back as long as he can before he's gone.

Then he disappears into the crowd, and I turn back toward the screen and find a place to sit down. The group of friends next to me lend me their extra blanket to sit on and offer me a slice of their pizza. I take it, feeling grateful for the generosity of fans. I wonder what Rico means by "no matter what happens tonight." What's going to happen?

The screen comes to life and the crowd cheers. I hear the familiar theme music pick up as the "Previously on..." begins, and I can't help it. Something in my heart twirls around and those old feelings come right back. Smokey and Heart share a charged moment on-screen, and the whole park cheers and hoots at the pure, unbridled *shippiness* of the moment.

Just like that, I no longer feel alone. I'm with my people, I'm smiling like a child, I'm right where I should be. And maybe SmokeHeart won't go canon in this finale, and maybe I didn't convince Jamie, but maybe I made a dent, and maybe the battle isn't over yet, as long as the fans love it, and the ratings go up, and Rico is a good person. Maybe there's hope. There's always season two.

The titles splash across the giant screen and the crowd cheers, then gets very quiet, because the finale is about to begin, and we're about to find out how this season ends, and this is the last new *Demon Heart* we'll get to watch for a while...or maybe forever.

I wrap my arms around my knees and fall into the story.

WHEN I OPEN THE DOOR TO HIS INSISTENT KNOCKING, Jamie storms into my hotel room and paces around the bed, his hands clenched in white knots.

"I'm sorry, Forest, I'm really sorry, but it's gone too far."

"What's going on?" I hang back by the door; his energy is making me nervous.

"Claire," he says.

Oh. "You don't have to tell me, man," I say, closing the door and coming into the room. "I'm pissed at her, too." I tried to call my agent about that damn fic she wrote about me, but his assistant said he'd have to call me back, he was in the middle of dinner with someone else.

"This goes beyond pissed," Jamie says. "We have to get these damn rumors off our back."

He sounds apologetic, but I don't know why. I don't really get what this has to do with me. I take a few steps toward him, but he edges back.

A knot starts forming in my stomach. I don't know why, but this just feels *wrong*. "I'm on board, man, just tell me what you need me to do."

When he speaks again, it's flat, emotionless. "Forest...I don't have a choice. You *know* that."

"What are you saying?"

The knot grows, sucking in all my fears, all my anxieties. I didn't try hard enough with Claire. I wasn't good enough on the panels. I'm not funny enough, I don't work out enough, it was those doughnuts, those *damn doughnuts*, why did I eat that Dairy Queen? No, it's my acting. The dailies are terrible, the editors told Jamie that there's not enough to work with. Or the execs called, told him he made a mistake, hiring me. They all made a mistake. I never should have gotten this job. I'm never going to get another role. I'm not good enough, I'm not good enough, I'm not good enough.

"You know Smokey dies at the end of one-twenty-two. We were going to resurrect you for the season two premiere, *if* there's a season two..."

Not good enough, not good enough, not good enough.

"But I can't do that anymore. Forest, the only way to get rid of SmokeHeart is to get rid of Smokey. I'm sorry." He reaches for my shoulder, but I pull away, dazed. I can't look at him.

Not good enough, not good enough, not good enough.

"I'm sorry, Forest. I have to let you go," Jamie says. "Smokey is dead."

I don't even hear him leave.

I don't even feel it when my knees hit the floor.

Just a haircut with a battle-ax.

45

claire

WITH MOMENTS LEFT IN THE FINALE, THE WHOLE crowd is rapt, silent. Smokey and Heart are in a foot chase, working separately, but together, each trying to track down and kill the Commander before he ushers in hell on earth.

Smokey has a lead on him; he chases the Commander through a warehouse district, finally catching up to him in an alley. He thinks he has the Commander trapped, and he pulls out his battle-ax for their final face-off, when a Demidragon emerges from the shadows, and heads straight for Smokey, his sharp claws glimmering in the moonlight.

There's a collective gasp as Smokey realizes that he's in some serious hot water. But Heart is nearby, I know he'll show up and help. He'll save Smokey. He *has* to.

The Demidragon and Smokey battle, but it's not a fair fight. The Demidragon breathes boiling-hot gas and has claws the length of a broadsword. Smokey's battle-ax is barely enough to defend himself as he dodges clouds of superheated dragon breath.

Finally, Heart rounds the corner of the alley, just in time to see the Demidragon take a final swipe at Smokey, *slicing open his torso.*

My eyes are glued to the screen in the dead silence of the park.

The Commander cackles, climbs atop the Demidragon, and flies away on its back, as Heart scrambles down the alley to help Smokey.

But it's too late. His injuries are too much. Smokey looks up at Heart with weak, dying eyes.

My breathing is shallow, because although I'm terrified for Smokey, *this*, this right here, is the perfect time for a love confession. On his deathbed, there's no more time. The truth should come out *right here.*

But Smokey only says, "I'm sorry I didn't trust you."

And Heart scrambles to put pressure on his wound, to stanch the bleeding, telling him, "It's fine, it's fine," getting emotional, realizing the extent of Smokey's wounds.

And Smokey whispers, "Heart. I'll be with you..."

And Heart just shakes his head, lip quivering, refusing to say it, because saying it means it's over.

And the tears are coming to my eyes just as they're coming to Heart's.

Smokey grasps his arm, eyes fluttering, and it's their last chance. "I'll be with you..." he tries again.

"'Til the dirt hits my chest," Heart gasps, and Smokey dies in his arms.

And Heart lets out a primal howl that echoes down the

alleyway, through the neighborhood, across the city, as the camera cranes up, up, up.

And the screen goes black.

And the credits begin.

And everyone stares, wondering what the *fuck* just happened.

Okay, okay, I tell myself. It's okay, they can't kill Smokey. They'll bring him back in season two. Heart will go down to hell and get him back himself if he has to. It's not over. Forest would have *said* something if he were leaving the show.

I look around the park, and the same conversation is taking place all around me. The volume in the park reaches a frenzied pitch as everyone wonders what just happened. Smokey's not really dead, no one believes it. It's just a cliffhanger, is all. Happens all the time on these shows. It doesn't mean anything.

I see the girl who offered me pizza gesturing with her phone to her friends with a furrowed brow. They pull out their phones, too, and I can see they're all looking at Twitter. I see another group with Twitter open on their phones, too.

I fumble as I pull my phone out of my pocket, and I have to squeeze my fingers into a fist a few times to stop my hands from shaking.

I manage to unlock my phone. Open the Twitter app.

And there it is, gathering retweets by the second.

Forest tweeted: *This wasn't supposed to happen, but it's over now. Smokey is dead. Forever.* There's a knot forming in my throat, making it hard to breathe. I take shallow breaths and focus on the grass below me.

Smokey is dead. *Smokey is dead.*

Heads crane around. The girls to my left are staring at me. Other people nearby take notice. Their whispers fill my ears, it's all I can hear.

Smokey is dead.

My screen slides down as *View 1 new Tweet* appears at the top.

I tap it. Another tweet from Forest:

Blame heart-of-lightness.

THE POUNDING IS INCESSANT.

I don't think it's the pizza guy.

"Forest!" she practically screams through the door.

Nope, not the pizza guy.

I roll off my bed and straighten myself up.

"Go away," I tell her. There's literally no one I want to see right now. Especially not her.

"Forest, open up!" she hollers, banging away. She's going to cause structural damage if she keeps going like this.

I cross to the door, but I don't open it. "Claire, go home. It's over. You've done enough." I say it sharply. Maybe if I can convey just how much I am *not fucking around* she might listen to me.

Silence.

Maybe it worked? Maybe she left?

"What did they say to you?" she asks, sounding almost defeated—a new attitude for her.

"Jamie said I'm fired because people like you won't shut up about SmokeHeart unless Smokey's literally dead."

I hear her let out a long breath. "He actually said that?"

"Yes."

"So it's true. He's dead."

"Dead, dead."

"Well, what the *fuck* was this all for, then?" She sounds almost primal.

Knock, knock, knock.

"Claire, I'm not coming out, just go *home.*"

"Pizza," a guy says.

I sigh, and lean my forehead against the door. Okay. Let's do it. I whip the door open, grab the slip from the guy, and start signing it.

I don't even look at Claire, but she's right there, wound tight like she's going to pop. She comes up right behind the pizza guy, making him very uncomfortable, and speaks at me over his shoulder.

"None of this would have happened if you hadn't been such a monumental asshole," she says with a scary fierceness.

"Hey, this is my *job*, okay, Claire? It's a lot more to me than it was to you." I look at her for the first time, and she's standing there like a wet dishrag that someone wrung out and left in the sink. Tear-streaked and rumpled, she glares at me.

I shove the receipt at the poor pizza guy and grab the pizza box from him.

"It's just a *show*," I say. "And not even a particularly good one. Move on. Go get a job or something. Have a life. Read a newspaper. Care about something in the real world."

The pizza guy slips out from between us and makes his escape.

"This *is* important," she says, wiping her cheeks, steeling herself. The old Claire coming back out. "That's why this never worked out." She waggles her finger between us. "Because you *still* don't think that representation matters at all. That it's not important for gay teenagers to see someone like them on TV."

"Who?" I demand, the irritation at her endless soapboxing finally boiling over into anger. "Who are these gay teenagers who care so freaking much about *Demon Heart*? Do you know any?"

She sputters, then spits out, "There's Tess."

"Then why are you here, and not her?"

I watch her fumble for an answer. Yeah, that's what I thought. "Why are you *really* doing this?"

"I told you."

"Claire—"

"I said I already told you!"

"You haven't told me shit about yourself, cupcake. Not really."

"This isn't about me."

"Of course it is, Claire. *What is your sexuality?*"

She shakes her head at me, pissed. Her hair, stringy and falling in her eyes, her jaw tight, she growls, "What's *yours*?"

My neck stiffens. "You think you know, do you?" I say. I put the pizza down in the doorway and dig my phone out of my pocket and hold up the page. "Yeah, I read all about it in, what's it called? 'Sugar and Cream'?" Claire goes pale. "This is a *major* breach of trust. You don't write sex scenes about someone you know."

"How'd you find that?" Claire takes a step back, unsteady now. "That's fiction," she says.

"It has my name on it—*and Rico's*. It has things I said to you in confidence. You made up shit about my dad." My voice is low, but I know she hears it. She drops her gaze now.

"It's just a story. Lots of people write RPF, there's nothing wrong with it."

"This isn't about that and you know it. People know you know me. They're going to think my dad *beat* me." I pull my T-shirt up and show her my back. "See? Nothing. No scars. But that doesn't matter now, does it? No, none of that matters as long as people get to read about me banging Rico in my trailer on my birthday."

"Everyone knows it's not real," she says.

"Do they? Because I'm not sure *you* know. Rico and I aren't in love, Claire. We're not secretly having sex. We're not making out after hours. We're. Not. Gay."

She shakes her head at me and curls her lip. "You're such a homophobe, and you won't even admit it."

"No, I'm just straight. There's a difference."

"If this was about you and some hot female costar, you wouldn't give it a second thought," she spits out at me. "This is entirely about your own internalized bullshit. Well, *get over it.*"

"You wrote *porn* about me."

"They're just dicks, you *dick*!" she shouts, throwing her hands up and grasping the back of her head. I'm worried people are going to start coming out of their rooms. She rubs her hands over her head and down her face, growling in frustration. Then she straightens her glasses. "I'm going home."

"So glad we talked. Thanks for the sympathy," I say. "Don't worry about me, I can always go on unemployment."

She stares at me, her eyes narrowed, full of spite. "I'm glad they killed you instead of Heart," she says quietly. "At least Rico doesn't hate us. I'm pretty sure he even shipped it." She starts down the hallway, mumbling, "I hope whatever role you land next gets you the kind of fans you actually want."

She turns the corner and she's gone, finally.

47

claire

MOM LOOKS UP FROM HER BOOK WHEN I MAKE IT back to our room.

"How'd it go?" she asks. I don't answer, I just haul out my duffel bag and start packing my things. My cheeks are hot, but I'm not crying anymore. I don't have any tears left for this.

Mom sits up in bed, getting that worried-mother expression. Oh, *now* she's worried. Where has she been this whole time? Why did she spend so much time learning how to LARP and not enough time telling me not to do foolish things like *feeling things* for other people and *caring* about stuff?

"I want to go home," I say.

"What's wrong, honey bunny?" She follows me into the bathroom where I start grabbing my toiletries. "What happened?"

I shove everything into a plastic bag and brush by her into the main room where I stuff the bag into my duffel. "I just...

I thought they would understand me here. But they don't. None of them do."

Mom rubs my shoulder. "I'm so sorry."

I flop onto the bed, partly just to get away from her. "I want to leave. Can we leave now?"

She must see that I'm serious, so she calls the airline and changes our flight, and within a few hours we're at the airport waiting for our plane back to Boise.

I don't want to open Tumblr, but I know I have to.

My notifications are chaos. I don't read the discourse; I'm not interested anymore. There was a time when I would have started typing an angry screed about everything that's happened, but it turns out it didn't matter. None of it mattered.

Nothing I did helped at all. It only made everything much, much worse.

I open a text post and stare at it. What do I even say about all this?

Sleepy passengers walk past us, pulling suitcases and clutching paper cups of hot tea. My mom snores slightly in the next chair. I tip my head back and lean against the cool glass of the windows behind me. I gaze up at the night sky above the airport.

Finally, I type: *I'm sorry. SmokeHeart is dead and it's my fault. I never meant for it to turn out this way.*

I publish it and wait a few minutes for enough people to reblog it to ensure it'll get out there.

Then I go into the settings and delete my blog.

forest ➡ 48

THE ANXIOUS ENERGY KEEPS RUNNING AROUND inside me until I can't stay in my hotel room anymore, so even though it's past midnight, I decide to go for a walk.

Outside, I shiver against the chilly night air and pull my collar up higher. It feels good to walk, though. I can feel the anxiety start to slip away as I round a corner and head past the darkened convention center. I wasn't expecting there to be people outside, but there's a long line of dedicated con attendees camped out overnight for something happening tomorrow. They're bundled up in their down jackets and fleece blankets, hoods cinched over their faces, playing cards, making one another laugh as low music fills the air. They are the dedicated, the passionate.

Maybe it would have impressed me before, even made me happy to see them so determined. But now I just see how it goes wrong, how quickly love can become zeal, passion can become fanaticism. How quickly I can go from having a promising career with opportunities in front of me to the gutter of Hollywood. Washed up at twenty-three. And for what?

I pass a convention sign with an arrow pointing toward the DEMON HEART MARATHON SCREENING and I remember that they're showing episodes until late tonight. I situate my hat low over my eyes and head toward the park a block or two away.

It's time to say good-bye.

Approaching the *Demon Heart* screening, I see the hundreds of fans lying out on blankets and lawn chairs on the sloping grass, watching our show playing on a large projection screen. It's dark out, and no one's looking anywhere but at the screen. I keep to the shadows formed by a cluster of trees toward the back of the park, find a spot, and watch with them for a bit. I recognize the episode right away. It's from late in the season, as Heart and Smokey try out a provisional truce. After destroying a monster that was wreaking havoc on a paddleboat casino together, they lean against a roulette table and share a beer.

"Take it, man, you earned it today," Heart says, holding out a cold one to Smokey.

I watch myself take the beer with a "Thanks," and hold Heart's eye for just a beat longer than necessary before clinking bottles with him.

I look around the park at the people watching. One girl nearby sighs, watching the screen, lovelorn, and her friend puts her head on her shoulder. "I know," the first girl whispers, rubbing her friend's arm. "I know."

This is shipping.

On-screen, Smokey and Heart share an earnest nod before

taking a drink, and the scene fades to black. Would they have made a good couple? No way to know, now. Jamie's name flashes on-screen and the park erupts into *boos*. I join them, low, under my breath.

Boo, Jamie. Boo, Forest. Boo all of us. Boo the whole damn show.

49

MS. NEWTON DRONES ON IN CALC ABOUT CONCEPTS I have no grasp of because I've missed so much class. Normally, I'd be anxious to catch up and make sure my A doesn't slip, but I'm just not feeling it anymore.

I've been back in Pine Bluff three weeks. If the kids here have any idea that I was momentarily famous on the internet, they haven't given me any indication of it. I didn't get a single "Hey, what's it like to hang out with C-list celebrities?" I didn't even get a "Were you sick or something?" It's like they didn't even notice I was gone. Except for Joanie Engstrom, who, when she saw me coming down the bus aisle my first day back, gave me a little smile and moved her bag for me to sit down before going back to reading her Bible. It's the friendliest thing that's happened to me yet.

Fine with me. I have two weeks left in junior year, and I'm just looking forward to a summer full of reading books (no more fanfic for me) and lying on my back on the trampoline in my backyard, pretending I live in a different country.

In Calc, I sketch myself in my notebook hiking the five-hundred-mile Camino de Santiago trail in Spain, far away from literally every person and every television in the world. When I run out of room, I flip the notebook over to continue the sketch on the back page, but I forgot that I had stuck a *Demon Heart* sticker there. Just the sight of it fills me with emotions so quickly it's like my hate-appendix burst, and my blood is filling up with deadly toxins that will kill me within minutes if I don't get the sticker out of my sight.

I start picking at the corner of it, but the sticker just keeps tearing rather than peeling and it won't come off, and my desk is filling up with little torn-off pieces, and I hate everything about it. Smokey and Heart looking at each other now, is just a taunt, a tease, a promise of something that will never come true.

I can't stand it anymore. I tear the entire back cover off my notebook. It makes a loud ripping sound, and everyone in the room turns to stare. Andrea Garcia is in that class; she stares. I don't care. When have I ever cared about what other people think?

I stand up, grab my backpack, and throw the entire notebook in the trash on my way out. Let me get a B in Calc. Who gives a shit about Calc?

I stride into the hallway and run directly into Kyle Cunningham with a flat *thud*. I stumble backward, and he tips his dirty hat up to see what just hit him. We make fleeting eye contact before I tuck my head down and try to push past him, but he grabs my shoulders and holds me there.

"Hey, hey, Claire Strupke. Where'd you go for so long? I

thought maybe you finally got the help you need, and they put you in a psych ward."

"Leave me alone, Kyle," I say, and try to brush past him again, but he keeps me in place with a strong grip.

"You want to come over tonight? I was hoping we could pick up where we left off."

"Andrea Garcia dumped you, huh?"

He hardens immediately. "I dumped *her*," he says brusquely.

"Maybe it's because you like to put your hands on girls who don't ask you to," I say, and push him away.

"Whatever, dyke," he says.

"Maybe I am," I say, catching him off guard. He gapes at me, his ugly mouth hanging open. I shove him to the side, sending him toppling into a bank of lockers, and keep walking.

Who knows? *Maybe I am.*

"SO ARE YOU BASICALLY WAITING BY THE PHONE, or..." I ask, sipping my nonfat cappuccino. Rico and I are finally back in LA, sitting on the patio of Aroma Café, surrounded by tanned and put-together industry types having conversations about scripts and stars and who got an overall deal where and for how much.

Rico sighs and takes a bite of his scone. "My agent is having an aneurysm; I'm actually concerned for his health."

I can't believe they've let it drag out for this long. After all our work at those conventions, our ratings for the finale were up slightly, but not spectacularly. The cast and crew of *Demon Heart* were supposed to know if they got a season two pickup weeks ago, but the network is dragging their feet for some reason that I'm not privy to.

Rico leans in, serious now, and adds, "I keep pushing for them to renew your contract, dude, but it doesn't look like it's gonna happen. I'm not gonna let it go, though. They can't do this show without you."

I wave him off. "It's over, Ric. I've accepted that."

"There's a million ways to bring you back. Reincarnation. Ghost. Hey, you could be a demon, like me!"

It warms me that Rico would fight for me, but he wasn't there when Jamie told me the news. Nothing is going to convince him to change his mind. "Jamie killed me off for a reason. He doesn't want me back."

"Jamie's an idiot." Rico leans back in his chair and nudges his scone toward me. I shake my head. No scones until I get another job. I have to get my eating habits back on track or I'm screwed. Rico crosses his legs and looks at me. "You talk to her lately?"

"Who?" He just shoots me a look. *Oh. Her.* "No."

"She's a good kid. Annoying as hell, but good," he says.

I just shrug, and he gets the message and moves on. "No matter what happens," he says, looking at me with a sad smile, "I'm gonna miss you next year."

"I'm gonna miss you, too," I say. And it's true. This last year would have been a living nightmare without Rico by my side. I don't know how I would have gotten through it. It strikes me that I should tell him that, then I think, Wait, I already did. That night in my trailer... and then I realize I'm remembering Claire's fanfiction. I start to chuckle to myself. Now who's the one mixing up fiction and reality?

"What's so funny?" Rico says.

"Oh, I was just thinking—" I say, and then stop myself, then think, Oh what the hell. "If Claire were here, she'd be—"

"—telling us to confess our feelings?" Rico laughs. "Okay,

how's this? I think you're a talented and committed actor and a good person, and working with you this last year has been an absolute pleasure."

Well shit. I guess the feeling's mutual. I want to tell him the same, but the only words ringing in my head are Claire's.

Oh, what the hell.

"Dude, honestly? I couldn't have done this without you. You've been wonderful. And I just figure I should let you know"—*deep breath*—"howmuchIloveyouisall. So . . . thanks."

Rico holds my look, this soft smile on his face that slowly turns into a smirk. "You know what Claire'd be saying *now*, don't you?"

"She'd be yelling at us to kiss. Don't you dare tell her we said any of that."

We both laugh.

"You should text her, see what she's up to," Rico says.

I shrug because, well, I've thought about it. The other day in West Hollywood, I saw a billboard for STD testing that had a stock photo of a close-up of two guys holding hands, one in a leather jacket and the other in a workman's jacket and it looked so much like SmokeHeart that I almost pulled over to take a picture for her, because I knew she'd laugh. I didn't, though. I'm still kind of pissed at her for that fic she posted. And besides, she hates me.

"When she left," I tell Rico, "we had a bit of an argument."

"You need to apologize?" he asks.

I dunno. No? Maybe? Probably? So does she, though. "I'm probably never gonna see her again, dude."

"You kidding?" Rico says, raising his eyebrows. "Mind

like that? She'll be running this town in ten years." He might be right.

A customer brushes by, knocking our table and causing our coffees to slosh onto the Spanish-tile tabletop.

"Reed?"

I look up. Holy shit. It's Jon Reynolds, holding an iced coffee, wearing new clear plastic glasses. I fix my hair real quick. I haven't seen him since that disaster of a panel back in Seattle.

"Hey, sir, hi." I get up and shake his hand while Rico mops up rivers of coffee.

"Hey, I watched a little of your *Demon Heart* show the other day. Turns out my stepdaughter and all her friends are goddamn lunatics about it, who knew? The two of you are good, real good. You got chemistry."

I exchange a look with Rico and bite my cheek not to laugh. "Thank you."

"Anyway," he says, "lucky running into you. I was just telling casting to bring you in to read for Tension."

No way.

"Oh! Yeah, yeah, great." *Be cool, Reed. BE COOL.* I want to ask why the hell he's bringing me in after watching that dumpster-fire panel. Did he not witness my complete meltdown? Was he not present as a room full of people who ostensibly loved me turned against me? I start to open my mouth but think better of it.

"Yeah, I know, that whole mess up in Seattle," he says, reading my mind. "Look, I have a teenager, I know how manic these things can get. Frankly, I thought you were great up there. I liked how you shut the whole thing down."

"Yes, sir," I say. Though I don't really know if that's an accurate description.

"This is just some fantasy for them," he says. "But for you, it's your whole life. You indulge these people once, and these little gay rumors will plague you your whole career. Not that there's a problem with the gays, but let's face it, we're never gonna cast that kid from *Glee* as Jack Tension, you know what I'm saying? There's a certain expectation."

I want to say, *So, what? Gay people can't play Jack Tension?* But I don't. I just need to get the audition, that's all. Just land the role.

"Anyway, we'll be in touch." He raps on the table before striding away.

I feel a little dirty. I don't want to look at Rico, but he just says, "Congratulations, dude!" and smiles hopefully. But I don't feel quite as jubilant as I should.

IT'S THE THIRD WEEK OF SUMMER VACATION WHEN the call comes. I'm deep into my sixth read of the Citybreakers books, lying on my back on the trampoline behind our house just as I'd planned, and enjoying the feeling of sunshine on my face, the overgrown vines blowing in the breeze. I haven't opened my laptop in weeks, haven't touched Tumblr, haven't looked at my email, haven't watched a frame of *Demon Heart*. Most days, I've been leaving my phone by my nightstand and not even looking at it except to plug it in when it needs a charge, keeping it on the pile of my things from the trip, my bags still unpacked, my expensive screen-printed poster still rolled up in its tube, never hung.

I am disconnected. I am outdoors. I am not looking at screens. This is what I needed. I'm also not talking to anyone. Not Tess, not my internet mutuals. My entire world right now is in Pine Bluff, in this house, this backyard. I keep hoping this will cure me, but I don't feel better.

I still ruined *Demon Heart*. I still ruined our ship. I still ruined everything with Tess.

I still failed.

I keep wondering what would have happened if I had gone to that first convention and never said anything, never asked a question. Just showed up, enjoyed the panel, and went home. Would I still love the show? Would I still have my fandom intact? Would Forest still have a job? Or was *Demon Heart* a powder keg that was waiting to explode, and I just happened to be the first spark that came along?

Mom and Dad have stopped asking me if there's anything they can do. We've found a way to work around each other, Mom moving me out of the way when she needs the dining-room table for her LARPing projects, Dad asking me if I like this word choice or that one when he wanders out of his office in the back shed, his pencil tucked behind his ear, his glasses up on the top of his head, reading a half-finished poem to me.

"Claire, telephone!" Mom hollers from the kitchen door. I stick my bookmark in my page and clamber off the trampoline to come grab the cordless from her, frowning because no one ever calls our landline for me.

"Hello?" I say.

"Claire." Rico's voice is light and smiling.

"Rico?" My heart lifts at the sound of his voice.

"Heyyy, it's good to talk again! How you been?"

How've I been? *Alone,* mostly.

"Good, good. How are you?"

"Well, it's pretty weird here," he says. "No one quite knows what to expect, so we're just sitting around, twiddling our thumbs, waiting for the decision to come down from on high. I've been learning to knit."

"You're knitting?" I laugh, because it's surprising and yet so perfectly *Rico*. I lean against the edge of the trampoline as I realize how much I missed him.

Weird to think I, a mere fan, missed hanging around Rico Quiroz, fandom icon, but it's true.

"Hey, Claire, I'd love to keep chatting, but I have to put you on speaker because there's some people here who want to chat with you."

And like that my good vibes evaporate. Of course this isn't just a social call. They want something from me. They always do.

"Yeah, okay," I say.

"Claire, it really is good hearing your voice," Rico says, low and genuinely. Then he resumes his normal voice. "Okay, putting you on speaker now. You're on with the fabulous Caty Goodstein and the very wise Paula Greenhill."

"Hi!" Caty chimes.

"Hello, Claire," Ms. Greenhill says.

Hearing their voices brings everything right back. The nervousness that I wasn't doing a good enough job, the excitement that I might make a difference. The crushing realization that I didn't. I take a deep breath and tip my head back to let the sunshine hit my face.

"Hi, guys, what's up?"

"Listen," Ms. Greenhill says, "first things first, I was really sorry we didn't get a chance to chat after the Seattle convention. I know a lot happened, between the panel and the screening and everything that went down on Twitter. . . ."

That's a nice euphemism for *Blame heart-of-lightness*.

"Yeah," I say.

"I feel like we left things on a bad note, and I was hoping to

give it another shot. What do you think, would you be interested in joining us for one more convention?"

I feel a zing of excitement at getting to go to another con,
but it's quickly followed by caution. The pain of how things
ended is still too fresh.

"I...I don't know."

"Claire," Caty says, jumping in. "It might help if we told
you the name of the convention. Maybe you've heard of it.
San Diego Comic-Con?"

I snap to attention. San Diego is the biggest, most important convention in the country. Everyone—*everyone*—goes to
it. I stand up straighter. I've wanted to go to this convention
practically since my first fandom.

But still...

The idea of going back, seeing Forest, seeing Jamie. I just
don't think I can do it.

"We know you deleted your blog," Caty says, barreling on.
"And that's totally fine, I get it. We'd set you up as the official
guest-blogger on the *Demon Heart* Tumblr. We'd also have you
doing media for some of the digital outlets that would be there.
You've still got a lot of interest swirling around you, girl, even
more so now that you've dropped off the grid. People want to
know what you think. So? What do you say?"

"I, um..." I stumble, wondering. Go to Comic-Con? Liveblog for the show? Be another PR shill for them?

"No."

There's silence on the other end. I picture them wordlessly
conversing about who should speak next. I save them the
trouble.

"I just don't want to go back into the same situation as

before, you know?" I say, rubbing my eyes under my glasses. "It didn't end well for me."

"It didn't end well for a lot of fans," Caty says. "That's why we want you back. To reset the conversation. A fresh start."

"I can't reset the conversation by liveblogging," I say. "If you want me to help out, you should—" I stop myself. Do I mean what I was about to say? Would I really do that?

"What?" Caty prompts.

"Tell us what you want and we'll discuss it," Ms. Greenhill says.

I shake my head, I can't believe I'm about to say this, but talking to these three, I'm starting to feel that I can still make a difference. They're offering me a voice in the conversation, and I'd be missing a big opportunity if I didn't take it, and then ask for more.

"Let me moderate the panel," I say. "At Comic-Con. Put me in charge of it."

Rico laughs—one short, exuberant bark—but no one else speaks. I imagine Caty and Ms. Greenhill are probably having another wordless conversation. I wait it out, wiggling my toes in the grass nervously.

Finally, Ms. Greenhill clears her throat. "Okay, let's do it."

Holy smokes, I didn't think that would work.

Rico lets out a hoot. "This should be fun!"

"I'm emailing you the info I need for your badge right now," Caty says.

I peek at the house, where my parents are watching me through the kitchen window. "Do you think I could get three badges?" I say. "I have a couple of old folks I need to bring with me."

The sky as we descend into San Diego is bright and clear, and I can see seagulls circling over the sparkling blue ocean. There's a man with a sign that says STRUPKES at baggage who takes us to the convention in a shiny black town car. Mom is freaking out and wondering what the taco situation in San Diego is like. Dad is quiet and, I would bet a dollar, composing poems in his head about this. I don't think either one of them has ever been south of Reno.

We see our first cosplayers when we're still miles away—a Peggy Carter mom holding the hand of a very young Luna Lovegood. I wonder if it's the girl's first Comic-Con. I wonder if she's as excited as I am. As we get closer to the convention center, the crowds get bigger and bigger, until they pack the sidewalks and move in waddling huddles. It's truly a spectacle.

Every single kind of fan is present in this place at this time. Most of the cosplays I recognize, but some of them are completely new to me. I see a whole group dressed like punk-rock Disney princesses and smile to myself. Beyond them, there's a group of pale, twitchy guys in oversize T-shirts who look like they haven't seen the sun since this time last year. To their left, there's a news camera interviewing a Castiel on the street. Next to Castiel is another Castiel. Actually, looking around, there are *so many* Castiels.

"Wow," Mom says, in awe, taking in the totality of the convention swarming around us.

"I know," I say.

The driver pulls up in front of a hotel. As we get out, Ms. Greenhill comes up to us, her smile huge.

"Claire! Trudi! Chuck, it's a pleasure to meet you," she says, vigorously shaking our hands in turn. "You guys ready to have fun this weekend?"

"I suppose so," Dad says. He's already overwhelmed, I can tell.

"You betcha!" Mom says.

"Yes," I say. And I *am* ready.

Ms. Greenhill nods at me warmly and holds out a manila envelope. When I tip it open, my badge slides out. *Claire Strupke. VIP.* This should all be old hat to me now, the fake-y, temporary glitz of conventions. But holding that VIP badge with my name on it in my hand, it still feels magical.

People travel from all over to come celebrate their favorite thing together in one place with other people who love that thing. Conventions are entirely based on mutual love of stories. I feel that love in the costumes of the people walking past, in the excited chatter of friends talking about what they want to go see first, in the eyes of the little kids gripping their parent's hand, just hoping for a glimpse of their fave.

No matter what my feelings about *Demon Heart* are now, I still adore this. I put my badge around my neck and nod at Paula. "Let's do it!"

"Great," she says, handing envelopes to Mom and Dad as well. "I've put an itinerary in there for you, too. We'll want to see you at the panel, but you're free until then. I've also put your room keys in there. Chuck and Trudi, you're together. Claire, you've got your own room. Thirteen forty-six. Go ahead and drop off your stuff, and I'll see you at the panel!"

RED ZONE 4 IS JUST SO SICK. THE GRAPHICS LOOK incredible, the story is immersive. I don't even know how long I've been sitting here in my hotel room playing it, but it's hours at least. This is my third time playing through the game since I bought it, and I know every stage. For the last month, I've done nothing but play Red Zone and work out. I'm calling it research.

In June, I auditioned for Jack Tension with the casting agent, who liked me, so I read for Reynolds, who liked me, so I read for the studio, who freaking liked me (holy shit!) but had concerns that I wasn't known enough. *They're vetting you*, my agent says. *Live the role*, my agent says. *Don't screw up at Comic-Con,* my agent says. My whole life could change with one phone call, and unless I make some kind of spectacular mistake here in San Diego, it's completely out of my hands. So I've decided if anyone asks about SmokeHeart, my answer is a simple "no comment," and until it's time to go onstage, I'm obsessively playing *Red Zone 4* and trying not to think about it.

Now, I'm deep into enemy territory with three clips and a hand grenade left when I hear the door beep and then open. No one else should have a key to this room. I slip off my headphones and say, "Hello?"

"Oh," I hear a voice say. I can't see her yet around the wall, but I hear her fumbling with her bags. "I thought this was room thirteen forty-six."

I know that voice. I pause the game and rise.

"It is," I say as Claire rounds the corner and sees me, finally. She looks different from the last time I saw her. Her hair has lightened like she's been spending a lot of time in the sun. She looks rounder, softer, less intense. She also looks surprised to see me as she glances around the room and notices my stuff everywhere.

"Oh..." she says. "Hi. I...thought this was my room."

"Pretty sure it's mine."

"Ms. Greenhill gave me the key."

"She gave *me* the key."

"Ah," she says knowingly as we both come to terms with the fact that we've been set up.

I take a seat on the bed again, but she continues to stand in the doorway. "So, you're back for another round," I say, trying for a playful jab, but it might have come out sounding too much like an accusation.

"Yeah, I guess so." She leans into the wall and picks at her fingernails. "I, ah, I deleted that fic you read off my account," she says. "I shouldn't have brought that stuff about your dad into it. Or Jasper Graves. I betrayed your trust, posting that. I'm sorry."

I nod. "Thank you." Well, well, well. Claire Strupke is capable of humility after all.

"I thought about deleting all of my fics," she says.

It makes me sad, thinking about the sum of her creative work just disappearing like that.

"Don't do that," I say.

"I'm just not sure I see the point anymore."

"What's Tess have to say about it?"

"Oh, ah..." Claire shrugs, meets my eyes fleetingly, then looks away again. "That wasn't anything."

"Kind of seemed like something," I say.

Maybe our convention tour turned out to be a major clusterfuck of epic proportions, but at least it seemed like one good thing had come out of it. Those two deserved to find someone who would make them happy. I'm still kind of rooting for them.

"Yeah, um, you know, I should go find Ms. Greenhill and get the right key," she says. "I'll leave you alone with your..." She gestures to the TV as she picks up her bag to go.

"Hey, Claire," I say, stopping her. I don't know what to say, but I know we can't leave it like this. With a few weeks of distance, some of the stuff I said to her in the heat of the moment makes me wince.

"I'm sorry I freaked out on you in Seattle. I lost my temper." She nods. "And I'm sorry I tweeted about you. I should never have done that."

"Thank you," she says, then narrows her eyes. "You just trying to butter me up so you get better questions?"

"What do you mean?"

"They didn't tell you?" Her eyebrows shoot up in disbelief.

"Oh man, okay. Um, well, I'm going to be moderating your panel."

"Oh! Wow." I snort. "Jamie's going to lose it."

"Probably."

"You gonna make it all about SmokeHeart?"

"I have to ask about it."

"Okay, but just a warning, all I'm going to say on the topic is 'no comment.'"

She shrugs but smiles, and it almost feels like maybe we're finding a way to be normal. I wiggle my controller at her. "I'm in the middle of a game here. Do you...maybe want to play with me?"

She frowns, dubious. "Did Ms. Greenhill ask you to do this?"

I hold up my hands and laugh. "I swear to god, this is all me."

She thinks about it, then drops her bag and comes over and takes the controller from me. "What're we playing?"

"*Red Zone*," I say, and she shoots me an amused look.

"Still on that?" she says.

"Once a fan, always a fan."

"Oh no, is that how that works?" she asks in mock horror. "You can never unfan something?"

"Sorry, dude, you're gonna be obsessed with this" —I draw circles around my face—"for*ever*."

She laughs, and it feels like a breakthrough.

Claire's actually pretty good at *Red Zone*. After thirty minutes of playing, she's killed almost as many enemy fighters as I have. We're closing in on the final battle when she asks me something I wasn't expecting.

"So, Jack Tension, huh? You think you're gonna get the role?"

"How'd you hear about that?"

"There were a bunch of gamer bros talking about it in the lobby," she says. "They seem stoked."

"Those are just rumors," I say.

"True ones?" She shoots an enemy who had the bad fortune of sticking his head up in the desert just as she was training her rifle on him. Dang, she's getting good at this.

"Studio hasn't approved me yet. They're worried I don't have the necessary appeal."

"The necessary appeal? Do I need to send them some URLs to fanblogs?"

I laugh. "I'm not sure that's the kind of appeal they're interested in."

"Ah," she says as she creeps through the remains of a bombed-out shack in the game, "they're not looking for girls."

"Well, it's a big action movie, so . . ."

"Yeah."

She lobs a grenade over a half-bombed wall, and as it explodes, it takes out three enemy fighters.

"All this gay stuff probably isn't helping you, either," she says.

"I wasn't going to say anything," I mumble. "But . . . no. It's not."

"I get it," she says. "No one's gonna make a movie with a gay action hero." She fires—*TAT-A-TAT*—into the brush, laying out several more enemies. "Even though that sounds rad."

She runs through the doorway of the next checkpoint, with me on her heels. The game dings our successful completion of the mission and goes into a cut scene, congratulating us on our work so far and explaining the next stage.

I drop my controller to my lap. "I've never wanted a role as much as I want this one," I say. "I mean, I don't envy them their decision—they have to find the right guy in the entire world to bet a billion-dollar franchise on. But I'm just sitting here hoping it's me and trying not to do anything that could jeopardize that."

"So basically, you're hoping SmokeHeart doesn't come up at the panel today," she says, not cruelly, just matter-of-factly.

I take a deep breath. "It would be easier for me if it didn't, yeah. But, Claire..." I rub my neck and think about the best way to say this. "I want you to know that I'm genuinely sorry for how I reacted. That first day in Boise, especially, and all those days afterward. I was uncomfortable, and I took it out on you. I'm sorry."

She nods and chews on her lip. I'm half-afraid I accidentally said something wrong in my apology and she's about to launch into a lecture. But instead, she says, "Thank you." Then, after a beat, she adds, "I know you can't do this, but it would be nice if you said that publicly. This is your last convention with *Demon Heart*, your last chance to tell people how you feel."

"I...don't know how I feel," I say, and that's the truth.

"Do you still think we're crazy?"

I remember the *Demon Heart* marathon back in Seattle, a park full of sighing fans. I think about Claire's fanfiction—surprisingly well crafted, emotional, and thoughtful. I think about her sitting me down over doughnuts and showing me the Tumblr fan experience. I think about what Rico always says: *You think too much, Forest.*

"No, you're not crazy."

She nods and half smiles at me. We both know this is progress. "It would mean something to a lot of people to hear you say that."

I know that's true, but I just don't think I can do it.

Claire looks at the TV, where our characters are being told to infiltrate a whorehouse popular with army men and weed out the "authentic whores" from "those enemy spy bitches." Her face changes. I've played through this level twice already, but it hadn't occurred to me how sexist it was until I saw Claire see it. I scramble for the remote control, searching the bed until I find it on the TV stand. I click it off so we don't have to hear it anymore. I feel sheepish and dumb, and I really don't like the way she's looking at me.

I expect her to say something about *Red Zone*, like *Some game*. But she doesn't need to. I already hear it in my head.

Instead, she just gathers her things. "I'll get going. See you at the panel." She heads for the door.

"Claire—" I don't know what to say, but I don't want her to leave like this.

"If *Red Zone* is what you want, then I want you to have that," she says. "I really do want you to be happy, Forest. I hope you get what you're looking for."

She slips out the door and leaves me alone.

What I'm looking for.

If anyone knows what I'm looking for, maybe they could give me a call and let me know? Because I have no idea. And every time I try to do something good, I end up screwing it up. I drop onto the bed, bury my face in the soft covers, and groan into them.

53

 claire

GETTING FROM THE HOTEL TO THE CONVENTION is more overwhelming than anything we've done so far. Making it harder are Mom and Dad, trailing behind me, distracted by literally any little thing.

"Who's that?" Dad asks, pointing at a cosplayer.

I look. "That's Poe. Remember? You like Poe."

"Edgar Allan?"

"From *Star Wars*, Dad." I'm trying to get them to safely cross this street without being hit by a pedicab or trampled by one of the literally gajillions of other people here.

"Who's she supposed to be?" Mom asks.

"Oh, I know that one," Dad says. "That's Xena the Vampire Slayer!"

"Close enough," I mutter as I take their hands and run them across the train tracks so they don't get run over while mixing up their badass female characters.

As we crowd up against other fans and wait for the light to change to cross the final street, Mom leans over and points to the guy next to us as she whispers, "What's he?" I look at him. It's a Jack Tension. And he looks game-perfect, down to the dusty fatigues and the replica assault rifle slung over his shoulder. The light changes.

"I don't know," I say, and lead my parents across the street.

Inside the convention center, the crowds don't lighten up. As we ride the escalator to the second floor, I can look down over the mob of fans and marvel at how many of us there are. It is simply awe-inspiring. I think the entirety of our little Boise convention could fit in one ballroom here. Looking out over the vast ocean of nerds, weirdos, and fans, I remember how far I've come from that first con in Boise. I wonder how far I'll go from here.

As we get closer to the ballroom where the *Demon Heart* panel is, I see that same Jack Tension cosplayer again, and then realize, no it's a *different* one. A little farther ahead, I see a guy in a Red Zone T-shirt, also walking the same direction as us. As we round a corner and the *Demon Heart* line comes into view, I see at least a dozen guys with Red Zone shirts, hats, or commemorative Comic-Con bags. Suddenly, the *Demon Heart* crowd looks much more like a Red Zone convention than anything else. I feel a knot of worry growing as we take our places in the line.

"Aren't you thrilled to finally meet them?" Mom says excitedly to Dad. "Forest and Rico, they're so dreamy, Chuck, you're not gonna believe it." Dad humphs like he's not excited, but I can see he is. There's so much energy in this line, it's impossible not to feel it.

"Okay," I tell them. "Once the line starts moving, just go

inside and find a place to sit. And try not to yell anything too embarrassing at me, okay?"

"We would never!" Mom says, clasping her cheek in horror.

"Right. I'll catch up with you after."

I turn to go make my way backstage when I see her.

About a hundred people up, wearing an adorable yellow dress, talking animatedly to someone next to her.

Tess.

I feel the knot of worry clench even harder. Has she seen me? Does she know I'm here? How is *she* here? *God*, she looks good. Who is she *with*?

I haven't talked to her since Seattle—since she texted to tell me she was going to a *sleepover* instead of watching the finale with me. She texted a few times after that, but when I didn't answer, she stopped trying. She must have seen that I deleted my Tumblr. I hope she knows it wasn't her fault. I hope she knows I don't hate her. But how would she know if I didn't tell her?

My hands are sweating at the very idea of talking to her. What if she's mad at me for basically shutting her out for the last two months? What if she doesn't want to see me? What if—my stomach drops at the thought—what if that girl she's with is her new girlfriend?

"I'll be right back," I say to my parents, and, sweaty palms be damned, I start up the line.

My heart is racing like I've just run a 10K. My vision narrows so I can only see her. Everyone else here is irrelevant.

I have. No idea. What I'm going to say to her.

I start with, "Hey, Tess."

She spins around, and her expression is this weird mixture of things I can't pin down. "Claire," she says. "Hi." She stares at me like I look different, or something. I'm pretty sure I look the same as always. So does she: amazing. She got a haircut since the last time I saw her, the shaved fade on the sides of her head perfectly fresh.

"You look great," I say. That yellow dress pops against her deep brown skin. It comes in nicely at the waist and then flares out, but it's not until I'm looking at it up close that I notice the tiny pattern. "Are those...battle-axes?"

"They are!" She smiles softly and juts her hip a little. "I had to special order the fabric, and I made the dress myself. Don't they look just like Smokey's?"

"They do," I say, impressed. She made this herself? And she's wearing fandom gear *in public*? It's subtle, but still... "I can't believe you made this, and you're *wearing it.*"

"It took some convincing, believe me," the other girl says, and Tess steps aside to show she's been standing with one of her friends from the sushi restaurant. I tense up at the very sight of her.

"Claire, you remember Jillian, right?" Tess says, and Jillian smiles at me.

"Yeah, hi." I'm looking back and forth between them, waiting for an explanation. I can't believe it—two months ago, she was afraid to even *talk* about nerd stuff with her friends, and now she's here with one of them *at Comic-Con.*

Tess rubs the toe of her red Mary Janes into the carpet. "You remember that sleepover I went to? Well, Harper basically had a meltdown."

"Completely," Jillian agrees.

"She told me that it's fine if I want to do nerd stuff, but it meant that she didn't really ever know me at all, and basically put our friendship on the line. But it turned out the other girls were cool about it, so she didn't have a lot of backup. And then she just kind of...caved."

"Yeah, she's all talk, no action," Jillian says.

"Anyway, later, Jillian asked to see some of my art, and I showed her, and I've just been a little better about talking about it since then."

"That's great," I say, a warm feeling taking over. But I try not to notice the way Jillian is standing so close to Tess, try not to focus on the easy way they talk over each other.

"Tell her about the store!" Jillian says excitedly, nudging her. My eyes linger on the skin of Tess's long, open arms where Jillian's fingers touched her.

"Oh, well, I set up an online store to sell some of my art," Tess says. "They put it on shirts and mugs and stickers and stuff. Someone in Paris bought a shower curtain with my SmokeHeart art on it!"

"Wow, that's amazing!" I say. "I'm really proud of you. Really."

"Thank you. I would have told you sooner, but..." She trails off.

"I'm sorry," I say, looking away. "I should've texted you back."

Tess shrugs. "Yeah. That would've been nice."

I cross one arm over my stomach and grab my other elbow, not sure what to say next. I look at Jillian, who's watching me carefully. Is she being protective because Tess is her friend or...

I try not to think about it. I want Tess to be happy, and it *is* my fault I didn't text her back. If she moved on, that's totally fair.

But I really hope she hasn't.

I have to ask. I don't know how, but I know I have to. I bury my hands in my pockets. "So, um, are you guys, like..." I look between them meaningfully.

Jillian doesn't get it, just stares at me. But Tess's eyes go wide right away. "Me and Jillian?" She starts laughing. "Oh god, no. No, no. Sorry, Jillian, but no." She reaches over and touches Jillian's shoulder, and Jillian catches on and starts laughing, too. My cheeks are burning up. I look away.

"Oh, okay, yeah, I was just wondering," I mumble.

Tess steps a little closer to me, and she must give Jillian a look or something, because she kind of turns her back and opens her phone to at least *pretend* like she's not listening to us anymore.

"I know I told you over text, but I wanted to say again," Tess says, "I'm sorry. I should never have pressured you to come out, I should never have outed you to your mom. You should be able to do it on your own terms, whenever you feel like you're ready."

I nod. I want to say thank you, but I'm afraid my voice will crack, so I stay quiet.

"Have you..." she starts, then lowers her voice. "On that front, have you...thought any more about it?"

"I've thought *a lot* about it," I whisper. "I've thought a lot about...*you*."

"You have?"

"I'm sorry I was dumb. I couldn't see that what you face is different than what I face. For me, it's just about whether I'm queer or not. Which is stressful enough." I laugh. "But for you, you have this whole other thing to deal with, too." She nods solemnly. "I'm sorry I didn't get that. That I *still* don't really get it. But I want to."

And I hold my breath that maybe what I see in her eyes is hope. That maybe I can stop being quite so dumb. That maybe I'm not the big freaking coward she thought I was. That maybe she and I could...

Then she leans in a little closer so that everyone else in this line fades away and it's just me and her. I can feel her breath on my cheek as she whispers, "I really want to try again...if you do." Then she pulls back a bit and looks me in the eye.

I do. I really do.

"I'd like that," I say, and watch as her face breaks into a smile. I want to say more, but my phone buzzes. It's a text from Caty: **Where are you?**

I look back at Tess. I really don't want this moment to end, but: "I gotta go."

Tess frowns. "You're not gonna sit with us?"

A smile pulls at the corner of my mouth as I realize she doesn't know. "No, I can't, I'm sorry. Find me after, though, okay?"

Tess nods. I wave at Jillian, who gives me a little smile.

I hurry off down the hallway. I pass my parents down the line, and they're giving me thumbs-up and waving. Oh god, they weren't watching that, were they? I feel my cheeks flush hot, and I put my head down and push through some service doors to an employee access corridor.

I bring my hand up to my cheek to feel where Tess's breath was on it just moments ago. My heart zips as I think about meeting up with her later.

I walk through the hallways toward the greenroom. I'm familiar with the ugly white industrial cinder-block look of these corridors now. It's ironic that the more successful you get, the uglier the hallways you walk through are. Maybe that's a metaphor for something.

The long walk gives me time to think about what I'm going to say onstage. I could use my very first question to ask about SmokeHeart, and then use the remaining time to ask follow-up questions about it. Or I could ask a bunch of regular questions and then use my last question to be about SmokeHeart.

I want to ask Jamie a million questions; I want him to say all the frustrating, complicated stuff he told me back in Ballroom 6E in Seattle, about how the TV industry works, about how he doesn't feel like he's in charge of his own show sometimes, and mostly about how he doesn't give a rat's ass whether we think his characters are gay or not, because he says they're not. I could press him on it today, I could get him talking. I could use this time onstage to finally expose Jamie's real opinions.

But how would that affect Forest?

Forest said his situation with *Red Zone* was very fragile at the moment, and it would be better if SmokeHeart didn't come up at all. If I push it, if I make a big deal out of it, will that sink his chances for that role? Will that tank his career?

And for what? At this point, Jamie has made it as clear as he can that he's never going to make it canon. Everyone has said that Smokey's dead for good, Forest is off the show. All I can do today is get some kind of cathartic release for the fans, but I can't make SmokeHeart happen. It's over.

Is it worth it to press them on it if it's not going to happen, and it might kill Forest's chances at his next job? The job he really wants, and is, let's face it, much better suited for?

I don't know.

When I reach the greenroom, I slip in through the doors and

stand near the back. I see Ms. Greenhill chewing out one of her assistants as he cowers. I don't envy him, but I smile a little, remembering how terrifying Ms. Greenhill can be and glad she's not directing that anger at me. I see Caty sitting sideways across one of the chairs, wearing a matching kelly-green pant-suit with a hot-pink belt. She looks up from her phone to give me a nod. On the far side of the room, Rico waves at me from the snack table. I realize to my surprise that I actually have some friends here. Is that sad? That my only friends are the cast and employees of the probably soon-to-be-canceled show *Demon Heart*? Or is that actually really cool? I can't decide.

I spot Jamie, hunched in the corner, completely ignor-ing me. I don't see Forest anywhere. Ms. Greenhill finishes dressing down her assistant and walks over, running her hand through her short black bob like she's wiping away his incompetence.

"Hi, Claire," she says. "Just a few minutes left. You ready?"

No, not at all. Why did I even demand to do this? I have no idea what I'm going to ask when I get up there, I have no idea how to hold my hands, or if my hair looks okay. I can feel the nerves creeping in the closer we get to showtime.

Ms. Greenhill reads the anxiety on my face. "You're gonna be fine. Honestly. We wouldn't have said yes unless we thought you'd kill it."

She gives me a comforting pat on my shoulder and moves off. My knees are starting to feel weak. Where the hell is Forest?

"I DON'T KNOW HOW THE PRESS GOT IT—WE'VE been having problems with leaks all year," Reynolds says, thwacking me on the back with a heavy hand. My agent told me Reynolds wanted to talk to me alone, so I waited like an idiot in the service corridor to catch him as he came out of a panel about the future of the video game in Hollywood. My agent also said the trades are running stories that the studio is circling me for the *Red Zone* role.

"I want you to be careful because there may be some Red Zone fans at your panel today. You know, eager to meet the new guy, see whatcha got," he says.

The idea of new fans, new expectations, it gives me heartburn. What ideas do they have about Jack Tension that they're going to ask me to comment on? What standards are they going to hold me to? I've barely gotten used to the *Demon Heart* fans.

But I don't say that. Instead, I say, "Sounds good."

"Now listen to me," Reynolds says, taking my arm and guiding me into a walk-and-talk. "This thing with the studio? It's tender. I'm talking *tender*," he says intensely. "They can still nix you at any moment and force me to go with Pratt."

I *knew* Pratt'd be in the mix for this!

He continues, "I want you to picture this situation as a burn victim. Weeping open sores. Do not poke. *TENDER*."

"I got it," I say to put an end to that metaphor.

"When you go out there today, I don't want you to say anything about *Red Zone* except, 'I would be incredibly honored to be considered for the part. I love the game.' Got it?"

"Yup."

"And don't say anything about *Demon Heart* except, 'It was a wonderful experience that I will cherish forever.'"

"Cherish forever?"

"You got it?"

"So I can't talk about *Red Zone*, I can't talk about *Demon Heart*. What the hell can I talk about?"

"Hell if I know, this is a damn spot," Reynolds says. "Just don't do anything stupid."

We arrive at my door and he slaps me on the back again, harder than before, and heads off.

I remind myself that I used to think Jon Reynolds was hot shit. Now he just seems smarmy. I take a beat before I go inside. I've been watching yoga videos on YouTube to mix up my workouts so it's not all weights and cardio. I take a few restorative breaths, and then let out a long exhale, making a big *ahhh* sound.

Don't talk about Red Zone, *don't talk about* Demon Heart. It's all so ridiculous. My whole job is to go out there and talk. Paula would love nothing more than if I bared my soul and gushed about personal shit and cried. That's the sort of thing that goes viral. Jamie would love for me to tell everyone to watch the show *Demon Heart* and nothing but the show *Demon Heart* and then share safe anecdotes about how much fun the show *Demon Heart* is to work on. Claire? Well, we all know what Claire wants, but that would really make Reynolds's head explode.

After one more restorative breath, I go in.

"There he is!" Rico hollers from across the room as soon as I enter. I haven't seen him in a few weeks and it's the longest we've been apart basically since we met. He crosses the room in a few strides and wraps me up in a big hug. "I missed you, Reed. What, I gotta go all the way to Comic-Con to see you these days?" He puts me down, then runs his fingers through my hair. "Oh, sorry, whoops, I forgot, don't touch the hair."

Over Rico's shoulder, I see Claire biting her lip, wearing the look of a shipper watching her OTP interact. (Yeah, yeah, I've learned the lingo, so what?) Rico tries to arrange my hair back the way it was, but I pull away from him.

"Stop, stop, you're making it worse!"

"I'm never gonna learn if you don't let me practice," he protests, laughing. I just push him away and fix it myself.

Claire is gesturing me over covertly like she's got the answers to the midterm to give me under the bleachers at lunch.

I go over to her. "Hey."

She's hugging her body with one arm and she's covering half her face with the other one. She looks up at me through her fingers.

"What is it?" I ask, popping into a crouch next to her chair so we can be eye-to-eye.

"Forest," she says into her hand. She moves her hand so she can talk clearly. "What do I do?"

I've only ever seen Claire stridently on a mission to convince everyone she's correct. Seeing her curled up, unsure, it's giving *me* secondhand nerves.

"What are you talking about? You're anxious about this panel?"

"No it's not that." She gives me a pointed look. "What do I *ask*?"

And I realize what she's saying. SmokeHeart. I take a deep breath to buy myself some time. I don't know what to tell her. I know what would make life easiest for me, but is that what I should say? Or should I tell her to follow her heart?

Earlier she told me that there are a lot of people who would like to hear me open up about SmokeHeart, that I could help heal some old wounds if I would just be honest about it. Maybe I should tell her to ask me about it. Press me until I can't *not* talk about it. But I know Reynolds would be pissed at me for saying something no matter how it comes out.

So here we are. Stuck.

"I know what it feels like to have everyone expecting something from you," I say. "Telling you what to do, where to go, how to sound, when to smile, what to say. I don't want to do that to you. You get to be your own person today." Claire frowns. "I think you should do what you think is best. There's no one I'd trust up there more than you."

She scowls. I haven't helped her at all. I give her a smile and stand up again. I don't envy her this job.

I pass Jamie sitting by himself in the corner, on his phone. He glances up and we accidentally make eye contact. I have absolutely nothing to say to him. He nods at me. I keep walking.

I'm happy to be here, happy to see Rico and Claire, and do my part to put my face out there if it helps my career, or helps Rico get a second season. But if I never have to talk to Jamie again, I'd be perfectly okay with that. One more panel and my obligations are fulfilled.

I go over to Paula's assistant Donna and say, "Whatcha got for me this time?" and she pulls this really beautiful vintage *Alien* T-shirt out of her bag. I can't believe it.

"I love *Alien*!" I say. "It's my favorite movie!"

"So I heard," she says.

I take off my T-shirt and slip the new one on. It's soft and fits perfectly. I turn around and Rico gives me a thumbs-up. "Thanks," I mouth at him from across the room.

Then Paula's hollering at us to get ready, and we gather our things and follow her toward the stage. It's showtime.

55

MS. GREENHILL LEADS ME TO THE SIDE OF THE stage. I've stood on the sidelines before, but never while knowing I had to step out from behind the curtain. I peek out and see the ballroom is huge, packed solid with fans. I don't know how I'm going to do this.

Ms. Greenhill takes me by the shoulders and looks directly into my eyes. "Claire, there is no one better suited to this than you right now. I want you to know that everyone here believes in you. You're going to be great. Now take a deep breath and hold it." I do. "And let it out slowly." I do. "Now go get 'em." She slaps me on the shoulder, and I stagger out from behind the curtain and make my way step-by-step onto the stage as the applause and cheering erupts from the audience.

The lights are very bright—almost blinding. I don't look at the crowd, just train my eyes on the podium at the end of the stage and focus on making it without tripping. When I get there, I put my hands on the hard wood surface of it, feeling it cool and steady under me as I lean into the microphone.

"Hello, everyone," I say, and I hear my voice projected supernaturally loud over the ballroom as the audience hushes. I think about how much more power I have, standing here on this stage, with this microphone in front of me, than anyone out there. I could say anything right now and they would all have to listen. My heart thumps with nerves.

"My name is Claire Strupke. Some of you know me as heart-of-lightness. I want to welcome you all to the *Demon Heart* panel at San Diego Comic-Con." The audience cheers wildly. I look into the crowd and I happen to see Tess in the fourth row, staring at me with huge, wild eyes. I wink at her, and she just looks even more shocked. Seeing her makes some of my nervousness subside. *Just imagine you're talking to Tess.* "Please welcome to the stage, from the show *Demon Heart*, Jamie Davies, Rico Quiroz, and Forest Reed." I can't be the only one who noticed that Forest's name got slightly more cheers than the others, including a distinctly male whooping. This is going to be interesting.

The three of them come out and take their seats behind the table. Rico and Forest smile encouragingly in my direction. *Doing great so far!*

"So," I say, "*Demon Heart* is at a critical point, having completed its first season, but not yet picked up for a second. That's unusual, for a show to not have a second season order this late in the year, isn't it?"

Jamie shoots me a look. "Yes, it is, thanks for bringing it up," he says drily. There's an uneasy laugh in the audience. Those are the first words he's spoken to me since that night in Seattle.

I shake it off and continue. "Fans are eager to know what's in store for the future of *Demon Heart*."

And here it is. The moment of decision. I could ask, *Can you address the issue of queerbaiting and how your show has contributed to it?* Or *In a world in which bisexual representation is so rare, how do you feel about the possibility that one or both of your leads might be bisexual?* Or even something snarky like *How do you feel about your show being the poster child for heteronormativity?*

I look out at the crowd, who are getting restless. Are they waiting for me to ask about it? Will they feel let down if I don't? I lock eyes with Forest, who is watching me intently, waiting. It's unfair that we ask this of him. That he feels like he has to put up a false front just so he can get the role he wants. Is he not an actor? What does it matter if his last character is gay? It doesn't mean they all have to be. But those are questions for the people in charge of his next project, not this one.

I turn my gaze to Rico.

"Rico, the first question is for you. How do you manage to memorize your lines that are in demontongue? That seems like it would be really hard."

Rico laughs and starts answering the question, talking about his elaborate and hilarious process involving making recordings of the lines and listening to them in his sleep. As he answers, Forest looks at me strangely, like I surprised him. He should be grateful; I'm saving his ass here. I'm doing this for him.

My next question is about how Forest learned to use the battle-ax. My next is about the costumes they wear. I start asking them questions about themselves that I know they have great answers to because I've spent so much time with them. I get Rico to talk about how much he loves those videos where returning soldiers surprise their dogs. I get Forest to discuss his love of Voodoo Doughnuts. I ask them questions a regular moderator wouldn't know to ask, and they're giving great answers, funny and authentic and real. I can feel the audience lapping it up.

Finally, it's time for the audience Q&A. There's a scramble as fans stand to move toward the microphone. I feel a little nervous for Forest. He might still get a SmokeHeart question, but at least it won't come from me.

The audience's rush to the microphone sounds a little physical, with some screeches and grunts and expletives, but the lights are too bright to see too much. One of the stage-hands flicks on a spotlight that hits the first person at the mic.

I notice right away that he's a man. He has a beard and he's wearing a giant black backpack that's the size of a small child. He leans in too close to the mic and asks his question. "Hey, Forest. I'm pretty interested in the fact that you might be the new Jack Tension. What can you tell us?"

Okay, fine, we'll get the *Red Zone* question out of the way first, and then we'll move on to *Demon Heart* questions.

Forest smiles at the guy and gives a line that sounds practiced. "All I can say is I would be incredibly honored to be considered for the part. I love the game."

"Do you even play Red Zone?" the gamer asks.

"I'm sorry, but just one question per person, please," I say as the gamer scowls at me and leaves the line. The next person steps up to the mic in a LAG KILLS shirt. Another freaking gamer.

He says, "Okay, but *do you* play Red Zone? And which character do you play as?" I roll my eyes and look back at Forest.

"Actually, yes, I play almost every day. I was just playing it this morning with a friend of mine." I feel my cheeks warm at that. *Friend.* I bite my lip and try to keep a smile from taking over my face. He sneaks a look at me. "And I play as Jack Tension." There's a titter in the crowd, and I realize that this seemingly innocuous statement about which character he plays *means* something to Red Zone fans. I wonder who else you can play as, and what that choice means about the player. I guess every fandom has its own set of insider politics and identity markers.

The next person steps up to the microphone and I am going to scream because it's *another freaking gamer.* "What other video games do you play? Like, *actually* play. Like, to the end," he says. Is this whole panel going to be video game questions?

I find Tess in the audience, and she rolls her eyes. I almost laugh. I can't wait to hear her commentary on this afterward.

Forest leans into his microphone. "You know what? I'm gonna put a pin in that one. It's a legitimate question, if a little condescending, but I'd like to see if there are any *Demon Heart* questions from the audience. This is a *Demon Heart* panel, after all, not a Red Zone one."

I'm impressed. The gamer fan grumbles and moves aside as he looks around to see if any *Demon Heart* fans are going to step up. A very small girl, about ten years old, squeezes past the gamers and reaches the microphone. She tries to speak, but the mic is too tall for her, so she turns and looks pointedly at the gamer behind her. He snaps into action and lowers the microphone. It makes me thaw a bit toward him.

Rico is completely melting over this girl. "Yes, hello!" he says. "Do you have a question for us?"

"Hi," she says. "My question is actually for heart-of-lightness."

I freeze. *Me?* I can see Jamie chortle out of my peripheral vision. I stand a little straighter, determined to answer it as best I can.

The girl says, "I just started writing fanfiction and some people were making fun of me for it and I was wondering if you have any tips?"

Oh. I have zero idea how to respond. It feels like all I've done as a fanfic author is make people mad. But, well, there's a small girl waiting for my answer.

"I think it's great you're writing fanfiction. It takes a lot of creativity and dedication," I say because that seems like a good thing to start with. My own feelings on it may be turbulent and complicated, but I still believe that much. "But it can be hard, too. When you're a fan, sometimes there are people who will try to make you feel bad about it. Sometimes it's jerks on the internet, sometimes it's people you know, like classmates or friends. Sometimes it's the people who are making the thing you're a fan of in the first place."

I look at Jamie, who is doing his best to tune this out, sitting back in his chair, sipping from his glass of water. "I know how easy it is to hear the messages from other people and start to feel crazy."

I look back at the girl. "But you're not crazy. And you should never be made to feel ashamed for loving the things that you love."

Weirdly, there's applause there. I guess that line connected with people. But the little girl isn't done with me. She asks, "But didn't you delete your blog? Are you going to stop writing now?"

And I guess the one-question rule is going out the window, because I respond, "Yeah, you're right, that was kind of BS, wasn't it? I'm not even taking my own advice. Here I am encouraging other people to write no matter what The Powers That Be are saying about them, but I'm not willing to do the same thing."

The crowd gets quiet, maybe they can tell that I'm not really filtering myself right now, I'm just thinking it through, out loud, in front of a few thousand people. "The reality is, I looked at myself and realized that I was spending a large percentage of my day—of my life, really—thinking and writing about characters who were dreamed up by someone who doesn't really care about people like me."

I find Tess in the audience again. She's got her hand on her cheek, but she's smiling at me, and I think there might be tears in her eyes. I don't want her to cry. This is *good*. This is a good moment. I want to wipe the tears off her cheeks and tell her I screwed up and please, yes, let's try again.

I think about kissing Tess, and how it feels better than any fic feels. I want to kiss her again more than I want Smokey to kiss Heart, and that's *a lot*. I don't know exactly what that makes me, but I know where to start.

And just like that, it's clear to me. Maybe this is it, the moment I figured it out. Standing on a stage at Comic-Con. Or maybe I've been figuring it out slowly and I just now understood it. Or maybe I knew all along and I was just scared to admit it. But I really, *really* like her. And I missed her. And all I want to do is tell her how I feel, and I don't care who else hears me. And I don't care what label they want to give me. I just need to tell her.

"I met someone recently who helped me realize that my connection to fanfiction is more personal than I thought," I say. "She's one of the most important people in my life, and I wouldn't have met her if it weren't for *Demon Heart* fandom. And she helped me realize something super important."

Okay, deep breath, here we go.

"And that's that . . . I'm queer."

And Tess's whole face changes as she laughs in surprise and looks completely full to the brim.

"And maybe some of you are, too, and maybe that's something you knew all along, but I only recently started figuring it out. And I don't know if I'm lesbian or bi or, like, homo-romantic pansexual or what, but I know I wouldn't have gotten this far in understanding myself if it hadn't been for fanfiction and the people I've met through writing and reading it."

And here it crosses my mind to look for my parents in the audience. They're easy to spot because Mom is waving her hands at me and Dad is throwing me big A-OK signals. *Dorks.* Dad's probably going to write a poem about this on the way home.

And for once, I'm not second-guessing myself. It feels *right*.

"If you know my work, you know that in my fanfic, I write Smokey and Heart as bisexual. They're not out on the show, but imagine if they were. Imagine what that would mean for all the people like me out there, who might be watching and waiting and *hoping* to see a bit of themselves on-screen."

I don't look at Jamie, or Rico, or Forest, not yet. "And while

I'm at it, I'm not just talking queer representation. Look at the show, look how white it is, how male. Where are the women, the people of color, aside from one? Where is any of the diversity that makes our world fascinating, and unique, and special? *Demon Heart* tells great stories, but in the end, all I see is Heart, Smokey, and a lot of straight white guys in rubber masks."

I adjust my glasses and get back on track. "Here's what I've come to accept. The show is never going to go canon with the SmokeHeart relationship. Smokey is dead; it's over. If seeing a SmokeHeart kiss on the show would have been important to you, you're out of luck. You'll have to rely on reading it in fic, because the real thing isn't going to happen. Whether you want to stay in this fandom and continue to make works that redefine *Demon Heart* in the way you want to see it—that's a personal decision you have to make for yourself. These guys have all talked on this subject before, and I'm not going to ask them to talk about it again today. I think they've made their positions pretty clear."

There, I managed to talk about it without asking Forest about it. I hope that's good enough. I hope that didn't hurt him too much.

There's silence in the hall. I can't tell if any of that was inspiring or disappointing or what, but it was honest, at least. All I really have left is my honesty.

"I think we should move on to the next question," I say.

"Claire, wait."

RICO HAS BEEN MAKING DAMN FACES AT ME THIS entire time. Very practiced, neutral faces that don't betray anything to anyone who might be filming or photographing him, but I can tell from the extremely slight way he narrows his eyes and bores them into me that he wants me to do something. But what can I do? *What the hell can I do?*

When Claire starts talking about her own experiences, I feel my heart split open. After seeing her with these high walls for so long, watching her tear them down and open herself up to a room full of people and cameras and reporters and who knows what all? It takes a lot of bravery to do that.

There's a little boy in the front row who is here with his mom. I just keep looking at his face, watching as his eyes grow bigger and bigger until they're like baseballs bulging out of his head. When Claire comes out as queer, he grips two hands to his chest and his mom puts her arm over his shoulders as big, fat tears run down his face. I don't know if Claire sees him, but I have to tell her about it after. This moment is touching people. Her *words* are touching people.

And then, after all that, she says she's not going to even ask us about it. After all that, she's still protecting me, making sure I don't have to answer the question or put my career on the line. That's when Rico's knee connects hard with mine under the table.

He's not wrong.

I have to do something.

I look at him, and for a moment, I see what Claire sees. A warm, gentle, thoughtful, obnoxious, fun-loving weirdo who wants to make sure everyone feels heard and has a good time. If there's anything he's taught me, it's that I should take more risks, worry less. Stop thinking so much.

I reach my hand toward Rico discreetly, thankful that there's a tablecloth between us and the crowd, blocking their view. I take his hand and he looks at me with a little half smile. I squeeze his hand and raise my eyebrows at him. A question: *Do you want to do this?* Rico squeezes back, and I see his eye crinkles go into full effect. *Yes, I do.* Damn I love those eye crinkles.

I hear Claire ask for the next question from the audience and I drop Rico's hand and say, "Claire, wait."

She looks at me with this stunned expression that makes me laugh as I push my seat back and stand up. I'm nervous, and I'm worried I'll knock my chair over or do something clumsy as I stand, but I don't. I wriggle my microphone out of its holder. It's game time. Take the shot, Reed.

I say, "There are a lot of people who don't want me to talk about this today. And, to be honest, I wasn't going to."

I cross to Claire, who's shaking her head a little and whispering, "You don't have to say anything."

"Yes, I do," I whisper back. I open my arms for a hug, and she looks at me a moment, and then accepts it. I wrap my arms around her and whisper into her ear, "I'm so proud of you," and as I do, my voice hitches. Because I *am*. So damn proud of her. I wouldn't be doing this if she hadn't shown me it was possible.

Over Claire's head, I can see Jon Reynolds standing in the wings, giving me a finger across the throat: *Cut it out.* I give Claire a pat on the back and turn away from him. Let him find out what I'm going to say along with the rest of the room. And if Red Zone wants to be dicks about the deal after that, well, that's out of my control.

I grip the microphone tight and forge ahead. "A few months ago, I didn't know anything about fandom or shipping or any of this stuff. But then I started meeting y'all, and I kept hearing the same thing over and over..." I walk to the edge of the stage. I can feel a spotlight struggling to follow me. Let's make that spotlight operator work for his money, shall we? I hop off the stage and the audience cheers. They have no idea what's coming. I have, well, just an inkling, and it scares the hell out of me.

I'm white-knuckling the mic, as I start walking into the audience. I take a breath. *Relax, Reed. Breathe. Don't think so much.*

I look into the bright spotlight, and I feel the eyes of thousands of fans on me. "I keep hearing that Smokey and Heart are in love." There's scattered whoops and hollers for that.

I shade my eyes against the spotlight, peering at people until I find what I'm looking for. *There.* In the eighth row, a twentysomething girl who looks to be about Rico's size, cosplaying as Heart.

"Do you mind if I borrow this?" I ask. She nods at me, dazed and exhilarated, and shrugs out of her yellow workman's jacket and hands it to me. "I'll give it back," I whisper as I take it from her.

I walk back up toward the front, and Rico, seeing me coming, hops out of his chair and meets me at the edge of the stage. I toss the jacket up to him. He grins at me, looking pretty excited to be taking part in whatever it is I'm planning.

"For a long time, I didn't want to hear it. I thought the same thing the whole world thinks when teenage girls open their mouths: 'You're emotional. You're delusional. You're hysterical.'" I turn around to make eye contact with Claire. "I was wrong."

I lean against the front of the stage and rub my sweaty palm on my jeans. "Look, I mean, I admit I didn't really get it at first. It took a while, you know, for me to get my head out of my ass."

"I love your ass, Forest!" someone shouts from the audience, and there are titters all around.

"I love his ass, too," Rico says, low, his mouth right on the microphone. The crowd erupts in laughter, and I have to will my cheeks not to turn pink. Rico laughs with them, enjoying making me squirm.

"Thank you. Both of you." I push off the edge of the stage and head back into the audience. "The point is," I say, getting this back on track. "Everything you saw on-screen, that was real. That really happened, and it's really part of the show. No one can take that away from you, not me, not Rico, not Jamie." I jerk my thumb at Jamie, who looks permanently indignant, like people keep stealing his parking spot at Whole Foods and there's not a damn thing he can do about it.

"All the feelings you feel when you watch the show? Those are just as real as anyone else's. What you think about *Demon Heart* is just as important as what Jamie thinks, or what some critic thinks, or what *I think*." I stop at the boy in the front row, who's clutching his arms across his chest. "You're not hysterical. You're not delusional. Your opinions are valid," I say, and he nods at me with big, teary eyes.

I relax my grip on the mic. The plan is falling into place. I spot a girl wearing a leather jacket like Smokey's and I head toward her. When I gesture, she immediately slips it off and tosses it to me with a big thumbs-up. She's on board. I notice that the strap is broken on the shoulder, just like mine, and just like that other girl I met a few cons back. I have come to love meticulous cosplayers.

"If you see *Demon Heart* as a love story, then it's a love story," I say. That gets a cheer, too. The energy in the room is building.

Someone from the back hollers, "Hell yes it is!" and there's another cheer.

I hear someone under their breath say, "What a chode," as I pass. I shoot him a look. He's one of the gamers who asked me a question before. I choose to ignore him. He came to a *Demon Heart* panel. He's gonna get demons and a whole lotta heart. As I pass, I hear him get to his feet and walk out. I see a few other people around walking out, too. Let 'em.

"Okay, Forest, I think that's enough," Jamie says. Oh, look, he lives! After basically sleeping and scowling through this entire panel, and indeed, every single media event so far, Jamie Davies is showing a little life.

"Sorry?" I say, then I put the microphone down on the edge of the stage so I can slip into the Smokey jacket.

"You don't get to dictate what should or should not happen. It's not your show," Jamie says.

I pick up the mic again. God, this jacket fits well. And it smells a bit like perfume, which is kind of nice. I'll have to tell that girl later when I give it back that her jacket smells great. "Yo, Jamie, due respect, but it's not your show, either. Once we make it and put it out there, it's not ours to say how people see it."

"Fine, but none of you get to decide what happens next. *I* do. And my writers. That's how this whole thing works."

Here's where Claire butts in. "You get to decide what's canon, but you know what? Canon can be wrong."

I climb back onto the stage. Rico's smiling at me like a maniac. I feel like I'm finally being someone he can be proud of. I feel like I'm finally listening to myself instead of reacting out of fear.

It feels good.

"This is ridiculous," Jamie says. And then he straight-up walks offstage. That's okay, I'm not doing this for him. In fact, he'd rather kill my character off than see this happen, so I don't have a lot of sympathy at the moment.

I turn back out to the crowd. The cheering is growing steadily, as people start to anticipate what's coming. The energy right now is incredible.

"I didn't get that at first, Claire, but you helped me get there."

Claire's watching me intensely, her hands gripping the sides of the podium.

"Get what?" she asks.

"That you as a viewer get to pick what your own personal canon is. That yours doesn't have to be the same as mine, or Jamie's, or anyone else's."

"Yeah, I think that's true."

"But sometimes, I get the sense that you're disappointed that your specific canon might not ever make it to the screen."

"Definitely," she says. Her face freezes in this stunned half smile, like she's trying to figure out what I'm up to. Just wait.

"Okay, well, maybe just in case, some people might want to film this?"

There are already about fifty phones pointed at us, but I see a dozen more fly into the air. My heart is in my throat. I can feel every single eye in the room on us.

"Okay?" I whisper to Rico, and he turns to face me with a nod.

"Okay," he says.

I watch him do a little shoulder shrug, neck stretch that I recognize from the moments on set just before *action*. He's getting into character. I close my eyes and find the part of my brain that always knows how Smokey will react next.

It takes a moment, because my heart is racing and my adrenaline is pumping, but I take a few long breaths, and slowly, the crowd fades away.

As Smokey, I open my eyes and look at Heart.

How long have Heart and I been fighting? Thinking that because of our nature, we had to be enemies, when all along we wanted the same things: peace, justice, freedom from hell. I spent so much time thinking he was my enemy that I never considered that that tightness I felt in my chest at the sight of him wasn't fear or anger. My obsession with him, the way I couldn't take my eyes off him when he was in the room, the way his name made my stomach curl up and my knees loosen—I had never known what it was before because I'd never felt it with anyone else.

It's simple, really. I just never let myself think about it.

I'm in love with Heart.

I tell him this with my eyes, and I feel it coming right back, his lips pulling up into a smile, his face wide open and welcoming. The warmth of knowing washes over me. Heart loves me, too. What happens next isn't even a risk anymore, because I know exactly what he'll do.

Standing on the edge of that stage with him, I've never felt so connected before. I raise the microphone to my mouth so everyone can feel what I'm feeling.

"Heart." I pause to wait for the cheers to die down. "I'm with you..."

I hand the microphone to him. Without breaking eye contact, he speaks directly to me. "'Til the dirt hits my chest."

I'm aware, then, of another cheer. Happy for the familiarity of the line, exhilarated about what might come next, just like me.

He puts the mic on the table and the cheer dies down. We're enveloped in utter silence as I hold his gaze for...

An...

Eternity.

Then I step forward, and he steps forward, and my breath and every other breath in the room catches in our throats.

And I allow myself to admire the sharp corners of his jaw, the smooth brown of his skin, the lines in his face from years of experience and living and laughing, and his deep warm eyes, which are looking at me like I'm the only person in the room.

And then I drop my gaze to his lips, which are curling upward in anticipation, and I know he's waiting for me to move first.

So I lean in, and I close my eyes, and his mouth meets mine.

And we kiss.

My hands move up to cup his cheeks, and I can feel him slipping an arm around my back and pulling me a little closer.

His mouth is warm on mine, and I can feel him holding back a smile. His hands move up my back, strong, yet gentle, letting me know he's got me, it's okay, I'm okay, *this is okay*.

I run my hand around his neck and up into his hair, and I'm astonished by a feeling in my gut that says, *This is hot.*

This *is* hot. Before, I might have been afraid of that feeling, but today I don't run away from it, I just let myself feel everything I'm feeling.

And then he slips his mouth open and my tongue dips in, and the kiss deepens until I can feel it everywhere. His whiskers scratch my cheeks, and there is a tightness in my chest and I'm a little afraid I might cry, but I don't, I just let the feeling wash over me and fill me up.

I don't know for sure that this is what Smokey wanted; I can't promise that he was in love with Heart, but I have to admit, it does feel right.

Gradually, I begin to hear the screaming of the crowd, which can't be ignored anymore because it's truly deafening. A thousand flashes of a thousand phones are firing at once, and I slowly, slowly become aware of reality.

We finally pull apart, and I open my eyes and find him right there looking back at me, cheeks flushed, smiling.

I bring my hand up to rest it tenderly on his cheek. His hair is a mess from where my fingers ran through it. I realize this might be my only chance to do something I've always wanted to do. I touch his eye crinkles, which only makes them crinkle harder. His hand lingers on my back, like he's not ready to let this moment go, not yet. Neither am I.

I look into his eyes and whisper, "Thank you." He nods and I wonder if he felt what I felt.

Magic.

As if to punctuate it, he gives me another kiss, this time on the cheek, and I have to bite my lip to keep from grinning as we turn out to face the audience and wave as the crowd goes absolutely bananas. I look over at Claire, and she's just staring at us, mouth literally hanging open. I wave her over, and she joins me on my other side like she's in a daze and it makes me laugh.

It feels like the three of us, arm in arm, could do anything.

57

I HAVE SO MUCH LOVE IN MY HEART FOR FOREST Reed right now. That is, I would if I still had a heart, which I don't, because my insides have completely liquefied and are pooled at my feet. I don't even know how I'm still standing—it's possible that I fainted and hit my head and this whole panel has been one long fantasy dreamed up by my subconscious.

But on the off chance this is real, I am going to die remembering this moment. I am going to watch the YouTube videos of those thirty seconds every single day until I am old and withered. I will make my children and grandchildren watch them. And they won't be impressed because in the future everyone will be gay, but I'll tell them of a time when it was different, when kissing another guy onstage at Comic-Con meant laying your job on the line, and put tears in the eyes of every queer and maybe-queer person in an entire enormous auditorium. When a gesture like that could make a difference.

This whole time, I thought the only person who had any

influence on this issue was Jamie Davies. And it's true, he's the only one who can make it real on the show. But you know what else is nice? Being *seen*.

Today Forest finally sees us. Today we ship it together.

The panel goes on a little longer as Forest and Rico answer as many questions as they can get to before their time is up and the con organizers have to actually come onstage (to no small amount of booing) in order to tell us to stop. Jamie never returns, and Forest doesn't get any more questions about *Red Zone*—maybe the gamers left, or maybe they just read the room and realized this was not their moment. I'd like to think they were quietly moved by what happened, and they all went on their phones and added *Demon Heart* to their Netflix queues.

I keep catching Tess's eye in the audience. She is honestly glowing, and she's smiling this smile that's a mixture of pride and wonder, and she is so cute I want a poster of the expression she's making to hang over my bed in my bedroom because I never want to stop looking at it.

When the time is finally up, I end the panel, and there's a standing ovation that makes my heart swell because I couldn't be prouder of Forest and Rico. They wave and wave and wave and finally make their way off the stage, and instead of following them, I jump right down into the crowd, pushing my way through to get to her.

Tess pulls me into her arms immediately and I'm kissing her and I don't care that there are a thousand people watching us and pushing past us and clapping for us, I am just so happy. And then there's a flash and I pull away and Mom just *took a freaking picture of us*.

"Mom!"

"What, honey bunny, you looked so cute!" She's standing next to my dad, who is clutching Mom's purse to his chest and looking like his heart might explode. *What a sap.*

"Do *not* post that anywhere," I say.

"Hi, Tess!" Mom says, ignoring me.

"Hi, Trudi; hi, Claire's dad," Tess says.

Dad looks like he's too choked up to answer, so he just lets go of Mom's purse with one hand and reaches over to shake her hand.

"His name is Chuck," I say.

"We're so proud of you," Mom says, bringing the phone back up to take another picture as people bump past us, streaming up the aisle toward the exits.

"Mom, stop!"

So she lowers the phone and looks at me with these big eyes. And Tess goes, "Awww," because Mom's antics still work on her.

"Good job, heart-of-lightness!" a random audience member says as she passes. I wave at her and smile, then look back at Mom.

"Okay, fine, you can take one more, but that's it."

I put my arm around Tess's shoulders and—*flash*—Mom takes another one.

"Claire!" someone hollers. I turn to see Caty waving at me from the front of the auditorium.

"Sorry, I'll be right back," I say, leaving Tess and my parents at the mercy of each other.

Caty gives me a big hug. "Oh my god, girl, that was like, *historic*! And you were amazing!"

"Hey! Was it okay?"

"*Okay?* That was *epic*! As long as I work in social, I'll never see anything else like that. The numbers are currently spiking through the roof. Not that you care about the numbers right now," she says, grinning at me. "What a way to go out with a bang."

"Go out?" I ask.

"Oh, yeah, next week Paula's moving me over to *Time Swipers*. Says it would be a shame not to spread my talents around." She shrugs. "I met with the team last week, there's some good stuff coming up in season two. You watch it?" I shake my head. "You should check it out. They have a femslash ship people seem to like...."

"Canon?" I ask.

"Not yet." She winks at me, then lowers her voice. "Can't say anything on the record, but you know I wouldn't steer you astray. This one's no bait."

"I was just thinking I should be getting into more femslash...."

She laughs. "I'll be honest, a lot of stuff came into focus for me when I started reading lady fic," she says, and holds my look. Caty reads fic? "Hey, I gotta get going, but it's good to see you. Keep in touch! You have my number. And give Forest a big wet one for me if you see him before I do. He was a star today. Really, iconic."

"I will."

I wave good-bye to her, then I look back at my parents. My dad is showing Tess something in his notebook—probably a poem he wrote about something that happened today. And Mom's taking pictures of them. It gives me these gross warm and gooey feelings. Tess catches my eye and smiles, and I head over to join them. What a day. What a freaking day.

forest ➡️   **58**

"OKAY, I'M DONE FOR A YEAR," I SAY, FLOPPING backward onto a couch in one of the endless greenrooms I find myself in these days and letting my arm cover my eyes. After our big splash at San Diego, Paula asked Rico and me if we would mind hitting a series of conventions before the new season of *Demon Heart* airs. This is our last one for a while and Rico flies out in the morning to North Carolina to get back to shooting season two.

Yes, *Demon Heart* got a second season. Yes, Jamie is still showrunning it. Yes, I'm still dead. No, SmokeHeart is not canon. That's how Hollywood works. It's not fair, it's not equal, it's not representative. At least not yet. But hopefully we made a difference. There were a couple hundred people who talked to me today who said we did. So, maybe.

"Put your hands out," Rico says, standing over me. I pull my arm off my eyes and squint up at him, and he's holding a

Costco-size bottle of hand sanitizer. I sigh and he pumps an excessive amount into my hands.

"Whoa, dude, relax."

"Trust me on this, bud. You just shook hands with two hundred and fifty people. Guaranteed, you have like six different strains of crud growing on your digits right now."

I rub the sanitizer into my hands until it starts to evaporate. "I don't need to see another fan for the rest of my life," I say. Rico gives me a look and I crack. He knows I don't mean it. "I know, I know. It's amazing, leave me alone." Seeing an endless stream of people looking you in the eye, voices cracking, hands shaking, telling you what you mean to them—it's wild and unbelievable and it fills you up, but it also sometimes overfills you. Afterward, I'm always happy I did it, but I'm also exhausted. Taking in other people's joy and fear in a concentrated period like we do during signings and meet-and-greets and photo ops, I always end up with an emotional hangover. But I wouldn't trade it for anything.

"How can you get tired of it?" Rico says. "The endless love and devotion, the repeated cries of 'Kiss, kiss!'" Rico cracks up. I roll my eyes.

They always want us to kiss again. We are never going to kiss again. (Unless the *Demon Heart* cameras are rolling, in which case, sure. But I'm not holding my breath.)

"C'mon, what do you need," Rico says. "You want a burger? Corn dog?"

"Something green," I say to him, and Rico nods and goes off in search of someone who can bring us some grub. This is our dynamic after these things, now. I lie flat on my back until the energy comes back to me, and Rico, who is always hyped up and ready to rock-and-roll after signings, goes off in search of something for us to eat. By the time he's back, I usually feel human again. It works.

I pull up my phone and shoot a quick text to Caty. **Signing over. Dead.** Then I use the emoji with *X*s for eyes. She writes back right away, **Purell immediately, you will NOT get me sick with your weird mutant fangirl diseases.** She follows it up with, **Meet you at the bar at 9. Bring your abs.**

I smile to myself and flop my arm back over my eyes. Caty and I have been seeing each other a little bit. She's one of the few people I know who doesn't constantly poke fun at me for making out with a dude at Comic-Con. She understands what it meant. Plus, now that she's not bossing me around, telling me what to tweet, she's actually really chill.

Maybe if Claire were here she'd be pressing me to figure out what the hell I was feeling during that kiss with Rico, but she's not here and I'm not worried too much about it. Maybe someday I'll figure it all out, but for right now, I'm just gonna live my life, and maybe get a drink with the cute girl with the out-of-control fashion sense once in a while.

"Is that a Forest Reed under there?" a voice says. Our greenroom at this con is in this big open lounge-y area that anyone with a VIP pass can wander into. Cautiously, I remove my arm from my face.

"Hey there. Zach." It's Zach Sanchez-Anderson, the *Time Swipers* showrunner. I only met him the one time, standing in the hallway back in Boise, with Jamie. I'm surprised he remembers me.

"Hi," I say, and sit up to shake his hand.

"Didn't mean to interrupt your nap," he says, and takes a step back like he could give me my space if I wanted him to.

"No, no, it's fine. Just, talking to fans, it kind of takes it out of me sometimes," I say. And then quickly add, "In a good way."

"Been there," he says, and I remember that this guy's writing resume goes back to *Star Command*...which means he knows Rico.

"Yeah, I bet you do."

"Hey, look...I know how fraught the conversation between talent and fans can be sometimes. And I know nobody's perfect. But I just wanted to say, I think you're doing a great job out there. You really know how to connect with people."

"Thank you," I say genuinely. Rico tells me this shit all the time, but it means something different coming from a stranger, and someone who really knows this world.

"And, hey, by the way, we have a guest arc on *Time Swipers* coming up that I think you would be perfect for. Guaranteed eight episodes, maybe more if the audience responds. You interested? I mean, I'm sure your schedule is bananas right now."

"It's...actually, it's not," I say. My agent is *laser-focused* on getting *Red Zone* to come back to me, but I'm pretty sure that's not going to happen. They got one whiff of my performance in San Diego and hightailed it.

I squint at him. "Is this Caty's idea?"

"Who, Caty Goodstein? No, I just love your vibe."

Good, I'd hate to think I got this job because my maybe-future-kind-of-girlfriend pulled strings for me.

"I've been watching you for a while, actually. I thought you were doing great work on *Demon Heart*, really nuanced stuff. It's a shame they let you slip away," he continues.

Seriously? "I'm definitely interested," I tell him.

"Lucky us! We'll be in touch, then," Zach says, and shoots me a finger gun. I wave as he moves off. I just got a new gig. Maybe my career isn't in the gutter after all. My god, I need a new agent. Why am I having to get all my jobs myself? I want a cookie.

I climb to my feet and wander over to the snack table in search of sugar and a sparkling water. As I reach for a chocolate chip cookie, my hand brushes someone else's.

"Sorry," he says, and my stomach zips because I know that voice. Carefully, slowly, I raise my eyes to confirm that yes, indeed, I am standing at a snack table next to *Jasper Graves*.

Suddenly all the air is gone from my lungs, my eyesight is fuzzy, my forehead starts to sweat. But I can't not say something.

"Cookies, huh?" I say stupidly. Jasper looks at me.

Jack Tension is looking at me.

"Love 'em," he says.

I can't quite make direct eye contact. I keep trying, but... I take a deep breath. *Just say it, Reed.* "Mr. Graves? Sir? I love your work, it means a lot to me, it's basically what got me into acting."

He turns to me, then. Looks me over. "Oh yeah?"

"Yup." Then I don't have anything else to say, so I go, "I don't want to bother you, I just wanted to say that."

Jasper squints at me, and I am frozen under his gaze. After a moment, he leans in, furrows his brow, and says, "You want to take a photo?" Not short, or rude, but like he actually wants to take a photo with little old me. And *obviously* little old me wants a photo, are you fucking kidding me?

When Rico arrives with our lunches, he sees me and Jasper Graves, posing for a selfie, and he cracks up laughing. "You're such a fanboy, dude."

It's true, I am.

MY MOM KEEPS COMING IN WITH TRAYS OF SNACKS, even though Tess and I are seriously no longer hungry.

"Mom, please stop," I say after she hands us a tray of cashew cheese kale chips and a bowl of masala-spiced roasted chickpeas. More internet recipes.

"I just want to make sure you ladies are taken care of," she says.

"Thank you, Trudi," Tess says like the suck-up she is, and I elbow her under the blanket we're sharing on the living room couch.

When Mom disappears again, I shoot Tess a look. "Stop encouraging her."

"Oh, she just wants to be supportive," Tess says, grabbing a handful of chickpeas. "I think it's nice."

She settles back into me, and I hit RESUME on Netflix. I pulled the TV out of the closet when she arrived and we haven't put it away since. We're shotgunning season one of

Time Swipers so we'll be all caught up before the premiere next week. The show, it turns out, is really fun and action-packed, and yes, there is a *juicy* interracial femslash ship that we have been absolutely *squealing* over.

Tess has been here visiting me for four days and we've barely left the couch. Not that there's anything to see in Pine Bluff anyway, but it's been nice to spend this time talking and getting to know each other better and—when we're absolutely certain Mom and Dad are out of the house—making out like crazy.

But Tess has to leave tomorrow to get back home before school starts, and I don't know what's going to happen next year, except that that I'll have Skype open almost constantly so we can video chat. And Tess keeps telling me I should apply to UCLA with her, and every time she says that, I can hear Caty's words about getting me an internship in LA ringing in my ears. But I haven't decided where to go to college. I haven't even decided whether to watch season two of *Demon Heart*.

My phone buzzes with a text, and I almost don't want to move in order to look at it because the way I'm situated across Tess's side right now is just too luxuriously comfortable to get up, but I do.

When I open the text I bust up laughing and hand the phone to Tess. It's from Forest, and it's a selfie of him with Jasper Graves. Forest looks so glow-y and delighted that I can't look away from his big, dumb face. He finally met Jasper Graves. I hope it was everything he dreamed it would be.

His text reads: **EVEN MORE HANDSOME IN REAL LIFE.**

I fall back into Tess, giggling.

"I kind of ship it," she says.

"Oh my god, I can't ship him with anyone anymore. He's too real now."

"Well, he's not texting *me* selfies, so I'm gonna go ahead and ship it."

I smile at the thought of Forest and Jasper finding a secret love together, but I know it's not real. It's just not Forest.

She nudges me. "You know what time it is."

I do. We haven't talked about it. I still don't know how to feel about it.

"It's almost nine," I say.

"Are we going to watch?"

I burrow my face into her shoulder. "I don't know," I mumble into her. "Do you want to?"

"I don't know," she says. "On the one hand, I'm mad at Jamie for being a jerk, and I don't think I'll like the show without Smokey. But on the other hand..."

"I want to know where they're gonna go from here," I say. I've had these same arguments with myself for weeks now.

"What's gonna happen to Heart?"

"Will he be emotionally destroyed after Smokey's death? Will he cry?"

"God, I hope he cries." She tips her head back against the couch and stares at the ceiling. I hope so, too. That's such good fic material.

"If we don't watch," I say slowly, "how will we know what the fanfic is talking about?"

Tess looks at me seriously. "That is a good point."

"Gotta eat your broccoli before you can have dessert."

"So true."

I look at the *Demon Heart* print hanging over the TV. It's

the hand-screened one Ms. Greenhill gave me when we were on the road. Mom framed it and hung it up, and it looks perfect there, and not just because it took the place of one of my mom's nude portraits. Looking at it reminds me of all the feelings I once had for this show, and all the feelings I might still have for it.

It's 8:59. Decision time. I look at Tess. She smiles. Who am I kidding? I need to know.

I grab the remote, hit the channel, and land just in time for the "Previously on..." to begin.

The theme song swells and all the old emotions come back. We sing along with the song as it plays under the clips from season one. I used to sit right here in this spot last year and watch these episodes every Monday night. The only difference was, I did it alone.

Now my knees knock against Tess's, and she's wearing an old *Demon Heart* T-shirt of mine, and I'm getting selfies from friends on the road. A lot's changed.

The "Previously on..." reaches the last clip. Smokey lies bleeding and dying in Heart's arms in the alley at the end of last season's finale. They stare into each other's eyes, and we say the lines right along with them.

Smokey and Tess say in unison, "I'll be with you..."

And I finish the line along with Heart. "'Til the dirt hits my chest."

Acknowledgments

THANK YOU TO AYA BURGESS, WHO WAS THE FIRST person I told the nugget of this story to while we waited in the dark for a concert to begin. After listening carefully to the whole idea, she said... "I don't get it." Thank you for always encouraging me, rooting for me, feeding me, and nudging me out of bed when the alarm rings even—*especially*—when you don't get the idea. It must mean you believe in me.

To Jim Ehrich, my wonderful agent, and the essential Helen Burak, who both read the original screenplay version of *Ship It* and saw a story people might relate to. This wouldn't have happened without you and everyone else at Rothman Brecher Ehrich Livingston.

To Brooke Bowman and the folks at Freeform Books for reading the script and seeing the bones of a book in it. To Kieran Viola, who helped this trepidatious screenwriter find my writing legs in the wide open sea of fiction and who never got frustrated when I forgot to describe what the room looked like.

To all the real-life friends, writing group members, internet friends, and fans, who read drafts of this story along the way. In particular, to Zach Gonzalez-Landis, who, despite never having read a word of fanfic in his life (until this book), has shown endless support for this project and read literally countless drafts. (I tried to count them; I couldn't.) Also thanks to my other readers: Heather, Catherine, Karen, Jillian, Beth, Augusta, Molly, Lyn, Flourish, Meredith, Corrie, Shannon, Kelsey, Brian, Laura D., Brandi, Amanda G., Hope, Riley, and many others. To everyone who read a version of it along the way and told me they saw themselves in it, this is actually for you.

To the many associations I'm a part of, which make my writing experience, my internet experience, and my life experience immeasurably better, starting with FTH, where I can confess my fannish side and be understood in a way I can't nearly anywhere else. Also to the AA Fems, SHOUTIES, Broads, Electrics, and Binders, where I can seek answers, intel, a script, a book, a name, a hand, a swift kick in the ass, or a ruthless online battalion. The internet wouldn't be tolerable without you.

To my *Riverdale* family, who taught me more about how to write than anyone else.

To my fandom families and internet friendships. When understanding my sexuality as a teenager seemed impossible, there were others on the internet who were going through the same thing, writing stories about it, and publishing them, for free, online. Without fanfiction and fan communities, my middle school experience would definitely have been atrocious. Also high school. Possibly also college. Definitely that period after college before I knew what I was doing. And again later, and again after that, and again last week. When the real world feels like one giant demon portal, fandom friends are there to help, ready to lend me their battle-axes. Because family don't end with flesh and blood.

To my family, especially my parents, who never made me feel weird about wanting to get into creative fields. Thank you for teaching me to be a reader, and for all the trips to Powell's, and for getting us the internet in sixth grade, which quite literally changed my life.

To every actor, creator, show, movie, book, or band I ever loved to an extent I'm told is unusual, thank you for the inspiration. This isn't actually about you, even if it seems like it's about you.

And to Aya again, because I promised you I'd thank you first and last, and you deserve it. Thank you for being unreasonably supportive. Now that this book is done, let's go watch some TV together.